# SHADOWED FLAME

A Witch & Wolf Novel

---

RJ BLAIN

Pen & Page Publishing

## Shadowed Flame
### A Standalone Witch & Wolf Novel

---

Matia Evans has it all, except for one thing: she can't see color. With an adopted family who loves her, a company she helps her father run, and more prospects than she knows what to do with, she's in no place to complain that her world is limited to shades of gray, black, and white.

Her inability to perceive color isn't the only strange thing about her: all souls have shadows, and she can see them. Unfortunately, there are humans who are worse than monsters. Worse, there are real monsters in the world, and they view humans as prey or as mates.

If Matia doesn't want to become a victim, a pawn, or a trophy bride of the supernatural, she must use every bit of her strength and cunning. Her freedom and survival depend on embracing the darkest parts of her soul, but if she does, she risks becoming the newest—and most dangerous—monster of all.

---

Copyright © 2016 by RJ Blain

All rights reserved.

No part of this book may be reproduced in any form or by any electronic or mechanical means, including information storage and retrieval systems, without written permission from the author, except for the use of brief quotations in a book review.

For more information or to contact the author, please visit thesneakykittycritic.com

Cover design by Rebecca Frank (Bewitching Book Covers.)

## Dedication

*To the Usual Suspects,
You keep things—like life—interesting.
Thank you.*

# ONE

*If my grandmother had been wise, she would have named him Hannah as a good luck charm against his clumsy nature.*

---

FOR THE THIRD time since arriving at work two hours ago, Dad tripped over his own feet and smacked face first into the carpet. The thump of him hitting the floor drowned out my sigh. I debated whether to get up and help him or stay at my desk and observe his efforts to restore his dignity.

If my grandmother had been wise, she would have named him Hannah as a good luck charm against his clumsy nature. Instead, I was saddled with it as my middle name, a ward against harm and a wish to prevent the Evans family curse from striking me.

In my opinion, I was far from graceful, but I had managed to avoid my father's clumsy fate. It made sense to me, although those who didn't know us well marveled at the fact I could walk in a straight line. If they found out I could cartwheel on a balance beam, they'd probably faint from shock.

Then again, few knew what I knew: I wasn't my father's daughter, and I doubted I would ever learn whose daughter I was.

"You could have some pity, Matia," Dad complained, rolling onto his side and propping his chin in the palm of his hand.

Blood oozed from his nose and dripped down to the stubble of his day-old beard.

No matter how many times everyone told me blood was a vibrant hue—a rich crimson —my traitorous eyes always told me another story. Blood was just another shade of gray, charcoal over the paler slate of my dad's skin. The carpet, like most of Dad's clothes, came in at a shade somewhere between black, black, and yet another shade of black.

Three words defined my world: black, white, and gray.

Instead of answering, I pulled out my cell phone and took several pictures to immortalize Dad's inability to handle the most basic task of walking without ending up on the floor.

Dad sighed, lifted his hand, and touched his nose. "This always happens right before a meeting."

There was so much I wanted to say, but as always, the words stuck in my throat. It was so much easier to keep quiet and turn my attention back to my work, work he needed me to finish if he wanted us prepared for the meeting we were scheduled to leave for in less than twenty minutes.

The graphs, the pie charts, the stock figures, and the projections blurred together, and I wondered why Dad made *me* prepare the damned presentation. Annamarie would've been happy to build it; she controlled the rest of our lives, presenting our schedule with a smile, ready to deal with the real world so we didn't have to, all so we could make it to the next business meeting without being late.

Annamarie could do a far better job than I could creating the presentation. As always, my eyes failed to comprehend the existence of color. Despite how many times someone pointed at the sky and declared with certainty its color was blue, all I saw was a gray paler than most.

Blue was a lie, just like the red of blood was a lie, no matter how many drops fell from Dad's chin to stain the carpet.

Maybe one day the doctors would figure out what was wrong with my head and fix it. If they did, I had thousands of photographs waiting to show me the real world, a world filled with color.

Until then, I'd keep on taking photographs. After I had snapped several pictures to print out later, I pointed at him, arching a brow.

Annamarie was going to kill him when she found the new spots on the carpet, and I'd take photos of her wrath, immortalizing the way her dark eyes glinted in the too bright glow of the recessed lighting overhead.

Maybe one day I'd know if her eyes were blue, green, brown, or whatever other shades eyes came in. Her hair was likewise a mystery, neither light nor dark, matching her skin.

I gave the pie charts a final glare before saving the file. As long as everyone else could tell the difference between the sections, did the colors really matter? Blue was gray, red was gray, green was gray, yellow was gray, and I wasn't sure which gray was which. With my luck, I probably used the most horrific combination of colors. My only saving grace was that Dad's associates were too dignified to vomit during a business meeting.

Instead of taking a picture, I'd print the presentation at home. The pages would join the thousands of other sheets I kept stored in my closet.

"I could go like this and set a new fashion trend. What do you think, Matia?"

Fighting the urge to sigh, I pointed at the doors leading out of our office. "No."

Dad grinned in victory at forcing a word out of me, hopped to his feet, and made it across the room without finding some other imaginary object to trip over. Opening the door, he bounced to our assistant's desk.

Annamarie wailed her dismay. "Mr. Evans!"

"I think I'm going to need a new shirt and tie," Dad replied, his tone wry.

"Jacket, too." Our assistant sighed. "I'll take care of it, sir. Please get cleaned up. Your car will be here soon."

"Thanks."

"Please don't strip out here, Mr. Evans."

Mumbling curses under my breath, I snatched my laptop and hurried to rescue Annamarie from my idiot father before he finished tossing his common sense to the four winds. I stormed into the reception area in time to watch the dark fabric of Dad's jacket hit the floor along with his shirt and tie.

"Please put your clothes back on, Mr. Evans."

"I thought I'd go like this. It'd make an impression."

Sometimes I really wondered how anyone took Ralph Evans, CEO of Pallodia Industries, seriously.

---

INSTEAD OF WAITING for Annamarie to find him a change of clothes, Dad made a run for it the instant she was gone, leaving me to follow or be left behind.

It was so, so tempting to make a hasty retreat to our office and hide under my desk until I died of old age. We left the safety of our reception area and headed through the executive wing of the building. Glass-fronted offices offered our co-workers and employees a clear view of my half-naked father, who strutted down the hall with his bloodied jacket and shirt draped over his arm. Why he had opted to wear his tie was beyond me.

At least he had wiped the blood off his face.

When Harthel, Vice President of the company, stepped out of his assistant's office, he halted, his mouth hanging open. Unlike Dad, who went to the gym every day and dragged me along with him, Harthel visited every last donut shop in New York City, doing his duty to keep them in business.

"Ralph?" The rank smell of the man's breath made me want to pinch my nose to spare myself. If the stench from his mouth wasn't bad enough, he was wearing a new cologne.

Why was breathing necessary?

Curious employees, ranging from administrative assistants and accountants to department heads, peered out of their offices to watch the fireworks.

While most of the men watched with wide eyes, the women focused their attention on Dad. I caught Harthel's assistant fanning herself, her gaze firmly locked on my father's chest.

Since dying of embarrassment didn't seem to be an option, I needed an exit strategy, stat.

Why had Dad decided showing off his physique was necessary?

Our employees were probably snapping photos on the sly. If at least one of them didn't surface in a tabloid showcasing my father as one of New York City's most eligible bachelors, I'd be torn between surprise and disappointment.

Newspapers paid a lot for photos, and Dad enjoyed the attention and positive press it brought to the company. Unfortunately, they were probably taking a few photos of me, too.

Dad and I were quite the team; the instant I had turned eighteen, I had joined him on the charts, claiming an even higher spot on the eligible bachelorette column.

Dad made the list because of his money and his looks. Me? I had no idea why the hell I was on it, but I wanted off the ride.

To make matters worse, the media loved father and daughter pictures, especially when the father's newest hobby involved sculpting his chest and abs.

Unfortunately for me, he was good at it. Some men had a midlife crisis and bought a new car, got a new wife, or dropped everything and went on a multi-month vacation.

My dad worked out and loved it.

Harthel cleared his throat. "Ralph? What's going on?"

Dad made a noncommittal noise in his throat.

Living as the CEO's daughter, partner, and general accomplice had rules. Rule one involved smiling. Smiling helped convince people I didn't want to stab them in the face to get rid of them. Rule two involved resisting the urge to stab annoyances in the face.

I really hated rule two sometimes, especially when Dad decided to pull an impression of *me*, refusing to offer his second-in-command an explanation for why he had blood on his clothes and was walking around half-naked.

In reality, Dad kept sharp, pointy objects away from me to protect me from the Evans family curse. If he learned about my violent thoughts, he'd either have a heart attack or give me the spanking of my life.

Dad wouldn't even care I was eighteen, an adult, and fully capable of making the decision to stab someone in the face. I'd happily serve a jail sentence if it meant Harthel wouldn't bother me—or anyone else—ever again. Dad would light my ass on fire so I wouldn't be able to sit for a week, but I'd earn it. He had raised me better; stabbing people for being intolerable jackasses was beneath me.

Inflicting physical harm was beneath an Evans woman. Financial and social ruin, however, was permitted and encouraged. As long as I smiled and didn't stab anyone—in the face or elsewhere—Dad would probably forgive me eventually.

Both rules sucked. Smiling made creeps like Harthel think I liked him when I didn't. I smiled so it wouldn't look like I wanted to murder him when I did. I smiled until it hurt.

My broken eyes made my discomfort around Harthel even worse. Not only did my eyes dislike colors, they hated greedy slobs and were determined to make certain I knew exactly what sort of man Harthel was. A miasma almost as vile as his Eau de Skunk cloaked him, radiating a chill potent enough I got goosebumps.

Dad dealt with my colorless world with far more patience than I deserved. The last thing he needed was to know shades of gray weren't the only things I saw.

Dark, cold tendrils stretched from Harthel towards my father. I stepped in the way, shivering as I came into contact with the shadows of the man's presence.

I wouldn't allow Harthel to contaminate Dad.

Dad had darkness of his own, but it had faded over the years, and I wasn't going to let some egotistical, corporate brown nosing so-and-so bring it back. "Please excuse us, Mr. Harthel. We have to leave for a meeting. Good day."

The onlookers sucked in a collective breath, and the weight of their attention crashed onto my shoulders. I clutched my laptop to my chest with one hand and grabbed Dad's elbow with the other to drag him down the hallway.

At the rate I was going, I'd blow through my self-imposed yearly allowance of spoken words by the end of the day, and it was only March.

---

WHILE ANNAMARIE HAD SCHEDULED our business meeting and ensured we knew when we needed to leave the office to arrive on time, she had neglected to inform me we had to fly to get there. Not only had she neglected to inform me of such a basic detail, but the fact we were taking a commercial flight seemed to have slipped her mind, too.

I triple checked my phone, looking over my calendar. Nope, there was no mention of any sort of flight anywhere. In fact, I had had several in-office meetings with Dad, and sometime during the thirty-minute ride to the airport, they had been canceled.

I had been conned, and our driver was in on it. Sam grinned as he handed me my passport along with a carry on bag. Dad waved our itinerary before stashing it in his pocket, ensuring I couldn't have a peek to learn the location of our business meeting.

At least my bag had just enough space for my laptop. A cursory glance informed me someone, probably Dad, had packed everything I'd need for an overnight stay. The only thing missing was my camera and the charger for my laptop. I turned the full force of my glare on Dad.

He ignored me, taking his luggage from Sam. The bloodied shirt, tie, and jacket were exchanged for new ones, but instead of dressing like a sane man, Dad draped them over his shoulder.

"Camera?" I whispered, pulling out my phone to act as a stand-in. I snapped shots of the terminal, of the people, and several of Sam, who kept grinning like an idiot while posing for me.

Taking pictures would distract me from having no idea what was going on or why. It would also provide me with some entertainment on the flight, since I hadn't thought to grab my tablet so I could read.

My laptop's battery was fully charged, but without any idea when I'd be able to acquire a new cable for it, I didn't want to use it too much.

"Go buy a new one," Dad replied, pulling out his wallet and handing it to me. "There's a shop in there somewhere with one, I'm sure. I have a few things to discuss with Sam, so I'll meet you at security. We're early, so we have time. No more than thirty minutes, though. If you can't find a camera you like, I'll get you one once we land. You can use your phone until then, right?"

Taking his credit cards and identification would serve him right, but instead of pursuing financial revenge, I left his things intact and stuffed his wallet in one of his jacket pockets. However tempting it was to remind him I was a paid employee, I shouldered my bag, snorted, and headed inside the airport.

I'd pay for my camera with my own money and ignore Dad's protests while proving I was capable of fending for myself.

I stopped just inside the doors, turned, and snapped several photos of Dad with Sam. Dad laughed and waved me off, and I responded by sticking my tongue out at him.

If I had to fly commercial, leaving my maturity and dignity at the doors was one way I'd survive the flight with my sanity intact. Security would be only the first of my nightmares. Security expected me to talk to them.

In a perfect world, I'd answer their questions with as few words as possible and breeze my way through. In reality, I'd open my mouth, nervousness would take over, and I'd stammer my answers, resulting in a lengthy questioning session.

Said session would end in tears, a missed flight, and a rebooking, which involved even more talking. I shuddered and marched through the pre-security terminal in search of a camera.

I found an electronics store with a selection of cameras, and while most of them were overpriced pieces of junk, I found a midrange camera sporting enough features to please the average photographer, which was what I'd remain until the day I died.

People liked things like color balance in their pictures. Lighting to enhance the colors of the real world meant little to me. At least I had an edge on black-and-white photographers. Sometimes I even allowed Dad to strip the colors from my pictures to show to his friends.

I turned my attention back to the camera. It had a larger body than most of the cameras, which intrigued me. A quick scan of the camera's features revealed it, unlike its brethren, used AA batteries.

I grabbed the box and tucked it under my arm, and on a whim, I snagged one of the slender portable cameras. To complete my hunt, I grabbed a camera bag and accessories I'd need to make good use of my acquisitions.

As a bonus, I found a charger for my laptop, which I snatched up on my way to the counter.

The store clerk wasn't interested in a conversation, ringing up my purchases and swiping my credit card with the customary greetings. I declined a bag with a shake of my head and beelined for the nearest bench so I could tear into the packaging.

Within five minutes, I had all of the necessary cables, mini tripod, batteries, and memory cards stowed in my new camera bag. I somehow found room to shove my laptop's new charge cable in my carryon. While fresh out of the box, the slim camera had a half-charged battery. Disregarding the instructions, I decided to put it to the test, stowing the larger camera in my purse.

My first goal was to photograph every last inch of the airport on my way to security. I'd work out my anxiety by snapping photos and find out just how long my new camera would last before it either ran out of battery or I trashed the button by clicking on it so many times.

"At the rate you're taking pictures, someone's going to think you're a terrorist scoping the place out," a silky smooth yet masculine voice rumbled in my ear. I squeaked, dropping my camera. The lanyard spared it from crashing to the floor. Instead, it took a dive down my blouse. With my face burning, I dug the camera out of my cleavage and spun on a heel to face the speaker.

What was it with men deciding not to wear their shirts to the airport? I got a really good look at his chest, which had a remarkable lack of hair. What sort of man waxed his chest?

I didn't care what color his skin was; in the airport's overhead lights, the sheen of his sweat made my fingers itch to find out if he was nearly as smooth as he looked. The thought only made my face burn hotter. Instead of looking up like I should have, my gaze dipped to his stomach to get acquainted with each and every one of his abs.

Dad liked working out and did a good job of it, but he didn't hold a candle to the honed perfection on display before me.

"Like what you see?"

Why did people always want an answer when they asked a question? It was so unfair. Deciding I had already embarrassed myself beyond redemption so it didn't matter what I did, I hopped back several steps, lifted my camera, and snapped a few pictures before beating a hasty retreat in the direction of the security gate.

---

I FOUND my boarding pass tucked in my passport, which solved a lot of problems.

With my ticket in hand, facing airport security seemed a far better fate than trying to explain my shameful behavior. I'd text Dad and let him know I had braved my worst nightmare on my own.

I'd use up the rest of my allotment of words for the year if it meant I didn't have another run-in with the sweaty man and his gorgeous, waxed chest. It was one thing to sneak peeks at a half-naked man; I did it all the time at the gym when I thought no one was looking. I caught plenty of men watching me when I worked out, too, and I didn't blame them for it.

Breasts had a tendency to bounce, and mine were no exception to the rule. No sports bra in existence contained mine completely. They were just too large. Most men, however, at least pretended to look at my face while sneaking peeks at my cleavage.

There were rules in polite society about objectifying someone of the opposite sex, and I had broken every last one of them in less than thirty seconds. To make matters worse, I had taken several pictures to immortalize the moment. Hustling across the airport at a pace that'd make Dad proud of my efforts, I popped the memory chip out of my camera, stuffed it in my purse, and swapped it out for a fresh one.

If security decided to turn on my cameras to prove they worked, they would find an empty memory chip and *not* the flexed muscles of a man too damned handsome for anyone's good, especially mine. Printing those photos would be the first thing I did when I got home.

In my haste to snap the shots, I wasn't even sure I had captured his face. With my luck, my camera shared my shameful lack of dignity, focusing strictly on his sinfully slick and smooth skin.

Grandmother, at least, would be proud. Hell, if she found out about the situation, she'd hunt the poor man down, lure him home, and do her best to make sure I wasn't actually a lesbian like she thought I was.

The condoms I kept in my purse's zippered pocket should have provided her with a few clues I was straighter than an arrow and interested in finding someone. I'd seen her rummaging through my things often enough when she visited there was no way she didn't know I had them.

Sometimes, I found more than I had stashed in my purse, probably a hint I should go get laid.

Unfortunately for me, while I was as straight as an arrow, when it came to love and sex, I couldn't hit the broad side of a barn at point blank range.

Condoms did me no good if I couldn't find a man to sleep with. Daddy's money attracted enough attention, but most men found my silence unnerving while I found their demands for conversation I didn't want equally disconcerting.

If I wanted to talk, I would. When I wanted to, I did. While I could probably dip into the shallow end of the gene pool for a night of fun, I wasn't quite ready to turn into a slut, no matter what my grandmother wanted.

I suspected she just wanted grandchildren, and since Dad wasn't putting out, she was fishing in the adopted granddaughter pool for a great-grandchild. At eighteen, I had plenty of time, and we all knew it.

So Grandmother snuck condoms into my purse, not realizing her son was a step ahead of the game and had taken me to the doctor at thirteen for birth control. I kept the condoms because I sure as hell didn't want to catch anything from my non-existent one-night stands.

Dad was a lot of things, but he understood other men, and he didn't take stock in the traditional belief girls and women were immune to sweat-slicked, bare chests.

Waxed bare chests.

Maybe I didn't fall in love easily, but damn, I had enough lust for two. I stifled a groan and beelined for security, integrating into the line so I could head to my departure gate and put the whole airport behind me.

I glanced at my boarding pass, my eyes widening as I realized I wasn't taking a direct flight. The first leg of the flight took me to Boston before connecting to London.

I blinked, rubbed my eyes, and checked the boarding pass again. The destination hadn't changed.

When I met up with Dad, we were going to have a long talk about why we were flying to London, England. Rule one would be discarded, and rule two would be up for negotiation.

The destination explained why we were flying commercial at least. Flying the corporate jet overseas cost so much even Dad hesitated to book it. I whimpered, and all thoughts of bare-chested men fled under the pressure of an unexpected trip to England with nothing more than a carryon.

The noon rush at the airport left the lines

a mess, but the security guards were moving people through at admirable speeds. In what felt like a blink of an eye, but was actually closer to forty minutes later, I was ushered through to one of the gates. I handed my passport and boarding pass over to the agent, who scanned it before handing it back.

"Where are you going?"

I hated security, but if I wanted to escape without having to deal with the gauntlet of additional questioning, I needed to pretend I wasn't shaking and that a film of sweat wasn't forming under my blouse. "London."

"Purpose of your trip?"

"Business meeting," I replied, keeping a close eye on the box with my carryon and my purse.

It passed through the machine, and the agent in charge of the device grabbed my bag and pulled out my laptop. "Turn it on."

I opened it up, and since I hadn't taken the time to shut it off, I tapped in my password, minimized the presentation, and turned the screen to the agent for his scrutinization. He tapped on the trackpad to prove it was an actual laptop before nodding his permission to put it away.

"When are you returning?"

Thinking fast on my feet was part of my job description, and all the other times we had gone overseas, we had returned within a week, so I replied, "In a week."

"Have a safe trip."

I blinked at him, and he blinked back before cracking a grin and gesturing for me to grab the box with my purse, my bag, and my shoes. I gathered my things, stunned I had cleared security without a fuss, and headed to the next checkpoint before he changed his mind about letting me through.

---

I FOUND a cafe and parked at a table for two, sighing from relief at the chance to sit down. Grabbing my phone out of my purse, I texted Dad to inform him I had navigated through the perils of security without a hitch and asked how long it would take him to make it through the gauntlet.

My phone rang ten seconds later, and before I had a chance to say hello, Dad blurted, "Go to the gate and wait for me there."

He hung up on me before I could do more than open my mouth in astonishment. Why would he call me to say that when he could have texted me? I stared down at the phone, tapping to return his call.

The call went straight to voicemail.

My creeped-out-o-meter redlined. Grateful I had already paid for my coffee, I got up, grabbed my bags, and debated whether to be a good daughter and do as told, or risk going through security a second time to find out what had gotten into Dad.

I didn't have far to go to reach the gate,

which meant if I decided to be a bad daughter, it wouldn't take me long to return to where I belonged. I selected Sam's number as I walked and held my phone to my ear while I dodged other travelers on my way back to the security checkpoint.

Sam's phone went straight to voicemail, too.

All things considered, the one person who probably knew what was going on was Annamarie. Swallowing a sigh, I hunted through my contact list, coming to a halt within sight of security.

"Miss Evans?" Annamarie answered, her tone shocked.

"Did Dad—" A flash of light drew my attention to the security gate, and before I could do more than turn my head to the source, a bang heralded a wave of heat and smothering darkness.

## TWO

*Dad had known something was wrong, and he had tried to warn me away.*

---

SOMETIMES, Dad woke screaming from a sound sleep, and I knew the nightmares were back. He had spent a lifetime—*mine*—coping with what he had done. The cries penetrating the ringing in my ears reminded me of those nights, the nights when he relived killing my mother.

Alcohol had evaporated from his life that night, but his change wouldn't bring my mother back, and my real father had never come for me. Like my Dad had done with his bottles, my real father had discarded me the instant my mother was gone. So, Dad had made me his responsibility.

I was grateful for that, I really was, but I still hated when he screamed. I hadn't known my mother or my real father, and with Dad around, I didn't need anyone else. Why did he have to scream?

I registered the sound around me in the

sleepy way I did at home, but the screams didn't quiet like I expected; Dad's cut off the instant he realized he was awake and no longer trapped in his nightmares.

Dad was never so shrill, either.

Noise enveloped me; the rare moments someone wasn't crying out or screaming, something crackled. The sounds were muffled, although I couldn't tell by what. A siren's shrill blare added to the cacophony, startling me into sucking in a breath.

Smoke filled my lungs.

The harsh fumes jolted me to full awareness. Bursts of light danced and flickered somewhere nearby, and my eyes stung from the haze surrounding me. Thanks to winter nights nestled warm in front of the fireplace, I recognized the crackle, the heat, and the shifting illumination as flame.

The memory of heading for the security gate at the airport crashed into me. Something had happened, something I couldn't remember. The throb in my head intensified with every breath. A groan slipped out, and the sound woke an itch in my throat and lungs, which heralded a rasping cough.

My chest hurt almost as much as my head. It took me longer than I liked to realize I was lying on my side. The flutter of anxiety in my stomach threatened to burst into full-fledged panic.

I, Matia Hannah Evans, didn't panic. I, Matia Hannah Evans, observed calmly and critically, prepared to dive in the instant Dad needed me to intervene and come to his rescue. Something had happened to make him call me to try to warn me away.

Dad had somehow known something was wrong, and instead of heading away from trouble, I had dived into it head first.

Was my father screaming? Had he, like me, been caught in the destruction? Bomb threats happened all the time. Not even in my nightmares had I ever imagined being at ground zero.

A tremble ran through me. Dad had known something was wrong, and he had tried to warn me away. Tears burned in my eyes. Was he trapped somewhere nearby, waiting for me to find him? The thought of him trapped in the rubble terrified me far more than the fact I had been caught in the blast.

Panicking would do me zero good. If I panicked, I couldn't do anything for either one of us. I took deep breaths, fighting against the urge to cough.

It was no different from work, if I thought it through a little. The first thing I needed to do was assess my situation. Once I knew what I had to work with, I could make a plan. I hurt, but I didn't feel the stabbing agony of a broken bone. If I had escaped without breaking anything, I'd consider myself ahead of the game.

I started with my fingers, wiggling them

one at a time. My right wrist throbbed. Shuddering, I rotated my right arm, gasping at the ache in my shoulder. It hurt, but it didn't feel broken.

If it were, I'd be screaming.

My left arm was pinned beneath my side, so I diverted my attention to my legs, starting with my toes. Warning jolts of pain shot up my calves, and I identified the cramp of muscles stuck in the same position for too long, which made me wonder how long I had been unconscious. I rotated my ankles.

My left one obeyed while my right twitched, and a stabbing tingle swept through my foot. Until I could get up and look at what was wrong, there wasn't anything I could do, which left me with the problem of my arm. While my hand was free, my arm was pinned beneath me, and wiggling my fingers woke the same sharp tingling sensation.

First, I needed to decide whether to roll onto my stomach or back. The smoke burned my eyes and decreased visibility to less than a foot.

Would someone who could see color have an easier time? Could red, green, yellow, or blue peek through the gray shroud of smoke, or did it restrict everyone to my colorless life? Under normal circumstances, I liked smoke.

Its color was one of the few truths I could rely on.

I decided my back was the safer choice. If

I could sit up, I could get a better idea of how much trouble I was in.

I flopped with the grace of a fish out of water. Something hard and hot poked me in the back, and I hissed at the scrape of a jagged edge against my skin. My breath wheezed, and the ache in my lungs intensified.

If I didn't get out of the smoke, I'd suffocate. Fear gave me the strength to lurch upright, half twisted due to the position of my leg. Through the haze, I could make out the debris pinning my foot, ankle, and lower calf to the floor.

Before its destruction, the airport had been a mix of stone tiles, carpeting, steel, concrete, and glass broken by utilitarian stations and an eclectic mix of casual, hip, and elegant shops and restaurants.

Broken chunks of concrete and tile tangled with twisted metal littered the floor. Smaller bits tumbled off me as I took stock of what had fallen on me. Most of the chunks were small enough to offer me some hope of being able to shift them aside on my own, assuming I didn't smother to death from the smoke first.

Shaking out my hands until the worst of the tingling faded, I buttoned my top all the way to its collar and lifted it so I could breathe through the fabric instead of inhaling unfiltered smoke. I had no idea if it would help, but with no other options, I decided it was better than doing nothing at all. I bit on the fabric to hold it in place and breathed out of my mouth.

I grabbed the first piece of debris and shifted it to the side. Once I was free, I'd find Dad, somehow.

---

THE SMOKE THICKENED while I worked, forcing me to stop and take breaks with increasing frequency. The stench of burning plastic deadened my sense of smell, and despite trying to breathe out of my mouth, I kept forgetting, and my nose, throat, and lungs burned. I didn't know how long it took to free my leg, but once I shifted the last of the twisted metal away, I rotated my ankles to restore feeling to my feet.

While I didn't think I had broken anything, I hadn't emerged unscathed. My head still throbbed. Dark smears streaked down my legs where I'd been cut by debris. Some of the gashes still bled sluggishly, although not enough to worry me. The burn in my lungs and chest bothered me the most. I wanted to cough, and I spent a lot of time clearing my throat to quell the impulse.

Coughing would only make it hurt more; I'd learned that lesson the first few times I had lost the battle.

The distant blare of sirens, the crack of crumbling concrete, and the groan of twisting metal kept the terminal from falling quiet. The screams had died down to low groans, and I shuddered. I got to my feet with the help of rubble. However tempting it was to ditch my heels, not even the smoke could hide the gleam of glass strewn between the rest of the debris.

I swayed with every step and flinched at the crunches beneath my feet.

A phone rang, its tones muffled. I listened to the chime, then discarded it as irrelevant.

It wasn't mine. It wasn't Dad's. I sucked in a breath, jerking in the direction of the sound. It didn't matter whose phone it was. With a phone, I could call Dad's. I couldn't call my own house to save my life, but Dad's number I knew. I scrambled in the direction of the device, climbing over broken chunks of concrete.

The chime faded, and I couldn't spot the screen's light through the smoke.

I waited, holding my breath in the hope it would ring again. It didn't. Sighing, I cursed my stupidity for wasting the first few rings. I wormed my way off the pile and lifted my arm so I could breathe through my sleeve.

The wreckage around me shattered my hopes one broken stone at a time. I had been on the fringe of the destruction. Dad must have been near the center of it.

The smoke and the crackle of flames somewhere nearby killed what was left of my hope. He wouldn't be meeting me near the gate. He wouldn't be meeting me anywhere.

It was a miracle I had survived.

What could I do? Beside the rubble, lost in the haze of fire and smoke, I felt tiny, insignificant, weak, and alone.

---

THERE WERE people alive in the rubble. I found the first woman by tripping over her. Like me, she was partially buried beneath what had once been part of the security gate. My hands shook as I touched her neck, searching for a pulse. I couldn't tell much about her, but her eyes were closed and her heart beat strong beneath my fingers.

I kicked aside debris so I could kneel beside her, taking in the twisted and broken metal and glass pinning her legs to the floor. Like me, cuts and scrapes covered her, leaving her skin darkened and smeared, probably from her blood.

Would pulling the weight off her help? I didn't know, but I couldn't leave her.

She lived, and like me, she was alone.

Grabbing hold of my sleeve, I gave it a few yanks where it had already been torn during the explosion, ripping it away in strips. Holding my sleeve over my mouth and nose so I didn't breathe in extra smoke wouldn't work, not if I wanted to use both hands, but I could at least fashion a makeshift mask for myself.

If I let the woman breathe in unfiltered

air, I didn't know what would happen to her. Her blouse was a thin, gauzy fabric like mine. I ripped the material and draped it over her mouth and nose, waiting long enough to watch the fabric flutter with her breaths.

It wasn't much, but I hoped it'd help her a little.

Like earlier, the exertion took a toll on me, requiring me to stop and pant each time I shifted the debris away. She had fared better than I had; while her legs were pinned, the metal and concrete had fallen around her instead of directly on top of her.

Once she was freed, I stared at her, wondering if it was safe to try moving her. If there was fire, I couldn't tell through the smoke, but I had no idea why she wasn't conscious. Had the smoke gotten to her, or was there some injury I couldn't see? Would moving her hurt her more?

She still lived, but if I moved her, I didn't know if I'd kill her trying to help her.

Never had I been so far out of my depth. I knew CPR; Dad had insisted I learn if I planned to go anywhere near a swimming pool so long as I lived. In reality, it had been for his sake as much as mine.

When Dad tried to drown himself being an idiot in the pool, at least *someone* could beat the life back into him.

I didn't think what worked at the pool would help the woman lying prone beside me. She was still breathing, so CPR wasn't necessary. I needed a real doctor, someone who actually knew what they were doing, to come help her, but there was no one. Sirens still sounded, but they were so, so far away.

I had moved the debris. It was a start. If others were trapped, I could free them, too.

When—*if*—help arrived, they'd be easier to move. My doubts piled up and threatened to crush me beneath their weight.

Was so little enough?

I didn't know, but there was nothing else I could do.

---

OTHERS HAD SURVIVED, and they wandered through the rubble. Some tried to help the people trapped in the debris, but one person couldn't do much alone.

I knew because I had tried, and I had failed. The debris weighed too much, and the smoke did too good a job choking off my breath. I had helped some, although I had no idea if they would survive.

Every person I stumbled across, trapped in the aftermath of the blast, woke my fear and left me cold and shivering. The first time I touched someone's neck—a man's—and found his skin cold and his body lifeless, I shuddered, and I checked four times to make sure he wasn't Dad.

The smoke blinded me, turning the familiar grays into a singular shade outlined in darker shadows. I had to draw close—within inches—to make out the man's features.

He wasn't Dad. The man's opened, sightless eyes stared into mine. Death left his mouth slack, and the charcoal of blood trailed over his lips.

I recoiled, shaking. There were others nearby just like him, gone beyond help. The hope Dad lived died away. If the blast hadn't killed those deeper in the rubble, the smoke and flames likely had—or would.

My mouth opened, but I couldn't force out a single sound. I staggered away from the man's body, covering my mouth with my hands. Others stood, staring at the ruins. They did nothing despite those still trapped in the rubble. Through the ringing in my ears, I could hear them crying out for help.

The thought my father was one of them chilled my blood. Alone, there was no hope of finding him, dead or alive. With others, the chance I could find him existed, however slim. I shivered, turning to the people avoiding the rubble, staring and doing nothing to help those trapped.

I headed to the nearest person. Through the haze, I couldn't tell much about her, just that she was a woman. She stood and stared at the debris, and I wasn't sure if she saw anything at all. Her clothes were torn and stained with dark splotches. I feared it was blood, but I couldn't tell for certain.

I never could, and the limitations of my

eyes hit me hard. How could I help anyone when I couldn't tell the difference between ash, soot, and blood? I couldn't even tell if the charcoal-colored stains covering me were from my blood.

For a long time, I stared at her, wondering what to do or say. All I could think about was how Dad would handle the situation. He'd take control, browbeat people into doing what he wanted, and be as quick with a smile as he was with a rebuke.

Dad wouldn't have hesitated. Silence wouldn't serve me, not if I wanted to find him.

I took the last few steps to close the distance between us. "You okay?" My voice was hoarse from the smoke, and the itch in my throat intensified to a burn. The first cough tore through me, and by the time I smothered the fit, I gasped for breath.

"How could this happen?" The woman kept staring at the debris. Like me, her voice was hoarse, but she didn't cough.

I didn't have an answer for her. Shaking my head, I followed her gaze. Her attention was focused on the dead man's body.

We couldn't save him, but he was a start. Swallowing back my queasiness, I wondered if I really wanted to take the next step. Even if I searched, would I find Dad?

Worse, what would happen if I did?

"We should move him." The words came out with far more confidence than I felt.

The woman frowned. "But he's dead."

"There might be others alive in that mess."

"But he's dead." The doubt and disgust in her voice annoyed me. As always, I hid my thoughts behind a veil of silence. Sometimes we ran into people at work who balked at certain tasks, and I couldn't blame her for her hesitation and horror at the prospect of moving a body. I wasn't thrilled with the idea, either. Instead of forcing her, I considered my options.

Remaining quiet wouldn't work, and it took every shred of my courage to say, "Go find others who are on their feet and able. Send them over and come back."

I kissed my word quota for the year goodbye, wondering if it would make a difference. The woman's dark eyes focused on me, narrowing in thought. There were so many ways someone could react to such a blatant order, but instead of the protests I feared, she nodded, turned on a heel, and headed for the nearest group of people.

Sometimes, people just needed a little direction in a crisis to help them focus their efforts. It didn't take long for the woman to recruit several people who weren't as squeamish to help with sorting through the rubble and dragging the bodies we uncovered out of the way. I took a few minutes to scope out the area, finding a section of wall near a half-destroyed shop.

At first, there were only seven of us struggling to dig through the debris in search of survivors, and I was the only woman. At my hoarse, clipped orders, several of the men dragged the dead to the wall, laying them together.

The entire time, I doubted. Was it wise moving the bodies? Would it help anything, or were we struggling through the choking fumes for no reason? My breath wheezed in and out of me. Others coughed, but the complaints I expected didn't come.

New Yorkers were tough like that. Later, the shock and anger would settle in. We still remembered. We'd never forget the day our skyline forever changed in a cloud of smoke, flame, and dust. Why were airports and planes so often targeted?

When I wasn't barking orders, I wondered, and I found no answers in my thoughts. Would we ever know the reason why? Did it matter?

I lacked a man's strength, but I moved the pieces I could, and the darkness hid my tears. Minutes slipped by, and I feared we would only find more bodies. When we found a woman alive, sprawled on top of smoking concrete, I held up my hand to stop anyone from touching her. "Is anyone a doctor? Nurse?"

My question was relayed through those gathered.

"I'm a paramedic." The man who approached had half of his face covered with a stained shirt, and his deep voice was muffled by the fabric.

"Your show." Stepping back, I gestured for him to come closer. "What can we do?"

"We're going to need supplies. Clean cloth, first aid kit, water. We won't find many left alive. We're long past the golden hour."

I'd heard of the golden hour before, the precious sixty minutes the injured had after an accident. As the seconds ticked away, their chances for survival plummeted. How long had I been unconscious after the blast?

Too long. It had been near noon when Dad had called and I had chosen to head for him instead of listening. LaGuardia was a place of glass and metal, a modern airport for a modern world. The lack of sunlight proved the paramedic right. At least seven or eight hours had gone by, and we were long beyond the golden hour. For one woman, however, we defied the odds. The chance we could save her—save just one more—drove me to face those who had shied away from our gruesome task. Most of them were women, although a few men dressed in the ruins of suits hung back as well. "Supplies. Find it. Cloth, water, first aid kits." I gestured to the half-destroyed store.

"Why bother?" one of the men snapped. "You heard him. We're past the golden hour."

I turned to him, looked him in the eye, and considered if I had the energy to find a window and commit the act of defenestration. Under normal circumstances, I would have settled for a glare, staring until my opponent looked away, unable to withstand my scrutiny.

Silence was a weapon as much as it was a shelter, but I didn't have the luxury of time, not anymore. "This is her golden hour. Help, or shut up and get the fuck out of the way. There's no room for a lazy coward here."

Heels were terrible shoes for ground zero of a detonation, but I pivoted without falling on my ass, sidestepped the bodies, and headed into the store. The first act of larceny was mine, but it didn't take long for others to follow my lead. I loaded my arms with tourist t-shirts, water bottles from the dead fridges, and found travel first aid kits scattered on the floor.

It wasn't much, but I'd make it be enough.

## THREE

What now?
―――――――――

BY EXPANDING OUR EFFORTS, we learned we were caged between two detonation points. The terminal's glass windows near the first gate had shattered, offering cold but fresh air through the cracks to those in the lounge. I wasn't sure how the thick windows kept together despite the damage from the explosions. Even with exposure to cleaner air, my lungs still ached. I fought for each breath, requiring me to breathe deeply each time I tried to speak.

When I wasn't wheezing, I was coughing, which made my task of organizing listless and confused victims all the more difficult.

Maybe the textbooks claimed the golden hour was only an hour long, but we kept finding survivors trapped in the destruction. Some were injured beyond our ability to help, and the pain in the paramedic's expression matched the tightness in my chest.

It wasn't much, but I ordered them to be

made as comfortable as possible and found someone to sit with them near the broken glass windows overlooking the tarmac. Huge lights illuminated a sea of tents, rescue vehicles, and stoked the hope of rescue.

Several stories up, all the intense glow did was offer us illumination to work by. One of the lounge stores had flashlights, but I doubted those below noticed us. The building still burned in places, forcing us away from where I wanted to be the most.

Someone touched my elbow, pulling my attention away from the flashing blue and red lights below. "What now?"

The woman was one of the later survivors we had found, pinned by wreckage but otherwise uninjured. Turning to face her, I took in those looking at me for guidance. In truth, I had no idea what to do. I made it up as I went, hoping my choices didn't cost someone —all of us—our lives.

"Set up a rotating shift. Hunt for survivors. Gather supplies; we might be here a while. Break holes in the glass to let more air in. Slowly." The last thing I wanted to do was provide more fuel for the flames, but we all needed to breathe. "Let's not stoke the fires."

My body burned with the need for air, as though I had run a race despite standing still.

"Where should we start?"

It was a good question, and one I didn't have the answer to. What else could we do that we hadn't done? I grunted, which led to a body-wracking cough. "Restaurants. There were a few mostly intact. Loot their supplies. See what they have that hasn't spoiled since the power went off. No dairy, no eggs. Likely spoiled. Nothing needing cooked. First aid kits."

"The employee-only doors were locked."

"Break in."

"How?"

How, indeed.

"I can help with that." Smoke did a lot of things to someone's voice, but I recognized the silky voice of the bare-chested man I had treated more like an object than a human being. Whirling around, I faced him. My cheeks flamed, and heat spread down my neck.

He wore a dress shirt, which was unbuttoned, partnered with a classic suit jacket. Dark smears stained the material, and I didn't want to think too hard about the source. Like almost everyone else, he wore a cloth mask over his nose and mouth to help protect against the fumes in the air.

"Thanks," I croaked through my mix of horror and embarrassment.

"You've got quite the head on your shoulders."

I wondered if he recognized me as the crazy woman who had taken pictures of his perfect chest without bothering to look up any farther than his chin. "See if you can find a cart."

"Sure. Anything else?"

"A time machine," I muttered, shaking myself free of the fugue clouding my mind to see what I could do to organize teams to brave the debris to look for anyone still alive.

---

IN NORMAL SOCIETY, names mattered. Introductions were made, forms of address established, and the way conversations and meetings played out were all founded on the initial greeting. A first impression could make or break negotiations, and I was a card my father had played early and often.

My presence worked in his favor, establishing him as far more than a businessman to those he worked with. I became his first impression, and he always took pride in introducing me.

In the ruined terminal, names no longer held weight or importance, so I wasn't concerned with them. If I remained a ghost in the smoke, it wouldn't bother me.

Hours had gone by without us finding a single survivor, and I put an end to the search.

It had been a miracle we had yanked so many away from the brink of death, but our extended golden hour was over. The paramedic had been joined by a doctor and a nurse, and they fought a different battle, one I could only help by making sure they had everything we could find for them to use.

They fought to save the lives still on the brink, extending precious minutes into hours. My body ached, and the worst of my pain was in my feet. Sweeping the debris, the dust, and broken glass out of the lounge had kept some of my fellow survivors busy.

I could have taken my heels off, but I left them on. Turning to one of the women who had a gift of browbeating people into cooperating, I said, "Gather everyone here. There's nothing more we can do but wait."

While the spotlights had turned the night into day, the dawn offered us a view of the ruins of LaGuardia. Terminal B hadn't been the only one hit; smoke rose from the distant buildings, and the other wings of Terminal B likewise burned. Grounded planes littered the tarmac, as did countless emergency vehicles.

"Jesus," someone gasped. The man staggered to the window. The blast had cracked the thick glass, blowing out some chunks of it while leaving enough to offer some protection from the late winter chill. In a week or two it'd be spring, but I had a difficult time believing in spring in the gray haze smothering the airport. "The whole place was bombed."

The scope of the destruction stretched as far as I could see in the early morning light, and I trembled. How many people were trapped in the other terminals of the airport, hoping for rescue?

How would those below even get to us? The boarding ramps had been destroyed by a second explosion in our terminal, cutting us off from the easy routes out. Until someone came for us, we were stuck.

A large hand pressed against my back. "You need to rest."

It was the man with the smooth voice, husky from the smoke. I turned to escape his touch, but my feet decided they had had enough of my abuse. Pain lanced up both of my legs, and before I could catch myself on the back of one of the lounge's bolted-down chairs, my knees buckled.

He caught me under my arms, lowering me to the carpet. Shifting one arm to support my back, he swept his gaze over me, staring at my heels. "Daniel?"

The paramedic made an appearance, narrowing his eyes as he took in my sprawled position on the floor. Crouching, he rested his wrists on his knees. "What happened?"

"She fell. Maybe her shoes?"

I watched the two men. Daniel was older, which surprised me. He was older than Dad by far, old enough to be my grandfather. There'd been no sign of age in the tireless way he worked.

The darkness hid a lot, and while we had found some flashlights, I had focused my attention elsewhere.

"You did all that work in those heels?" Daniel blurted, and in his tone, I heard his disbelief and what I hoped was respect. "Jesus, ma'am, your feet are going to be a bloody mess. Why didn't you have us check your legs? You never said you were hurt."

"Busy," I choked out. My voice was so hoarse I wondered if he understood me.

Twisting around without rising, he gestured to one of the women who served as his assistant. "Water and the cleanest shirt you can find."

A giggle bubbled out of me. Using the tourist trap shirts had resulted in interesting bandages, if the running jokes among the survivors were to be believed. The thought of wearing them on my feet was so absurd I burst into laughter. Those nearby stared at me as though I had lost my mind.

Maybe I had.

In a state of sick fascination, I watched Daniel peel my heels off. I wasn't the only one to wince at the bruised and blistered state of my feet. In a way, I was thankful I couldn't distinguish color.

My feet made Daniel's helper gag.

"You're not going to be walking anywhere in any shoes anytime soon, ma'am. Well, maybe a week. Give orders from a chair. Think you can keep her off her feet, Ryan?" The splash of water on my feet drew a pained gasp out of me.

The gasp led to coughing and wheezing, and by the time I controlled the worst of the fit, I couldn't sit up without help.

Ryan adjusted his hold on me, keeping me upright when all I wanted was to flop on the floor and sleep. "Won't be a problem."

"Smoke inhalation," the paramedic announced. "Hell, we've all got it to some degree or another. No surprise there. Keep her in the fresh air, give her as much water as she'll drink without throwing it up. You know how to do CPR, Ryan?"

My entire body went cold. While there had been cases of people surviving because of CPR, it was a losing proposition. Chest compressions took effort—more effort than most of us had left. The breathing component was intensive, too, although we had been taught in class the chest compression was the most important element.

If I needed CPR, I'd likely be leaving LaGuardia in a body bag. I knew it, and judging from the paramedic's expression, so did he.

"I'll keep an eye on her. Anything we can do?"

"Breathing exercises. Long and deep. I'll see if anyone has an emergency inhaler. What we need is an oxygen mask, but beggars can't be choosers. I'll get someone to break open the glass more. We could all use the fresh air. Ma'am, just focus on taking deep breaths. Don't talk unless you can't avoid it, and try to avoid coughing. Keep her awake, Ryan."

"Anything else, Daniel?"

"Got any miracles handy? We could use a couple."

"I'll see what I have in stock."

I laughed, which led to bone-jarring coughs. Working one arm under my knees while the other supported my back, Ryan lifted me up and carried me to the seats closest to the window. He ordered someone to move, freeing enough space for him to sit with me on his lap, my head nestled in the crook of his arm while my legs stretched out over the empty seats. The cold air bit at my aching lungs.

Fresh air didn't make it any easier to breathe, but I was too tired to feel anything more than resignation.

---

RYAN HELD me as though we were friends rather than strangers with the misfortune of meeting in an airport prior to it exploding. I listened to him talk of his love of the outdoors, especially up high in the mountains. If my lack of questions or replies bothered him, he showed no sign of it. Most people expected something out of me during a conversation.

All he seemed to want was someone to listen.

The smoke made his voice pleasantly husky. The animated way he spoke of the outdoors made me want to see his expression as he took in the landscapes he so adored.

When he spoke of a sapphire sky dipping

down to crystal snow, it was the sparkling white that drew me in and held me enthralled to his story.

I wanted to take pictures of such a place, adding them to my collection of colorless photos, hoping for the impossible dream of seeing the world through his eyes. I wanted to know what it was like to breathe in the cold air of a world untouched by man, high above everything, with the gold of the sun and the sapphire of the sky surrounding me while I stood on a mountain of white snow covering gray stones.

The mountains seemed like the perfect place for my world to meet the real one.

Ryan smiled, staring out the window while he talked, and I wondered what it would be like if a man smiled that way for me. Love, for him, was a faraway place, forever unobtainable to me.

Why did I always desire what I couldn't have?

"I want to take pictures of a place like that," I confessed in a whisper. My voice betrayed me, so hoarse and weak I could barely hear myself.

Ryan's gaze turned to me, and his smile faded. "Do you?"

"I want to see that shade of blue." If Ryan could love it so much, so could I, if only I had the chance.

His laughter warmed me, and he leaned over and picked up a bottle of water. Giving it a good shake before opening it, he offered it to me. "This should help your throat a little."

"Remind me never to trust you with soda."

"And ruin the surprise when you forget?"

The question touched on a future out of my reach. I had no idea what sort of future I would have—if there was one for me.

I had never imagined a world without Dad in it.

I took the bottle and took a long swig of the water. The smoke and the chemicals hanging in the air gave it a bitter taste. I wrinkled my nose, drinking anyway since the liquid eased some of the ache in my throat. "Thanks."

"Go ahead and drink it all. I can get another bottle."

I obeyed. If water held another coughing fit at bay, I'd guzzle down three or four if I had to. When I finished, he took the bottle out of my hand, grinned at me, and lobbed it up and out the window through a gap barely large enough for it to fit. "Score!"

I caught myself before I laughed.

"You know, you're different, and I like that. Don't change."

The direct way he spoke reminded me of the way Dad liked to give orders during a meeting. I should have been offended, but I was too used to people who didn't like the way I minced words or chose not to speak at all.

I liked the fact my quiet didn't bother him

even more than I liked his chest. It had never occurred to me there could be a man out there who didn't mind a quiet woman. Instead of answering, I made a thoughtful noise in my throat.

It was a mistake. The first cough burst out of me, igniting a fire in my throat and lungs, burning away everything other than my awareness of how much harder it became to breathe after each and every rasping cough.

---

WITHOUT FEAR and desperation driving me, there was nothing left to anchor me to the real world. My body rebelled at all the work I had done, leaving me trembling.

My awareness narrowed to the weariness in my body, the faint whistle of my breath, and the way my throat tightened as time passed. From time to time, my chest hurt, far beyond the ache I had endured when working despite the choking smoke. During my more lucid moments, I was aware of my entire body throbbing to the faltering beat of my heart.

Death had been something I'd known about since I was little. Every year in the late fall, Dad told the same story. Maybe he meant to absolve his guilt by being honest about my mother's death, but he made sure I never forgot.

In the same sure way the seasons flowed

into one another, death came for us all. Sometimes we went out with a bang, killed instantly in a car crash. When I had been a little girl haunting his shadow, he had called me his little miracle, a cat with one fewer lives.

Maybe Dad's open acknowledgement of the fleeting nature of life better prepared me for when I'd make the transition from life to death. Dad understood failure and accepted it readily enough, as long as it hadn't been a failure due to negligence.

Effort mattered to him.

It was easier to accept how tired and worn I was knowing I hadn't gone out without a fight.

When the pain ebbed and I floated in darkness, I wondered if death was the peaceful calm and quiet of the moment before sleep. That I had the presence of mind for thought at all intrigued me.

A steady beep convinced me I probably wasn't dead. I considered the sound, high enough in pitch to annoy me, infrequent enough to convince me it wasn't some sort of alarm or warning, and rhythmic enough I could use it to measure time.

At least, I thought I could. I made it up to three hundred beats before my muddled thoughts refused to comprehend the nature of numbers, forcing me to start over at one.

I blamed whatever was keeping my body so numb. Maybe I had become a ghost with a fetish for devices that beeped? I wanted to giggle, but couldn't, which disappointed me.

Maybe I didn't like talking all that much, but I enjoyed laughing. In the comfort of home, away from prying eyes, I watched comedies until I cried from my mirth, earning disgusted scowls from Dad, who never managed to get me to share the joke with him.

Sometimes, I laughed to make him wonder.

Maybe there was something to the belief someone's life flashed before their eyes before death. It wasn't a flash, though. I leisurely explored my memories, right up until the bitter end, when I had accepted I wouldn't find Dad in the rubble.

I had found so many others, but not him.

It was a mercy for both of us. Death ended many things, but Dad wouldn't have to live with me dying first. I was okay with being the second to go.

All I hoped was he hadn't felt a thing. Of all the people in the world, he deserved an instant, painless end.

He had endured enough because of me.

---

HELL WAS the steady beep in my ear. At first, I could ignore it, thinking it would go away. Lights in tunnels, out of body experiences, all the little myths surrounding death I could accept.

I wanted to throw something at the source of the sound, which was somewhere to my right. That I had a sense of direction convinced me death was either a very logical place, or I was somehow quite alive.

Beep. Beep. Beep. Beep. Beep. Beep.

Fucking beeps.

English had a lot of foul words hidden away in its vocabulary, and I practiced as many of them as I could in my head, my irritation at the sound growing the longer I was forced to listen to it.

The noise did serve one good purpose, however. As it annoyed me to whole new levels, the evidence I wasn't quite dead yet filtered through the numbness fogging my head. Both of my feet ached, and I only made the mistake of wiggling my toes once.

Pain was an excellent teacher, and as my nerves started reporting in, I wondered if I could make a strategic retreat back to the land of the suspected dead. The beep was wretched, but it didn't hurt me.

My chest throbbed, my feet were raw, and pain burst up my legs if I so much as shifted my weight. The prick of a needle near my elbow gave me the necessary clue to figure out the source of the infernal beeping.

Hospitals were filled with beeping machines. I had visited them often enough between charity events and appointments trying to figure out what exactly was wrong with my head. Life support machines and monitors were the common offenders, and they were necessary evils.

They kept people alive.

Sometime between piecing together the fact I was alive and figuring out I was in a hospital, I managed to force all of my fingers and toes to report in and confirm I was somewhat intact.

Mostly.

My memory of how I got to the hospital was fuzzy. I vaguely remembered something about my shoes killing my feet. After that, everything was a blur followed by nothing.

If I ever got on a plane ever again, I'd make a point of wearing sneakers with my business attire. Maybe I'd start wearing sneakers exclusively. I could afford to be eccentric. I got enough stares for my tendency to remain silent. What was wearing comfortable shoes compared to that?

I took my time preparing to open my eyes. Once I did, I had a feeling the gates of hell would truly open. I hadn't given anyone my name, and my purse was gone, likely blown to bits along with the rest of my identification.

I didn't want to step back into a world without Dad in it, but I couldn't hide forever. He'd been the one to teach me that.

The light hurt my eyes, and I squinted and waited until I could see without my vision blurring and sharp stabs of pain arcing through my head all the way down to my toes. All of the curses I'd been practicing in my head battled for dominance.

I settled for an oldie but a goody. "*Fuck!*"

Motion in the corner of my eye drew my attention, and a slack-jawed nurse stared at me, a clipboard in her hand. Her pen hit the floor, its clatter loud enough to drown out the wretched beep.

Hospital rooms had lots of little buttons, and the nurse slapped one of them. I blinked at the nurse, who blinked back at me, as though she wasn't quite sure she believed what she saw.

Was it that uncommon for someone to wake up spitting curses? Surely it had to happen often in a hospital. My throat itched, and my mouth felt like I had chewed on salty cotton balls.

Maybe she was impressed I managed to say a word, considering I was convinced my tongue had become a clay block in my mouth.

Before I could figure out if I could wrangle my mouth into forming another word, a man dressed in a doctor's white coat swept in. I liked doctors' coats. They were a truth; my world overlapped with normal people, bound together by the color white.

"Well, well, well. This is promising," the doctor said, his tone light with his satisfaction. "Margie, please make arrangements for a full set of tests."

"Yes, sir. She, ah, was vocal, too. She woke up and said a single word."

It was intriguing watching them watch me, talking to each other as though I didn't exist.

"What word?"

Some words were worth repeating, and if I was going to demonstrate I was conscious and aware, it was worth trying to speak a second time. "Fuck."

All in all, I sounded pretty cheerful. Morning breath wasn't a pleasant experience for anyone, but there should have been limits to just how bad it could get. It tasted like something had been roasted to a crisp and shoved down my throat to rot. The nurse's cheeks darkened, and she made a helpless gesture.

I was just glad I couldn't smell my breath.

"Get those tests scheduled," the doctor ordered, taking the clipboard out of the nurse's hand. "Let's try you with a sip or two of water and see how that goes. You've been a very sick young lady."

If there was an understatement of the year award, his comment was a strong contender for the top prize. The water was cold and soothed my mouth. The first few sips didn't even reach my throat, my mouth was so desperate for moisture. I would have kept drinking until I floated away, but the doctor pulled the bottle out of my reach.

"Is that better?"

I nodded, which was when I discovered there were objects stuck to my forehead. The movement triggered a mild headache, and I decided I'd use up next year's stockpile of spoken words to cut to the chase. "My name is Matia Hannah Evans."

I proceeded to give him my home address, place of employment, and every other relevant bit of information on my life. I even had my insurance policy number memorized. Once done, I explained what had happened, giving him a full account until I reached the blank spots in my memory.

By the time I was done, my voice was so hoarse I was impressed I wasn't spitting blood. While I talked, the doctor dutifully wrote down the information I gave him. For the most part, he listened in silence, interrupting only to request a repeat of certain bits of information. When he asked if I had any family, I hesitated.

Once I spoke the words, I wouldn't be able to take them back. If I spoke them, I'd be fully acknowledging the likely truth. Taking a deep breath made my lungs ache. "I don't know if my father survived."

"Do you know his number?"

I gave him my father's cell phone number, and after a moment of thought, I also gave him Annamarie's number, explaining she was our assistant.

"You're young to have an assistant."

I blinked at the doctor and said nothing.

"What's your father's name?"

"Ralph Evans."

The doctor choked on his own spit. "Are you serious? Ralph Evans? The businessman?"

"We were at the airport when the bombs went off. I'd gone through security before him, so we were separated."

"Excuse me for a moment, Miss Evans." The doctor left the room, pulling a cell phone out of his pocket. He stayed right outside of the room, watching me. He spoke for a few minutes. Without hanging up, he returned, holding the phone to my ear.

"Matia?" The hope in Dad's voice hurt so much I burst into tears.

"Daddy?" I hadn't called him that in years, and I didn't care. I didn't care I blubbered the word, or that my tears made my eyes sting, or that my hitched breathing stabbed my lungs and throat.

"It's okay, Matia. I'm okay. It'll take me a few hours to get to you, but I'm coming, okay? Don't you go anywhere."

I stared at the various machines attached to me and wondered how he thought it'd be possible for me to leave the bed let alone stage an escape. Torn between laughter and helpless sobbing, I agreed.

Then I started coughing, and the doctor took the phone away, claiming they had to run tests, although he probably wanted to make sure I didn't cough to death.

## FOUR

*You'll be taking her home tonight.*

---

THE DOCTOR RAN me through so many machines I didn't know which end was up. Four hours after the start of the gauntlet, the verdict was in. I had survived, although the jury was still out on whether or not I'd live a normal life again.

With luck and some divine intervention, I'd be back to normal in a few months. Well, as close to normal as I got. The vision tests flummoxed Dr. Simmons, making me laugh—and cough—as he tried to figure out clever ways to confirm my vision hadn't been impaired by my healing concussion.

The real problems all involved my lungs; it was a miracle they still functioned at all. Three days in a machine designed to purify my respiratory system had helped, but Dr. Simmons was a good doctor.

He told me the truth.

I had lived, but it'd only be a matter of time before the chemicals I had breathed would come back to haunt me. While asthma wasn't a certainty, it was a likelihood. Cancer would also be highly probable. How the cancer would manifest would remain a mystery until it showed up.

More likely than not, my lungs would never fully recover.

At least my feet had healed while I had been sedated, and while they were tender, I could walk without much discomfort.

Dad showed up in time to hear Dr. Simmons give me the rundown of the things I wouldn't be able to do for the next few months while I recovered. Running and heavy physical exertion topped the list. Standing frozen in the doorway, Dad stared at me with his eyes wide, his face pale, and shaking so hard Sam took his jacket out of his hands so he wouldn't drop it.

"Mr. Evans." Dr. Simmons rose from the stool next to my bed to shake hands with my father. "She came out of sedation with no problems, her breathing has stabilized, and her blood oxygen levels are low but acceptable. We kept her sedated longer than necessary to err on the side of caution, but so far, so good. You'll be taking her home tonight. You will need to acquire a few pieces of equipment for her care at home, mostly for emergency situations. While she's through the worst of it, there's always a risk of complications developing."

Dad's expression went carefully blank,

and I realized he was relying on his negotiation skills to get through the conversation. Before he could start asking a million questions, I needed to stop him somehow.

Why did so many problems have to be solved with talking? My throat still hurt, and the last thing I wanted to do was say anything at all. "In English, he means I need to keep oxygen or something around in case my lungs file their pink slips." I would also get several inhalers for emergencies as well as a list of prescriptions a mile long.

Some of them served one purpose: to lower the risk of developing cancers and lung diseases.

Dr. Simmons hadn't sounded too hopeful about their effectiveness.

Still, a five percent increase in my chances of dodging a terminal bullet was worth it to me, even if it meant I'd potentially suffer from dizzy spells and God-only-knew what else.

I figured I'd tell Dad about all that later. Much later, maybe after I developed whatever demonic cancer had surely invaded my lungs from breathing in so many chemicals and smoke. Maybe I'd hold on long enough for Dad to die of old age first.

Not likely.

Dad's gaze snapped to me, and he stepped to the side of my bed, bending down to cup my face in his hands. He kissed my forehead and sighed.

Relief had a sound, and I heard it in the way his breath left his body. When he inhaled, the wavering I heard was the only sign of the tears he held back, probably for my sake.

"I thought you were dead. When Annamarie called…"

I didn't know what to say. Every thought that popped into my head was a lie, and I couldn't bring myself to say anything at all. Instead of coping with the quick, painless death, he'd have to watch my health deteriorate while I tried my best to pretend nothing was wrong.

Dr. Simmons cleared his throat. "Her long-term prognosis isn't bad, which is something. It could be far worse."

Dad's hold on me tightened before he released me and turned to face my doctor. "Define 'isn't bad.'"

"She won't be running in any races any time soon, but there's a chance for a full recovery. This isn't a guarantee, just a chance, Mr. Evans. If her recovery falls in line with other severe smoke inhalation cases, however, the development of asthma is extremely likely. Cancers are a high possibility, as are other respiratory illnesses. Frankly, it's a miracle she suffered through only one mild infection after her arrival."

Dad turned and sat on the edge of my bed, and I sighed at the purposeful way he kept between me and my doctor. I wanted to throw something at Dr. Simmons for revealing the consequences of the explosion.

In truth, it was probably for the better. I wouldn't have to gather the courage to tell him myself.

"Okay. What happens next?"

"You take her home. You'll need to make arrangements for certain pieces of equipment. I've also taken the liberty of contacting a specialist in Manhattan to continue her care. She'll need to have her blood oxygen levels monitored to make certain her lungs are functioning sufficiently. There will be treatments in the future to help strengthen her respiratory system. I recommend working with a nutritionist to account for her change in physical condition. Substantial weight gain is a possibility if she's been used to an exercise regime. I'm assuming this is the case, as her good physical condition substantially helped with her survival. I have prescriptions for her. It is really important that you make sure she takes all of them at the appropriate intervals, or it could impede her recovery. There will be several inhalers she will need to keep with her at all times. The pharmacist will go over the specifics with you."

"She can come home? Now?"

"She will need to come back in for checkups, but you can take her home. I'll authorize the discharge. I'm afraid there will be quite a bit of paperwork since we didn't have an identification on her when she was admitted.

One of the nurses will help you." Dr. Simmons grinned, and the expression made him look ten years younger. "Bed rest for several days would be wise, preferably with supervision. Follow the directions for the inhalers carefully. If she has difficulty breathing, call an ambulance. Do not attempt to drive her in yourself. Am I understood?"

"Understood, Dr. Simmons." Dad hopped to his feet, caught Dr. Simmons's hand, and pulled the startled man into a hug. "I can't thank you enough."

The doctor's laughter surprised me. "Mr. Evans, it's me who should be thanking you. Because of you and your company, this hospital had the machines required to save her life. Without your donations of finances and equipment, I would have been making an entirely different type of call today."

My father was silent long after the doctor left the room.

---

IT TOOK ALMOST six hours to finalize my discharge. Sam left long enough to get the prescriptions filled, returning with a long list of things I had to do to safely take the medications.

While Dad dealt with the paperwork, I went through my medications with Sam's help. I was impressed by the persnickety nature of the drugs. "You're serious? I have to do a full mouth rinse and gargle or I'll get *what?*"

"Thrush, Miss Evans."

"Thrush? I'll get a bird in my mouth?"

Sam laughed long and hard. "No. It's an oral yeast infection. Just gargle like a good girl every time you take the medication. You'll be fine."

"I'm an adult, and I'm going to need adult supervision to take these pills," I complained, prodding at the bag.

"I don't think it'll be a problem. Getting Mr. Evans to go to work without you, however, will be a challenge."

Instead of answering, I kept digging through the bag. There were twenty different prescriptions plus three inhalers. I wrinkled my nose at the most obvious sign my already abnormal life was taking a turn for the worst.

"There was a guy named Ryan," I blurted.

"Ryan?"

"From the airport."

"What about him?"

"I wanted to thank him." Through the exhaustion, the hard work, and the challenges, he had been there. He had been there right up until my memories went completely blank.

I wanted to go where he had seen his sapphire skies and capture it on film.

"After we get you home, I'll see what I can find for you. What can you tell me about him?"

"Just his name," I admitted, my face flushing. "He was past security at Terminal B."

"They've released the passenger list, so I'll have a look and see what I can find. No promises. He could be an employee of the airport, and they haven't released the employee list to the general public." Sam pulled out his phone and tapped in a note. "I'll do what I can."

I doubted LaGuardia allowed their employees to run around without their shirts on, but I had no intention of telling anyone I had drooled over a man's sweaty chest and had taken photos to immortalize the moment. "Thanks. I'm going to need a new phone and laptop…"

"Your laptop, phone, and cameras were recovered, along with your purse. I'm afraid the larger camera was broken, but the smaller one still works. Your laptop was damaged, too, but we managed to recover the hard drive. Your phone is dead, but we recovered all of your pictures."

"Seriously?"

"Very. They started returning personal belongings a week ago. We got the call they had found your things yesterday morning."

I swallowed. "How has Dad been?"

"I won't lie, Matia. We thought you were dead. I took him to his parents right after we were released from the airport. He wanted to stay, but Terminal B had gotten hit the worst and was all but gone. We didn't have a whole lot of hope you had survived. We got lucky; we had been delayed heading to the security gate. When the bombs went off, we were on the edge of the explosion. I got him away from the smoke and outside with a little help from someone in the same situation. It took both of us, because he wanted to look for you. He fought us every step of the way."

That Dad and I had such similar thoughts both warmed and distressed me. "I looked for you and Dad, too."

"I'm sure you did." Sam ruffled my hair and smiled at me. "Maybe you're a full-grown woman now, but you're still his little girl, and you're definitely cut from the same cloth."

Sam was one of the few who knew I was adopted, but his words made me smile regardless. He had been with us from the very beginning, learning right along with Dad how to take care of a kid with more issues than most magazines.

Sometimes, it was easy to forget he was our driver and occasional bodyguard and not a part of the family.

---

THE MEDICATIONS MADE ME DROWSY, and by the time Dad had finished with the discharge papers, I was asleep on my feet. I made it all the way to the car without wheezing, coughing, or falling flat on my face, which I viewed as a major victory.

I meant to sit in the back with Dad, but he herded me to the front, laying the seat back and buckling me. My protests, which consisted of trying to bat his hands away so I could do it myself, were ignored. When I was situated to his liking, Dad kissed my forehead and sat in the back behind Sam, probably so he could keep an eye on me.

Sam dominated the conversation on the drive home, giving my father the complete rundown on every last one of my medications. Neither seemed to want my input, so I snuggled into the leather seat and contemplated if I could actually fall asleep in a moving vehicle.

Each time I closed my eyes, I remembered the bang of the explosions, smelled the smoke, and heard the screams. I stared out the window into the darkness, watching the highway lights go by.

The lights had a color to them—at least, I thought they did. If they didn't, why would their light seem so gray to me? Was the night sky truly black, or was it some shade of blue? Could a sky capable of making someone like Ryan smile ever become colorless? Was a sapphire sky pale or dark? The snow I understood; I'd gone skiing with Dad in the past. Maybe my world was limited, but spraying powder in the sunlight sparkled all the same.

Snow was white, at least some of the time. I'd heard some folks claim snow had a blue hint to it, and I wondered how white could become blue.

I fell asleep while wondering where I could find snow-tipped mountains with sapphire skies and woke up to Dad talking to someone on the phone. I listened, resisting the urge to stretch so I wouldn't interrupt his conversation.

It was about work, although I didn't recognize the names of the men he addressed. I tried to discern what sort of account negotiations were underway. The few times Dad mentioned equipment, it was for construction, which made up almost half of the company's holdings.

When Dad finally hung up, I indulged in a stretch, wincing at the pop and crack in my joints. I was in my own bed, although I had no memories of reaching home. "Why aren't you at work, Dad?"

"You're here, that's why."

Great. Dad was in super-protective mode, not that I blamed him. I would be, too. However, super-protective mode meant misery for me; every move I made would be scrutinized, and the first time I wheezed or coughed, hell would rain down on my head.

If Dr. Simmons was to be believed, there would be a lot of coughing and wheezing in my future. Getting Dad off to work would be my first mission. Once successful, I'd soak in the jacuzzi until I turned into a raisin.

I yawned, groped for one of the spare pillows, and covered my head with it. "What time is it?"

"Nine."

"Night?"

"Morning."

"Weekend?"

"No."

"Go to work, Dad," I hissed.

"You're here. I'm not going to work."

Three things annoyed me most in the world, and Dad was going for three of three. First, I hated when Dad skipped meetings. If he missed an important meeting, I'd end up with even more work to catch up on. Second, I hated when someone watched me sleep. It was bad enough a lot of people had done nothing other than watch me sleep and monitor my vitals for a week and a half. Third, I hated feeling dependent on others for basic things, including sleeping in my own bed.

"Do you want me to get out of this bed and chase you out the door?"

"You will do no such thing."

"Go. To. Work."

"Matia!"

"Work."

"Someone has to watch you. The doctor said so. You heard him. I'm not leaving you alone."

"Call Grandmother. She can keep me company today, tomorrow, and however many days it is to the weekend."

"It's Monday."

"How many days have you missed?"

Dad didn't reply, although I heard him huff.

One of the more annoying additions to our apartment was the inclusion of landlines in every room. Even the bathroom had one, much to my disgust. For once, it worked in my favor. I rolled over, groping for the handset. I managed to get the receiver in the vicinity of my ear before reaching for the base.

Speed dial was my friend, and with the press of two buttons, the phone was ringing. Sam picked up on the third tone. "Hello?"

"Take my father to work, please. He's in my room stalking me."

Laughter filled one ear while Dad's protests filled the other.

"I can be there in twenty minutes, Miss Evans. Will you be joining him?"

"Wait, that's an option?"

"Is what an option?" Dad demanded.

"It's an option, and probably the one least likely to give Mr. Evans panic attacks. Don't forget to pack your medications and inhalers."

"Thirty minutes," I ordered, hanging up.

"Thirty minutes until what?" Dad rose from the chair he had stolen from the kitchen, glaring down at me with narrowed eyes.

"Until we go to work. I have to shower, get dressed, and pack the stupid medications.

We're going." I flung the blankets off, decided I really didn't want to know how I had gotten into my pajamas, and slipped out of bed.

"You can't go back to work yet."

"Sam says otherwise."

"Sam isn't your father!"

"Dad, can you at least *pretend* everything is normal? Please?" I could already feel my throat itching with the need to cough, and I swallowed back the urge. "I'm okay. I feel fine."

It was a lie, and judging from the way Dad frowned, he knew it. My feet hurt from standing, my chest still ached in the wrong sort of way, the way that warned me breathing was a privilege I was no longer entitled to.

"I only got you back yesterday."

"So trot me into work, put me on display, glow your way through your meetings, and leave me in our office while I check my email. That should keep me busy for a week. You can even come in and make certain all is well. I'll even kidnap a few employees to fill me in on what I've missed so I have all the supervision you could ever want. If you leave me on bed rest, I will kill someone by the end of tomorrow. I'll shove heads on pikes and mount them to our balcony, just you wait and see."

Dad stared at me, his mouth hanging open. Had I grown a second head, nose, or some other stray body part? I headed to the bathroom, careful to take my time so I wouldn't exert myself, peeking in the mirror.

The problem with being colorblind was the fact I had no idea how I looked. Gray was gray, and when it came to complexion, apparently there were lots of shades of healthy—and unhealthy—colors.

"What is it?" I demanded, poking my head out of the bathroom.

"You're very talkative this morning."

Oh, right. With my dubious relationship with spoken words, I supposed my speech was enough to floor Dad. I'd have to be a lot more careful about keeping the rude things I wanted to say locked in my head instead of speaking them without care for the consequences. "Have you ever doubted my intelligence?"

"Well, there was this one time you—"

Several incidents came to mind, and each one was more embarrassing than the last. "*Dad!*"

"Do you really want to go to work?"

"Yes. You will be fired if you do not go in to work."

Dad sighed, shook his head, and stalked out of my room, throwing his hands in the air in his frustration. "You're a mean boss. Fine. Have it your way. We'll go to work. I will work, and you will sit on the couch and watch movies, play games, or do things unrelated to work. Got it? There will be no working. You're supposed to be on bedrest, young lady. That does not mean go to work."

Instead of fulfilling my dream of becoming a human raisin, I took a quick shower and changed into a pair of jeans, button-up shirt, and a sweater. With jeans, it didn't matter what color my blouse was, and since the sweater covered it completely, no one would notice I had dressed myself, something I hated doing so much Dad or Sam dealt with my clothes or dealt with my mismatched attire. I finished my casual ensemble with my favorite pair of sneakers. To add to the image of having no fucks left to give over my appearance, I piled my hair on my head in a messy bun and declared my efforts complete.

When I emerged from my bedroom, Dad gawked at me with wide eyes.

"If anyone tries to tell you this is not business attire, they're wrong."

The knock at the door saved me from justifying my choice of clothing. Sam took one look at me and laughed, giving me a thumbs up to signal his approval.

There were worse ways to start a day.

FIVE

I groaned at the thought of having
to deal with the fat weasel.

---

INSTEAD OF SUBJECTING me to the steps required to get to the elevator from our normal parking spot, Sam had dropped us off in front of the doors, drawing the attention of every single employee outside on their smoke break.

Not only had New York City outlawed smoking indoors, but it was against company policy; too many of our employees had asthma. Considering I had joined the ranks of inhaler-toters, I was grateful for Dad's decision to cater to their health needs.

Once inside, I wouldn't have to worry about my lungs filing for divorce from the rest of me. The three steps to the lobby were enough to wind me, but I forced my breathing to stay slow and deep.

Quick, shallow breaths led to coughing and wheezing.

While I didn't know any of the employees by name, they recognized me, and offered their hellos and smiles. I returned the smiles. On a whim, I murmured, "Hello."

I heard them whispering when I followed Dad into the building. He held the doors open for me, and I was pretty sure he was counting my every breath just to make certain I was still alive.

The stomach-churning stench of Eau de Skunk gave me advance warning of Vice President Harthel's presence in the lobby. I glanced around, catching sight of the rotund man near the security desk, chatting with one of the guards.

"Chuck," my dad called out, and I groaned at the thought of having to deal with the fat weasel.

Mr. Harthel spun around like Dad had jabbed him in the ass. "Ralph? What are you—" The man caught sight of me and his mouth dropped open.

My eyes decided to start playing tricks on me again, and the inky miasma surrounding Mr. Harthel reached out in my direction. I slinked to my father's side, seeking shelter from my imagination in the comfort of his presence.

Dad wasn't usually the type to welcome public displays of affection, but he wrapped his arm around me and pulled me close. Super-protective mode had some benefits, and not even the tendrils of darkness dared to approach my father when he was playing guard.

"She wanted to come in today," Dad explained. "Any problems I should know about?"

"N-no problems, Ralph."

Maybe I had taken enough medication to down a horse before leaving home, but I didn't miss the way Mr. Harthel's gaze slid away from me without making eye contact with Dad. Sirens—the kind I'd heard wailing in the distance at LaGuardia—rang in my head.

The shroud enveloped Mr. Harthel like a second skin, staining him with the darkest of blacks.

"Good. I'll be with Annamarie shuffling my schedule for the day." Dad checked his watch. "Will you be in your office in an hour?"

"I can be."

"Good. We'll talk then."

My creeped-out-o-meter redlined, and I shuffled closer to Dad, torn between following him to the impromptu meeting in Mr. Harthel's office or hiding in ours to avoid any contact with the company's vice president.

The hike to our office exhausted me, but pride demanded I make it without falling over in a faint, panting like a dog, or coughing to death. My breath wheezed, a faint whistle I hid from Dad by humming a cheerful melody.

As soon as he turned his back for more than ten seconds, I'd go fishing for one of my inhalers. I had used one once in the hospital at the doctor's insistence so I'd know how to use it if—when—I needed it. That I hadn't lasted a full day without requiring it bothered me almost as much as the idea of leaving Dad to face Mr. Harthel alone.

The nice thing about Mondays was the fact everyone was so focused on catching up from the weekend they didn't look up from their work when we passed through the executive floor. It wasn't until Dad opened the door for our reception I was noticed.

Annamarie surged to her feet, made a strangled noise in her throat, and fainted.

Dad knocked half the stuff off her desk, including Annamarie's monitor, in his effort to catch her as she fell. Fortunately, success was measured in preventing our assistant from hitting her head on the floor. While my father missed catching her, she did end up sprawled on top of him, her head pillowed on his chest.

I closed the door for privacy, sighed, and took advantage of Dad's position on the floor to use my inhaler. It helped a lot faster than I expected. Once certain I wasn't going to wheeze or cough, I crossed the reception to glare at my father. "You didn't tell her we were coming in?"

"It slipped my mind."

I picked up Annamarie's phone, referenced the employee list, and called the nurse for Annamarie and tech support to bring up a replacement monitor. Neither of the men I spoke to recognized my voice, and I didn't introduce myself. Some things, at least, hadn't changed.

---

WORD SPREAD of my presence in the office, resulting in a steady stream of curious employees wanting to verify I truly numbered among the living. While Annamarie recovered on the couch in our shared office, I sat at our assistant's desk, restoring everything my father had knocked over and onto the floor.

It gave the onlookers a chance to peer at me from the doorway like I was some critter in a zoo. The bolder ones came right up to Annamarie's desk, leaning over her replacement monitor to take in my less-than-professional attire.

"What a pity. No one told me today was Casual Monday." The head of the accounting department, Mrs. Frank, arched a perfectly threaded eyebrow at me. I liked her, which is why I didn't start pushing the buttons on Annamarie's desk in the hope one of them opened a trap door under the woman's feet.

"I told Mr. Evans he'd be fired if he didn't show up for work today." The drugs were making me run my mouth again; I needed to figure out how to keep my lips zipped, stat.

Mrs. Frank laughed, reached into her purse, and pulled out an unopened package of cough drops, setting them on the desk.

"Give your voice a rest, use those, and drink some hot tea. It'll help. Is Mr. Evans in his office?"

"I'm in here, Margret."

Cough drops hadn't been a part of my recovery arsenal, which made them even more appealing. I ripped into the package, grabbed one, and unwrapped it, popping it in my mouth. "He's supposed to meet with Mr. Harthel in ten minutes."

"I'll make sure he gets on the move," Mrs. Frank promised, strolling into my father's office.

Most of our employees were like Mrs. Frank, pleasant and interesting to be around. I bit my lip, wondering if I really wanted to let Dad meet with Mr. Harthel alone.

I couldn't. Grumbling my annoyance under my breath, I did a final pass over the things on Annamarie's desk, straightened the photo of her with her young son and husband, and followed Mrs. Frank.

Annamarie was sitting on the couch, blowing her nose while my father sat beside her.

"See? She's right there, safe and sound," Dad said, pointing at me. "Sorry to leave you to clean the mess, Matia."

Mindful of Mrs. Frank's advice to rest my voice, I smiled instead of saying anything, and leaned over to give our assistant a hug. She clung to me hard enough she surprised a squeak out of me, which made Dad laugh.

"I'll send Rachel up to cover for you, Annamarie," Mrs. Frank said, reaching around me to pat our assistant's shoulder. "Take your time and go clean your face. I'll wrangle these two to see Mr. Harthel before the board meeting."

"Board meeting?" I blurted along with my father and Annamarie.

"You didn't know?" The alarm in Mrs. Frank's voice placated me. "Wait. You didn't know, Annamarie? It's in forty minutes."

"No. Who ordered it?" Letting me go, Annamarie surged to her feet, brushed by me, and stormed to her desk. I grimaced the instant she passed through the door. "What happened to my monitor? This is a mess!"

"Good intentions, poor execution," Dad called back. "At least you didn't crack your skull on the floor or your desk, right? Right? That counts for something, doesn't it?"

"Mr. Evans!" our assistant wailed.

I sighed at the hell we were putting the poor woman through. "She needs a raise. What board meeting?"

"Mr. Harthel planned it on Friday. I thought you had called it, Ralph?"

"This is the first I've heard about it." When Dad started clenching his teeth hard enough his jaw twitched, I knew there'd be trouble and a lot of it. While the vice president could call for a meeting of the board, he needed to involve both Dad and me in the process.

Maybe Dad was the primary face and

CEO of Pallodia Industries, but I had earned my shares over the years, enough to put me on the board in my own right. Granted, half of my income was in shares, an arrangement I had made when I had been fifteen and officially joining the company. After accounting for my rank in the business, which fell somewhere beneath Dad but above most of the various heads of departments and the vice president, I should have been the second person notified of a board meeting.

If I added the shares Dad had put aside in my name I hadn't earned on my own, if an issue went to a stockholder vote, the other shareholders would have to gang up to overrule me if I chose to vote instead of abstaining as usual.

Abstaining was my way of letting the company maintain its vitality. Dad voted early and often, and I was content with my role as observer.

When I needed to vote, I did. If I needed to again, I would.

What was Mr. Harthel up to? Was he seeking to undermine Dad, taking advantage of the attack on LaGuardia? By eliminating Dad and me from a vote, he'd be in a far better position to get what he wanted—whatever that was.

I wouldn't put it by him, which only served to make me angrier.

Angry me had a foul mouth, and it took every bit of my will to avoid punctuating my words with curses. "Why are you involved, Mrs. Frank?"

As a department head, Mrs. Frank usually attended the meetings, but she didn't rank as a major stockholder; her shares and rank combined got her into the meetings, but her influence ended there.

I shoved my hands into my pockets, glancing in the direction of my desk. Instead of my usual no-name brand I picked for myself, it was an Apple, Dad's preferred brand.

I hoped it had everything I needed loaded on it.

Mrs. Frank sighed. "The minutes."

Normally, it was Annamarie's job to record the minutes for the board meetings, and I exchanged glances with my father. It didn't happen often, but the darkness surrounding my father had returned, wafting from him.

Maybe I wasn't really all that sure what my confused eyes were seeing, but I had an idea of its cause: fury.

There was definitely no way I could leave Dad to meet with Mr. Harthel alone. Dad would break our second rule with a cheap pen if I left him unsupervised. I headed to my desk and packed up the new laptop. Worsecase scenario, I'd use the cloud to pull up my backups for the unexpected meeting.

I'd just have to wing it.

So much for a relaxed day lounging on the couch pretending to work. I plastered a smile on my face. "Annamarie, would you please pretend you know nothing of this meeting?"

"Miss Evans?" Annamarie rolled her chair into the doorway, her mouth hanging open. "I-I mean, of course, Miss Evans."

Dad's eyes widened before narrowing. "What are you planning, Matia?"

"Regular conference room for the meeting, Mrs. Frank?"

"No, the one two floors down."

Interesting. I kept smiling. The first thing I needed to do was convince Dad to cooperate with me and prevent him from revealing the fact we knew about the board meeting. "Think you can pretend you know nothing of the meeting, Dad?"

He scowled. "I can. Why should I?"

"I'm asking you to?"

"You drive a hard bargain, Miss Evans. Fine. Why am I pretending I know nothing of this meeting?"

"It's more fun this way," I replied. "I think I'll head down a few floors and crash a party. Come in maybe twenty minutes late, would you, Mr. Evans?"

Mrs. Frank coughed, covering her mouth with her hand. "I had no idea you were such a devious, wicked young lady, Miss Evans."

"If only you knew. Whatever you do, don't encourage her," my father muttered wryly, shaking his head at me. "I'll one-up you. I'll call Chuck instead of going to his office. I'll make him break a sweat if he wants to be on time for his own board meeting. I'm sure I can think of something to keep him occupied. Annamarie, can you pull copies of the company bylaws, employee agreements, and general policies? I think I'm going to need them. Margret, if you could send Rachel over, I could use another set of eyes going over them."

"Yes, sir!" both women replied, moving to execute my father's orders.

I tucked the new laptop under my arm, grabbed my purse, and stole Dad's access pass. "You'll just have to get someone to walk you around, Dad."

Heading to his desk, Dad grabbed a pass on a lanyard and held it up. "Then I'll just take yours."

I grabbed mine, which had my latest company photo on it before tossing Dad's back to him. It was new, and I wondered when it had been issued. "Well, fine then. Be that way. I'm going downstairs for a coffee so I don't murder someone due to my lack of caffeine."

---

WHILE I WANTED to go to my favorite coffee shop across the street, I headed for the one on the ground floor of the office building. It had several booths in the back, offering the illusion of privacy.

It was enough for my needs. With a coffee

in hand, blacker than the darkest pit of hell, I opened the laptop.

I had no idea why Dad had a love affair with Apple computers, but I'd deal with the unfamiliar operating system. Thirty minutes wasn't enough time to figure out how to load Windows on it, if I could even load Windows on it. At least I knew enough to figure out how to locate my files.

They probably wouldn't work on the laptop, but I found the entirety of my ruined laptop's hard drive on the system. I pulled up the list of board members, and relief swept through me when the file opened.

It seemed Dad's claims Excel and other Microsoft products worked on Apple laptops were true. I had no idea how to access the corporate-wide private servers, so I hoped nothing major had changed with the list.

Twenty-five men and women would be cramped in the smaller conference room, but two floors down from the executive level was the ideal place to keep something under wraps. The entire floor served exclusively for meetings too large for individual offices, and it wasn't uncommon for the board members and executives to head down during the day, so no one would notice anything unusual.

Most preferred the larger conference room on the executive level for the main board meetings, which meant one thing to me: Mr. Harthel was trying to hide the board meeting, probably from Dad.

If the man had made the plans on Friday, I hadn't been a factor in his scheduling. I clenched my teeth. Dad—along with everyone else—had thought I had died. Too many 'what if' questions rattled around in my head.

What if I hadn't woken up coherent and well enough for the doctor to be comfortable letting me leave the hospital? I wondered about that. The time I had spent unconscious was long enough I was astonished they hadn't kept me in for observation. But, it had worked out.

If I hadn't come into work, we wouldn't have found out about the unplanned board meeting. I had no idea what Mr. Harthel was putting up for vote, but I'd crush him and hope he choked to death on the darkness cloaking him.

No one fucked with Dad on my watch. I had a bit of an advantage in my unexpected appearance at the office. My casual clothing would also help unsettle everyone. When I opened my mouth, a lifetime of silence would work in my favor.

Almost dying in an explosion had loosened my tongue. I'd have to implement a third rule to keep from embarrassing myself. Smile. Don't stab anyone. Don't curse, at least not too much.

I really wanted to know what the Vice President of Pallodia Industries hoped to accomplish without Dad in the way to stop him.

The list of board members told me nothing, and neither did my old calendar.

The only loose end I could pursue was the business meeting we had never reached. Could the missed meeting have something to do with Mr. Harthel's decision to go behind my father's back?

I had difficulty believing it, but I had no other ideas and no more time to think it through. Making the best of a bad situation was my role at Pallodia Industries, and I'd make certain every member of the board remembered it by the time I was done with them.

---

I STOLE a security guard's baseball cap out of his back pocket and flipped him a salute and a wink. Startled laughter followed me as I prowled the meeting floor of our building.

Without a real plan, I figured I'd catch the attention of security and make certain they were nearby in case hell broke loose in the conference room. With his cap on my head, I snared my first guard, who caught up with me and fell in step beside me, invading my personal space long enough to flip my access badge. His startled inhale made me smirk.

"Miss Evans? Is that really you? What on Earth…?"

"Could you quietly bring a few friends to hang out around the conference room where the board meeting will be held?" I kissed away all hope of a quiet year and invoked the first rule, smiling until it hurt. "Around the corner, prowling about, just nearby, please."

"Of course, Miss Evans. Is there a problem?"

"I might be starting one." I liked the way my tone promised trouble.

Dad never should have let me come to work hopped up on half a pharmacy. By the time I was finished in the board meeting, security might be taking *me* off premises. I wanted to pop Mr. Harthel's malicious little bubble and get rid of him, but unless I caught him directly violating company policies, I couldn't do anything other than bait him and the other board members and hope for the best.

"Understood, ma'am."

I tipped the brim of his baseball cap. "Thank you. I'll be borrowing this for a bit, if you don't mind."

"Can I get a picture of you wearing it?"

I laughed, leaned against the hallway wall, and posed, dipping the brim down and flipping him another salute. "Photograph away, sir."

If the images of a casual, rumpled, disheveled, and thoroughly unappealing me circulated through the media, I didn't care. Maybe it would remove me from the eligible bachelorette pool.

"Thanks, Miss Evans. No one would believe it otherwise."

"No, thank you for your hard work. Do you know if any of the executives or board members have arrived yet?"

"No, ma'am. You're the first on the floor."

"I'll be in the conference room propping up the wall or something." In actuality, I'd be inside the room's kitchenette, preparing coffee and pretending I was one of the caterers. I'd probably have to make room for the real caterers, who wouldn't be happy I was in their way while they tried to prepare the conference room for a meeting of stuffy sophisticates.

"Yes, ma'am. Give a shout if there are any problems."

"You can count on it. Thanks."

The main conference room on the floor, and the only one large enough to hold the entire board, was on the far side of the building, requiring me to hike so far my breathing wheezed by the time I arrived.

I sighed, fetched my inhalers out of my purse, found the one the doctor assured me would work on minor incidents, and gave it a try. It lacked the punch of the first one I had used, but after several deep breaths, I no longer sounded like a whistle. Steadying my nerves, I swept into the conference room, startling the two women inside.

"You're not supposed to be in here,"

Brenda Cartney, the coordinator of everything food-related in the building, blurted.

I grinned, flicked my cap off, and pressed my fingers to my lips, closing the door behind me. "I'm not here, Brenda. I'm a houseplant some idiot put in the kitchenette."

The older woman's mouth dropped open. I didn't recognize the caterer, which didn't surprise me; so many of them came and went from the building I wondered how many companies Brenda had to hire to keep us supplied in a business where daily meetings were the way of life.

"Pretend you didn't see me, okay?"

Brenda's mouth opened and closed, but no sound emerged. I swept by her, setting my laptop on one of the side tables out of the way. I draped a newspaper over it to hide its presence before taking up residence in the kitchenette. The silence continued for another few moments before one of the women moved, and the chink of porcelain announced they had resumed work and were finishing the preparations for the board meeting.

I waited in silence, wondering what I'd hear once the meeting began.

## SIX

*Maybe he'd have just cause to listen to me now.*

---

TO KEEP BOARD MEETINGS EFFICIENT, Dad had one woman—Brenda—serve as the caterer in the room while business was conducted.

She had signed an iron-clad NDA, and I couldn't remember many times the board had invoked the black-out option for sensitive discussions. I heard the chatter of the gathered executives from my hiding spot in the kitchenette, crammed between the wall and the refrigerator. I had been forced to shove the damned thing six inches to make enough space for me to fit.

Mr. Harthel didn't have the sense to activate the black-out option. Maybe he thought he was a lot of things, but Brenda reported to Dad—and to me. Once I was finished with my clandestine activities, I'd have to pull the woman aside and take advantage of her vast wealth of knowledge to figure out what the hell was going on within Pallodia Industries.

I flexed my hands as a way to contain my desire to pace and tilted my head to listen. The opened doorway on the other side of the thin wall allowed me to hear the conversations in the conference room.

According to the kitchenette clock, Mr. Harthel arrived ten minutes after the meeting was supposed to start. Dad's delay accomplished one thing: *we* were never late for a board meeting, and as often as not, we were there first. Respecting the time of our employees, the executives, and other board members came in as one of Dad's top priorities, and everyone knew it.

By showing up late for the board meeting he had called, Harthel sent a message to the other members. I smirked, squirming in my cubby so I could cross my arms over my chest. The opening of the meeting went smoothly, and Mrs. Frank ran through the attendance for the minutes. Once she finished, the room fell quiet.

Dad wouldn't have wasted a single second before diving into business, and I wondered how many of the board members were thinking the same thing I was. Without his presence, the conference room felt empty despite knowing how many people were seated around the massive table.

"Well, Chuck, you brought us all together. What's going on?" While I didn't always see eye-to-eye with Percival Luther, the lawyer was one of Dad's biggest assets, handling the company's most sensitive matters. For all our differences, Percival belonged in the role of vice president, something I had complained to Dad about in the past without any results.

Maybe he'd have just cause to listen to me now.

"We need to vote regarding Ralph's ability to operate the company in light of the tragedy involving his daughter."

Brenda stepped into the kitchenette, set her coffee pot down on the counter, and stepped out of view of the executives. Focusing her attention on me, she pointed in the vice president's direction. Fury splotched the woman's cheeks dark as coal. Was the color staining her cheeks red?

I missed my phone and its camera, as I wanted to immortalize her righteous wrath. To control her and keep my presence secret, I pressed my finger to my lips.

She jerked her head in a nod, acknowledging my order.

"Do you have a recommendation to submit to the board, Chuck?" The sharp edge in Percival's voice warned me of trouble for someone, and I wondered who.

Loyalty seemed to be a fleeting thing at Pallodia Industries, and I wondered how long corporate betrayal and treachery had been going on right under our noses.

"Yes, I have a recommendation. I believe we should enact an involuntary leave of absence to permit Ralph sufficient time to handle his personal matters. Missing the meeting in London has caused us substantial problems. We need to recover and fast, ladies and gentlemen." Papers slapped to the wood surface of the conference room table. "This details the restructuring I think will ensure Pallodia Industries can maintain its superior position in the market."

Brenda wrinkled her nose and made throttling motions, and I nodded to my accomplice-in-crime. Murder and the resulting jail time started looking like a good idea.

"I have taken the liberty of printing each of you a copy of the proposal. I've also created the appropriate sheets for ratification of the proposal should the vote pass."

"You're in quite the hurry to move on this. Ah, I see you've appointed yourself as the CEO of the company in Mr. Evans's absence."

"I am the second-in-command of this corporation, Mr. Luther. It is a direct shift to fill in the gap his absence will cause."

"Actually, Miss Evans is the official heiress of the corporation and second-in-command, Chuck." Of all the executives, I liked Armand Davies the most. In more traditional companies, he would have ranked as the chief operations officer, although in our hierarchy, he came in right beneath Mr. Harthel and equal in rank to almost everyone else in the room.

One day, I'd have to talk to Dad about restructuring the corporation so it made sense to those outside the company. Hell, too many days, the ranking structure didn't make any sense to me, and I lived and breathed it most days of the week. I often wondered if Dad had gotten tired of trying to figure out the company's structuring and put me in charge of it when I had been a toddler. I hadn't come up with another theory that made sense.

"Miss Evans is no longer a factor in the operation of this corporation, Armand."

It was my turn to make strangling motions, and it took every bit of my willpower to stay where I was when I wanted to storm into the conference room, grab a chair, and find out how many times I could beat him with it before my abused lungs gave out on me.

Brenda refilled the coffee pot and returned to the room to serve the board members. The silence stretched on, and I listened to the squeak of the chairs, the shuffle of cloth on leather, and the taps of pens on pads of papers.

Someone typed, and I suspected it was Mrs. Frank. Knowing her, under the guise of recording the minutes, she was probably reporting every word to Dad until he decided to come crash my party.

Armand grunted and more papers slapped to the desk. "Until Miss Evans's death is confirmed, she is the executive vice president and official heiress of this corporation. Her functionality has always been as an executive vice president, a role above yours, Vice President Harthel. I can provide you with a listing of the current company structure if you need a reminder of her position. You do not have the authority to decree she is not a part of the proceedings. I do not have a death certificate in my filings, and not only does she hold a higher rank, she is a major shareholder."

Instead of silence, quiet murmurs filled the room. After what felt like an eternity and hadn't been more than five minutes, Percival said, "Armand is correct. You are wasting our time, Chuck."

"The man's daughter is dead, Mr. Luther!" Harthel bellowed, and I heard the crack of his hand on the table. "He is unfit to guide this corporation as necessary."

The eruption of noise and board members shouting over one another made me sigh. Brenda bolted into the kitchenette, her eyes wide and face pale. "This is insanity!"

It was insanity I had to deal with. I wiggled out of my hiding spot, grabbed one of the pitchers of water, and stepped into the fray. Men and women alike were on their feet with the sole exception of Mrs. Frank, who had pushed her chair back, her laptop on her lap.

No one, save her, noticed me. Adjusting my grip on the pitcher, which easily held more than a gallon of ice-cold water, I swung it in an arc, its contents spraying over the collection of executives and upper management.

Some shrieked, some cursed, and every

eye focused on me. As recognition struck the board members, silence fell.

"Sit down," I ordered in a hoarse rasp, setting the glass pitcher down on the counter so it made a heavy thump. Reaching up, I peeled the baseball cap off my head, turned it around, and crammed it back over my hair.

One by one, the men and women sat, and more mouths hung open than not.

"What exactly do you think you're doing, Mr. Harthel? You were perfectly well aware my father and I were in the building today. You were on the phone with him before coming here. It seems you neglected to inform him we were having a board meeting today. Why might that be?"

The speech was enough to wind me, but I refused to reach into my purse for one of my inhalers. All I'd do was prove the wretched man was right.

Harthel's face paled to a gray fringing on white. "M-Miss Evans."

"Give me a reason I shouldn't call a vote to have you demoted until you demonstrate you have the integrity to remain an executive." I got the sentence out without choking on any of the words, but I was aware of the faint wheeze of my lungs failing to keep up with me.

"Use your inhaler, Miss Evans," Mrs. Frank ordered.

I glowered at the woman, muttered a few curses, and obeyed. If she had noticed halfway across the room, my pitiful state was obvious to everyone else, too. I didn't pay attention to which one I used, but it helped, and I sighed my relief. "Well? Mr. Luther? You're the best qualified here to give me a breakdown of legal reasons I shouldn't propose a motion to demote Mr. Harthel until he remembers the principles of this corporation."

Percival, who was seated not far away and had caught the full brunt of my pitcher of water, jumped to his feet and held out his chair. When I didn't move, he grabbed hold of my elbow, dragged me to his seat, and pushed on my shoulders until I sank down onto the leather cushion. "I would need to look over the specific bylaws, but—"

"Unnecessary, Percival. I have the appropriate sections with me," Dad announced, sweeping in through the conference room door. He held a thick stack of papers in his hand, which he tossed on the table. The security guard I had recruited trailed after him. "Get out of my building, Mr. Harthel. You're fired. Security will see you out. Your personal belongings will be couriered to your home address."

Catching my attention with a wave of her hand, Mrs. Frank turned her laptop to face me, and the image of the conference room was displayed on her screen in one window. A black panel occupied the other half of her screen.

Harthel opened his mouth to say something, and Percival cleared his throat, standing behind me with both of his hands on the back of my chair. "Chuck, you lied to the board. It's a direct violation of this company's policies. Make your excuses to HR in a formal letter, but I will remind you all conversations in this room are recorded."

"Get him out of here," Dad ordered, stepping out of the way of the security guards.

Harthel spewed incoherent curses and fought the men, requiring three of them to haul him out of the conference room. Once he was gone, Dad closed the door. "Well, it's been an interesting morning. As you can tell, I am in the office today and should be all week. Annamarie is in the process of working out my schedule. I'd like all of you to stop by her desk and make arrangements to meet with me one-on-one. For now, we need to discuss Mr. Harthel's replacement. Any nominations, suggestions, or volunteers?"

I jerked my thumb over my shoulder in Percival's direction. "He'd do a good job."

"While I'm flattered, Miss Evans, I'd rather remain in my current position. I feel I can do the company the most good where I'm at now."

My father stared at me, his eyes narrowing. A creepy-crawly sense of dread worked its way down my spine. "Why are you looking at me like that?"

"I motion that Miss Evans should handle

the hiring of Pallodia Industries' new vice president."

I groaned. Not caring the table was still soaked from my temper tantrum, I slumped over the glossy wooden surface. "I do not second this motion."

"I second the motion," several voices chorused.

"All those in favor?"

Every hand except mine went up in the room, which still meant I could overrule the decision if I really wanted.

"All those against?"

Every eye focused on me.

"Abstain," I hissed, and flipped them all my middle finger, evoking laughter from everyone except my father, who glared at me.

"Motion passes. In the interim, we will split Mr. Harthel's work over as many personnel as possible. You'll be in charge of that, too, Miss Evans. You can spend the rest of the day pouring through Mr. Harthel's emails and files. I had his passwords changed and access blocked on all company devices before I so rudely interrupted this meeting. I expect you in our office as soon as the meeting is finished."

Without waiting for a reply, Dad swept out of the conference room.

"Yes, sir," I grumbled to myself, shoving myself upright. "Any other business?"

No one said a word.

While I wanted to find some corner to

hide in, nipping rumors in the bud seemed wiser than letting people come to their own conclusions. "I was released from the hospital yesterday. Technically, I'm not supposed to be here today, but Dad wouldn't come in without me, so here I am. Apparently, I have correspondences to review. If you need me, I'll be stealing a computer from Mr. Harthel's office. If you want to talk, schedule an appointment with Annamarie. Mrs. Frank, will you please handle the closure of the meeting?"

"Of course, Miss Evans."

I nodded my thanks, gathered up my laptop, and left the meeting, wondering what had driven my father to fire Harthel, who had been a part of Pallodia Industries for as long as I could remember.

---

WHEN I ARRIVED at Harthel's office, several people were waiting outside of his door, which was closed and locked. I scowled at the barricade, contemplating how to gain access without breaking something.

"Who has the key?"

"We're not sure, Miss Evans," one of the men replied. While he wore a dress shirt and slacks like every other man in the building, something about his rumpled hair, lack of a tie, and general nervousness screamed tech to me.

"Got one of those fancy hammers you use to beat computers on you?"

A smile answered me, and stooping down to one of the carry cases on the floor, he pulled out a rubber mallet. "One of these?"

While Dad only bought the best for the building, interior glass was glass. I grabbed the mallet and put all of my annoyance behind my blows. It took three solid smacks to break the glass window above the lock. Instead of shattering into a million pieces, it broke apart in sheets. I crunched out a hole large enough for me to slip my hand through and open the door. "Oh my, it seems like the window was somehow broken. What good fortune."

For my next trick, I handed the tech my laptop. "I want a full, unmodified copy of his system put on this, if it fits. I want the actual computer locked up. No one is to touch it. Preserve the system. If you need a replacement desktop, send me a purchase order for it and I'll take care of it myself. I also want access to his emails and full collection of passwords."

The tech took my laptop and nodded. "Shouldn't be long to copy, ma'am."

"I'll be in my office." I left the workers to their job, and on the way, I gestured to Mr. Harthel's assistant, who got up from her desk. The poor woman didn't look too stable on her feet as she followed me down the hallway.

Annamarie was at her desk, her eyes

widening as I swept through the door with Mr. Harthel's assistant at my heels. "Miss Evans?"

"I'd like you two to work together. I need Mr. Harthel's full schedule for the next month merged with my calendar. Tech is loading his data onto my laptop, so hopefully I'll be able to salvage at least some of his work. Laura—your name is Laura, right?" I blinked at Mr. Harthel's assistant; she wasn't much older than me, and if memory served, she had been with the company for less than three months.

"Yes, ma'am. Laura Madison, ma'am."

"Okay, Laura. I know this is sudden, but you're going to be working beneath Annamarie. Annamarie, figure out an equivalent or better position for her, would you?"

"Why not as your personal assistant, Miss Evans? You could use your own instead of waiting until you think your father doesn't need me."

My mouth dropped open, and I blinked several times.

Having my own assistant hadn't crossed my mind since Annamarie planned everything. Then again, my father and I had so much overlap in our schedules it wasn't that much extra work to keep both of us in line. "Next you're going to tell me I need my own office."

"There's the empty corner office on the other end of the floor."

I narrowed my eyes. "This is a set up, isn't it?"

"There's even a reception office attached to it, just like this one. Empty, lonely, and needing someone to fill it."

I knew the office. Most of the time, I forgot it was even there. Once upon a time, it had served as a glorified playpen to keep me contained when I had been too little to attend meetings with Dad. Once I had outgrown it, I had forgotten all about it.

"Someone really hasn't claimed it?"

"No one has claimed it. I'm not even sure when someone was last in the office or its reception."

I turned to Laura. "How do you feel about cleaning if it comes with a job promotion?"

"I'm not being fired?" the woman squeaked.

I snorted. "Why would I fire you? You haven't done anything wrong that I'm aware of. Print your resume, bring it over, and see what it'll take to make that office habitable. Are you allergic to dust?"

"No, ma'am."

"Matia, please. You take care of those offices and leave the rest to me."

Laura's eyes widened so much I feared they'd pop out of her head. Whether she was afraid I'd change my mind or used to someone who demanded immediate obedience, the woman fled.

She returned in the time it took her to

walk to her desk and back with the resume, handing it to me with shaking hands. She ran down the hallway, slowing long enough to close the reception door behind her.

I blinked, staring at the single sheet of paper in my hand. "Am I that scary, Annamarie?"

"Miss Evans, until today, half the company has been convinced you're mute or just really, really shy. Today, you're talking more than your father, and trust me, that's an accomplishment."

"Just because I don't like to talk doesn't mean I can't," I protested.

"No, you just don't waste words. There's nothing wrong with that. Still, you should let your voice rest. You sound terrible."

I did, but at least I wasn't wheezing. I pulled out a cough drop and popped it into my mouth. "Dad's going to whine, isn't he?"

Annamarie giggled. "Between you and me, Miss Evans, he'll mope for at least a week and probably invade your office until you kick him out. Don't worry about him. You deserve your own space—and your own assistant, too. Laura's a hard worker."

"A hard worker who was going to be looking for a new job."

"Well, it's a good thing you have a new job for her, isn't it?"

## SEVEN

*There's something you need to see.*

---

WHEN I FINALLY MADE MY way back to my shared office, Dad was sound asleep on the couch. One of his legs was stretched out on the cushion while the other hadn't quite made it up before he had decided to doze off, using the arm rest as an impromptu pillow.

It was common enough for one of us to take a nap after hours, although I hadn't seen him pass out so early in the day in ages. I covered him with a blanket and headed to my desk, looking over the things I'd have to move.

It wasn't much. Annamarie handled everything with a paper trail, filing the sheets away and removing them so it wouldn't clutter our frantic lives. My desk had seen better days, likely searched during my time in the hospital.

It'd fill a box with room to spare.

It was tempting to swipe everything off onto the floor to deal with later, but I tidied it into unorganized piles and reviewed Laura's resume. The woman was a fresh college graduate, which meant she was likely twenty-one or twenty-two. Unlike many in the office, instead of the standard business degree, she had opted for an English major.

Before becoming Harthel's assistant, she had worked at a coffee shop as a barista. I narrowed my eyes, wondering why Harthel had hired her. Taking the resume to the reception, I dropped the sheet on Annamarie's desk. "Your thoughts?"

Annamarie picked up Laura's resume, and her eyes widened. "This is it?"

"I want a background check done on her. Find out where he found her and why he hired her. I'll keep her as long as she's competent."

It wasn't Laura's fault Harthel had hired her when she wasn't qualified for the job. Why had he kept her for three months, though? Unless she had relevant experience hiding somewhere I wasn't aware of, she would've been flying blind from her first day of work.

"Of course. Anything else?"

"Does Dad have anything scheduled for the next few hours?"

Annamarie shook her head. "Not until four. I thought it'd be wise to keep his schedule light today."

"He's asleep on the couch. Don't let anyone disturb him, not unless it's an emergency. Even if it is, route everyone to me first."

"He's so worn out," our assistant whispered, glancing behind me at the office's open door.

It wasn't my fault, yet it was. I sighed. "I know. He needs the normality, and so do I."

"You feeling okay?"

"Tolerable. Not a fan of this whole wheezing thing," I admitted, wrinkling my nose. "Not a fan of the inhalers, either."

"Don't you even *think* of trying to move things out of your office on your own, Miss Evans. I will have security take you and Ralph home if you try."

Annamarie would, and we both knew it. I surrendered, holding my hands up in acceptance of the ultimatum. "Understood."

"Good. I've pulled up Mr. Harthel's calendar. There's something you need to see."

The first thing to catch my attention was the five o'clock meeting with the company we had been scheduled to visit in London. I sucked in a breath, pointing at her monitor. "Does Dad know about this?"

"No. I didn't know about it."

"Call them and reschedule the time and location. Work with them. You said Dad had a four o'clock?"

"Yes."

"See if they'll move it to four. I'll handle it myself."

"Ambitious. I'll pretend I know nothing of

your four o'clock, then. The meeting location is a restaurant. How do you want me to handle it?"

"Give them a call and see how they want to deal with the time shift. Pick a different restaurant, too. I'm going to look at this empty office. When the tech comes back with my laptop, guard it for me, okay?"

"Will do. I'll let you know as soon as I can get a hold of the meeting contact."

---

THE CLEANING CREWS hadn't been to the reception and the corner office on the other side of the executive floor in a long time; there was a sense of abandonment to the place, which was partnered by a thin layer of dust on the hardwood floors. The glass was clouded, and I grimaced at the thought of the effort required to restore its clarity.

It'd probably be easier to shatter the windows and replace them with something newer.

Every office between the corner and reception was likewise empty, and I wondered about the waste of space. I could think of plenty of good men and women who deserved an office upgrade.

At least the lack of employees gave me a chance to work without an audience.

"Miss Matia," Laura blurted, staring up at me with wide eyes. She was on her knees on the floor cleaning up a puddle of sudsy water.

"I'm pretty sure we have mops somewhere in this building. We have a janitorial staff, too. I didn't think it needed so much work." I grinned at her, grabbed a towel from her collection of them, and tossed it on the puddle before going to work with my foot to help clean up the mess. "Do I want to know how the main office looks?"

"No. I don't think anyone has been in there in years. There's dust everywhere."

"Anything to move out?"

"No, nothing at all. It's empty."

"Okay, I'll have a look inside to see what sort of space I have to work with." While I was pretty certain the office was actually larger than the one I shared with Dad, I wanted to confirm my memories matched the reality of the situation. "You're going to need a bigger desk, a better chair, and other odds and ends. Once we have the reception floor dried, go hunt someone down in HR and have them put you in touch with the best folks for a renovation and new office furniture. Annamarie can help you set up a purchase order if you haven't done one before."

"I haven't," the woman mumbled; she stared down at the soapy puddle in front of her.

"I learned everything I know by sitting down and doing it, Laura. If you don't understand something, ask questions. If you're worried you won't remember, take notes. If you need a good binder to help you track your notes, I'll buy one for you. If you don't have a cell phone capable of organizing everything, the company will provide one for you. I'm not going to lie to you. You're going to have a difficult job. The hours are long, and I might end up calling you at four in the morning because I need to be across the country by noon the next day for an unexpected meeting."

"I don't have a cell phone. I can't afford one." The hopelessness in her voice made me pause.

I didn't know every employee's salary, but Laura was my responsibility. "How much is your salary?"

"My contract has me on hourly wages, ma'am."

"How much?"

The number she gave me wasn't much over minimum wage. In New York, in the heart of Lower Manhattan, minimum wage was a death sentence for someone's finances. Long hours and overtime weren't enough to make up for that.

Rage rooted me in place, and I was glad Dad had fired Harthel. If the man had been anywhere in the building, I would have hunted him down and shoved my foot so far up his ass he would've started singing soprano. I drew several deep breaths.

"Change of plans. We're going to Human Resources. Leave everything where it is."

Laura squeaked and surged to her feet. Her skirt was damp, and her top had water stains on it. I took off my sweater and handed it to her, straightening my blouse while she wiggled her way into it. "Am I in trouble?"

"No, you're not in trouble. I'd say step lively, but I am sticking to a leisurely stroll. I have a few stops to make first."

"Yes, ma'am," my new assistant whispered.

My first stop was Annamarie's desk. She took a look at me and then at Laura, and her eyes focused on the fact the woman was wearing my sweater. "What's going on?"

"I need a few favors, Annamarie."

Dad's assistant grabbed a pen and a pad of paper. "Ready."

"I need the corner office totally cleaned out, top to bottom. Dust bunnies have made a nest in there, and it's uninhabitable. The windows for the reception are opaque. They'll need to be replaced. I'll also need every office not in use in that wing cleaned out and resupplied. New desks, new chairs, the works. I want it done by Friday. If the windows will take longer, get me an estimate. Send me the purchase orders, and I'll review and sign off on them."

"Okay. What else?"

"Laura will need a company cell phone and a full plan for it, as well as a personal-use allowance."

"I can have it by the end of the day."

If my guess was right, Laura couldn't afford an internet connection, and while she likely had a computer, it wouldn't do everything I'd need. "Next up, she'll need a company laptop and desktop for home use, plus all accessories. I want it set up so both machines can access the internet through wireless tethering."

"I'll get a hold of the tech team and get an ETA on when they'll be ready."

"Thank you. Also, I'll need a new cell, too."

"The order was already placed, ma'am. You should have yours in a couple of hours."

"Thanks, Annamarie. Come along, Laura. We have a lot to do and little time to do it in."

"Don't forget to use your inhaler if you need it, Miss Evans. Laura, consider watching her your top priority."

"Yes, ma'am," Laura replied, straightening.

Assistants. Couldn't live with them, couldn't live without them.

---

THERE WAS something satisfying about storming into Human Resources on a warpath. The elevator ride four floors down was in silence, which Laura spent fidgeting while pale gray smoke swirled around her.

Sometimes, my eyes played tricks on me, but the insight into the woman's state of mind intrigued me. It wasn't the inky maliciousness of Harthel's presence, but a darkening of her spirits. I guessed it was brought on by fear, anxiety, and uncertainty.

I'd be anxious, too, if my entire career was turned upside down in the matter of a few hours. Trips to Human Resources meant trouble in most people's minds, and Laura hadn't been in the company long enough to know how Pallodia Industries operated.

If the new equipment hadn't been enough to tip Laura off she was about to have a very good day, I'd make sure to catch her if she dropped into a dead faint when I settled on her new salary.

HR's receptionist gaped at me as she rose from her chair. "Miss Evans?"

"I need someone to pull out Laura's file and make some adjustments."

The receptionist sat back down, picked up the phone, and made a call. A minute and a half later, she directed me to Abby Thatcher's office, the head of HR. Laura swallowed and clasped her hands in front of her.

"It's fine, Laura. Abby is pretty laid back, and you're not in trouble."

Well, Abby was normally laid back, but I had tossed a pitcher of ice and water all over her and most of the other members of the board not too long ago. With luck, I hadn't fallen too far out of the executive's good graces.

"Miss Evans." Instead of staying seated, Abby got up, circled her desk, and clasped my hand in a firm shake. Then, with a soft laugh, she pulled me into a hug. "Today was the most fun I've ever had in a board meeting."

My face burned. "I'm glad you enjoyed it. I'm stealing Harthel's assistant, but there are a few issues I need to discuss with you."

"I have someone pulling her file right now. It won't be long. Sit, sit. You look exhausted."

I was, although I hadn't noticed it until she had mentioned it. I flopped onto the chair, kicked off my shoes, and stretched my legs.

"If you want to prop your feet up on my desk, I don't mind."

I laughed, which birthed several painful coughs. Once I recovered, I propped my feet up and groaned as I got a chance to really stretch out. "Laura disclosed her wages to me, and they're unacceptable, so we're going to fix it."

Laura collapsed onto the chair beside me and clutched the arms as though she was ready to fall to the floor. "It's really not necess—"

"Bull-fucking-shit it's not necessary. Cents over minimum wage is unacceptable for a member of this company. Abby, how the hell did this happen?"

Abby's eyes widened. "Who set up your file, Miss Madison?"

"Mr. Harthel took care of everything, ma'am."

"Miss Madison, we do not hire anyone at

minimum wage in our company—or anywhere near it, for that matter. While specific employee payment rates are confidential, all salaried employees are paid at least five dollars over the minimum wage per hour, plus bonuses."

"I'm paid hourly."

Abby's eyes narrowed. "Who was handling your timesheet?"

"Mr. Harthel, ma'am."

Abby picked up the phone, smashed two numbers, and made a low sound in her throat, resembling a dog growling. "Margret, I need a full copy of Mr. Harthel's expense reports, including authorization of employee bonuses, authorized expenses, and payouts. I also require all accounting information for Laura Madison, his assistant. How long do you think it'll take for Miss Madison's information? Okay. Call me back."

Hanging up, Abby sat straight in her chair, flexing her hands. "I apologize, Miss Madison. As the head of HR, it's my responsibility to make sure these situations do not occur."

Laura stammered something, so nervous I couldn't understand a word she was trying to say.

While I wouldn't blame her if she cracked under the pressure, I wanted to turn the attention away from her and back to me. "The only one to blame is Mr. Harthel. The damage has been done, so instead of beating ourselves up over it, let's fix it. Can we issue a bonus to bring her wages on par with the average for the rest of our entry-level secretarial staff, Abby?"

"Easily. Once I have a copy of her timesheet, I can have the bonus authorized by accounting for the next payment cycle."

"Issue it as a one-time direct deposit. Accounting can complain to me later for the inconvenience."

"I'm paid by check, ma'am."

I froze, staring at Abby, who met my gaze with an expression so neutral I pitied whoever took the fall for Laura's employment. Checks weren't common in our company; direct deposit worked best for everyone, ensuring stable payments for our employees. "Company check?"

"I just cashed them, ma'am. Mr. Harthel signed the checks, though."

Abby's phone rang. "Thatcher."

There was a long moment of silence. "Okay. I'm going to send Miss Madison to your office. I will email you in a moment with the relevant details." Abby hung up. "Miss Madison, please go down the hall towards reception. Mr. Westley is in the third office to your right."

Laura got to her feet, excused herself, and fled.

I got up, closed the door to Abby's office, and locked it so no one could walk in on us. I clacked my teeth together. "It's a damned good thing Dad fired Mr. Harthel."

"I had absolutely no idea it was possible to slip an employee into the company and bypass HR, Miss Evans. We—"

"As vice president, he had full authority to override many of the company protocols. What I need to know is why he slipped her in. I've seen her resume, Abby. She's not qualified for this level of work. I'm taking her as my assistant and having Annamarie teach her the ropes, spreading some of the workload around." At the first sign of wheezing, I dug into my purse for the weakest of my inhalers.

The last thing I needed was to end up back in the hospital.

"Sit before you fall down."

I obeyed, sighing as I stretched out and used Abby's desk as a foot rest. "If she's an illegal immigrant, I want her legalized. If she's in trouble, I want her removed from the situation and placed elsewhere. If she's living in the slums, I want the company to rent an apartment on her behalf, somewhere close to work. We will pick a rent of no more than twenty-five percent of her after-tax wages and function as an intermediary between her new landlord and her. I'll cover the difference in her rent out of my pay. Have someone from legal draw up an agreement for the lease if this becomes necessary. Maybe she's Harthel's mistake, but she's now our mistake, too, and we don't abandon employees who haven't done anything wrong."

"Understood. What was on her resume?"

"English major with a bachelor's degree. She was working as a barista before being hired by Harthel. She doesn't even know how to fill out a purchase order. Harthel was keeping her around for some reason, though. Likely scheduling and answering basic emails, which anyone can do."

"That's going to cause you problems."

"As long as she's good at scheduling, she can learn the rest. Even if she's not good at scheduling, I'll steal a couple of interns to help out. Dad could use Annamarie full-time without her splitting all her time between us."

"May I make a recommendation?"

I waved my hand in invitation.

"Offer Miss Madison the opportunity to pursue better education. Employ her with flexible hours, allowing her to go to school. We have programs in place to cover the costs of education. This would allow her to develop her skills and grow into the position. Working with you would be a good experience for our paid interns, as well. Annamarie can oversee the schedule and ensure there are no mistakes while avoiding the majority of the work."

"Salaried?"

"Of course."

"How long will it take HR to open a file for her?"

"Twenty to thirty minutes. Her banking situation may be a problem, depending on the type of account she has."

"I'll walk her down the street to our bank if I need to. I have a feeling I will need to detour her to some department stores for position-appropriate attire. I'll use my company credit cards. I'll expect the clothing and other things I purchase to be deducted from my pay."

"We have a fund for business expenses. Use it. That said, wouldn't it be better to do her background check first?"

"Annamarie is already on it."

"Good. Is Ralph aware of the situation?"

"Dad is asleep on the couch. He'll probably stay there for a few more hours."

Abby grinned at me. "When are *you* going to bother with a degree, Miss Evans?"

"Bite me, Abby. When I retire, if I feel like it."

I'd probably be forced into retirement a lot sooner than I liked, but no one needed to know that.

EIGHT

You look terrible.

---

I LEFT Laura in the capable hands of Human Resources and returned to my office—Dad's office. My every step dragged, and I wanted nothing more than to take over the couch for my own purposes, but unfortunately, my day was just beginning.

I couldn't go to a meeting with Mirage Resources dressed like I'd come off the street. Well, I could, but it wouldn't make a very good impression.

When Dad woke up and figured out I had spent the entire day going non-stop, he'd go right back into super-protective mode, smothering me in his efforts to safeguard my health.

Annamarie narrowed her eyes when I stepped into the reception. "You look terrible."

"Is Sam free? I need a change of clothes for my four o'clock."

"No. He was drafted to deliver Mr.

Harthel's things to his condominium complex."

"I don't want Sam anywhere near Harthel," I hissed. The coughing fit took me by surprise, and by the time it subsided, I was doubled over with my hands braced on my legs. "Fuck."

"Use your inhaler. Sam was given instructions to hand the boxes to the security guard of the complex for delivery. Your new phone is ready, by the way." Annamarie opened a drawer and pulled out a new cell, the same model as my old one, and offered it to me.

I straightened, digging into my purse for the inhaler with the biggest punch. Once I could breathe without wheezing, I took my replacement phone and stuffed it into my purse. "Okay. I'll need a cab to Fifth Avenue. I can't go to a meeting looking like this."

"Since we're on the subject of your four o'clock, they agreed to the rescheduling. Considering the original reservation was for dinner, I made arrangements for a shift to a new location. I picked a rather nice Italian restaurant. I hope that's suitable?"

"Italian sounds great. Thanks, Annamarie."

"Are you sure you want to go shopping on your own?"

"Positive."

"Matia." While Annamarie hadn't been a mother for long, she had mastered the talent of imbuing my name with the promise of trouble if I didn't heed her, a perfect imitation of Dad's tone when I was being stubborn over something.

"I really do not want to deal with the rumor mill when people realize I am colorblind," I hissed.

"Every single person who has ever seen one of your pie charts knows you are either colorblind or completely incapable of color coordination. You're going to end up with a neon pink blouse with a pumpkin orange skirt."

"And they'll both be gray to me. Who cares?"

"I do."

"I'll talk to someone in the store," I muttered.

"Why don't you take Laura with you?"

"She's with HR being sorted out."

"You could always go as you are."

"No."

"Pink blouse and orange skirt," Annamarie warned.

"Is that combination really that bad?"

"It's horrific. You're a beautiful young woman, Matia, but orange is *so* not your color."

"I was planning on asking them to select the best black blazer, skirt, and white blouse they had and just go with that."

"You're going to a business meeting, not a funeral."

"It counts as a funeral. Mine. I'll have to talk."

"You also have to take your medicine." Annamarie got up from her desk and headed to the water cooler in the hallway outside of the reception, returning with a glass, which she handed me. "Sam gave me the rundown of what you need to take if you need help figuring it out."

There was no point in fighting her over it. I plunked down on one of the reception chairs, dug through my purse for the horrendous number of bottles, and read through the directions, setting aside the ones I needed to take. I ended up with fifteen different pills.

The rest of my life came in all sorts of shapes and sizes. Instead of complaining about it, I knocked them back and guzzled water to make sure they all made it down my throat.

"Mr. Harthel has probably already made a mess of the negotiations. Why not show up just like you are, unsettle the whole lot of them, and steamroll them? Knock them off balance from the start, control the conversation, and make them dance to your tune. The restaurant doesn't have a dress code. Even if it did, the instant you whip out the company credit card, they won't care if you're dressed in rags."

I was tempted to contact HR and suggest Annamarie belonged in negotiations instead of slaving away taking care of me and Dad.

Then again, she wouldn't be taking care of me for too much longer, not if Laura worked out.

I surrendered with a sigh. "I'll be in my office writing up a job description for the vice president position. I don't want to be bothered unless it's Laura or urgent."

Annamarie, as gracious as always in her victory, smiled and nodded.

---

WHEN THREE O'CLOCK ROLLED AROUND, I woke Dad so he could get ready for his meeting. I returned to my desk and resumed browsing the internet to find what qualities we really needed in a vice president.

Dad groped for his phone, blinking blearily at the screen. "Why didn't you wake me sooner?"

Instead of answering him, I grunted, clicking on the next job description for Vice Presidents. The list of requirements was longer than any other example I'd seen, and I doubted Dad and I could meet the minimums if we pooled all of our experience together.

"Matia, I needed to *work*. You made us come in to work."

"So go work. You have a four o'clock meeting."

Lurching off the couch, Dad staggered to his desk, picked up his wallet and pass, and glared at me. "You could have woken me up for lunch at least."

"So go eat lunch and go to your meeting. I have a few things to finish here."

Dad sighed. "You're supposed to be resting."

While there were perks to Dad when he was being protective, if I wanted to make my four o'clock, I needed to get him out of my hair—and make a solid game plan so Dad wouldn't figure out I was leaving the office until I was long gone.

I pointed at the door and focused my attention on my laptop, which the techies had returned to me with a full copy of Harthel's files.

"Matia."

The snap of my fingers broke the silence, and I gestured to the door again. "Go."

"I guess I'll just go to my meeting straight from lunch," he complained.

All I could do was hope Dad finished sulking sooner than later. "I was fine the entire time you were dozing on the couch. I'll be fine the entire time you are at lunch and attending to your meetings."

"Meetings?"

"Don't you have a five o'clock, too?" I knew he did; it had been Annamarie's idea to load in as many impromptu meetings as she could fit, giving me until eight—possibly nine—to make my way back from the restaurant to the office. Sam would be on call to pick me up so I could finish pulling the wool over Dad's eyes.

He checked his phone. "A six, seven, and eight o'clock, too, apparently. Wonderful."

"Gives me time to deal with this. Go get lunch and get to your meetings."

"Not even going to give your old man some sympathy?"

"No."

"So cruel, Matia."

I stared at him until he left. The instant the door closed, I smiled. In twenty minutes, Sam would pick me up for my meeting. I had already reviewed the information from the original meeting. It helped I had done the majority of the work on the proposal, from inception to final presentation. Harthel's data, while complete, was an unorganized mess, and I hadn't found his notes for the meeting—if he had any. I had my doubts.

Checking his email had been one of the first things I had done. Like his computer, his emails were an unorganized disaster. He had hundreds of emails dealing with Mirage Resources, and I hadn't had time to read through them all. The newest ones confirmed the original place and time of the meeting. Dredging through the newer emails hadn't helped any, either. It had taken a twenty-email exchange to settle on the meeting time.

I'd need hours I didn't have to unravel the tangled mess.

I also had the problem of Laura to deal

with. Bypassing HR was no easy task, yet Harthel had pulled it off flawlessly. HR would be examining the circumstances and likely have proposals on how to close every single loophole Harthel had used to sneak her in.

I needed to know why he had done it, and I had the feeling it had something to do with her background check. Picking up my landline, I punched speed dial for Annamarie's desk.

"What can I do for you?" Annamarie asked.

"Has Laura's background check come back yet?"

"I'll call downstairs and find out." Annamarie hung up.

While I waited, I grabbed a pad of paper and pen, backing my chair from my desk so I could spin in slow circles. What did Pallodia Industries really need in a vice president?

Integrity came to mind first, and I had no idea how to weed out the scumbags from the good-natured people we wanted working for the company. I narrowed my eyes and turned back to the job hunting sites, browsing through the staggering assortment of executive roles available.

Certain skills and experience were needed for such an important role, but integrity, a strong work ethic, and the ability to think in stressful situations rose to the top of my wish list for a candidate.

I could have hired a head hunter to investigate other businesses for a candidate, but I didn't want someone just out for their next paycheck. Money mattered; Laura was proof of that. The hope in my new assistant's eyes when she realized she was moving up in the world reminded me just how much it mattered.

There was no denying the truth; I was a spoiled rich girl. I didn't worry much about household budgets, although I was the one who tracked how much we spent versus how much we made.

Dad had insisted we live within our means, and I even paid my fair share of the rent and bills, but with two of us contributing, I could have lived a lavish lifestyle without ever dipping a toe into our savings.

Maybe once everything blew over, I'd talk to Dad and get some perspective on the real world—the one our employees faced each and every day. Was our company-wide minimum wage close enough to a solid living wage?

I didn't know, but I did know one thing for certain: I wanted whoever replaced Harthel to know what struggling to get by was like from bitter experience. It'd help give us the insight we needed to run the company better for all of our employees, and it would give us someone who'd work hard to keep the job once they had it.

I wouldn't find such a person with a typical job description, that much was certain.

My phone rang, and I picked it up. "Yes?"

"Her background check is completed." There was a slight hesitancy in Annamarie's voice.

"Bring it in." I hung up.

Five minutes later, Annamarie knocked and entered, carrying a manilla folder, which she dropped on my desk. Her lack of expression told me far more than I think she wanted me to guess.

"What's the problem?"

"It's her credit."

"Is that all?" I canted my head to the side and arched a brow. "How is it a problem?"

"She's worse than bankrupt."

"And?"

"Are you sure you want someone incapable of handling her finances working on sensitive material?"

I wanted to get angry at the question, but I forced myself to bury my irritation and hide it behind a smile. "Does she have a criminal record?"

"No."

"So it's just her credit?"

"I took the liberty of calling her landlord to inquire on her as a tenant. She's under an eviction notice, effective at the end of the week."

"That makes it easier to relocate her to a better apartment nearby. See what you can do so she has a new apartment on Friday. Somewhere in a good neighborhood with a reasonable commute. Find out her current travel times and shave off a few minutes here and there as you can. If you're too busy, get HR to handle the apartment acquisition or whoever else would take care of corporate-acquired housing."

"You're serious."

"No one can survive in this city on minimum wage living alone, Annamarie. She has student loans. She was a barista. Hell, the fact she has no criminal record is damned impressive. Desperate people do desperate things—including working under an asshole like Harthel. What I want to know is how he found her, why he kept her, and what he was trying to hide bypassing HR."

My next words would either sink me or lift me up in Annamarie's eyes, and I knew it. "The pay she was given was the real crime here, and we're the ones who need to clean up the mess. I'm giving her a chance to prove she deserves the job. I absolutely refuse to make her a homeless woman when it isn't her fault. Harthel's behavior does not reflect on her performance and integrity. It does everything to show we do not treat our employees in a way they deserve. Okay. She has a poor credit rating. So what?"

Annamarie's mouth hung open, and she spluttered before falling silent.

"If an apartment can't be found for her by Friday, make reservations at a hotel for her and have her things put into storage in the interim. I'll pay the balance myself."

"We have a budget for corporate-sponsored housing. I'll make sure it's done," Annamarie whispered before retreating to her desk.

---

AT THREE-THIRTY, when it was time to leave for the dinner meeting, I was ready to go home and sleep. Instead of succumbing to the temptation of canceling the meeting altogether and rescheduling for another day, I packed up my laptop, stuffed it into my oversized purse, and ignored Sam's slack-jawed stare. "Yes, I am going to the meeting like this. No, I don't have time to change. They can deal with it."

"It was my idea," Annamarie chirped from the reception.

"You're going to make an impression, that's for certain."

"If Dad asks you, you know nothing, Sam."

"When did she get involved in corporate clandestine operations, Annamarie?"

"This morning, apparently. I think it's the medications. She'll talk your ear off if you give her half a chance. Not a bad thing, considering she's fielding a dinner meeting."

"Dealing with the fallout from this morning?"

"Yes. Try to be back by eight-thirty, Miss

Evans. I'm not sure I can coerce any other executives into meetings tonight to cover for you."

If dinner took three hours, I was going to need bail money. Once again, Sam brought the car around to spare me the steps in the parking garage. I slid into the back, buckled in, and sighed from relief at having escaped the office.

"Day from hell?"

"I threw a pitcher of ice water over the entire board while Dad was looking over company bylaws."

"Was that before or after your father fired Mr. Harthel?"

"Before."

"Nice baseball cap. Who did you steal it from?"

I had forgotten I was wearing the hat. "One of the security guards on the meeting floor. I meant to give it back."

"I'm sure it'll keep until tomorrow. You'll need to text me thirty minutes before you want to be picked up if you don't want a wait. If you sneak a nap, I'll even wake you up when we arrive."

"So I can be bleary-eyed on top of hoarse and casually dressed?"

"You'll make them feel important if you look utterly ragged."

"You're just saying that to make me feel better."

"You caught me."

"Seriously, if I fall asleep now, you won't wake me up. How much sleep has Dad been getting lately?"

"Not enough."

"I noticed. He spent several hours out cold on the couch while I dealt with work. Does he need to see a doctor?"

"No, but you do tomorrow afternoon at three."

The last thing I needed was Sam slipping into the same protective mode as Dad. "Noted. I'll be there."

"Good. I'll pick you up at two—one-thirty if you're at the office tomorrow."

I groaned. "Nothing closer?"

"Sorry, Matia. I don't pick the appointment locations. All I do is drive the car."

Arguing about it wouldn't change anything. "I stole Harthel's assistant. Dad doesn't know yet."

Sam snorted. "It's about time you got an assistant of your own."

"Did you run into the slime dropping his things off today?"

"Fortunately not. The building security guards claimed the boxes and signed off on them. I was gone before he came to retrieve them. Would you rather I wait near the restaurant for you?"

"No. It'll probably be two hours—maybe longer, depending on how long they want to talk. If I'm lucky, I'll be out in an hour flat, but I don't have high hopes of that."

Sam sighed. "You're supposed to be resting, you know."

"I have all three inhalers, I brought all my medications, and I even figured out how to take them on my own. I'll be fine, Sam."

"Call me if you need anything, okay?"

"Okay, okay. If I need anything, I'll call." I sighed, wondering if I'd ever be fine again after what had happened at LaGuardia. "Oh, any luck on finding Ryan?"

"No luck, sorry. There was one Ryan on the passenger list for Terminal B, but unless your gentleman is a woman named Danielle, it's not a match."

I wasn't surprised, but I sighed from disappointment anyway. Finding a man using a photograph of his sweaty chest was likely impossible, and without the ability to identify his hair color, eye color, and skin tone, I'd have an easier time finding a needle in a haystack.

## NINE

*For such a young woman, you're shrewd.*

---

WHILE THE ITALIAN restaurant Annamarie had selected wasn't New York's finest, it came close. Sam's chuckles rang in my ears long after he had left me on the curb to rot. Sighing, I pushed my way inside, wondering how I'd get through a business meeting in a restaurant where formal funeral attire wouldn't have been out of place.

The host took one look at me and grinned, dipping into a bow. "Your party has already arrived, Miss Evans. Please follow me."

Several someones would face payback for not warning me about the restaurant, but I'd save Annamarie for last as thanks for sparing me the hassle of explaining who I was and warning the restaurant staff I wasn't wearing anywhere near my finest. I followed after the host, adjusting my purse on my shoulder. At the very least, if anyone laughed too hard at me, it weighed enough to make a viable weapon.

Rule two was overrated anyway.

When the host led me to a table set up for twelve people and eleven men were waiting for me, it took every bit of my willpower to plaster a smile on my face and at least try to pretend I wanted to be meeting with them. I'd been to many business meetings over the years with Dad, but never had I seen one quite so unbalanced.

Larger meetings tended to include at least one token woman in the group. I'd grown up living the reality of that role, although Dad used me to his advantage whenever possible.

The only man to rise was directly to my left, and his mouth was partially open, although I couldn't tell if he was surprised or horrified. His hair was a darker gray than his skin, which was a duskier hue than his companions.

They were all younger men dressed in their best suits, although the variations in tones assured me they weren't all in black and white formal attire.

Without allowing my smile to slip, I offered my hand. "I hope I didn't leave you waiting long, gentlemen. Since Mr. Harthel can't attend, I'm Matia, the representative for Pallodia Industries."

Eleven pairs of blinking eyes stared at me. Deer trapped in the headlights of an oncoming car were more responsive. "Is this when I should make an assumption regarding communications with Mr. Harthel? Unfortunately, due to the nature of his being let go this morning, I am working with old information."

I sat, pulled my chair to the table, and stashed my purse between my feet.

"Mr. Harthel was let go?" The gentleman to my left sank onto his seat, thrusting out his hand. I clasped it in a firm grip, applying as much pressure as my slender fingers allowed, which was met with an equally firm squeeze on his part.

There was a challenge in the man's shake, which I answered by ignoring it altogether. I freed my hand and took a sip of water to soothe my throat. "A polite way of saying he was fired for lying to the board in a meeting this morning."

"I see. Well, I'm grateful you could make time in your schedule to meet with us on such short notice, then. I'll admit, we were expecting Mr. Harthel. I'm Dalton Sinclair, the Vice President of Marketing for Mirage Resources. Let's skip the formalities, shall we? Please call me Dalton."

"Pleased to meet you, Dalton."

He made introductions around the table, and the eclectic mix of accountants, marketers, secretaries, and attorneys intrigued me. I smiled and nodded to each one of them, hoping I wouldn't have to call any of them by their names.

Remembering Dalton's was going to be difficult enough.

"From my understanding, Mirage Resources is based in London. Is that correct?"

"Yes, that's correct. Unfortunately, our CEO was unable to make the trip. Most of us are from our New York office. To prevent any misunderstandings, what do you know about the negotiations?"

Before I had a chance to answer, the waiter came, and I invited Dalton to order wine if he desired, choosing hot tea to help with my throat. I was intrigued when they followed my lead, all choosing non-alcoholic beverages.

Recapping the initial negotiations as a part of the discussion process wasn't completely unheard of, and I covered the benefits of the medical research equipment Mirage Resources would sell to Pallodia Industries. With the license for the patents, Pallodia could expand into several important markets.

Harthel had likely ruined all the numbers work we had done, but I laid out the original opening bid, which totaled over a hundred million dollars for the purchase of several patents and licensing of several more.

I stopped frequently to take sips of my tea and water, horrified at how hoarse my voice was. At least I didn't wheeze despite how much talking I was doing. It was bad enough I had to resort to a cough drop.

Using an inhaler in front of so many businessmen would do a lot more harm to my reputation than good.

We were interrupted several times by the waiter, who took our orders and returned with our meals, which we ate when we weren't talking. I barely tasted my food; spaghetti normally appealed, but with so many watching me, I couldn't bring myself to eat more than a few bites, instead choosing to fill the silence with everything I remembered from the proposals and information I had compiled for the meeting.

The entire time, the representatives of Mirage Resources looked troubled, exchanging looks when they thought I wasn't watching. Dalton frowned, glancing across the table at one of the attorneys. "Mr. Harthel had made a drastically different proposal."

"Before discussion continues, I'd like to make it perfectly clear any discussions for a merger, share sales, or personnel acquisitions weren't intended to be brought to the table."

Someone at the other end of the table snorted, and a wave of chuckles and titters worked its way to me. Dalton was the last to crack a smile. "For such a young woman, you're shrewd. What made you come to the conclusion he had proposed one—or more—of those things?"

While I couldn't remember their names, I did remember which two men were the attorneys, and I gestured to them. "As the sellers, you wouldn't bring a pair of corporate attorneys for starting negotiations. They'd be involved later in the process, after we had a written proposal ready for examination. Their presence means you wanted a direct and immediate legal guidance, which implies a broader scope of negotiation—or a more serious acquisition on your part."

"You're familiar with negotiations, I see. What is your rank at Pallodia Industries?" Dalton looked me over, his eyes narrowing.

I gave him the time to speculate and wonder at my attire, taking a sip of my water. "Executive Vice President."

Several of the men choked and coughed, and Dalton's eyes widened. "*You're* the Executive Vice President?"

"Mr. Harthel probably told you he was aspiring to—or already held—the position, didn't he?"

Dalton wasn't the only one who flinched. I blinked as the missing pieces fell into place. With me out of the picture, Harthel was the likeliest one to take my place, which was probably the reason for the board meeting. After seeing me in the lobby, he had the choice of continuing the farce or informing the entirety of the board he hadn't followed protocol. If he had managed to force Dad into a leave of absence, he could have secured his position in the company, either ousting my father or taking over my role.

"I apologize, Miss…?"

"Evans. No apology necessary, Dalton.

You're not responsible for Mr. Harthel's actions, and I hope we can restart negotiations so they're beneficial to both of our companies. If you are all located in New York, I'd like to propose we conduct further meetings at our office building—or yours, if you'd prefer. I'd also like to extend apologies on behalf of Pallodia for our inability to make the initial negotiation meeting."

"Evans? The same as the CEO's?"

I chuckled. "The same. I'm afraid he had meetings tonight and wasn't able to attend. Should we continue negotiations, you'll meet him."

Dalton stared at me for a long moment before offering a smile, which made him look almost as young as I did. "That would be beneficial for both of our companies. If you can provide me with your information, I'll send over a copy of the files Mr. Harthel had given us for review. Do you think a meeting later this week is possible?"

"I think it's a possibility." I dug out my wallet and breathed a sigh of relief that someone had inserted new business cards. I didn't have enough for everyone, but I handed over the entire stack to Dalton. "I'll be in and out of the office tomorrow, but give me a call at your convenience and we'll set something up."

"I'll do that, and I'll inquire about the CEO traveling here to join us. If you could provide written documentation, it would help speed things along."

My smile became genuine. "Email me. I still have copies of our original proposal."

---

I MISJUDGED how long it would take us to finish dinner, resulting in me waiting outside of the restaurant for Sam to arrive. While the other businessmen left, Dalton Sinclair remained, leaving me to wonder why he stuck around when he could have returned home.

I propped the restaurant up, stuffing my hands into my pockets. "Waiting wasn't necessary, Dalton."

"It's rude to leave a lady waiting on her own." He relaxed, and with no care for his suit jacket, he joined me in leaning against the wall. "Please excuse how forward this is, but we were under the impression you had died in the LaGuardia bombing."

"My purse was lost in the debris. Since there was trouble with my ID, I was listed as a Jane Doe for a while. Once they got that sorted, I went home. My father was rather busy, so he hadn't notified anyone I was returning to work until I showed up." I shrugged. "Terminal B was a mess, and it was quite a while before they managed to reach the section of the terminal we were located in."

"Terminal B was the hardest hit."

"I got lucky." I still had no idea how I had made it out of Terminal B, but I believed Ryan was behind it. Without any matches on the passenger list, I had little hope of finding the man again, especially since my only photos of him involved his bare chest.

If I showed Sam the pictures, could he help me track Ryan down? I doubted it.

"Sounds like it. Had I known you were still recovering, I would have suggested we postpone the meeting."

I shook my head. "Problems like this tend to escalate if left alone, and considering Mr. Harthel's behavior, it couldn't wait. I'd rather not leave either of our companies with an unfortunate mess to clean up—one larger than the one we're already dealing with."

If Dad ever found out how much ass kissing I was doing to the contact at Mirage Resources, he'd kill me. Salvaging a deal with the other company would serve as a starting point for making up things to him, since he had suffered far more than I had as a result of our aborted flight from La-Guardia.

I doubted my guilt would ever go away. My entire life had been before me, and every time my breathing began to wheeze, I recognized that life would be a lot shorter than I had anticipated.

"Mr. Harthel's deal wouldn't have gone through, anyway. It was shit. The one you prepared, that's the deal the boss in London wants. Mr. Evans came up with quite the proposal."

I laughed, and it triggered a cough so strong my eyes watered. Reaching into my purse for an inhaler, I fought the itch in my throat, somehow managing to contain it long enough I could ensure I'd be able to take another breath.

"You okay?"

I had cough drops for a chaser, waving Dalton off. It took several minutes for me to recover enough I could speak without croaking. "I was warned they'd be like that. I'll be okay. Thank you."

Dad would kill me if he found out I was lying to clients.

"I had heard rumors Mr. Evans was masterful at preparing bipartisan proposals, but I hadn't believed them until we saw the preliminaries. I don't suppose you'd be willing to share trade secrets, would you?"

My voice was raspy when I laughed. While Dad had been heavily involved in the Mirage Resources proposal, it had been *my* work. Originally, Dad was going to do the majority of the presentation, leaving a few choice tidbits for me. "Sure, I can share a trade secret."

"Oh? What's it going to cost me?"

"This one's on the house."

"I'm intrigued."

Watching for his reaction, I resumed my relaxed stance against the restaurant's rough exterior wall. "I'm very pleased you liked my proposal."

Dalton's eyes widened a little, so slight I wouldn't have noticed if I hadn't been watching him. "*Your* proposal?"

"He was the one doing all the talking for the proposal. I was the one doing all the thinking. Unfortunately, also the pie charts."

"There has been a rumor about those, too. There were also a few rumors Mr. Evans's daughter was best known for her ability to go through an entire meeting without saying a single word."

"It's a secret. I—"

The squeal of rubber and a flash of headlights drew my attention to the street. A taxi cut across the nearby intersection and plowed into the front of a car parked on the curb in front of the restaurant, sending a shower of plastic, metal, and sparks flying.

The impact launched the taxi over the sidewalk and directly into the light pole, plunging the street into darkness.

The car kept going and smashed into the side of the building, and the stench of burning gasoline and rubber filled my nose. Time slowed, and in the distance, sirens wailed.

My throat clenched and cut off my scream. I clapped my hands over my ears, willing the sounds and the smells to go away. My entire body turned cold, and a shudder ripped through me. Backing away, I shook my head to deny the wreckage of twisted metal and plastic.

I needed to escape, so I retreated into the crowd of people gawking at the accident. My first few steps faltered, my breath wheezing as my heart thundered in my chest. Each step came faster, until I broke into a run, leaving the ruins behind me.

---

THE STENCH of Eau de Skunk woke me. There was no mistaking the wretched excuse for a cologne, and my entire body jerked with my desire to distance myself from the source of the smell.

A hand seized my jaw, clutching so tightly my teeth dug into my cheeks. I struggled, and pain stabbed from my wrists and up my arms to my aching shoulders.

"Wake up, you stupid slut," Harthel hissed, and his breath was even more putrid than his cologne.

I gagged, and a rattling cough tore through me. When he released me as though I would contaminate him, I fell to a cold tiled floor. The tip of his dress shoe plunged into my stomach and drove the air out of me.

My mouth opened and closed. My lungs burned, but my body remained paralyzed between breaths while the edges of my vision darkened.

Harthel kicked me again, and dead air

wheezed out of me without flowing back in. The darkness in my vision spread until all I could make out were the tips of the man's polished shoes. One foot moved out of sight.

Moments later, he hit me again, catching me between my breasts. Pain blossomed through my chest, and a single breath wheezed into me. After the first, my lungs remembered what they were supposed to do, but it took all my strength to force air in around my constricted throat.

Harthel shifted his foot to my chin, working his toe beneath my jaw to force me to turn my head. "You and your father are going to regret firing me. I've already sent him one video so he could listen to how terribly difficult it must be for you to breathe right now. Too bad that's the last thing he'll ever hear from you. It's a race against time, and it's one he can't win. Taunting him is only half the fun. The other half will be making sure he sees every last bruise I beat into you before I get tired of playing with you."

I couldn't answer him even though I wanted to spit curses at him.

Crouching beside me, Harthel pressed his fingers to my throat to check my pulse. The black aura surrounding the man intensified, and his touch chilled me to the bone. "I don't want you to die quite yet. Where would be the fun in that? I considered raping you, but I don't think I want your special brand of filth touching me like that. Instead, I'll just give your pathetic father the fear I may have raped you. Fear is so much more potent than the reality, isn't it?"

"Bastard," I choked out.

Harthel rose, stepped over me, and smashed his foot down on my bound hands. "I guess I'll begin with your hands, then. How long *does* it take for bruises to form? Let's find out, shall we?"

# TEN

### How could a nightmare hurt so much?

---

HARTHEL LEFT me in the bathroom to rot. It took a little over a day for Harthel's blows to mottle my skin in a way that satisfied him. He enjoyed talking about their colors and how the black, blue, red, purple, green, and yellow marring me pleased him. The man's laughter accompanied the snap of his cell's camera. On the hour, every hour, he came back to worsen a bruise or add a new one.

Then he'd read me the taunts he sent to my father. Sometimes, he mentioned how much I wheezed. Once, he had implied a few kicks to the chest was almost as good as CPR.

My entire body throbbed to the erratic beat of my heart, and while I struggled for every breath, the wheeze and burn in my lungs didn't worsen. If it did, I'd probably die. The realization settled over me, resignation numbed me, and I fought in the only way I knew how.

Harthel cherished reactions, be it a twitch,

a gasp, or tears of pain. Denying him what he wanted hurt almost as much as the force behind his blows. My tears burned, but keeping my eyes closed helped stop them from falling. Holding still made what he did worse, especially when he refused to ease the pressure of his foot. If Harthel hadn't broken one or more of my ribs, they were so bruised even the faintest touch sent fire scorching through my body.

One moment blurred into the next, and I finally found relief when I fainted.

The respite didn't last long; Harthel dumped me into the shower and turned the cold water on so my muscles stiffened and the ache penetrated deep to my bones.

When my blouse soaked through, Harthel ripped it open, popping off the buttons and leaving my chest and stomach exposed. He left my bra on, not that it helped hide the evidence of his beatings. Every inch of bare skin was mottled black and other dark tones, which I assumed were blue and purple. The man voiced his satisfaction with a huff.

I closed my eyes while he took his photographs with his cell phone. I wasn't even sure when—or how—I had burst a vessel in my right eye, but the other bruises were bad enough. There was no doubt in my mind Harthel was sending images to my father.

When my eyes were open, the tendrils of the man's dark aura stretched throughout the bathroom and tiled sitting room. It brushed my skin, numbing me in its wake.

"Son of a bitch," Harthel snarled.

The bathroom door was open, allowing me a clear view of the man while he worked at an armchair and small table. Instead of working on his computer, he had his cell out.

"Are you behind this?" Rising to his feet, he stomped to the bathroom, holding his phone display in my direction. I stared at him, marveling at his idiocy. How could I do anything?

My hands were bound together and were tied to the faucet to make certain I couldn't go far even if I wanted to. There was enough slack in the line for him to move me as he desired but ensure I couldn't get out of the shower. He'd done the same to my ankles. Both were unnecessary precautions.

It took all my strength to keep breathing. Earlier, I had been able to lift my head, but I leaned against the frigid tiles. I shivered, although I was grateful for the cold water's numbing embrace.

I hurt, but the pain was remote and distant.

"Did you do this?" Harthel's voice turned shrill, and he waved the phone in my face. Water splashed on the screen.

When I didn't respond, he pointed at one of the icons.

The phone's GPS tracking had been enabled, and a weak laugh worked its way out of my throat. "How could I?" I rasped.

The coughing fit my words triggered ripped through me, and the incessant pressure in my chest intensified.

Harthel's eyes narrowed. "Don't get smart with me. I could just kill you now instead of giving your pathetic father a chance to find you. He won't, not when I take my phone and get moving, of course. But he'll try. Then he'll live with knowing he failed to find you while you were dying a slow and painful death."

"Bastard."

Slapping his hand over the shower faucet, Harthel turned the water off before stepping into the shower and onto my bound hands. The shriek made its way out my throat but emerged as a croaked groan. "Keep your mouth shut. I could just kill you now."

Harthel's phone rang, and after wiping the display on his slacks, he stepped back several steps and answered, "Harthel."

While I understood the GPS tracking on the phone could isolate someone's location, without any idea where we were, I didn't know if it would help—or if Harthel would ditch his phone and leave, taking me with him. Or, as I both hoped for and feared, leave me behind.

If he left me, I could try to find some way to break free, although I doubted I'd succeed. The water had seeped into the ropes binding me, making them swell and dig into my wrists. Keeping still kept them from tearing into my skin, although I had, from time to time, seen discoloration in the water streaming around me towards the drain.

Whoever had called Harthel had a lot to say, and the man's expression changed from smug satisfaction to suspicion. "How did you get this number?"

In a way, I missed the cold water; it numbed me, and without it, the pain of Harthel's assault on my hands shot up my arms into my stiffened shoulders. The worst was my chest and ribs, which had been targeted the most. The fact my lungs hadn't ceased functioning altogether amazed me.

I wheezed, but I could—did—keep fighting for every breath.

"You have no proof of that." Harthel's body tensed, and he twisted to level a glare at me, his expression accusatory. "Let's assume, for a moment, I am—"

Whatever the person on the other end said, it made Harthel's face pale to white, and the black miasma surrounding him retreat, coiling around his body to add to his rotund bulk. "Fine. Here's my one and only offer. I'll leave the little slut, but it's not my problem if she dies before you can find her. Since you think you're so smart, I think you can find her on your own."

Smiling, Harthel crouched beside me, his gaze sweeping over me. "You don't even know if I have her with me or if I've left her somewhere else. You know nothing."

With the man so close, I could hear the person on the other end of the line. "Your last photograph came with a time stamp from twenty minutes ago, taken by your cellular phone, which has not changed position since the picture was taken. She's with you. Put her on the line. If she's dead—or dead by the time I reach her—they will need tweezers to pick the shredded remains of your carcass out of the tree tops."

"I'm afraid she's beyond talking," was Harthel's smug reply. "I could put her on the phone. Would you like to listen to her wheeze? That's the best she can do right now. I'm sorry, but she doesn't have an inhaler with her. It doesn't matter, anyway. You won't be able to find me—or her. You talk big, but it means absolutely nothing."

"You're located near Whiteface Mountain, skirting the primary ski resorts."

Harthel stiffened. "You've been tracking this phone for less than five minutes."

"That's all the time I needed to find you. No matter where you go, I can—and will—find you. You better hope the girl can talk, because if she can't, you'll find out just how serious I am. You can try to run, Mr. Harthel, but there's exactly one road out of where you're at, and there's still snow up in those mountains. Go ahead, go off the beaten path. I'm sure you'll freeze to death before someone finds you. I could have sworn the weather mentioned something about a late-season blizzard. Stop posturing and put the girl on the phone."

"You're seriously trying to tell me you're going to let me go if I put the girl on the phone and leave after you've confirmed she's still alive?"

"You're going to untie her, and when you're done, you will not touch her again if you value your life. You will put her on the phone, I will speak to her, and when I am finished, you will run like the little coward you are. If you run fast enough, you might not meet me on the road. That's your only chance. Am I understood?"

Harthel swallowed, and the lump in his throat bobbed several times. "Fine. I'm putting the phone to her ear now."

The phone scalded my chilled skin, and a shudder ran through me. It took several deep breaths and a few raspy coughs before I could whisper, "Hello?"

"Here's what's going to happen, little lady. You're going to sit tight until that fat fuck leaves. Once he's gone, survive, no matter what it takes. It won't take too long to get to you, okay?"

I cleared my throat several times before choking out, "Okay."

Harthel took the phone back. "You've talked to her."

"Untie her and get your pathetic fat ass

away from her. So help me, if you're within a twenty mile radius when I arrive, you're a dead man. Don't you ever think of going near her again. Got it?"

"Fuck you," Harthel snapped before hanging up.

While he cut my hands and feet free, it didn't stop him from stepping on me in the process. When something in my wrist broke, I slid into painless darkness.

---

I WOKE IN THE TUB, and I had avoided drowning to death by a mere inch. Water lapped at my chin, and the splash of it overflowing accompanied a crackle I knew all too well. The hint of smoke in the air sent terror icing through my veins. I jerked, and my body thrashed in the water.

My vision blurred. Blinking away the sting of smoke-induced tears, I struggled to sit up. Pain flared through my chest and ribs, and I submerged, the water closing over my head.

The water seemed far too deep. Had there been a jacuzzi or a hot tub in the room? Ski lodge, if the man on the phone had been correct. I didn't remember one. I didn't remember much beyond the pain-filled blur between Harthel's kicks.

I lurched out of the water, groping for

something to hold onto so I could keep my head above water.

My feet found purchase on an uneven, roughed surface at the bottom of the tub. A blast of cold air in my nose drew my attention to the snow falling on me and melting in the cold water overflowing the tub.

My hands and fingers didn't work like I expected, and I couldn't secure a grip on the water-slicked porcelain. A flash of light and wave of heat woke my fears; a scream burst out of me.

The sound that emerged from my throat, however, wasn't a scream. It was a high-pitched, squeaky yip.

I never yipped. I never squeaked, yipped, or whined like a dog, yet the noises I made matched a puppy's terrified cries. The water dragged at me, and I groped for the side of the tub again.

It should have been easy to find a grip with my fingers, except I didn't have fingers. I had paws and claws, and the water soaked fur I shouldn't have had.

Debris fell from the crumbling, burning ceiling, splashing into the tub and sizzling. Wood cracked against my back, and another pained yip burst out of my throat. I clawed at the rubble in the tub in my effort to keep my nose above water.

Not a human's nose, but the elongated muzzle of a dog.

I panted to catch my breath. While my

chest burned and I wheezed, I could fill my starved lungs with air.

I had to be in a nightmare, one where the world burned around me while I was trapped in a dog's body, unable to escape. I'd burn and drown, and fear gripped my throat and tightened until I suffocated. Another whine burst out of me, and I scrambled over the submerged debris until I cowered beneath the running faucet. The water cascaded over my head, streaming over my eyes and running along both sides of my nose.

The water would keep me from burning to death. If I died from the smoke and flames in my nightmares, would I die in the real world, too? My entire body ached, as though I had been pounded to dust before I had been stitched back together as a small dog of some sort.

I wanted to scream, but all I managed was a pitiful whine.

The creak and crack of burning wood drowned out my cries, and I recoiled as another section of the ceiling collapsed into the bathroom. The snow fell harder, and somewhere nearby, another crash shuddered through the entire building.

The flow of water cut off. I whimpered as the stench of smoke clogged my nose and filled my lungs. I tried to tell myself it was a nightmare, but how could a nightmare hurt so much and feel so real? The water clung to me and numbed most of my pain, but the throb in my ribs and chest mirrored my human body.

How could a nightmare hurt so much?

I dredged up the strength to claw at the debris and the side of the tub in my effort to escape, but the water dragged me back and held me hostage. Bone-deep lethargy sank into me, and with the last of my will, I flopped as close to the surface of the water as I could before collapsing. The tip of my nose and muzzle rested on fire-scorched wood. The rest of me submerged in the water, chilled from the persistent cold and snow blowing in through the ruins of the burning lodge.

---

THE NIGHTMARE REFUSED TO END. The flames burned hot and furious, and it didn't take long until only the blackened, charred skeleton of the building remained. Flashes of light penetrated through the rising smoke in the dying daylight. Ice formed over the surface of the tub and frosted over me.

It hadn't been much, but I had managed to claw my way up so my entire head was free of the water, not that it did me any good. If I stayed submerged much longer, I'd freeze into a furry ice cube.

As a human, I could have crawled out of the tub and at least taken shelter where the ruins smoldered, coaxing warmth back into me. Then again, as a human, the falling debris likely would have killed or drowned me. For better or for worse, my smaller size let me avoid being crushed.

It wouldn't save me from hypothermia, and I was aware of the shivers coursing through me.

If I wanted to survive, I needed to move, but my limbs refused to obey my demands. I managed to make a front paw twitch—the one Harthel hadn't broken with his heel while cutting me free and leaving me to die.

The logical side of me believed he had placed me in the tub of running water and set the fire to finish me off. By doing so, he would have kept his word to the man on the phone.

The caller had wanted me to survive. The cold air stung my lungs, and I made one last attempt to climb up the ice-slicked debris to freedom. My claws dug in and jammed in the grain of the wood. My hind legs twitched before acknowledging subservience to my demands. Focusing my strength and effort on my hind paws, I thrust myself up, the frozen water and frost crackling in my fur.

I tumbled over the edge, fell onto the smoldering wreckage scattered on the bathroom floor, and collapsed in a panting heap.

---

WITHOUT THE NUMBING of the cold water,

my body reported so many sources of pain I couldn't move, let alone stand. I shuddered on the bathroom floor while snow fell though the ruined building, covering me in a blanket of white.

When night fell, ribbons of light marked where the building still smoldered. The heat of the dying fire failed to reach me. I'd been told to survive, but hopelessness chilled me as much as the mountain's snow and freezing wind.

Fur, at least, provided some measure of protection against the cold and the snow. If I had been dressed in my opened blouse, flimsy bra, and jeans, I would've long since frozen to death. Tremors twitched through my body, and I stared at my paws, the only part of me I could see without moving my head.

In the flickering illumination of the dying embers, they were gray, like everything else in my life. The embers were pale, fringing on white.

Even in my dreams—my nightmares—I couldn't capture a glimpse of any color. I sighed. If I moved, it'd only take a few feet to reach one of the piles of embers and the warmth they radiated.

I lurched to my feet—my paws. The instinct to shake and rid myself of the snow clumped to my fur rose. The instant I braced and made the whipping motion, a yip tore out of my throat. Throbbing pain concentrated around my chest and ribs and my right front paw. The rest of my paws ached, but they tolerated my weight better. Stabbing jolts seared through my head.

Focusing all my attention on the glowing point ahead of me, I forced one paw in front of the other. The logistics of working four paws in unison made me stumble and stagger the first few steps, but I kept upright. I was forced to climb over chunks of wood scattered over the floor.

The snow and ice hid hot cores within the debris that singed my pads when I broke through the protective layers of cold. I yipped and whined, scrambling over the debris to reach the ruined wall.

My eyes hadn't betrayed me; warmth radiated from the glowing embers, and I huddled as close as I could get without getting burned. Through the gaps in the crumbling structure, a world of white stretched into the darkness.

In the morning, I'd wake up from one nightmare and enter the next, but at least I'd be human.

## ELEVEN

I had to take a detour.

THE BOUNCING BEAM of a flashlight played over the ruined structure. I blinked away the pain from the glare, huddling closer to the dying embers, which no longer provided enough heat to hold the late-season winter storm at bay.

Feet crunched through the snow, and someone cursed, soft and vehement. I sniffed, and my nose identified a fresh scent. The hint of male in the air caught my attention and held it, and the part of me that was still definitely human recognized the sweet, spicy aroma of cinnamon.

A new part of me, the one that liked having a fur coat, four paws, and sensitive nose, had certain ideas of what males were useful for, which fell in line with what had led me into photographing a man's—Ryan's—naked chest at LaGuardia.

The fear Harthel had returned chilled me even more than the snow and ice, and I whimpered. I cowered among the debris. A soft whine escaped before I could control the impulse.

Thrusting his hand through a gap in the burned-out structure, the male grabbed hold of my neck and pulled me through the hole. A yip burst out of me as pain seared across my ribs and through my chest.

The backdrop of falling snow turned the man into a dark shadow, his figure tall and far more slender than Harthel's obese bulk. He towered over me, lifting me up by my scruff before cradling me in his arm. With his other hand, he unzipped his jacket, which my nose identified as leather.

While I squirmed and yipped and whined in my effort to free myself, he kept a firm hold on me. When I stopped struggling to catch my breath, he stuffed me inside his coat and pinned me to his chest, zipping it up until only the tip of my nose was exposed to the cold.

"There you go, beautiful. You sit tight and warm up. I'll have you to the car in no time."

My nose didn't recognize the male, but I recognized his voice as the caller who had threatened Harthel.

Holding one arm beneath me to keep me in place, he turned and left the lodge behind. I shuddered with his every step, and the pressure of his jacket against my sides made my ribs throb in beat with my heart. While he trudged through the snow, he murmured reassurances. Dark shadows marked his original path, which followed what I assumed was a road or a trail cutting through the forest.

Headlights guided us to a dark-colored SUV. Its engine was still running, and after he opened the passenger side door, he eased me out of his jacket and set me on the seat.

He closed the door, circled around the SUV, and slid behind the wheel, reaching up to turn on the car's overhead light. Despite the illumination, my pain-blurred eyes couldn't make out his features. "Sorry it took me so long to get here. The cops thought it was a good idea to close the main roads, so I had to take a detour." Reaching into the back, he grabbed a blanket, which he tucked around me. I fell into exhausted slumber to the gentle touch of his fingers stroking my fur.

---

I WOKE to warm water drumming my back, and the weight of my soaked fur pinned me as effectively as the methodical hand stroking my back and sides. The sweet scent of vanilla soap filled my nose. My muzzle, head, and ears remained out of the showering warmth. Blinking, I took in the granite counters and mosaic tiles of a kitchen, my gaze focusing on the bright light of the time on a coffee maker.

Something about the numbers, which informed me it was two minutes after five, puzzled me. The gray was too bright, too vivid, but it wasn't white, either. I stared at it, wondering if the dim overhead lighting in the kitchen was somehow affecting the clock on the machine.

Maybe an animal's eyes saw the color gray differently than human ones. I wasn't even sure what sort of animal I was. Not a cat.

Cats didn't have longer muzzles like I did. A dog, probably. Did raccoons have long noses? Wait, I had paws. I definitely had paws. My front ones were draped over a very masculine arm, right along with my chin. They looked like dog paws, not that I had much experience with canines of any sort.

Dad didn't like dogs, and dogs didn't like Dad.

I had the strangest nightmares. Maybe it wasn't even a nightmare, but the afterlife. I remembered fighting to breathe and the cold shower, and the way my body hurt, the snap of the bones in my wrist, and the incessant pain. No one could live through so much. Death made sense.

It made a lot more sense than a person—me—becoming a dog.

I sighed.

The faucet turned off, and the arm I rested on shifted beneath me. Moments later, a hand stroked over my head, starting above my eyes and working over my ears to my neck. "Almost done, beautiful. There was a lot of soot and blood in your coat, but it's almost all out.

Just sit tight a little longer, okay? Then I'll get you dried off and warm, and I'll make you something to eat. You've got to be starving."

Did dead dogs need to eat in the afterlife? I didn't think so, but the thought of waking up to be tormented by Harthel again sent a shudder through me, as did my thoughts of Dad.

I had no way to tell him I wasn't really hurting any more, even if I had slipped into a fantastical dream where a man with a nice voice didn't think it strange I was a dog instead of a woman. There were benefits to being a dog, though.

Dogs didn't go to work. Dogs could sleep whenever they wanted. Dogs got away with atrocious behavior, including shoving their noses where they didn't belong. Dogs could take up enough couch space for three and get away with it, too.

I didn't want to be a dog in the afterlife. I didn't want an afterlife at all.

I wanted to go home and tell Dad everything would be okay even though it wasn't. I wanted to find a way to glue back together the shattered pieces of my life. I wanted to live.

I didn't want Harthel to win, and he had. Maybe my body no longer *hurt*, but my bones still ached and reminded me of what he had done and how he had enjoyed slowly beating the life out of me one kick at a time.

When I kept quiet and still, the man resumed his work, turning the faucet back on to rid my fur of the evidence of what Harthel had done to me. I closed my eyes.

The dream would end eventually, and reality would come back with a vengeance—or I'd realize I was actually dead. After all, women didn't become dogs, and there was no way anyone could survive what I had endured.

Some things were just impossible.

---

REALITY EXERTED itself the first time I tried to stand without help. Agony seared through my paw, up my leg, and flattened me, tearing a yelp out of my throat. I slid from the granite counter into the sink and shuddered against the stainless steel, whining with every breath.

My cry brought the male with the sweet cinnamon scent at a run, and my sensitive nose recognized the sharp bite of anxiety. The knowledge wasn't mine; humans couldn't identify such smells, could they?

Working his hands beneath me, he lifted me out of the sink while I panted, shaking in the aftershocks of the pain. He stretched me out over a towel, and his fingers stroked down my leg to my throbbing paw.

"He'll pay for every broken bone." While his anxiety remained as an undertone, his scent changed, and after a moment of consideration, I decided the putrid odor was his fury. Puzzled over the strength of his emotion, I turned my gaze to his face.

While the kitchen remained dimly lit, the shock of recognition swept through me and numbed me to everything but Ryan's face. The shadow of a new beard marked his jaw, but he hadn't changed much from what I remembered.

Of course I'd insert someone like Ryan into my dream. I had wanted nothing more than to see his snowcapped mountains and sapphire skies, but I hadn't been able to find him, not while I had been alive and human.

His attention was focused on my paw, and I yipped when his fingers found the injury. I whined.

Something in me stirred and demanded I twist my ears back and bare my teeth to show my displeasure at the pain. I heeded the instinct, and I added a growl of my own accord.

A sense of approval at my contribution warmed me from the inside.

"I'll wrap your paw so it doesn't hurt as much, but there's not much I can do for it. It has to heal on its own." Ryan gently lowered my paw to the counter and splayed his hands flat beside me. The heated scent of his rage strengthened. "It'll only take a few days. It shouldn't even take that long. If I had gotten there sooner…"

The anguish in his voice confused me almost as much as his ignorance. Broken bones took weeks to heal, sometimes months. I'd gotten lucky at LaGuardia. I had recovered from most of the cuts, scrapes, and bruises in the time I had been in the hospital, helped by the doctors and nurses who had fought to save my life. Ryan had, in a different way, saved me, too.

My memories of LaGuardia remained blurred, but he had been there when I had needed someone the most.

I had no idea how our paths had crossed again. If the limited amount I had heard on the phone was any indication, he didn't even know my name. Yet, somehow, he had called Harthel and lived up to his word he would find me.

In the real world, the one where I was alive and human, it was an impossibility. He didn't know my name. I hadn't given it to him. I had known his—or what he liked to go by—but Sam hadn't been able to find him.

How *had* Ryan found me? Nothing made sense, and I had no way of asking.

Harthel had sent the photographs and videos to my father, but Dad didn't know Ryan. Dad would have come on his own, his aura blacker than a night without stars. My eyes were still broken, but if Ryan had an aura, I was blind to it.

Ryan growled, straightened, and stalked out of the kitchen, returning several minutes later with a first-aid kit, which he set on the counter beside me. Removing a roll of self-adhering wrap, he took hold of my leg and started bandaging.

The pressure of the bandage hurt, but I swallowed my whines and watched him. When he finished, I couldn't see any part of my paw and most of my leg was likewise covered.

"I hope you like beef, because I wasn't planning on guests. It might be a while before the snow lets up enough to go to the store." Without waiting for me to reply, not that I could, Ryan went to his stainless refrigerator, pulled out enough paper-wrapped packages to feed five, and went to work.

---

THE STEADY THUNK of Ryan chopping through meat accompanied his muttered curses. I wasn't sure what he was upset about, but his cutting board would never be the same. His more enthusiastic strikes left grooves in the wood, and he had to yank on his knife to free it.

Vegetables didn't seem to be a part of Ryan's idea of dinner. I should have been bothered by the exclusion, but watching him cut meat into cubes and roll them in pale flour flecked with spice roused my appetite.

Standing with one of my paws completely encased in bandages proved a challenge, but I stayed upright. While Ryan had dried the water out of my fur, the need to shake washed over me. Any weight on my injured paw hurt, but I ignored the discomfort to indulge in a full body shake.

My motion caught Ryan's attention, and he paused in his chopping to watch me. "Be careful. It'll hurt like hell if you fall."

I kept my distance from the edge and limped my way in his direction, halting at the sink, which served as an effective barricade. Eyeing the ledge behind the sink, I wondered if I could crawl my way across.

The first victim of my attempt to cross the distance was the dish soap, which I knocked into one half of the divided sink. Ryan set his knife down and arched a brow at me.

Without the soap in the way, I eased my way behind the faucet. Two sponges and a dish cloth joined the soap in the sink by the time I made it halfway across. My final opponent was a porcelain dish holding two sink stoppers.

With a soft laugh, Ryan reached over, picked it up, and set it in the sink. "Not very satisfying prey, I'm afraid. Once you've recovered and have gained some size and weight, I'll take you on a hunt. You'll have to tolerate being an indoor wolf for a while."

I froze, staring at him. *Wolf?*

Impossible.

When I didn't move, Ryan leaned towards me, stretched out his hand, and pressed his finger to the tip of my nose. "Wolves are far superior to poodles, don't you think? They're also far better than one of those yipping ankle biters. You'll find others of our kind do not appreciate being called werewolves, but why try to cover the package with a pretty name? I should be apologizing for what I've done to you, but I won't. I can't. The alternative wasn't acceptable."

I blinked and crossed my eyes so I could look down the length of my muzzle at his finger. Part of me wanted to bite him. The rest of me was confused and intrigued. Indecision kept me still, and Ryan tapped my nose a final time before turning his attention back to his cooking.

What alternative?

Death, I suppose, was a rather unacceptable alternative. But why did Ryan care?

I made my way along the shelf behind the sink and sat on the other side, focusing my gaze on the meat he was cutting. Hunger cramped my stomach, and I licked my lips.

Raw meat, including sushi, had never been something I had been brave enough to try. I wanted to grab the biggest chunk of meat Ryan hadn't finished cutting up so I could sink my teeth into it. I swallowed, and a pleading whine worked its way out of my throat.

"It's been in the fridge too long for you to eat raw, beautiful. The last thing I want is to give you food poisoning right now. You're healing too slow as it is."

I turned my ears back. While I didn't

know much about wolves, I was pretty certain the species scavenged for food and had no problems eating old meat. The gnawing pain of hunger distracted me from the other aches in my body, even my paw. The slick granite made it difficult to walk without sliding, so I adopted an odd waddle in my attempt to get closer to the cutting board.

"Oh, no you don't," he said, reaching over and grabbing me by the scruff of my neck. He lifted me up, staring me in the eyes. "You can't trick me. I've seen just how stubborn you are. You're not getting raw meat. It'll make you sick, and you're sick enough."

Tucking me in the crook of his elbow, Ryan carried me out of the kitchen into an unlit living room. He dodged the dark outline of a coffee table on route to an armchair situated beside a small couch. Grabbing the throw pillows from the couch, he tossed them onto the floor before setting me on top of the pile. "Your job is to rest. My job is to cook. When it's ready, you can eat everything you want."

Ryan crossed his arms over his chest and glared at me, although the corners of his mouth twitched as though he fought to hide a smile. I sniffed, and my nose agreed with my assessment; he wasn't angry, and his amusement added a sweet undertone to his scent.

When he returned to the kitchen, I contemplated the little bit I had learned. Were werewolves real?

My paws and fur told me yes while the logical side of my head screamed no. Dreams, nightmares, and drug-induced hallucinations made sense to me.

Women couldn't become wolves.

My doubts, however, remained. What if they *could*? What if I had?

If I had, if I wasn't actually dreaming, how had I become a werewolf? I had never been bitten by a dog, and the closest I'd ever been to a wolf was looking at one at the zoo as a child. Glass and concrete had separated us, although I still remembered the cunning gleam in its golden eyes.

What had Ryan done to me? How had he done it?

I narrowed my eyes and watched Ryan from my nest of pillows. All I knew of him was his love of the snow and sky. All he knew of me was the fact I had a stubborn streak a mile wide and had gone to extreme measures to search for Dad before changing my motivation to help myself—and others—survive the bombing at LaGuardia.

With luck, maybe he didn't realize or remember I had taken photographs of his chest before my life had turned into a miserable, pain-filled hell.

TWELVE

The weather works in our favor.

---

FOOD REVITALIZED ME, and true to Ryan's word, he let me eat as much as I wanted. Instead of water, he gave me a bowlful of broth to go along with the meat. I ate until my sides bulged and my ribs ached from the pressure of so much food in my stomach.

Crouching down beside me, Ryan watched me while I engaged in a staring contest with the last chunk of meat in the bowl he had set down within easy reach. "Finished?"

I snatched the piece of beef and growled, retreating with the last of my meal until I hunkered beneath the coffee table. I choked it down so it wouldn't get taken from me.

Laughing, he shook his head and picked up both dishes he'd set down for me. "I wasn't going to steal it from you. There's plenty more if you want some later. It's too damned cold for you to go outside, especially since a stiff breeze could probably knock you over right now, so I'll set the bathroom up so you can reach everything you need."

I'd never been one for truly vivid dreams, and the times I had had one, they never involved such mundane things. Whether unaware of my embarrassment or choosing to ignore it, Ryan headed to the sink, rinsed the dishes, and put them away in the dishwasher. I emerged from my hiding place, limping in his wake to observe his behavior as he restored the kitchen to perfection, finishing with wiping down the counters.

"I'd start the dishwasher now, but it isn't hooked to the generator. It could be a while before power comes back. The generator has its work cut out for it running the necessities, the emergency lights, and the other stuff in this place." Ryan leaned against the counter, crossing his arms over his chest. "The weather works in our favor, though. You need the time to heal and get used to things. I hadn't wanted it to be this way. I meant to wait until the full moon, but that didn't work out so well, did it?"

I sat and cocked my head to the side, pricking my ears forward in what I hoped he'd recognize as my interest.

"I've botched this, to say the least. I just couldn't let you die in the airport, but I couldn't let you change, either. I wasn't even sure if it would work, but I was desperate. I should have asked you first. There's a lot of things I should have done. I'm not supposed to make anyone into a werewolf. I don't have a pack. Haven't had one in years. Still don't want one. I work better on my own."

Ryan paced around the kitchen, pausing now and then to adjust something on the counters or wipe away some spot of dirt. Limping after him, I sat within several feet, stretching my neck in order to look up at him.

"Under normal circumstances, I would have told you everything first. I would have told you what to expect, how things would change for you, and help you adapt. The ritual would have been done by a proper Alpha instead of a rogue like me. A lot of things would have been different. You would have had a choice. You didn't exactly have a lot of choice, though. You don't seem like the quitting kind to me, and you would've died in the airport if I hadn't done what I did."

The bitterness in Ryan's voice was matched by a subtle souring of his scent. He leaned against the counter and studied the floor at his feet as though the veined pattern in the tiles hid the mysteries of the universe.

I waited.

"I should have found out your name and contacted you. Found out if you were interested. Date you, convince you I was the type of man you wanted around, and *then*, once I was certain you wouldn't go running and screaming for the hills, show you what I am. What I wanted you to be with me. You would have sworn not to tell a word, because we can't. Fenerec—that's what us werewolves call ourselves—are usually killed if we slip. They might consider my circumstances. Maybe."

Ryan went back to pacing, and I stayed out of his way. An unsettled feeling spread through me. The implication Ryan would be put to death froze me to my bones.

"I'm *supposed* to be one of the smart ones. One of the ones in full control. That's why they let me loose without a pack. That's why they call *me* in when a pack fucks things up and they need someone to clean up the mess. That's why I was even at the airport, because word got around some wolves were doing shit they weren't supposed to be doing. Too bad they hadn't figured out an entire pack had gone rogue and decided to go the terrorist route for money." Ryan balled his hand into a fist and thumped the counter. "A lot of people are dead because *I* didn't figure it out, either—not until it was too late."

His sigh carried too much weight, and I limped forward to sit beside his feet.

Until I had become a dog—a wolf—I never would have believed emotion had a scent. I never would have believed how adept my nose could be at identifying which emotions were which.

A shadow surrounded Ryan, cloaking him as his guilt and anxiety strengthened. With my nose's help, I understood what the miasma surrounding him meant. Strong, negative emotions bled from him, affecting more than just his scent.

Unlike with Harthel, I didn't get a sense of malice from Ryan, but it didn't keep me from shivering.

"So, here we are. I'm in deep shit because I broke almost every taboo by making you a wolf so you'd live. I'm in deeper shit because I went outside of channels and did an unapproved op on my own. If I don't show up with you—as a human with control over your wolf—both of our heads will roll." Ryan lifted his hands and ran them through his hair. "Every fucking instinct I have wants me to keep you as a wolf to give you a chance to heal, but you can't learn control until you've gone through the ritual sickness. That's the period when your body—your human one—goes through some changes because you're not quite human anymore. It usually takes three or four days. For you, it'll probably take longer. Once the storm blows over, I'll have Inquisitors knocking at the door demanding an explanation."

I turned both my ears back and showed him my teeth. The temptation to chew on his ankles until he gave me an explanation I understood competed with my natural inclination to wait in silence.

Ryan sighed. "I don't want to put you through the pain of changing forms."

With his help, I could return to being a

woman again? I grabbed hold of his jeans in my teeth and growled a warning. If he even thought about denying me a chance to ask him questions, to understand what had happened, I would chew his ankles until he pled for mercy.

"You've been hurt enough."

I growled again, jerking on his jeans. He sighed his surrender.

---

THERE WERE different levels of pain, and I was intimately familiar with most of them. Every time Dad went to the gym, I experienced the dull ache of used muscles and the stiffness associated with exercise. Illness had a different sort of pain, but I had been fortunate enough to avoid it most of the time.

I'd endured sprains and other injuries in gymnastic classes before I had gotten too involved with work to continue the sport, but Harthel had introduced me to the agony of broken bones.

Nothing prepared me for the searing burn of changing from a small, wolf's body to a woman's. I wasn't sure what Ryan had done to me, but he touched my shoulder, and my entire body shattered to pieces. A wolf so small shouldn't have had the mass to transform into a human body, yet my bones cracked, stretched, reformed, and grew while my fur melted away to raw skin.

It hurt too much to scream, although choked cries found their way out of my throat. I shuddered, and I could smell blood in the air—mine.

Through it all, Ryan remained crouched nearby, not quite touching me, but close enough his breath caressed the back of my neck.

When the pain transitioned to the dull ache of bruises, I went limp, shuddering on the cold bathroom tiles. My breathing wheezed, although I was able to gulp down entire lungfuls of air.

"Thirty-nine minutes," Ryan murmured, rising from my side. "Longer than I like, better than I feared. Lie still for a few minutes. I'll fill the tub. In about an hour, the first of the ritual sickness symptoms should begin. In the meantime, I'll try to answer all the questions I can."

Moments later, the sound of running water filled the bathroom. Ryan's back was to me. It was then I realized I was naked from head to toe. My face burned with my embarrassment, and I lurched upright.

Every muscle and bone in my body protested the movement. I shuddered, bracing my weight on one hand so I wouldn't flop back to the floor. Blood and bruises darkened my skin, leaving nothing untouched from Harthel's blows. My ribs and stomach were the worst, the bruising so dark they were black. I flexed my hands, and while both of my wrists ached, nothing felt broken.

The little hope I had of dreaming crumbled apart at the reminders of what Harthel had done to me. The evidence was branded onto my skin, denying me the ability to pretend I had dreamed it. I wanted to wake up so everything would disappear, but I wouldn't.

I didn't even have to pinch myself to confirm I was awake; touching my leg was enough to hurt. I swallowed, shivering from more than just the cool bathroom tiles.

Ryan turned to me, and his gaze focused on my face before sweeping down, taking in every inch of me. His stare focused on my ribs, and the muscles of his cheek twitched. Kneeling beside me, he reached out and traced his fingers over my ribs, applying enough pressure I clenched my teeth.

"Your name isn't Ryan. I looked for you." My words rasped out of my aching throat.

"You looked for me?"

"Passenger list. You weren't on it."

Ryan chuckled, shaking his head before rising to his feet. After he checked on the tub, he turned to face me, and smiled. "Ryan's my middle name. I like it more than I like Dexter Cole."

"Dexter Cole," I echoed, considering his name. I liked it, but I liked Ryan better. "Matia Evans."

For a long moment, Ryan said nothing, his

expression puzzled. "I've heard that name before. Who are you?"

"Corporate paper pusher," I grumbled, shaking my head. "Some idiot thought it'd be funny to put me on an eligible bachelorette list for New York, too."

Ryan snapped his fingers. "Everyone was talking about the father and daughter pair up on the bachelor and bachelorette list. Is that why that asshole grabbed you?"

Wrinkling my nose, I sighed and wondered just how much I wanted to tell Ryan. "No. He wanted revenge because my father fired him."

"He did that to you because he was fired." Ryan balled his hands into fists and turned to the tub, shutting off the taps.

With the help of the toilet, I got to my feet. I had to lean against the wall to keep from falling to the floor.

Ryan turned to face me, his eyes narrowing as he looked me over again, his attention focusing on my feet. "Your feet don't hurt?"

"They mostly healed while I was in the hospital," I whispered.

Closing the distance between us, Ryan took hold of my elbow in a gentle but firm grip, pulling me in the direction of the tub. Before I had a chance to try to climb in on my own, he placed his hands on my hips and lifted me up. I gasped at the heat on my feet.

Ignoring my wordless protest, he lowered me in.

The water was deep enough to cover me right up to my chin, and I leaned against the back with a heavy sigh.

"If you want bubbles, I'll start up the jets. I don't have a lot of soaps. I don't usually bring anyone here."

"The jets would be good," I mumbled, fighting the urge to submerge and give myself the illusion of hiding. Bubbles would hide the bruises for a little while, too. "Dish soap is fine."

Ryan laughed, crossing the bathroom to a panel on the wall. "I can do better than dish soap. I'm probably the only man who has his generator set up for the jacuzzi and chooses to sacrifice the television and other appliances to make up for it. The coffee maker, refrigerator, emergency lights, water heater, and the jacuzzi are all hooked up. I use an oil furnace, too. Never know when the power will go out in the mountains."

"Sounds like you have your priorities straight to me."

The jacuzzi rumbled to life, and I sighed when the jets hammered at my sore, aching muscles. Closing my eyes, I leaned back, resting my head against the ridge of the tub. "Thank you."

"For what?"

"Everything. Helping me. You didn't have to. I don't even know how you found me."

Ryan crouched in front of the sink's vanity, opened one of the doors, and pulled out several bottles, which he set on the edge of the jacuzzi. "That Harthel fellow made a few mistakes. I didn't find out who he was sending the photographs to, but he used a special server to mask his location. Unfortunately for him, the server's owned by a friend of mine. He noticed the odd activity and decided to take a peek at what Harthel was doing. My friend gave me a call and dropped the info in my lap after doing a traceback to Harthel's IP address. Harthel had hired him to mask some other activities, so he had the man's number, which he gave to me. I recognized you right away and decided to take matters into my own hands."

I gritted my teeth, leaned forward, and grabbed one of the bottles, squinting to read the label in the dim lighting. Lavender worked for me, so I opened the cap and dumped some of the soap in. The jets worked their magic, and within moments, the soothing scent filled my nose.

"He was sending them to my father."

"I regret giving that fucker a chance to escape." Ryan growled, low and deep. "I'll be right back."

Marching out of the bathroom, he left me alone to relax in the water. The jets massaged my muscles while reminding me of every bruise mottling my skin. I sighed and closed my eyes, wondering what I'd tell Dad.

When Ryan returned, he had a cell phone in his hand. Perching on the side of the jacuzzi, he unlocked the device and tapped at the screen. "I'll talk to your father. Ralph Evans, correct? The businessman."

I flinched. "I don't know what to tell him."

"Leave that to me. I plan on twisting the truth a little to help cover the fact you're healing far faster than possible. There are certain rules we werewolves have to follow. I'll teach you over the next few days. Fortunately, even the Inquisition would be hard pressed to get anyone up here during this storm, so we have some time. Not as much time as I would *like*, but time. We have options."

"You broke the rules helping me."

"I did." Ryan sighed, shaking his head. "I broke quite a few rules, actually. It won't surprise me if the Inquisition decides to put my head on a silver platter. Trust me on this one, you want absolutely nothing to do with silver now."

"Why?"

"You really don't know anything about the Inquisition?"

It was my turn to shake my head. "Nothing. Never heard of them before today."

"That'll complicate things. Think of them as the police of the supernatural world. Their job is to make certain Normals don't know about us and prevent them from becoming victims to rogue werewolves, witches, and other magic users. It'll take days to give you a full debriefing on it—days we don't have right now. I'm planning on telling your father I found you by serendipitous accident, you were coherent enough to give me his number, and that your injuries look a lot worse than they actually are."

"He'll want to come."

"I'd like to see him pull that trick off in this weather. There's nowhere nearby suitable for a helicopter. The way up here is treacherous enough even if you know where you're going. Let me worry about the logistics. Do you know your father's number?"

I dutifully relayed Dad's cell number. "Tell him I'm sorry."

Ryan smiled, reaching over to brush my wet hair away from my cheek to tuck the stray strands behind my ear. "You'll be able to tell him that yourself soon enough. For now, rest while you can. The next few days are going to be unpleasant for both of us."

## THIRTEEN

Please put some clothes on.

---

RYAN MADE himself comfortable on the ledge of the jacuzzi and dialed Dad's number. The temptation to hide in the bubbles had me sinking deeper into the water. The werewolf arched a brow at me, pressed the button to connect the call, and held his cell to his ear.

"Hello, is this Mr. Evans?" Ryan's expression remained neutral. I heard my father's voice on the other end of the line, tired and too soft for me to understand over the rumble of the jacuzzi's jets. "Sorry to bother you at such a late hour, but my name is Dexter, and I'm calling on behalf of your dau—"

Dad's voice took on a hard edge, and Ryan's mouth quirked into a grin. "No, sir, I am not calling about a ransom request. I certainly didn't kidnap her. I—"

Once again, Ryan was interrupted, and the shade of his eyes brightened. He offered the phone to me. "Here."

I lifted my arm out of the water, grabbing

for the phone. "If it ends up in the water, it's not my fault." I placed his cell to my ear, sighed, and said, "Hi, Dad."

"Matia? What is going on? Are you okay? Those pictures…"

"It was Harthel. Dexter happened to be in the area and found me. I'm fine. Mostly fine. Bruised and sore, but fine." I sighed, tempted to sink back into the jacuzzi. "We're stuck in a blizzard."

"You don't have your medicine. You are not fine. I saw those pictures. There is no way—"

Ryan snatched the phone out of my hand and placed it to his ear. "Mr. Evans, sorry to interrupt your conversation, but she's quite tired and shouldn't talk much. I have a fully stocked first aid kit here, which includes emergency inhalers. Yes, I'm aware of her asthma. Most of her injuries appear to be superficial, and I'm taking every precaution with her health. She's a very lucky young lady. No, I didn't see him. Unfortunately, I had the choice between helping her or chasing after the culprit. I chose her."

I huffed, sank down to my chin in the water, and batted at the bubbles. "I have horrible luck."

"Matia says she has horrible luck," Ryan relayed, shaking his head and arching a brow at me. "Mr. Evans agrees with you."

I retreated into the relative safety of the bubbles, mumbling curses under my breath.

Ryan spoke to my father long enough to give him the address of the cabin, explaining how it might be a while until the roads were cleared enough to reach it. I learned Ryan had a snowmobile, but it had been put into storage for the summer. When Ryan left me alone in the bathroom, I flicked at the bubbles and wondered how everything had gone so wrong so fast.

By the time Ryan returned without his phone, my stomach was doing flip flops, and instead of soothing, the jets agitated my nausea. I swallowed.

"You're turning a shade of gray-green," Ryan reported, pausing in the doorway to turn off the jacuzzi. Once the jets gurgled and died away, he plunged his hand into the jacuzzi, hunted down the stopper, and pulled it free. "Time to get you out of there and into bed. Mr. Evans will be calling back in the morning to check on you."

I should have been bothered by my nudity and the bruises mottling my skin, but I was too tired and queasy to fight Ryan as he helped me out of the tub and went to work with a plush towel. It took all my concentration to stay on my feet and ignore my queasiness.

When the nausea finally won, Ryan held my hair out of the way and didn't say a word.

WHEN MY STOMACH wasn't rebelling, I alternated between burning and freezing. In the brief periods when I felt almost human, I slept until the fever took hold again. I had faint memories of talking to Dad several times, although the specifics of the conversations slipped away from me. In my more coherent moments, I was aware of intense hunger driving me, forcing me to eat despite my awareness of the misery I'd suffer as a consequence of obeying the gnawing, growling demands of my stomach.

Through it all, Ryan remained close, sometimes pacing the bedroom, sometimes hovering in the doorway, and sometimes lying stretched out on the bed beside me, watching me with quiet intensity.

It didn't take me long to realize when his eyes brightened, Ryan's wolf watched me.

Part of me was no longer human, too, and she liked his attention and wanted more of it. Despite my incessant nausea and fever, my wolf wanted me to shunt aside my discomfort and pursue the patient male.

The longer he waited, the more my wolf wanted him.

When I finally woke feeling more like a human than a zombie, Ryan was sleeping on top of the covers beside me, dressed in a rumpled t-shirt and a worn pair of jeans. I had no recollection of dressing, but I wore a long dress shirt too big for me. He snored, a soft, rumbly sound my wolf enjoyed listening to.

Hunger cramped my stomach, and I eased my way out from under the duvet, wincing in anticipation of pain.

I stood, my body creaking protests at having been immobile for so long, but the discomfort I expected didn't manifest. I stretched both of my hands, and while my fingers were stiff, there was no other evidence of my time with Harthel.

Once I satisfied the demands of my appetite, I would deal with figuring out what happened next.

My wolf didn't want me to leave Ryan, but I ignored her whining. While I was attracted to the man, and had been even before I had started sharing my head with her, I wasn't about to go jumping my two-time rescuer.

But damn, I wanted to, and my wolf knew it.

I made my way to the kitchen, careful to keep quiet so I wouldn't disturb Ryan. Dim overhead lights guided my path, and I dodged around the armchair partially blocking the hallway leading into the living room. The curtains covering the cabin's large front window were closed, and I detoured to peek outside. Everything was dark, but I could hear the hiss of snow and wind against the glass.

From what I could tell, the accumulation came up to my knees, but I couldn't tell if the snow had blown against the window or if it had continued to fall while I had been ill. My wolf wanted out, and her restlessness drove me to pressing my hands to the glass.

Winter cold numbed my skin, and my wolf whined her impatience and desire for fresh air. I glanced in the direction of the front door, shifting my weight from foot to foot.

It had been too long since I had been able to take a deep breath of fresh air without my chest and lungs hurting, and my desire to experience the winter bite of a blizzard lured me across the living room. There was no sign of an alarm system, just a chain, a deadbolt, and a regular lock. I found it amusing Ryan used the chain in addition to the two locks.

If someone made it past the deadbolt, the thin chain wasn't going to help much.

However, the chain would prevent the door from flying in my face if the wind was too strong, so I left it in place. All I wanted was a deep breath, not to let in too much cold air.

I cracked open the door, shivering at the sting of wind-driven snow, and breathed in, savoring the crisp, clean scent that flooded my lungs. I was aware of my wolf's attention to every little subtlety in the air. The snow had a scent, which she ignored. The hint of wood warned me a tree had fallen somewhere nearby. Even without her help, I was able to pinpoint the harsh bite of gasoline and smoke.

Underneath it all was a spice undertone

partnered with the musk of wolves, and my desire to escape into the snow chilled to wariness. I closed the door and locked it.

Hunger forgotten, I returned to the bedroom, hovering in the doorway while debating if I should wake Ryan and tell him about what I had scented outside. My wolf whined in my head, and I was aware of her desire to find somewhere dark and confined to hide.

"Ryan?"

The soft snoring I found comforting ended in a snort, and the man bolted off the bed so fast I sucked in a breath, tensing. He was at my side before I had a chance to retreat, and his nose flared. "What's wrong?"

"There are wolves outside."

Ryan's eyes narrowed and brightened, and he breathed in deep. "Your wolf wanted fresh air."

Over the years, I had learned to listen to tone as much as watch body language when trying to keep one step ahead of businessmen who believed me inferior because of my age and gender. I relaxed at the lack of accusation in Ryan's tone, although the stiffness in his stance concerned me. "I did, too."

His smile softened his expression. "Once you're fully over the ritual sickness, we'll hunt."

My wolf's excitement roused at Ryan's words, and my reservations clashed with her desire for fresh meat and blood. In order to distract myself, I considered my health—or lack of it. "Won't I slow you down?"

"What do you mean?"

Would I ever get used to acknowledging my shortcomings? I clenched my teeth, straightened my back, and forced myself to look him in the eyes. "My asthma."

Ryan sighed and shook his head. "You won't slow us down. I'll explain later. First, I want a look at these wolves."

Something about his tone warned me of trouble. "Is there a problem?"

"Depends on who has come calling." With his cheek twitching, Ryan stalked in the direction of the front door, and I followed in his wake. He hesitated near the kitchen. "If they're Inquisition Fenerec, it'll probably be okay, as long as I can convince them you're not a threat. Follow my lead."

"You mentioned something about the fact you weren't supposed to…" I shrugged, uncertain of what he had done wrong by saving my life.

"Secrecy is important to the Inquisition. No one is supposed to know we exist, and I took a lot of risks at the airport."

"I don't understand."

Ryan scratched his scalp and shrugged. "When you had trouble breathing, I began the ritual on you, and I took a few precautions to keep you from shifting for the first time. It was risky. It might not have worked. I hadn't done the ritual before; I'd been taught how, but I wasn't supposed to use it without being sanctioned. If I had fucked it up, we'd both be dead right now along with anyone who had witnessed it."

My eyes widened. "Why?"

"Fenerec are dangerous. Never doubt it for a second. We're a threat to Normals, and the Inquisition exists to prevent us from preying on humans incapable of defending themselves. I'll have to explain the rest later. I want you to stay behind me and keep calm. Don't let your wolf take control. If she perceives a threat, she'll want to."

While I didn't have any reason to believe he was lying to me, I didn't feel very threatening, and if I was at risk of my wolf taking over, I couldn't tell. She seemed content enough to lurk in my head.

I had no idea how Ryan expected me to keep control—or how I'd even know if I was losing control in the first place. All I could do was try. I fisted my hands, lifted my chin, and said, "Okay."

RYAN'S PREPARATIONS worried me and my wolf, and by the time he finished triple checking his gun, I wanted nothing more than to find a safe place to take cover. He held the weapon in a firm grip, headed to the door, and unlocked it. Unlike me, he let the wind blow it all the way open.

I shivered from the cold on my bare legs, pressing my hands to my legs to keep Ryan's dress shirt from billowing. Snow swirled inside, and I backed away, torn between keeping my eye on Ryan and trying to spot the wolves in the snow.

Their scent strengthened. Through the pale haze outside, shapes moved, but instead of the wolves I expected, four figures approached.

"Come in." Ryan kept his gun low and pointed at the ground, his finger clear of the trigger. "That all of you?"

"That's all of us," a man replied, and my eyes widened with recognition.

Dalton Sinclair had been the last person to see me before Harthel had kidnapped me, forcing Ryan to finish turning me into a werewolf—a Fenerec. My nose told me wolf, and my wolf confirmed my belief.

"Dalton? Dalton Sinclair?" I blurted.

How could Dalton be a werewolf, too?

Ryan jerked in my direction, his eyes widening. "You know him?"

"We've met. Small world, Miss Evans." Dalton stomped inside.

"You were there, on the street where the car went off the road. Were you hit? Were—"

"I'm tough to kill, Miss Evans. If someone wants me dead, they'll have to do a lot better than that." After the other three men entered the cabin, Dalton closed the door and locked it.

My face burned when I realized our late-night visitors were naked. I slapped my hands over my eyes, which resulted in a few throaty chuckles. "Please put some clothes on."

The only man I wanted to see naked was Ryan, and before I even considered sleeping with him, I needed to get my head screwed on straight—and learn a lot more about life as a Fenerec.

My wolf's attention focused on Ryan, and I was aware of her desire for me to latch my teeth onto his throat until he submitted to us. It took every bit of willpower in my possession to lower my hands and head for the kitchen. I paused at the oddly bright light of the coffee maker, shook my head, and started to brew a pot to keep my attention focused somewhere safe.

Ryan followed me, setting the gun on the counter. "I'm going to assume since you neglected to bring clothing with you that you're not here to get rid of us. There should be something that fits you in the bedroom closet down the hall."

I listened to the soft pad of feet on the floor, heading in the direction of the bedroom I had been sharing with Ryan.

My nose warned me Dalton was still somewhere nearby.

"We were in a hurry. And no, we're not here to get rid of either one of you. I've been assigned to handle your punishment, but I'm not in the mood today. Bad puppy. Don't do it again."

"Are you being serious? That's it?" At the disbelief in Ryan's voice, I risked a glance at him. His eyes were wide, and his mouth hung open.

"Very. I do expect for you to give me a complete explanation of everything that has happened, however."

"Please put some clothes on," I repeated, careful to keep my gaze fixed to the countertops or coffee machine.

"It is a bit chilly in here." Dalton chuckled and headed down the hallway.

I sighed my relief, slumping over the counter. "That was awkward. How do you know him?"

With a quiet laugh, Ryan gave my elbow a nudge with his. "You're feeling better. No more nausea?"

"I woke up hungry. Not so hungry now." I wrinkled my nose and glared at the coffee machine. "So, how do you know Dalton?"

"He's an Inquisitor. Most Fenerec packs stick to a set region, but Dalton and his team tend to travel all over the world. They're called in whenever there is a problem outside of a pack. I wasn't very subtle when I went hunting after you. They tracked my phone here." Echoing my sigh, Ryan settled in beside me, resting his elbows on the counter. "I was worried they'd be hostile."

"I remember."

"There's something going on, though."

At the worry in Ryan's voice, I straightened and shifted my weight from foot to foot. "What makes you think that?"

Ryan glanced over his shoulder. "Don't let his appearance fool you, Matia. Dalton Sinclair is someone you do not want to cross, and when he is playing nice with those who have broken the rules, there's a reason for it. He wants something. What, however, I don't know, and that worries me."

## FOURTEEN

*He saved your scrawny ass, pup.*

---

MY WOLF DIDN'T LIKE SO many males nearby.

It wasn't fear driving her, but some other instinct I didn't understand made her wary of them. Half the time, she wanted me to keep between the four men in the sitting room and Ryan, who stayed with me in the kitchen. The rest of the time, she urged me to bare my teeth and drive them out into the snow.

"Relax," Ryan whispered in my ear.

It took a great deal of effort to force myself to lean against the counter and pretend every muscle wasn't tensed and ready for something—anything—to happen.

Dalton cleared his throat and propped his feet up on the coffee table from his spot on the middle of the couch. "Let's get down to business. Cole, I know you're concerned, especially in light of your recent behavior. Had the circumstances been any different, we'd be having an entirely different conversation right now."

Ryan stiffened beside me, and my wolf identified the sharpness in his scent as anxiety. "What do you mean, sir?"

"Dalton. Sinclair, if you absolutely feel you must stand on formality."

"I'm a rogue, sir. I've violated several taboos. Why are we having this talk when you should be dealing with me?"

"Let's start at the beginning, since Miss Evans has no idea what is going on. It's best if she understands everything, as I require her to be a part of this conversation without feeling like an outsider or interloper." Dalton crossed his arms over his chest, his gaze focused on me.

In the dim illumination, the man's eyes had a disconcerting gleam to them, as though they glowed of their own volition, in a too bright gray that unsettled and intrigued me. My wolf whined in my head, and her presence faded, retreating to some dark recess, leaving me to deal with our four late-night visitors.

"I haven't had a chance to teach her much," Ryan confessed.

"Of course not. I'm not criticizing. You did as you needed to do, and you did so with admirable caution and care. That, in part, is why the Inquisition has chosen to turn a blind eye. I need you to tell me everything that happened from the beginning, however."

Ryan flinched. "It's a long story."

"I have time."

Dalton's companions made themselves comfortable; two flanked him on the couch while the third opted to sit on the floor with his back resting against the coffee table. Breathing in deep, I tried to make sense of the smells, but with my wolf in hiding, I was only able to pinpoint the five signatures of male wolf, with Ryan and Dalton having the strongest scents.

With a heavy sigh, Ryan retrieved two stools from the other end of the kitchen and offered one to me before sliding onto his. "Are you aware of my last assignment, sir?"

"No. My instructions were to rendezvous with you and handle the situation however I saw fit. I have orders to give you a new assignment, should I be satisfied with your stability."

Ryan snorted, and when his posture relaxed, I hopped up on my stool at the kitchen counter to listen to the conversation. While I had made coffee, I was the only one who had a cup, and I grabbed my mug, taking a cautious sip while enjoying its warmth in my hands.

"Is your last assignment relevant to the situation?"

"Yes."

When Ryan refused to elaborate, I fought my urge to grin. The tactic was one my father and I used in business arrangements often; by forcing Dalton to ask questions, Ryan was holding his ground. Sometimes, being forthcoming had benefits; offering information could be used to garner good will. It could also be taken as a sign of weakness.

If Dalton wanted anything out of Ryan, I had a feeling the man would have to work for it.

Dalton sighed, and I had the feeling he understood the situation as well as I did. "I'd rather not be here all night playing games, Cole."

"Ryan."

"Not exactly the sort of progress I was hoping for, but I'll accept it."

"I was assigned to track down a rogue pack. The trail took me to La Guardia. By the time I figured out what they intended to do, it was too late; I got caught in the blast after security. I had been sent in with three other operatives; one was killed, the other two were in the airport before security." Ryan sighed and shook his head. "We got sideswiped, sir, and once we figured out what was going on, it was too late. As it was, I was down and out for several hours before I managed to get back on my feet."

"You were also at La Guardia, Miss Evans."

I nodded, but if Ryan meant to railroad Dalton into directing the conversation, I would play the same game. Ignorance caused many problems in the business world, and I had no doubt the same applied to Fenerec.

Until I knew more about what was going on, I didn't want to say too much.

Ryan shifted on his stool, and I was aware of his attention on me. "I started the ritual in La Guardia and used wolfsbane to prevent her first shift. She was dying. She would have died if I had done nothing."

"That was risky, Ryan."

"I refused to let her die without doing something."

"You forced the ritual on her." Dalton sat up, cocked his head to the side, and watched Ryan, his expression neutral.

"By the time I began the ritual, she was no longer capable of agreeing. I made the decision for her. I accept responsibility."

Dalton waved his hand in dismissal. "What is done is done. The fact she is seated beside you is evidence enough she wanted to live. How did you give her the wolfsbane if you performed the ritual when she was incapacitated?"

While I found it unnerving the two males discussed me as though I weren't there listening to them, I kept my mouth shut. I had questions, but I knew myself well enough to understand once I started asking for clarifications, I'd derail the conversation.

Once Dalton finished, I'd take over and demand answers.

"I gave it to her in a bottle of water. She was having trouble breathing because of smoke inhalation. I was hoping they'd reach us before I needed to act. They would have been several hours too late if I had waited."

Ryan clacked his teeth together. "I had no choice."

"Your wolf didn't give you one, did he?"

Ryan shrugged and remained silent.

"All right. So, you performed the ritual and somehow managed to stall her first transformation, which was enough to prevent her death. That explains a few things—when I met her prior to her kidnapping, she didn't have the scent. I had assumed you had performed the ritual after you had tracked her down."

I clenched my hands into fists. "It was Harthel."

"We know. We found out shortly after Ryan went on the hunt for you. One of Ryan's contacts notified the Inquisition of the situation. You owe him, Ryan. He saved your scrawny ass, pup."

"I understood the risks."

"I suspect you did. I've been ordered to ask you about your interactions with Harthel."

Ryan sighed. "My contact saw Harthel's activities and decided to look into it. When he saw the videos and images, he contacted me. I recognized her, had my guy activate the GPS beacon on Harthel's phone, and tracked him down. Once I had a fix on him, I called him and made my demands. I gave him the choice of leaving her alive, or I was going to kill him and leave bits of him all across the state. He was going to kill her, so my first concern was driving him away and buying enough time to get to her. She had her first shift sometime after Harthel left but before I arrived."

"Did you burn the cabin he was holding her at?"

"No. It was already burned when I arrived."

"Harthel did it?"

Something about the way Ryan tensed worried me, and my nose confirmed his anxiety. My wolf roused. She whined, her uncertainty strengthening with each passing moment.

"Ah," Dalton said, and I froze when the man's full attention turned to me. "I was worried that might happen."

"You smelled it, too?" Ryan whispered.

"I'm going to do you a favor, puppy. My pack's going to do you a favor, too. None of us are going to mention you willingly performed the ritual when you knew what she might be. You're going to lie so well no one can scent it on you. Understood?"

"I don't understand," I snapped, and at my wolf's encouragement, I growled.

"What do you remember? All of it, Miss Evans, from after the business meeting until now."

I shuddered. "The taxi hit the restaurant. After that, it's a bit of a blur. Harthel meant to get revenge on my father over being fired."

It was the truth, mostly. I couldn't bring myself to admit just how afraid I had been.

Drawing a deep breath, I forced myself to face what Harthel had done to me. Words brought it back to life, and I remembered the pain, the chill of the water, and the heat of the flames. "He wanted to hurt my father, so he beat bruises into me. He wanted to make my father suffer. I think he meant for me to drown."

"When I arrived, the water in the tub was still running," Ryan confirmed.

Rising to his feet, Dalton stepped over the Fenerec on the floor, paced to the window, and shifted the curtain to stare outside. "Why?"

"Matia?"

I shrugged. "Why would he want revenge on my father? That's easy; we fired him. Don't ask me what Harthel was thinking. I don't know. He kept me in the shower for a while. I don't remember him moving me to the tub. Last thing I remember was him stepping on my hands."

Rage tainted Ryan's scent. "What do you remember?"

"I woke up in the tub. The cabin had already burned. I climbed out. That was when you found me."

"You don't remember the fire?"

I shook my head.

"Typically, fire witches don't start manifesting flame without warning signs." Dalton approached, leaned over, and looked me in the eyes. I leaned back, holding my breath.

"Back off," Ryan growled.

Panic and fear seared through me, scorching through my head as my wolf reacted to the promise of violence in Ryan's posture. With a snarl, I slid my way between Ryan and Dalton, baring my teeth at my wolf's demand.

Instead of the anger I expected, Dalton laughed. "All right. Don't worry, Miss Evans. I'm not going to do anything to your male."

My wolf approved of Dalton's acknowledgement Ryan was ours, although I wasn't entirely sure if my wolf wanted him for a mate or meal. Ignoring my hunger had been easier when the four males had first arrived, and I had been uncertain of their intentions.

"Matia?" Ryan's hand was warm on my arm, and he tugged me back. "It's not wise to challenge Dalton."

I whirled, pulling free of Ryan's hold to face him. With a growl, I snapped my teeth, clacking them together. The action was as much mine as it was my wolf's, which pleased her more than it did me, although I found it intriguing.

With him, I didn't need to smile, and we knew it. Instead of stabbing, I would bite, and my wolf reassured me it was the way of the wild and expected of us. My gaze lowered to his throat, and at my wolf's encouragement, I licked my lips.

Dalton grabbed hold of the back of my neck, startling a yelp out of me. "That's quite enough, little puppy. You can make Ryan your chew toy later, after we've finished talking."

When I growled, Dalton tightened his hold on me. I was aware of the man's thumb sliding over my skin before pressing down hard. A faint tingle was the only warning I had before a jolt of electricity zapped down my spine.

My legs refused to work, and when my knees buckled beneath my weight, Ryan caught me, pulling me against him. "Sinclair!"

"Don't be dramatic, Ryan. She's recovering from ritual sickness. Perhaps you have forgotten this, but I haven't, and there's little as dangerous as a hungry bitch who hasn't learned to control her instincts yet. Once she's had something to eat, we can continue our talk."

---

ALL FIVE MALES joined forces in the kitchen and emptied Ryan's freezer and refrigerator. Once they demolished those supplies, they plundered an outdoor storage unit, returning with armfuls of packages wrapped in brown paper.

The kitchen wasn't large enough for five men, but none of them seemed to mind the cramped quarters. If anything, Ryan relaxed in the company of the other males, which pleased my wolf.

I learned two important things about Fenerec from watching them. First, the males looked human, but human men didn't enjoy such close contact. At first, I wondered if they were all bisexual, but my wolf's rejection of the idea was so intense it triggered a headache.

Second, food was serious business.

"That much?" I had lost count of the times I had asked.

"It might not be enough," Dalton replied, giving me the same answer he had before.

"I don't see how that's possible." Every bit of counter was covered in meat, and I spotted a fifty-pound bag of potatoes in the process of being cut up by one of Dalton's companions, Gavin. Gavin was the most vocal of the other wolves, filling in the quiet with an ongoing commentary regarding politics, something I tried to ignore whenever possible.

Dalton chuckled and washed his hands before worming his way out of the confines of the kitchen, grabbing a mug of coffee on the way. "Fenerec have high metabolisms, Miss Evans. We require a substantially higher caloric intake. Five to ten times the amount of a human. We may look human, but we're not. That's part of the reason you were so sick."

"Five days, and she spent most of it either sound asleep or in the jacuzzi. She didn't throw up nearly as much as I expected, but she had a pretty intense fever," Ryan reported.

I frowned. "When I was in the hospital, the doctor said I had an infection of some sort, but I didn't ask him about it."

Dalton pulled a phone from his pocket, dialed a number, and placed a call. "Dalton Sinclair. I need you to pull medical records for Matia Evans. You can probably get the information from her father, Ralph Evans. He'll cooperate. Give me a call back when you have everything. I'm looking for a diagnosis of an infection from when she was hospitalized following the La Guardia bombing."

After hanging up, Dalton returned his phone to his pocket. "I was going to wait, but I suppose there's no point now. Ryan, one of the major reasons your actions are being ignored is because Miss Evans was already on watch by the Inquisition; she's Fenerec-born. When I met her, the scent was very subtle, so unless you were looking for it, you may have missed it."

Ryan straightened, his eyes widening. "I had."

"Your wolf probably picked up on the scent even if you hadn't." Dalton sounded amused. "Poor puppy, you were helpless from the start."

"I'm *what*?" I blurted. "What are you talking about? What scent?"

"At least one of your parents is a Fenerec," Dalton answered, his eyes brightening as his wolf showed through. "Depending on circumstances, Fenerec-born are sometimes initiated into the Inquisition at an early age, or they are left in the dark. You were left in the dark to allow you a chance to lead a normal life. Of course, you have made yourself exceptional on your own, but that doesn't surprise me. Fenerec-born aren't fully human, although they aren't Fenerec, either."

"One of my parents was a Fenerec?" I shivered from more than the cold, and my wolf was both intrigued and concerned. "Does Dad know this?"

"He knows. The Inquisition tries to be careful in its selection of homes for Fenerec-born children. Fenerec can be volatile. When a Fenerec's mate dies, it can have dire consequences. Some go mad and have to be put down. Your father is also Fenerec-born, and he volunteered."

"I know. He killed my mother." It hurt saying the words, but I had come to terms with the truth long ago.

Dad had defeated his shadows over the years, and I had never been able to truly blame him for what he had done. He had paid for my mother's life with his own.

"It doesn't bother you?" Dalton sipped his coffee and watched me.

I scowled, wondering why the discussion had turned so personal. Without a reason to hide the truth, I sighed and shrugged. "Why would it bother me? Most drunk drivers just go on with their lives. Some get someone else killed. Dad? He's spent my entire life trying to undo what he had done. He doesn't drink anymore. He doesn't even drive—doesn't have a license. I can't get one. He made a mistake, and it cost my mother her life, but he took me in. It's not like I remember my mother or father—my birth ones, that is."

"You can't get a license?" Dalton demanded. "Why not?"

Another sigh slipped out of me, and I tapped my temple with a finger. "Brain damage from the accident. I'm monochromatic."

"Monochromatic," Dalton echoed.

"Completely colorblind. Since I can't distinguish color, I can't be licensed to drive."

The Fenerec males exchanged long, silent looks. Dalton stared at Ryan before facing me once more. "The process of becoming a Fenerec should resolve any physical problems."

"What?"

"I mean you shouldn't be colorblind any more if it was caused by an injury. Of course, it might be a gradual return of sight since it is an older injury, but by the time you've finished transitioning, you probably won't even have any scars. We have extraordinary healing abilities."

A chill ran through me. "That's impossible."

Dalton's brows rose. "You readily accept

you can become a wolf, but you have a problem believing your colorblindness can be cured?"

Taken aback by the realization Dalton was right, I sat back, frowned, and wondered if I dared to hope my colorblindness could be cured. When morning came and the sun lit the world, would I finally be able to see color?

What would I do if I couldn't?

Hope was a dangerous thing.

## FIFTEEN

*Food was serious business.*

---

IT WAS the coffee maker's bright light that frayed my last nerve. I glared at it and growled, fighting against the urge to break the damned thing for catching my attention all the time. Whenever I caught a glimpse of it out of the corner of my eye, it distracted me.

"What's bothering you?" Ryan poured a mug of coffee and set it on the counter beside me. "It won't be much longer for dinner. Well, breakfast at this point."

The coffee helped, and I forced my attention to the dark brew.

"Too much change at one time," Dalton stated.

I glanced at the man, who had taken over the entirety of the couch as though he owned the place. Instead of answering him, I sipped my coffee and reminded myself an Evans woman was above stabbing someone. It took every bit of my willpower to force a smile. "Sorry. The light's bothering me."

Ryan turned to his coffee maker and frowned. "What's wrong with it?"

"I'd say don't come between a man and his coffee, but I'm not volunteering to stop her if she decides to wreck it." Dalton laughed. "Annoyed bitches are truly a force to be feared. No one wants to face off against an annoyed, hungry bitch. You could have just tossed one of the steaks in the pan and given her something to chew on while waiting for the rest."

While my wolf thought biting was far superior to stabbing, she wanted to act, and I took deep breaths until I could speak without growling. "It's just too bright."

"We Fenerec do have sensitive eyes," Ryan acknowledged. "You need to get used to it. It's important we hide our nature from the Normals. It's not uncommon to have problems with the transition. The scents alone can be overwhelming. I had trouble with the changes in taste. Before I became a Fenerec, I really liked spicy food. Now I have to be far more careful with it. What humans perceive as hot is pretty rough on a Fenerec."

"Good to know," I grumbled.

Dalton grunted, lurched off the couch, and came into the kitchen, grabbing a mug and pouring himself a cup of coffee. "It's red. The light's red, and it's an obnoxiously bright one at that. With our ability to see in the dark, bright lights are an annoyance at the best of times."

Red was the color of blood, which had always seemed like a darker gray to me. How could something so dark seem so bright? I narrowed my eyes. Was it the intensity of the light bothering me, or was there red lurking in the illumination?

Gray was gray until it wasn't anymore, and I doubted what my eyes were trying to tell me. Was I seeing red, or did I just want to see red so much the light came across as too bright, too *something* to fit in the world I knew?

Ryan pulled out his phone, tapped at the screen, and made thoughtful noises.

"What are you looking up, Ryan?" Dalton leaned over to look at the screen.

"You'll see." Leaning away from the other Fenerec, Ryan turned his phone so it faced me. "What do you see?"

I frowned, took the phone from him, and stared at the picture of a fruit stand. It never ceased to amaze me how many different shades of gray were in fruits and vegetables. Something in the lower corner drew my eye.

Grays were gray until they weren't anymore, and I had no idea what I was looking at, but it wasn't gray, it wasn't white, and it wasn't black, either. Ryan's phone slipped out of my numb fingers.

Dalton caught it before it hit the tiles.

"Yellow and green peppers with a single red one in the corner," Ryan reported, and I heard smug satisfaction in his tone. "It's red, Matia. You're seeing the color red."

"But that's impossible," I whispered.

The Fenerec laughed, and Dalton clapped my shoulder hard enough to stagger me. "You'll just have to get used to it."

---

ALL OF MY LIFE, red had been gray, and I had a difficult time figuring out what exactly red was despite my eyes telling me the color wasn't gray. It was bright, and it was different, and I struggled to make sense of it. My wolf was just as confused about the color as I was, which didn't help matters for me any.

What else was the darkness hiding? What would I see when the sun finally rose? Excitement, hope, and dread warred within me, and I found it difficult to tear my gaze away from the coffee maker's light.

What if Ryan was wrong?

What if he was right?

"I'm going to turn it off if you don't eat," Ryan warned, nudging me with his elbow. "Eat. You've gone too long without a good meal."

The entire kitchen was overrun with food, and the other Fenerec were tearing into the meal like it was their last. I hungered, but it was hard to focus my attention on my plate with my dream of seeing a world in color almost in my reach.

"I'll unplug the maker until she's eaten

enough," Dalton said, pausing in his feeding frenzy long enough to pull the cord.

I scowled at the darkened display.

"I'll turn it back on once you've eaten. The sun'll be up soon, and we can do some vision tests to see how your sight is coming along." Ryan put my fork into my hand. "This can be your first lesson about Fenerec in groups. We're not in a pack, and our guests are in a pack. In situations like this, it's best if there are no hungry Fenerec. Hungry Fenerec operate on instinct, and hungry Fenerec hunt. Let's not prey on our guests."

"Fenerec prey on each other?" A chill ran through me. "Are you serious?"

"Not like that; we aren't cannibals. We do, however, get territorial when hungry. You're still recovering from ritual sickness, so those instincts are starting to come to the forefront. It isn't uncommon for fights to break out between rival packs. It's one of the reasons I'm an authorized rogue. I don't get into fights with the locals—not usually."

"Ryan's submissive," Dalton explained.

I had a feeling the first thing to come to mind wasn't what Dalton meant, although my wolf was very intrigued by the idea of making Ryan submit. "Ryan's what?"

Dalton laughed. "Submissive. If he isn't suppressing his natural instincts, other Fenerec are typically driven to protect him. Ryan's unique in that he can force certain dominant instincts, which he uses to his advantage. It's also the reason he was willing to let us into his home. If he were dominant, he wouldn't have even considered it without a fight. It's what makes him a really good peace keeper, too. Packs tend to fall in line if they're worried about hurting a submissive wolf, and Ryan's submissive enough it lets him get away with things a dominant simply can't."

My wolf was as confused as I was. "I don't understand."

"You'll get a better feel for it once you're ready for a hunt and a dominance contest. Normally, you would have gone on a hunt when you had your first shift, but your circumstances didn't allow it. That's not unusual when the ritual is done on the sick or injured, and you were both. Once the weather clears, I'll take you and Ryan on a proper hunt."

Ryan tensed beside me.

"Eat," Dalton ordered. "I won't explain anything else until you do. And Ryan, relax. You couldn't challenge any one of us, and you know it."

I obeyed, and with the first taste of the rich meat in broth partnered with token chunks of potato, my stomach demanded to be filled. Years of eating in polite company kept me from humiliating myself, but my wolf wanted more, and she wanted it *now*.

Fortunately, Ryan expected my reaction, and as fast as I cleared a plate, he had a new one ready. My wolf approved of his prompt offerings of food.

"All right. If you can listen and eat at the same time, I'll give you both a briefing," Dalton said, pushing his empty plate away. The other wolves scattered; two of them headed for the sitting room, although I heard one of them head in the direction of the bathroom. He discovered the jacuzzi, and it didn't take long for the rumble of the jets to start.

Ryan laughed. "That took longer than I expected."

"Your hot water heater isn't going to survive our visit." With an amused laugh, Dalton got up and headed to the fridge. "We're going to eat you out of the house, too. I'll take you shopping to replenish your supplies after the snow's cleared."

"The Inquisition will comp me," Ryan replied, shrugging.

"Only because I'm going to tell them you were justified."

Ryan's scent was tinged with his annoyance, and Dalton had a sweeter undertone to his, which distracted my wolf from our shared hunger. "Please no fighting in the kitchen. You'll spill something."

"Never spill a woman's dinner. Never, ever spill a bitch's dinner. This is my advice to you as your friendly local Alpha, Ryan."

"Friendly?" Ryan countered in a mutter.

The sweetness in Dalton's scent strengthened. "When I want to be."

If Dalton was going to prod at Ryan, I'd

add my jabs in, too. "What do you expect from a business shark, Ryan?"

"Shark?" Dalton demanded.

"Better than bottom feeder, barely."

Someone in the sitting room snorted. "She's got a point, Sinclair."

"Watch yourself or be put in your place," the male warned.

My wolf's interest piqued at the challenge in Dalton's voice. What would Dalton Sinclair do if we challenged him? I had been facing off against men since I'd been little, and it felt no different from the verbal boardroom brawls I'd witnessed over the years.

"Fenerec posture a lot, don't they?" I asked Ryan.

"Whenever possible. It's a game to the dominants. The Alphas just expect everyone else to do what they want."

"That's rather obnoxious."

"You're telling me."

Dalton sighed. "You're going to teach her bad habits, Ryan."

Considering I had a list of behaviors to embrace so I wouldn't succumb to my desire to act on violent impulses, I already had enough troubles. If my wolf amplified those thoughts, I worried I would finally succumb to them. "What sort of bad habits?"

"Challenging Alphas. Not wise. Females are rare enough among our kind that an Alpha won't kill you outright, but until you're mated, you're a prime target."

Ryan's growl startled me into staring at him. His eyes were too bright to be natural, and I couldn't tell if the dim emergency lights gave them the appearance of glowing, or if there was something more to the intensity of his stare.

"An unmated bitch can even make a submissive male challenge for the right to her," Dalton explained. "You're safe from me and the rest of my pack, who are mated already. Ryan's the only eligible male here—part of why we were sent. Why rock the boat?"

I was missing something, and I had the feeling it was something important. "Please explain."

"Fenerec mate for life, Miss Evans. In a way, you're fortunate. Fenerec mating season is already over for the year, so our mating instincts are fairly dormant until winter. That said, males and females hunt for their mate year round, although they'll often wait until the winter rut to finalize a mating bond. Not always, but often. You'll have a chance to adapt to being a Fenerec before dealing with amorous males seeking your attention."

Ryan growled again, and I met his glare with one of my own. "Don't pick fights in the kitchen."

Cocking his head to the side, Dalton said, "Technically, I'm the one picking the fight."

"Maybe so, but I have a substantial amount of sway regarding your company's business interests at the moment, and don't think I've forgotten that, Mr. Sinclair. That's still *my* proposal, and I have no intentions of backing off on it just because—" I blinked, and my head went blank at trying to put to words everything that had happened.

"You became a Fenerec?" Dalton suggested.

"I take it absolutely no one can find out I can become a wolf, correct?"

"Correct."

"What about my father? Him, too?"

"Your father's parents happen to also be Fenerec, so he's well aware we exist. He might not be enthused over you having undergone the ritual, but I'm sure he can cope with it."

I considered the man through narrowed eyes. "How do you know that?"

"We were briefed by the Inquisition prior to coming here, that's how. You may not be aware of this, but Pallodia does a great deal of work with Fenerec-owned businesses. Fenerec often use business as a way to indulge predatory skills in a bloodless hunt. Fenerec enjoy business negotiations, especially with one another. Money is an excellent way of keeping score."

The growl from Ryan annoyed me into jabbing him with my elbow. "Will you stop that?"

"He's being too familiar with you."

The silent stare that had worked so well for me in the business world also affected Fenerec, and after several minutes, Ryan shifted nervously on his stool. I kept staring until he voiced a single whine.

"It seems becoming a Fenerec has made you quite vocal compared to your reputation, but I see you still wield silence as a sword." At the amusement in Dalton's voice, I leveled a glare at him, too.

"I've used up my quota of words for the next decade."

"Or you're catching up on them," Dalton countered.

"Maybe. Please stop picking a fight with Ryan."

"I'm an Alpha. I'm supposed to pick fights with him. I want him in my pack, and unless he challenges me, I can't initiate anything. Don't steal my chance to have such a nice submissive for my pack."

I stabbed my fork into a chunk of meat, shoved it in my mouth, and chewed on it, waiting for the Fenerec to elaborate.

"He means because of my position in the Inquisition, I'm protected from subjugation unless I specifically initiate a dominancy challenge, Matia," Ryan supplied.

"Define subjugation for me, please."

Ryan sighed. "It's the process of bringing a Fenerec into a pack, and it's typically done as a part of a dominancy challenge. Sometimes, Alphas will subjugate a Fenerec if the Fenerec's Alpha can't hold onto him or her. In my case, I don't have an Alpha, so I would be dominated and subjugated at the same time.

Most Fenerec prefer to stay with their origin pack."

"If an Alpha can't hold onto their Fenerec, they don't deserve to be an Alpha," Dalton muttered.

With his scent sour with annoyance, Ryan got up, plugged in the coffee maker, and went about brewing a new pot. "There has been a lot of competition to build stronger packs on the east coast. The west coast Fenerec are notably stronger in dominance contests than we are. It's pack politics. Submissive Fenerec are uncommon, which makes us in high demand. Females are always in high demand. A mated female brings potential puppies to the pack, and an unmated female brings prestige and male candidates to join for a chance to court her."

Dalton chuckled. "To make a long story short, Ryan's like every other male of our species. You're an eligible female, so he wants to court you. If I take you into my pack, he'll want to join me to get a chance to have you as his mate."

"Don't you dare," Ryan snarled.

"You going to challenge me for her?" Dalton snarled back.

Dalton's pack in the sitting room made a point of avoiding looking in the direction of the kitchen. "They're not going to stop, are they?"

"Not until you're mated," Gavin replied, his voice light with laughter, although he refused to make eye contact with me, Dalton, or Ryan. "Dalton has been after Ryan ever since he came to the New York area several years ago. Ryan's the Inquisition's first contact for problems in the city. If Dalton can bring Ryan into our pack, it'll up our standing substantially. In turn, the Inquisition's agent will have more support, which would make them happy, we get a submissive, and that'll make our pack stronger. We're not like regular wolves. In a lot of ways, our pack's strength is defined by our weakest member, but because Alphas and dominants exist to protect submissive pack members, we're made stronger because of it."

"I don't see what that has to do with me."

"If Dalton subjugates you, Ryan'll follow. He wants to court you—hell, he wants to court you bad enough he risked his life to save yours by performing the ritual in a *very* public place, if my understanding of the situation is correct. You've been coming between Dalton and Ryan all night, and we're taught to listen to those cues. Ryan's probably more submissive than you are, so you and your wolf are defending him."

"You're talking too much, Gavin," Dalton complained.

"I'm just trying to stop the fights before they start. We're all tired, and we have a job to do. If you want them, try honey first. Better yet, just tell the bitch to drag her male to the bedroom and see if the mating bond sticks. We can go play in the snow for a few hours while they get it out of their system. They're going to drive us insane if we have to put up with the posturing, and you'll antagonize Ryan. If you antagonize him enough, he might even try to suppress his submissive tendencies. You don't really want a fight to the death over a female, do you?"

My wolf and I both fixated on Gavin's comment about the bedroom. "Fenerec really decide who they stay with for life in the bedroom?"

Dalton sighed. "Sometimes a mating bond takes hold without sex, but it's pretty uncommon."

"Well, that explains my grandmother," I muttered.

"Pardon?"

"She's always sticking condoms in my purse."

Dalton choked, Ryan laughed, and the other Fenerec shook their heads.

"What? If you think that's bad, the first time I saw Ryan, I objectified him and managed to only get a picture of his stomach and bare chest." I shrugged and lifted my hands in helpless surrender. "Do you know how difficult it is to get someone to sleep with you when you don't like talking? I like listening. If I have something to say, I'll say it. Otherwise, I won't. Is that difficult to understand or something?"

Ryan chuckled, and there was a heat in his

scent my wolf found very interesting. "It's true. In the airport, she seemed quite content to listen to me talk. Honestly, I thought you were just trying not to cough."

"I'd still like to see your mountain," I reminded him.

"So you said."

"So, if I were to say I wanted to sleep with him, that doesn't make me a slut by Fenerec standards?" I asked.

"It doesn't make you a slut at all. Males are expected to do the same. It's normal behavior for us," Dalton confirmed. "Whether the mother is Fenerec, Fenerec-born, or human, our puppies are usually human and become Fenerec later in life. Fenerec-born puppies have some of their Fenerec heritage, including a heightened interest in sex, especially during the winter."

"Expected? I'm expected to sleep with anyone I want? How are you not overrun with babies?"

The Fenerec fell quiet, and even Ryan stared at Dalton.

"Did I say something wrong?"

Dalton sighed and shook his head. "No, you didn't. Unless you purposefully try to have puppies, you won't. First, Fenerec females aren't usually fertile until winter, neither are males. Females, Fenerec or otherwise, have to induce male fertility, so there's no such thing as accidental puppies. Should a bitch become pregnant, she has to avoid transforming to her wolf for the entire pregnancy. After the first month or two, should the female transform, she'll miscarry. It's difficult for us to have puppies. Not impossible, but difficult. Fortunately, the Inquisition has taken steps to prevent miscarriages lately. Yellowknife and Seattle have very strong Alphas capable of preventing bitches from transforming. Unfortunately, there's a very long waiting list to be transferred to one of those packs. Human mothers don't have nearly as many problems, but there is a higher percentage of miscarriages when the father is a Fenerec. Most women choose to have children while human and become Fenerec after they've had children."

When Dalton fell silent, I wondered what the man wasn't telling me.

Gavin cleared his throat, catching my attention. "Dalton wants to build that sort of pack here on the east coast. Washington's Alpha pair is capable of helping one female through a pregnancy at a time, and that's the best we've got. They're good, but some pairs have been waiting decades for a puppy. That's why he's been so determined to get Ryan into his pack. A submissive wolf brings out an Alpha's protective instincts, and our pack doesn't have a submissive. Our pack doesn't have any Fenerec females, either—our mates are all human."

Ryan groaned and slumped over the

kitchen counter, covering his head with his arms. "That's a dirty tactic, Gavin."

With a shrug, Gavin replied, "It's the truth, though. The east coast Fenerec need a strong pack. One Fenerec bitch here had a puppy last year, Ryan. One, and it was Washington's pack who pulled it off. That's it. One. Every other mating failed because we just don't have strong enough Alphas. Yellowknife and Seattle can't handle the full burden of our race's survival. The European packs are no better off. Seattle's hosting six European bitches, Yellowstone has seven more, and everyone on the other side of the pond is holding their breath, because that's the *entirety* of their mated female population."

"The entirety of Europe only has thirteen Fenerec women?" I whispered.

The Fenerec refused to meet my gaze, and Dalton sighed. "The plague hit Europe really hard a while ago. The Inquisition brought a lot of the survivors to the United States. Canada has guardianship of the wizard who figured out a cure to the plague, and we have the witches capable of making it dormant. You'll probably get it and require immunization, but we're used to that now."

"Plague? What plague?"

Dalton smiled, and I could tell it was forced by the way his cheek twitched. "One that almost wiped out the entirety of the Fenerec species. We survived, and we're recovering, and we have the Inquisition to thank for that. Europe was hit the hardest. The woman who came up with the cure lives in Canada, and it took her time to figure out how to teach the witches to cure it. It probably would've been easier on the Inquisition if they had let our kind die out. They wouldn't have to deal with so many problems that way."

My wolf growled in my head, and I voiced her discontent. Dalton held his hands up in surrender. "I'm just telling it how it is. We Fenerec aren't exactly a peaceful species. You've seen it first hand. Rogue Fenerec were the ones behind the bombing at La Guardia. Ryan's been assigned to bring them to justice. It's your job to help him and prove you're not a risk to the Inquisition at the same time."

My wolf quieted, and in her silence, I heard the promise of death and violence against those who had forced Ryan to turn me into a werewolf.

## SIXTEEN

*Assuming she can keep her teeth to herself, she'll fit in just fine in operations.*

---

MY WOLF THIRSTED for the hunt, and I should have been bothered our prey was a pack of Fenerec. All she cared about were my memories of the explosion at La Guardia and how close to death I had come.

While I had no memory of Ryan binding me and my wolf together, she did, and her fury at those who had hurt and killed so many burned bright.

"When you say we're to hunt them, does that mean we get to deal with them?" I wanted to growl my eagerness, but to control the urge, I turned my attention to the beef and potatoes in front of me.

My hunger no longer gnawed at me, although I continued to eat until I couldn't handle the thought of another bite. Eating gave me a chance to control my wolf's impulses, including her desire to head for the door and go kill those responsible for the airport's destruction.

Dalton drummed his fingers on the counter. "There are two ways the Inquisition deals with rogue Fenerec. They use them or they kill them. While technically Ryan's a rogue, he's more of a sanctioned operative. He lives outside of an Inquisition-controlled pack, but he works directly for the Inquisition. While most Fenerec call him a rogue, he's not one, not really. While you're a rogue, because you're *Ryan's* rogue, they'll look the other way. Ryan's too valuable as an operative to waste, and the Inquisition wouldn't want to antagonize him. That's why they want you to partner with him to deal with the rogues. It satisfies the Inquisition's need to confirm if you're worth sanctioning."

My wolf growled at the threat, but instead of echoing her noise, I stared at Dalton before turning my attention to Ryan.

Ryan fidgeted and refused to make eye contact with me.

"If I join a pack, does that mean the issue of how I became a Fenerec is no longer an issue?"

"That's typically how it works. Your Alpha would take responsibility for you. Unless the rogue Fenerec has broken one of the taboos, the Inquisition prefers to see a Fenerec relocated rather than killed. Unfortunately, most rogues have violated the taboos."

"What are the taboos?"

"There are a lot of them, but the most important one involves telling unauthorized Normals about the Inquisition. Unauthorized rituals, such as the one Ryan did on you, are also considered taboo, but they'll consider circumstances, especially in cases like yours. Killing Normals is taboo as well. Anything that compromises the safety of Fenerec, witches, and other supernatural is taboo. One day, I'm sure the Inquisition will be exposed to the public, but until that day comes, we hide among them. Even if we are exposed, I suspect the rules won't change much. While we can be killed, Fenerec are tough, and so are witches. Normals are fragile, especially when compared to Fenerec."

"And if Ryan and I find this rogue pack and kill them?"

"Well, you'll be considered the darlings of the Inquisition to say the least. They're upset enough this group almost killed a submissive—Ryan, that is. Add in the number of Normal lives lost? They want this dealt with immediately."

"But we're two against how many? An entire pack?"

Ryan growled, and I fixed my gaze on him. Once again, his eyes were bright and glowed with a light of their own. "There's no way an untried bitch and I can take out a pack of that size. There are at least twenty of them, maybe more."

"I'm authorized to help you."

"Your pack has fifteen members. The rogues still have the advantage."

The way Dalton smiled chilled me to the bone. "We may be fewer in number, but I will take quality over quantity any day, Ryan. Most in my pack have spent their lives like you, as operatives for the Inquisition. Our operations were in the battlefield. We weren't approached for this job. We volunteered. Take that as you will."

Ryan tensed. "Black ops. All of you?"

"You'd be the first we'd allow in who wasn't, and only because your skills lie in other areas. Fenerec need a pack. Being submissive makes it easier for you to handle being a lone wolf, but you can't suppress your instincts forever."

My wolf was offended at the way Ryan pointed at me. "And her?"

I couldn't tell which one of us had the urge, or if it was something we decided together, but I launched off my stool and latched my teeth to Ryan's throat, growling a warning.

Dalton grasped the back of my neck and squeezed. "All right, puppy. Maybe Ryan deserves it, but we can't talk if you're busy trying to get into a dominancy battle with him. Ryan, once she's gotten better control over her instincts, I have the feeling she'll be quite the little schemer. I've seen her business work; I thought the proposal was from her father, it was that advanced. He's taught her negotiation, she's got good ideas, and she's able to find bipartisan solutions to problems. Assuming she can keep her teeth to herself, she'll fit in just fine in operations."

Letting go of Ryan's throat wasn't in my wolf's plans, and she liked the way he stayed still, waiting, with his attention fully on us. If I tightened my hold on him, it could go one of two ways. I could rebuke him, something my wolf considered but disliked compared to our other option.

With a single nip, my wolf was certain we could keep Ryan's attention on us.

Dalton's hold on my neck tightened. "Matia, release him. This should be all the lesson you need to understand why she needs a pack."

I growled, lifted my hands, and grabbed hold of Ryan's shoulders, tangling my fingers in his shirt.

"She's just got a hold on me. That does not mean she needs a pack."

"Probably hasn't decided if she's going to kick your ass for disrespecting her or if she wants you for pursuits entirely inappropriate for the moment."

Ryan laughed, and his throat vibrated against my mouth. Unable to resist the temptation, I flicked the tip of my tongue against him. He tasted a little salty and a little sweet, and my wolf's interest in him intensified.

"You're pretty relaxed for a man with his throat in a bitch's teeth," Dalton muttered.

"I'd be more relaxed if you let go of her neck. I've always been of the opinion it's easier to just let a new Fenerec learn about their instincts by experiencing them. If I feel threatened, I'll fight back. I don't. Of course, she's testing the waters with her teeth on my throat, and it could go either way. What can I say? I'm willing to take the risk."

"Of course you are, you want her for your mate." Disgust laced Dalton's tone, although his scent sweetened. My wolf found the dichotomy interesting.

I didn't care. What would I do with Ryan? I gave his neck another lick before releasing him. When I straightened, Dalton let go of me and stepped out of my reach, stirring my wolf's desire for the hunt.

"Your instincts are out of control," Ryan observed, taking hold of my hands and prying me off his shirt. With his attention on Dalton, he said, "We can't risk exposing her to Normals yet. Letting her loose to hunt the other Fenerec would be disastrous."

"If I might be so bold, Ryan, I have an idea," Gavin said from his spot in the sitting room.

"What idea?"

"Challenge her. Winner takes all. Do you want her for your mate bad enough to take her and her wolf on? If she's going to shake out dominant, you're going to have to prove you're worthy of her anyway. If she wins, you submit to her and join our pack. If you win and she submits to you, you claim her as your mate and function as her Alpha until you decide it's in your best interests to join our pack anyway, especially if you want a puppy down the road."

Dalton crossed his arms over his chest. "Ryan's submissive. He can't function as an Alpha."

"If it means the difference between life and death for his mate, you better believe he'll step up to the plate. He's already proven he can dominate stronger Fenerec if he's cornered."

Without me holding him in place, Ryan scooted out of my reach. If it weren't for his smirk, I would've worried he was angry at me for biting him. "I'm not getting into a fight with her. She might have weighed over fifteen pounds during her first shift. She fit in my jacket. My *leather* jacket. A challenge is completely out of the question."

Humming thoughtfully, Dalton hooked my stool with his foot and drew it closer. "Did she grow any before she shifted back to human?"

Ryan shook his head. "No."

"Agreed, then. A challenge is out of the question. She might pick up a few pounds during her second shift but not enough to face off against you. It wouldn't be a fair challenge."

I gave the stool a nudge in Ryan's direction and sat beside him, keeping a close eye on him in case he decided to run.

If he did, my wolf was eager for the chase.

"Miss Evans, he's not prey," Dalton murmured.

I tilted my head to the side, matching Ryan's smirk with one of my own. "Why do Fenerec require packs?"

Dalton leaned back against the counter, watching me with a bright gleam in his eyes. "Smart question. We run the risk of our predators taking over, that's why. We find stability in family units, which are our packs. When we have others to protect and others to support us, we can maintain the balance between human and wolf. Fenerec on their own may run wild. Once the wolf takes full control, a witch might be able to save them, but usually not. Think about how you're behaving right now. As a human, you'd never behave this way, would you? As a human, you were polite to a fault, quiet, and you made every last word count."

It was true, but my wolf didn't understand what was wrong with the change.

We had a mate to catch and defend, and we both liked Ryan. My wolf did not mind if Ryan submitted to her—or us. If he did, we could safeguard him. The here and now mattered more than the future to my wolf, and that's where we differed.

Tomorrow needed to matter as much as

today. My wolf's disapproval chilled me, but I ignored her.

"It doesn't go the other way? The human in me can't hurt the wolf?"

Dalton shook his head. "Think about your life. What instincts did you have? Few, if any. Humans have lost them. The part of us that was human is not strong enough to subjugate the wolf, not completely. Your wolf might sleep from time to time, but you'll no longer look at the world through human eyes. You're no longer a human. As you age as a Fenerec, if you don't lose control of your wolf and run wild, you'll find you'll become a blend of who you once were and the wolf you are now. Younger Fenerec run a higher chance of running wild, but the older ones are far more dangerous if they turn."

"So a pack helps prevent this?"

"Yes."

I stared at Ryan. "And what about him? He doesn't have a pack."

"Eventually, maybe in a few years, maybe in decades—perhaps even in centuries—his wolf will take over. The part of him that's human will disappear, leaving him an uncontrolled, vicious animal—a very smart, vicious animal. The Inquisition will be forced to kill him. It's a slower process for submissive Fenerec, usually. Ryan's always been an exception. Don't let his appearance fool you. He's an older wolf."

Looking Ryan over, nothing about him looked very old. "How old are you?"

"Old enough," Ryan replied, his voice as tense as his body.

"As a Fenerec, he's older than I am. He's in his fifties, maybe early sixties. It isn't uncommon for a male Fenerec to spend decades searching for a mate, although Ryan's been at it longer than most. Many Fenerec are hesitant to search among human women for a mate because they fear the Inquisition, which leaves witches, Fenerec-born, and those who are approved to be introduced. Fenerec females will pick human males, too, although it's less common. How old were you when you underwent the ritual?"

"Twelve," Ryan mumbled.

"Submissive females are in high demand as a mate; males generally have an instinct to protect females, which puts submissive males at a distinct disadvantage. They don't offer protection to females, and most females have a natural inclination for the strongest male they can hunt down." Dalton snickered and made himself a mug of coffee. "Welcome to life as a Fenerec."

"Do you have a mate, then?"

"I do. She's not my first. We've been mated for ten years now."

"She's human, though, right? You said your pack doesn't have any Fenerec females. So, as a female Fenerec, I'll be expected to find a mate, probably a Fenerec, and belong to a pack?"

Dalton shrugged. "My mate is human—for now. It probably doesn't seem all that important to you, but come winter, you'll get caught up in the rut like the rest of us. It's not exactly optional for us. Our wolves' instincts come out strongest in the winter. As for belonging to a pack, it'll be necessary. If you have no control over your instincts, you'll be a risk to yourself and others. Maybe you don't realize it now, but you're a lot stronger than you were before, and you can easily kill someone without meaning to. Isn't that right, Ryan?"

Ryan lowered his eyes to the floor, sighed, and nodded, and in his scent, my wolf detected his misery.

I wondered, as did my wolf, but I kept quiet. Maybe later, once I had a chance to get to know him better, I'd ask what had happened to make him smell so sad.

"We've given you a lot to think about, Miss Evans. Why don't we take a break for a bit? Ryan, take her to bed so you both can get some rest. Give her a chance to think things through. You've got to be tired from standing guard during her ritual sickness. I'll hold down the fort and start making plans to deal with the rogue pack. We'll put our heads together and see what we can figure out. I know you've already been questioned about the attack, but I want us all to talk about it when we're fresh."

With a growl so soft I barely heard it, Ryan rose from his stool, his gaze still lowered as though he was afraid of what Dalton might do if he dared to make eye contact with the other Fenerec. I stood, sliding my way between the two males, baring my teeth at Dalton in silent warning.

Instead of angering him, my defiance and aggression made Dalton smile, which annoyed my wolf into growling in my head. I didn't let her take over my voice, however, backing out of the kitchen with Ryan.

I didn't like the way Dalton looked down on Ryan, and I really didn't like the way Ryan bowed so easily beneath the pressure of the other Fenerec's stare. Before I could voice my displeasure, Ryan took hold of my elbow and dragged me to the bedroom. My wolf relaxed when we entered the room we had shared with him for so long.

With a heavy sigh, Ryan flopped onto the bed.

There was still too much I didn't understand, and I hated my ignorance. When I worked with my father, I always had the option of finding someone who had the answers I needed. Corporate life was so much easier to understand than Fenerec. Too many emotions boiled under my skin and made it hard to concentrate on the facts.

I made decisions on *facts* not *feelings*, and with a wolf sharing my body, emotions I had no control over crested like waves battering the shore before they retreated only to surge again.

While Dalton could have answered my questions, my wolf was uneasy around the Alpha, which left Ryan as my only viable option. I didn't mind; Ryan had done nothing but help us both, and I was grateful for everything he had done.

Because of him, I lived, and I wanted to repay him for the risks he had taken for me. I would begin with thanking him.

"Hey, Ryan?"

Soft snoring answered me. I smiled, worked the blanket out from beneath him, and stretched out beside him before covering us both.

# SEVENTEEN

*Miss Evans, he's not prey.*

---

I WOKE to Ryan growling in my ear, his breath warming my skin. I jerked, scrambling to sit up, searching for the cause of his irritation and found the bedroom dark with light streaming in where the curtain didn't fully block the window.

"What is it?" I whispered, my body tense and my wolf wary, waiting for the threat I couldn't see.

"We're going out for a while," Dalton said from the doorway. "Sorry to wake you. We'll be gone for a few hours. It's stopped snowing, so we're taking advantage of the opportunity. We'll be back with replacement supplies, Ryan. The Inquisition found a snowmobile I could borrow and took care of the shopping, but it'll take a bit to get back up here. Couldn't you have lived a bit closer to the main road?"

"No," Ryan grumbled, burrowing under the blanket.

"We'll be back, and when we are, we'll figure out what our next step is." Dalton retreated down the hallway, and Ryan relaxed beside me.

There were a lot of things I didn't understand about Fenerec, but my wolf believed Dalton had somehow frightened or worried Ryan.

What I didn't understand was Ryan's reaction. "Why did you growl at him like that?"

"If he hadn't woken me up, I wouldn't have growled at him," Ryan muttered.

There was far too much I didn't know about Ryan, and my wolf was eager to learn more about our prospective mate. "You growl when you wake up?"

"Not usually. He's in my territory."

Understanding struck hard and fast. While the cabin belonged to Ryan, Dalton was the dominant Fenerec. Although I didn't understand what made Ryan submissive and Dalton dominant, Ryan either wasn't willing or able to drive the Alpha away.

"You haven't growled at me for that."

Ryan chuckled, and the sound rumbled in his chest. "I want you in my territory. If growling will keep you in my territory, I'll growl at you all you want."

My wolf was intrigued, as was I. However, with Dalton out of the way, I wanted to start learning so I could make informed decisions. I couldn't keep letting my wolf's urges take control.

The first thing I needed to do was understand Fenerec, their packs, and what life would be like for me in the future—a future I hadn't anticipated having after the destruction at La Guardia. "Can you explain packs to me?"

"I'm not the best one to explain. I haven't been in a pack for decades."

"Why not? Why don't you want to be in a pack?"

"You're a business woman."

"Yes."

"Consider a business. You're at the top of the ladder, right?"

I chuckled and shook my head. "Not quite."

"Close enough. You're near the top. You're responsible for everyone beneath you, aren't you? You're from a pretty big company, so maybe you don't know everyone personally, but you're still responsible for them."

It was true, and it had been a part of why I had laid down the groundwork to have Laura become my assistant. She—everyone—was my responsibility, and it had been as much my failure as Human Resources's she had been mistreated by Harthel.

Would I be able to return to work? Would I ever be able to contain my wolf enough to pretend I was still just another human when I wasn't?

I clenched my teeth and lifted my chin. "That's right. I'm responsible for them."

"In the corporate world, I'm the equivalent of the night-shift janitor, the person who does a job but is never actually seen—I'm the person who comes and cleans up everyone else's messes. Many Fenerec need someone or something to protect. I've been in three packs, and they've all been the same. To protect is to control for Fenerec. So, I always end up kept in the equivalent of a jail, but because they're Fenerec, the jail is filled with creature comforts. They're all the same."

The bitterness in Ryan's voice was partnered with an acrid stench. When I breathed it in, it left a sour, bitter taste on my tongue. My wolf didn't know what the smell meant, but she didn't like it.

It reminded her of sickness.

"What about it bothers you?"

Ryan sighed. "Most submissive Fenerec want to be in the company of others. I like being alone. I like having the time to think."

My eyes widened as I considered his words. In the airport, Ryan had spoken about how he loved the solitude of the mountains and their endless sapphire skies, skies I had never believed I could see for myself. The hope I would one day bear witness to the shade of blue Ryan so loved grew stronger.

Solitude was something I enjoyed, too. It let me think. It let me step away from the rigors of the world, regroup, and prepare for the future.

"That's part of why you go up to your mountain, isn't it?"

"Yes."

I bit my lip to contain my sigh of disappointment. I wanted to see Ryan's sky, but I didn't want to invade his privacy, not when it meant so much to him. "Are all packs like that? Containing you because you're submissive?"

"Yes."

"Is it true the—that the human in you will die, and they'll have to kill you?"

"One day," he acknowledged.

"Is there no way you can be in a pack and still be free?" My voice cracked, and I cleared my throat. "Is there no way to make it work?"

"If I were yours, would you let me go whenever I wanted? Maybe I'd be gone a day, maybe a week, maybe a month—maybe I'd stay up in my mountain for a year, alone."

My wolf's anger and dismay cut through me, and her emotions stole my breath. Her denial strengthened with every passing moment. I ground my teeth together, using so much force pain radiated from my jaw.

We had gotten along so well, my wolf and I, and refusing her wishes hurt. Fighting her was like driving a knife into my own stomach and twisting the blade.

I valued my freedom and independence, I valued being able to make my own choices, and I valued deciding for myself what sort of life I would live. The idea of someone caging me, no matter how comfortable the prison, left me sick to my stomach.

No one deserved that. I understood, and because I did, I forced myself to nod. "I would. I'd hate it, I'd hate every minute of it, but—"

Ryan crushed his mouth to mine and kissed away the rest of my words.

---

AS A HUMAN, I had always enjoyed sex when I found a good partner. As a Fenerec, need and desire ruled, and even without my wolf's urges spurring me, I wanted Ryan. One kiss from him was enough to make me burn.

Ryan toyed with me, and with any other man, I would've hated it. With him, my wolf loved every moment he left me breathless and wanting. Had I been the one in control, I would have gone for what I wanted most first.

I wasn't, and by the time Ryan finished with me, I was sprawled on top of him, bathed in sweat and gasping for air. Pressing my nose to the side of his neck, I breathed in deep, savoring the way the spice of his scent mingled with mine.

"That wasn't quite the response I was expecting," I confessed, contemplating if I had enough energy to roll off Ryan. The warmth of his skin conspired to keep my body relaxed, and I made a contented noise in my throat. "I like being alone sometimes, too."

"I really value my freedom."

I laughed and drew circles on his chest, his skin slick beneath my fingers. "I can tell. If I'd known it was so easy to get a man to sleep with me, I wouldn't have so many unused condoms in my purse."

Ryan had far more strength than his lithe body suggested, and he used it to flip me onto my back and pin me beneath him. His breath washed over my throat. "I'm the jealous type, beautiful."

Instead of being alarmed by a man trapping me with his body, a sense of security blanketed me, a feeling I hadn't realized had been stripped away from me until I became aware of it settling around me and my wolf.

Dad had given me that feeling, but it had begun to crumble after La Guardia and had been crushed to powder by Harthel. Relief so strong it stole my breath flooded through me.

I wasn't alone.

Other men I had let go before my jealousy could rear its ugly head, but Ryan had already worked his way under my skin, and I'd fight to keep him and the sense of safety he brought with him. "So am I."

Ryan chuckled and kissed my throat before working his way up to my lips. After several gentle, feather-light kisses, he murmured, "Good. You deserve unwavering loyalty. Any man foolish enough to stray from someone as beautiful as you doesn't deserve to have you. I'm also greedy and don't like to share."

My stomach chose that moment to gurgle its demands for food, and Ryan barked a laugh. "My father liked complaining he was always competing with my mother's stomach for her attention."

I blushed. "I'm sorry."

"Small price to pay. However, if I don't want to become your breakfast, I better check if there's anything left in the fridge. If it's stopped snowing, we could go hunt."

My wolf's interest piqued. "Hunt?"

"Hunt. As wolves. You'll have to learn how eventually. I'll teach you the basics in the cabin."

"Let's hunt."

Ryan chuckled, dropped another kiss on my lips, and rolled off me. "If that's what you want, that's what we'll do. It's a good time to start teaching you how to be a Fenerec. It's a good chance to see if you can figure out the trick of transforming, too."

"I'm not sure what to do," I confessed.

"When I want to change into my wolf, I concentrate on my wolf's shape, his body, and him. However unhelpful this sounds, after that, it just happens. Part of your problem will be the fact you have no familiarity with your wolf. My wolf can sense yours and can call her out, though, just as I can sense you—the human part of you—and call you out and help initiate your shifting." Ryan sighed, and his expression turned wry. "Dominant Fenerec have an easier time forcing someone else to shift—or stopping a transformation from happening."

"But you can?"

"I do a lot of things I shouldn't because I must."

"Would it help if I watched you change?"

Ryan shook his head. "If anything, it'll make it more difficult, I think. There'll be time enough to watch me go through it later. Experience it a few times for yourself first. You have enough to come to terms with already."

There was something about the way his voice turned guarded I didn't like, and I narrowed my eyes, shifting on the bed so I could watch his every move. "Why would I have a hard time coming to terms with the fact you can shift into a wolf?"

Ryan grimaced. "It's not the fact I can become a wolf. It takes me half an hour on a good day. Your wolf won't like it."

"Why not?"

"It's painful, that's why. Until you've experienced the pain of transformation a few times, your wolf will have a difficult time accepting the necessity of it, which will make it harder on you. Once you've begun transforming, the process will happen on its own, so I'll shift while you're shifting, too."

"How long should it take me?"

"It took you almost an hour your first shift, but you were hurt. You probably don't remember much about it, do you?"

While I had some memories of when Ryan had brought me to his cabin, they were blurred, and I had difficulty making sense of them. "A little, but not much."

"Give it a try. See if you can coax your wolf to the forefront and take her shape."

Although I was aware of my wolf's presence and her eagerness to hunt, I couldn't figure out how to break through the barriers separating us. After a few long minutes trying to puzzle it out, I shook my head in defeat.

Ryan shrugged and didn't seem surprised by my failure. "You'll figure it out eventually. Don't worry about it. It gets easier with each transformation. When the full moon rises, you'll shift, and you'll probably catch the hang of it then. Tell me when you're ready. This will hurt, and there's nothing I can do to help with that."

I swallowed, worried about what I was getting myself into, and nodded when I was ready.

Ryan cupped my face in his hands, stared me in the eyes, and my world narrowed to the agony of every bone in my body breaking at the same time.

---

WHEN I FINALLY FINISHED THE transition

from human to wolf, Ryan was waiting, his tail draped over his front paws, sitting straight and majestic, with every last strand of his fur neatly groomed to perfection. Despite Dalton's belief my eyes would heal and I would see color, he was the familiar shades of gray I expected from the world, a dark slate compared to the lighter tones of his cabin.

My disappointment lasted only as long as it took for me to realize just how large Ryan was as a wolf. He towered over me so much I had to lean back to get a good look at his head.

His nose and muzzle were the purest white, as were the tips of his ears.

Rising, Ryan shook himself, unsettling his smooth fur so tufts of it stood up every which way. He dipped into a playful bow, warbled at me, and batted me with his paw.

I fell over and rolled onto my back, astonished at how little effort it took him to knock me over. With my wolf's help, I figured out how to get back onto my paws, mimicking the way Ryan had shook out his coat. With his tongue lolling out of his mouth in canine laughter, he knocked me over again with a single swipe of his paw.

My wolf's desire to rise to his challenge burned in my bones, and I lurched upright and lunged at him, snapping my teeth in rebuke.

Ryan warbled and turned, cast a look over his shoulder, and brushed the long hairs of his tail against my nose. With his tongue still hanging out of his mouth in open mockery, he headed for the bedroom door, choosing to ignore my presence behind him. My wolf recognized the taunt for what it was, and her desire erupted into a need to put the male in his place despite his far larger size.

I howled and chased after Ryan, slipping and sliding when my paws hit the hardwood floor of the hallway. Crashing into the wall hurt, and I yipped as I sought to find my balance. My prey halted at the threshold between the kitchen and living room, watching me with pale, bright eyes. One of his ears twisted back as I tripped and flopped to my belly on the floor.

My wolf's disgust at my clumsiness dulled the edge of her annoyance over Ryan's mockery. Scrambling upright, I slowed to a careful prowl, aware of the way I couldn't find any purchase even when using my claws to keep me from sliding on the floor. I flattened my ears and warbled a complaint.

Ryan's tongue lolled out, and he jumped for the carpet, flicking his tail in silent challenge. Baring my fangs and growling, I stalked after him. Maybe I had no hope of overpowering such a large wolf, but I'd catch him all the same. When I reached the carpet, I crouched and launched in his direction.

With a single step to the side, he evaded me. The instant my paws hit the floor, I dug my claws in deep, twisted around, and lunged for him, snapping my teeth at his side.

Ryan knocked over the coffee table dodging out of my reach, and I recoiled and yipped from the noise. The furniture made a convenient barricade for my prey; while it wasn't large enough to offer him complete coverage, I was too small to jump over it. Howling my annoyance at being thwarted, I raked my claws down the table's underside. I darted for the end, reaching around to bite at his tail.

I caught a few hairs with my teeth before he took off for the kitchen.

A small size offered me agility and should have granted me speed, but Ryan always kept just beyond my reach, going as far as smacking me with his tail if I bored him. The living room lamp fell prey to my clumsiness. Ignoring the shattering of the glass bulb, I propelled off the wall and crashed into Ryan's side. He jumped back, smacking into the television.

It teetered on its stand and fell towards us, and with a heavy sigh, Ryan stepped over me. The large screen smashed across his back, and glass showered down to the floor. I hunkered under Ryan's belly, tucking my tail at the minefield of glittering shards strewn across the carpet.

Ryan sighed and stood still, supporting the ruins of his television so it wouldn't crush me under its weight. When I took a single step to navigate my way through the shards, he growled at me. I froze, whining at the rebuke, retreating to my original spot, lowering my head.

Through Ryan's legs, I got a good look at his living room and the rubble of what had once been his furniture. While I had managed to destroy the lamp, Ryan had broken off three of the four legs of his coffee table, added several long gashes to his couch, knocked over the end table and flattened it, destroyed the sound system, and had managed to bring down the curtain and its rod. The few paintings and decorations on the wall had toppled to the floor.

The kitchen hadn't fared much better, although I had no idea how we had managed to knock open the cabinet doors and spill their contents all over the tiles.

Ryan shifted his weight, grunted, and bucked the television off his back, sending it on a crash course with his couch. A tangle of cables and devices followed, smashing to the floor in a cascade of plastic and glass.

Any other man I knew would've begun mourning the destruction of his property, but all I could detect from Ryan's scent was his amusement, as though the evidence of my chase was a badge of pride rather than an unexpected expense or concern.

Ducking his head beneath his front paws, Ryan snagged me by the scruff of my neck and lifted me. I yipped and tucked my tail and paws. I wasn't sure how he managed to navigate the minefield of glass shards, but Ryan carried me to safety before setting me down beside the door.

The scratch of a key in a lock startled me into retreating towards the kitchen. Before I could make it far, Ryan stepped on my tail, pinning me in place. I growled and batted at his paw, which earned me a huff.

A moment later, the door opened and Dalton let in cold air and snow, which swirled over the floor. The Alpha paused in the doorway, blinked at us, and stared in the direction of the living room.

"I'm not sure I should ask," the man said with a sigh in his voice. "I see you weren't exaggerating about her size, which leads me to far more questions than you can answer right now, Ryan. Is there a reason your home has been destroyed?"

With far more dignity than I thought possible for the situation, Ryan bobbed his head.

"Just answer me this: any problems?"

Ryan shook his head.

Heaving a sigh, Dalton shook his head, once again taking in the destruction of Ryan's home. "All right. I'll take care of the mess so you don't shred your paws. Go blow off steam, but don't be out long. It's cold, and it'll only be getting colder. The others will be up in a few minutes, but I'll tell them you're going for a run. Don't lose your bitch in a drift. They're bigger than she is."

Laughing, the man squeezed by us and headed into the kitchen. With his tongue lolling out of his mouth, Ryan released my tail and nosed me in the direction of the door. I stared at the snow, casting a scornful look at the Fenerec males.

A drift would be overkill; the snow piled against the door towered over me, and not even the trail Dalton had broken was shallow enough for me to navigate without help. Ryan didn't seem to care, snatching me by my scruff and lifting me up before plowing his way towards the forests surrounding his cabin.

# EIGHTEEN

*If you could stop making work for your guests, I'd appreciate it.*

---

RYAN CARRIED me high onto his mountain where the gusting winds swept the rocks clean of snow. Setting me down, he dragged his tongue over my fur, soothing where he had bitten into my scruff. The cold air nipped my nose, and crisp scents filled my lungs with each breath.

Even in his cabin, I had been aware of the smells signifying civilization, but on the peaks of Ryan's mountain, the reminders of humanity slipped away, leaving me with an unbroken view of pale skies, pristine snow, and dark rock.

If there were colors in my world, I couldn't see them, no matter how long I stared up at the sky in search of the sapphire Ryan loved.

Ryan nudged my shoulder with his nose, huffed, and took several steps in the direction of the peak, pausing to make certain I followed him. The rocks were cold beneath my paws. The difference in our size worried me. He walked without any sign of the snow bothering him, while I had to hop to make my way through the snow, which came up to my belly.

Would I one day grow to such a large size? Ryan had mentioned wanting to hunt, but beside him, I was aware he could swallow me without having to chew first. I shivered from more than the cold.

While I was aware of my wolf's presence, she was distant, and I got the sense she had no interest in what I did, leaving me to discover the wonders of the wild on my own. After having been contained within a human body, I was a little dismayed by her lack of interest in the fact I was a wolf.

She was content to leave the matter of the hunt to me while she slept.

In a way, I couldn't blame her. The reality of the chill biting through my fur and stinging my nose was a lot less thrilling than the idea of it, which had lured me from the warm comforts of Ryan's bed.

Maybe I'd like the mountain top better when the wind didn't threaten to knock me over each time it gusted. I scrambled after Ryan, struggling to keep up with him as he followed a path I couldn't see. He abandoned the open slopes for pine forests, and the thick boughs overhead kept the worst of the snow off the ground.

A musky odor hung in the air, and I

halted, lifting my head in my effort to identify it. Something about the scent roused my wolf, but after a moment of consideration, she slipped back into slumber, leaving me ignorant of its source. Ryan snuffled, and both of his ears pricked forward.

Instead of his brisk, purposeful stride, Ryan slid into a prowl, every step slow, smooth, and silent. He weaved his way through the trees, his head held low, although I was aware of how he scanned the forest in search of something.

I followed in his wake, forced to hop from paw print to paw print to keep up with him. My attention was so focused on picking the path of least resistance I didn't notice Ryan had stopped until I collided with his hind legs. I shook my head and peeked around his bulk.

A herd of deer foraged, plundering from one of the few deciduous trees lurking among the pines. They scraped their hooves against the bark and ripped away the newly budding leaves, oblivious that a wolf equal to them in size watched and waited, biding his time.

For what, I wasn't sure, but I froze and stared at the deer, wondering if Ryan meant to take on so many animals on his own. There were at least fifteen of them, including several bucks with large racks of antlers.

I shivered at the thought of the sharp-looking prongs tearing through fur and flesh.

If the risk of being impaled by antlers

bothered Ryan, he showed no sign of it. Stalking forward, he circled around the herd so he could come at them from behind. Uncertain of what I was supposed to do, I trailed after him, grateful I was small enough I could hide in the snow while aware of the fact the deer could flatten me beneath their hooves if they took exception to my presence.

The deer were so enthralled by their foraging efforts they didn't notice Ryan until he was within striking distance. One of the animals made a deep, short sound, and the others threw their heads up in response.

Ryan surged into motion and threw himself at one of the does on the fringe of the herd. With an audible tearing, which sent shivers running through me, he clamped his jaws around her hind leg, giving a massive shake of his head. The dull crack of a bone breaking beneath his teeth heralded the animal's scream. Instead of keeping a hold on her like I expected, Ryan snarled, growled, and lunged at the remaining herd.

They scattered, vanishing into the trees.

Ryan's prey tried to run on three legs, trailing behind the rest of her herd, dark splotches of her blood staining the needle-strewn snow. Falling silent, Ryan circled his prey, both his ears cocked back, as though deciding how best to start eating her.

The fresh scent of blood stirred my hunger and my wolf, and her eager whines filled my head. I crept forward, my gaze locked on the doe, who let loose another shrill scream.

Ryan lunged forward, seized the doe's throat in his jaws, and drove her to the snow. Her cries turned to gurgles, which Ryan silenced with a shake of his head.

Part of me, the part of me still decidedly human, wanted to turn tail and run. The rest of me smelled the blood in the air and hungered. Ryan's bright, pale eyes focused on me, and he lifted his head, his white muzzle stained dark. Swallowing, I gathered my courage and plowed through the snow to join him.

His ears pricked forward, he pawed at the doe's carcass in what my wolf recognized as an invitation. She was far larger than me, and I stared at Ryan in rebuke, wondering what he expected me to do with a deer at least ten times my size; my entire body was smaller than her head.

Ryan taught me and my wolf how to best feast on deer, and when I had eaten my fill, he devoured the rest.

---

ONE DEER WASN'T sufficient to satisfy Ryan's hunger, and I learned not all prey fell so easily as his first doe. He stalked after the herd, carrying me when I walked too slow for his liking. With the herd aware of a wolf hunting in the woods, they scattered whenever they caught his scent, bleating their fear.

Undeterred by the herd's flight, he stalked after them, driving them higher up his mountain, cutting them off from the safe havens of the valleys far below the peaks. I had no doubt Ryan could have easily chased down any of the animals, but he took his time toying with them.

I liked his caution, especially whenever I got a good look at the bucks' antlers. There were three of them, although judging from their size and small racks, two were still young. The third, the largest of the animals, was the real threat, and I watched the buck with wary regard. My wolf's concern echoed my own, but instead of whining my dislike of hunting something so large and dangerous, I watched him.

Ryan's gaze often locked on the buck, and he licked his muzzle, his eagerness sweetening his scent.

The forest thinned as we headed up the mountain slopes. I gave up following Ryan every step of the way, watching as he darted back and forth, blocking the deer from escaping downhill using the force of his presence alone. The wind strengthened as we climbed upward, and the smoother ground made way for boulders and crags until the peaks jutted high over head in sheer cliff faces marred by cracks in the iced stone.

It was there, with few places left to go,

Ryan threw back his head and howled. The sound echoed from the peaks, and the ground trembled beneath my paws. I whined, tucked my tail, and scrambled for one of the stones uncovered by the incessant wind.

Thunder rumbled despite the clear skies, and the deer bleated their terror. They scattered, and Ryan charged for the largest of the bucks. They collided, wolf fangs against dark hooves. The buck's hind legs lashed out, thumping against Ryan's side, staggering him from the force of the blow. I growled, flattening my ears while I watched, my wolf itching for me to join in the fray despite our small size.

With a snarl and bared fangs, Ryan threw his weight on the buck's back, sinking his teeth into the back of the animal's neck. Something about the way Ryan clawed at the buck's hide puzzled my wolf. The buck screamed and thrashed, revealing the underside of the tender throat.

I hopped down from my boulder, gathered myself, and plowed through the snow, ducking between the buck's flailing hooves. My wolf took control, and she sank our fangs into the buck's soft throat, tearing at the thick hide to reach the blood and meat beneath.

Ryan snarled, shouldered me out of the way, and finished what I had started with a single bone-crunching bite. Warbling a complaint, I pounced on Ryan's forepaw, nipping at his thick fur.

With a swat of his paw, he knocked me into the snow, bared his fangs, and growled at me. My wolf's shock and dismay froze me in place, and when she retreated, I whined and backed away.

Sighing, he reached out and pinned me in place, his paw pressing between my shoulders. A lick to my muzzle reassured my wolf, and I waited to see what Ryan would do.

He turned his attention to the buck, settled in beside the carcass, and ate. All the while, I was aware of him watching me.

---

THE DEER HAD FLED, but their flight hadn't saved some of them. The broken bodies of three does littered the churned snow below a ledge not far from where Ryan had downed the buck. I peered over the edge, grimacing at the evidence of an avalanche having slid down the slope, toppling the smaller trees in its path. The third deer was mostly buried, with two of its legs jutting through the snow.

Picking me up in his mouth, Ryan loped down the mountain, bypassing the cliff to reach the fallen prey. Setting me on an exposed rock, Ryan made his way to the nearest deer, grabbed its legs in his jaws, and began tugging it down the slope.

It wasn't until I followed him to the trees I realized we weren't far from his cabin, and his home had narrowly missed being buried by the avalanche. Leaving the first carcass near his front door, Ryan headed off for the next one. I sat on his porch, draped my tail over my front paws, and shivered while waiting for him to return.

He was dragging the third doe up the stairs when the door opened and Dalton emerged.

The man crossed his arms over his chest, sighed, and shook his head. "I told you we would replenish your stock, Ryan."

Ryan dropped the doe's carcass onto Dalton's feet, sat, and lolled his tongue, but I didn't understand what the wolf found so amusing. It comforted me my wolf didn't understand, either.

"We'll take care of them. Why don't you go inside? If you could stop making work for your guests, I'd appreciate it, Mr. Cole." Dalton bent over, grabbed the doe by her leg, and hauled her to the edge of the porch. With a grunt and heave of his shoulders, he draped her over the railing, leaving her to fetch the other two animals. Ryan nosed me inside the cabin.

The rest of Dalton's pack, armed with cleaning supplies, looked up as we came in.

Ryan braced his legs and shook the snow out of his coat, and I lolled my tongue at the dismayed cries from the other males. Mimicking him, I got the worst of the water and snow off my fur, basking in the cabin's warmth.

I would have been content to lie down, but Ryan picked me up by the scruff and carried me in the direction of the bedroom, flicking his tail dismissively at the other wolves.

Laughter followed in our wake. Tossing me up onto the bed, Ryan returned to the door long enough to nose it closed before jumping up beside me. Pinning me down with a paw, he went to work grooming out my fur, and only when he was satisfied, did he release me.

Then he pressed his nose to mine, and I felt a faint pressure in my head before the stabbing pain of transformation lanced through me.

---

CHANGING from wolf to human hurt far more than the other way around, and by the time the pain eased, I wondered why anyone would willingly shift their shape. I groaned, crawled my way under the blanket, and threw it over my head.

"It gets better with practice," Ryan assured me, and he slid beneath the blankets with me. The warmth of his body and the caress of his breath on the back of my neck relaxed my wolf. I grumbled wordless complaints about her ability to immediately forget the torture of broken bones and muscles stretching, snapping, and reforming.

Fenerec had to be insane, all of them.

"Once you gain size, I think you'll figure out how to hunt just fine. You had the right idea with the buck." Ryan chuckled, sliding his hand over my hip before pulling me close to him.

"Ryan," Dalton called from the other room.

Ryan growled. "Insufferable Alpha."

I peeked out from under the covers. "So ignore him."

With a shake of his head, Ryan rolled away from me and left the bed, pulling clothes out of his dresser. He tossed a shirt and a pair of sweat pants at me. "The man's a menace. He'd come in here and drag me out of bed by my feet and haul me into the other room naked."

Ryan looked as good shirtless as he had in the airport, and my wolf appreciated the sight of him almost as much as I did. "You could go out in just your pants."

"And you could go out just wearing my shirt," he countered. Then he paused, blinked, and shook his head. "Forget I said that."

Jealousy had a scent, and my wolf liked when it mingled with Ryan's cinnamon spice.

I grabbed the shirt and pulled it over my head, kneeling to test its length on me. Unable to resist the urge, I tugged it down as far as I could in a faked display of modesty. "I would be showing a lot of leg."

"I'll do anything, just put the sweats on. Please."

Flashing him a grin, I grabbed the dark sweats. "Anything?"

"You're a wicked little bitch, aren't you?"

"It's not my fault you look so good without your shirt."

"I had noticed how much you seemed to like my chest before. It was rather difficult not to."

I blushed. "I'm sorry about that. I shouldn't have done it."

"Where was that camera of yours focused, anyway?"

There was a tap at the door. "Ryan?"

Ryan sighed. "Just a sec."

Remembering Ryan's admission of feeling trapped by other Fenerec, I pulled on his sweats and ran my fingers through my hair in a haphazard effort to tidy my appearance. After snagging my fingers on several tangles, I gave up and wrinkled my nose. "I don't suppose you have a brush, do you?"

"Bathroom."

I slid off the bed and headed towards the door, only to have Ryan slip his arm around my waist and pull me to him. All it took was a light press of his lips to mine to ignite my wolf's interest in him all over again. Add in my own desire, and it took every last bit of my will to not yank the man to the bed. My breathing turned ragged, which Ryan answered with a throaty chuckle.

"Maybe that'll keep your attention on me

for a while," he murmured, pulling away from me.

I had no idea how he thought I'd be able to concentrate on any male other than him; my wolf was fixated on his scent and was the jealous type. I had been the loyal *and* jealous type even before I had become a Fenerec, and I had noticed him *before* my life had been turned upside down.

"I'm not interested in any of the other males," I replied, lifting my chin.

"That's promising."

"I told you I'm—" I narrowed my eyes. "You're teasing me, aren't you?"

Ryan delayed answering by pressing his lips to mine once more. I gave his shirt a tug before working my way down. He captured my hands in his with a throaty laugh. "Later."

Grandmother would have been proud of my one-track mind with a destination right back to bed. "You could just ignore Dalton and pay attention to me."

"I heard that," Dalton muttered from the other side of the door.

There was something satisfying about twisting around and mule kicking the door, especially when Dalton spat a startled curse. "Go away, Mr. Sinclair. I'm busy right now."

"But I need to discuss something with Ryan, Miss Evans."

"When I'm finished with him."

"If I wait until you're finished with him, I'd probably die of old age first. There'll be plenty of time for you to hunt him later, I promise."

"I want to hunt him now."

"Just give the Alpha male his way, Matia," Ryan murmured, tugging me towards the door. "It makes them happy and lets them think they're still in full control."

"I heard that, Ryan."

"Maybe you wouldn't hear things you didn't like if you stopped listening at my bedroom door," Ryan complained, releasing me to yank open the door. Dalton was crouched in the hallway and stared up at us, his eyes pale.

One day soon, I needed to figure out what made someone submissive. Without any sign the other Fenerec frightened him, Ryan lifted his bare foot and placed his heel on the center of Dalton's forehead and shoved, sending the man sprawling. "You may have just robbed me of the best hours of my entire life."

I frowned, wondering what he was talking about.

Laughing, Dalton hopped to his feet before giving Ryan a companionable slap on his shoulder. "You'll survive for a few hours."

"I might not. I really might not. Just look at her, Dalton. Just one look, though, or I'll be forced to gouge your eyes out."

"Control your male, Miss Evans," Dalton ordered.

My wolf's unease became my own.

Ryan didn't want anyone controlling him.

I remembered his words and his reaction to mine. Clenching my hands into fists, I took a single step forward and bared my teeth in a snarl. "I will do no such thing."

"And why not?"

"He doesn't like it. Back off."

Instead of the anger I expected from the Alpha Fenerec, Dalton smiled.

## NINETEEN

*Take your shirt off.*

---

DAD WAS SITTING at the counter sipping coffee with several wolves from Dalton's pack; for a long moment, all I could do was stare at him.

One of them was even a wolf with his large head resting on Dad's knee, staring up with imploring eyes. I had no idea what the Fenerec wanted, but my father was doing an admirable job of ignoring the massive animal, either unaware or uncaring he ran the risk of being swallowed whole. I doubted the Fenerec would have to chew for long.

With a frown, I counted bodies, realizing there were two extra Fenerec. I drew in a breath and held it, and my wolf and I worked together trying to sort through the numerous scents in the cabin.

One of the Fenerec was a female, and I tensed, turning an accusing glare on Dalton.

Males wouldn't target Ryan, but a female was another matter entirely. I scowled, sighed, and went into the kitchen, hugging Dad from behind and resting my chin on his shoulder.

Other people would have jumped or been alarmed, but Dad kept still, although I was aware of him glancing out of the corner of his eye to confirm it was me. With Dad around, another layer of my missing sense of security fell back into place, and I relaxed against him.

There were a lot of things I needed to say, but the words stuck in my throat. I needed to tell him I was sorry for everything, for scaring him again, and for becoming something far from human.

I could smell his anxiety, which was fading away under the stronger scent of his relief.

Reaching up, Dad gave my hair a ruffle and a pat. "Are you all right?"

Was I? Could I ever really be all right? I was alive, I could breathe, but everything had changed. I didn't know what would happen, either, which didn't help me one way or the other.

Before the destruction at La Guardia, my life had been so carefully planned.

Everything had changed, and change brought uncertainty.

Change also brought with it excitement and the thrill of the unknown. Without Ryan, I'd probably be dead. Without him, I probably never would have left the airport.

I'd hold him accountable and enjoy every

moment of it; my wolf's eager whines filled my head.

"I'm all right," I replied, and it was the truth. "Thanks to Ryan, that is." I wasn't above using Dad to keep Ryan around, and Dad was the type to repay debts. Straightening, I tugged on my father's arm, pointing at the male my wolf and I both desired. "That's Ryan. He was at the airport. Ryan, this is my father."

The Fenerec using Dad's knee as a headrest turned both ears back, and my wolf's unease strengthened. My nose confirmed my belief the Fenerec was male, but there was something about the way the wolf stared at me with too bright eyes that put me on edge.

I didn't get a chance to think about it for long; Dad stood, caught me in his arms, and held me in a hug so tight the air rushed out of my lungs in a squeak. When he let me go, he turned to Ryan, who was standing beside Dalton and watching me with pale eyes.

Maybe one day, I'd truly understand the significance of the shifting shades of a Fenerec's eyes. Part of me recognized the color as Ryan's predator, his wolf, showing through, although I didn't understand why. I sniffed, struggling to sort through the many scents in the air. The relief from my father was the strongest, although there were undertones my wolf recognized as wariness.

Dad either didn't know he was surrounded by predators or didn't care. Striding to Ryan, he held out his hand and said, "I'm Ralph. Seems I have a lot to thank you for, Mr. Cole."

Ryan shook my father's hand. "Ryan."

While my father was a lot of things, I'd never taken him for the violent kind, but before I could do more than gasp, Dad grabbed hold of Ryan's shirt and tossed him on the floor. The next instant, he had his knee pressed to the Fenerec's throat. "Rules are simple, Mr. Cole. If you hurt her, there will be a line of people ready and waiting to disembowel you. I'll be at the front of it. Since I don't have your Fenerec strength, I'll ask Mom and Dad to help. I'm sure they wouldn't mind. Right?"

The male who had rested his head on Dad's knee showed his teeth, and the female made her appearance, voicing a single warning growl.

I stared at the pair of wolves, realization sinking in they were my grandparents. I breathed in deep. While Dad lacked the spiced sweetness of Fenerec, my wolf recognized subtle similarities in their scents. Pointing at them, I blurted, "Grandmother?"

The female lolled her tongue and displayed a canine grin.

"I'll keep that in mind," Ryan replied, lying still beneath my father. "You're pretty strong for a Normal."

"Fenerec-born."

"You're still strong."

"I'm going to have to be if I have to start beating Fenerec to keep them from making any inappropriate advances on my daughter."

I closed my eyes and rubbed the bridge of my nose. "Dad, Grandmother has been putting condoms in my purse for years. I think we're beyond this stage of the game. He's been perfectly appropriate, thank you. Stop trying to scare off my male."

"Your male?" Dad growled.

I opened my eyes to narrowed slits. "Mine. I'm plenty old enough to decide who I sleep with, when I'll sleep with him, and how often I'll sleep with him. If I want to take him on the hallway floor in front of everyone, I can."

Ryan gave a throaty chuckle. "Kinky."

"There's no need to publicly claim your male, Matia," Dalton muttered, shaking his head. "I apologize for her, Mr. Evans. She hasn't quite managed to learn to control her aggression yet."

Laughter was the last response I expected from Dad, and his chuckles startled me. "She'll figure it out. She's smart. As for you, Ryan. I meant it. Hurt her, and I'll make sure you regret it. Understood?"

"Yes, sir."

"Good." Dad hopped to his feet and offered Ryan his hand. It surprised my wolf the Fenerec accepted the help. "Take your shirt off."

"What?"

"Your shirt. Take it off."

I covered my mouth with my hands, my eyes wide as I gawked at my father. "Have you lost your mind, Dad?"

"No. Take your shirt off, Ryan."

Heaving a sigh, the Fenerec obeyed. "Why am I doing this?"

Dad crossed his arms and stared at Ryan's bare chest. "I only want the best for my daughter, and that includes everything. I won't have a scrawny weakling protecting my little girl. Turn around."

My face burned from my embarrassment. "Dad!"

Turning in a slow circle, Ryan chuckled again. "Do I pass your inspection, sir?"

"How are your skills?"

"*Dad!*"

Dalton hopped onto one of the kitchen stools. "He doesn't mean skills in bed."

"This isn't up for discussion," I snarled.

"Relax, Matia. Let your father satisfy himself. It's expected, and Fenerec-born males can be just as stubborn as Fenerec when it comes to their puppies. It's better to just let them work it out."

"Dad will not be satisfying himself using Ryan." Everyone stared at me. When I realized what I had said, I sucked in a breath. "I didn't mean it that way. Dad, leave him alone."

"I don't mind putting myself on display." With a wicked grin, Ryan struck a pose and flexed his muscles. "I'm enough to make other Fenerec jealous."

"It's true," Dalton conceded. "Ryan really is a prime piece of real estate. He's submissive, Mr. Evans, which I think you'll find is a good match for your daughter."

"He won't be able to control her," Dad snarled, whirling to face Dalton. "That's a problem."

Dalton shook his head. "No, she'll be fixated on making sure his world is perfect and happy. She'll probably be a strong dominant one day, and having a submissive around will keep her grounded. It's an ideal situation. That's not the real reason I brought you here, though."

Something changed, something that made the gathered Fenerec tense, and my father's scent turn sour. My grandparents growled, and the low, rumbling sound put me on edge.

The acrid bite of anger grew and overwhelmed all other scents. It came strongest from my father, but was shared by everyone else, even Ryan.

"What's going on?"

For someone who wasn't able to transform into a wolf, Dad was good at growling. "We need to talk about how we're going to deal with Harthel."

Dalton nodded. "We also need to discuss the rogues who attacked La Guardia airport. We're going to put together a plan, and we're going to deal with them."

At first, I thought my wolf's burning desire was for revenge, but after I took a moment to really think about the emotions bleeding into me, I realized she wanted something far more important than vengeance.

My wolf needed justice, for me and for everyone else who had become a victim within the airport. Ryan deserved a chance to redeem himself for his failures, too, a chance to erase the darkness in his eyes and spirit when he spoke of those he hadn't been able to save, me included.

---

DESTROYING Ryan's living room and kitchen ruined Dalton's plans, and the Alpha snarled at both of us about it. Without the couch and several of the stools and with the glass still embedded in the carpeting, there wasn't enough room for us. At the barked order from the Fenerec, Ryan herded me in the direction of his bedroom so we could shift to wolves and make the journey down the mountain.

"It was inevitable," Ryan muttered, closing the door behind him.

The flex of his bare muscles absorbed my attention, and I licked my lips. "I'd do it again."

"You deserve far more time than we have. Later."

My wolf warbled complaints in my head,

and her lust for the man made it difficult to think about anything else. I clenched my teeth, forced myself to take long, even breaths, and waited until the burning need lessened to something I could tolerate and ignore. "Does it really get easier? Shifting, that is."

"You'll get used to it. It'll always hurt, it'll always be a little tiring, but you'll get better and faster at it. With luck, you won't have to shift again until the full moon." Ryan offered me a smile. "Your father is an interesting man."

"Dad knocks you on your ass, so you think he's interesting?"

"That's nothing more than standard Fenerec posturing. In his case, it's a learned behavior. It was interesting he brought his parents to back him. Most men try to fight their battles alone, especially when it comes to their daughters." Ryan's eyes brightened, and he closed the distance between us, flicking his tongue over his lips. "And make no mistake, beautiful. He's right to try to warn me and put me in my place. Unfortunately for him, you're already mine, and I have no intentions of letting you go."

I should have been alarmed and offended by his claim, but my wolf adored Ryan's display of aggressive possessiveness. Her influence kept me silent and rooted in place.

Something in my expression pleased a

smile out of Ryan, and he dipped his head to press his lips to mine.

I didn't realize he had tricked me into relaxing my guard until the pain of changing forms swept through me and refused to let go.

---

I WARBLED complaints at Ryan for forcing me to transform again. Aching and trembling from exhaustion and the aftermath of such intense pain, I could barely stay upright, which spurred me into snarling and snapping my teeth.

The way Ryan lolled his tongue at me, his scent sweet with his amusement, infuriated me into howling.

Howling brought my father, who opened the bedroom door. A pack of Fenerec, all wolves, crowded behind him.

"I haven't heard a tantrum like this since you were six." Dad stepped into the room, dodged the discarded clothes littering the floor, and stooped to grab me by the scruff of my neck. He lifted me up and turned me so I was forced to look him in the eyes. "I raised you better than that, young lady. I brought a muzzle, and I will use it if necessary."

I snapped my mouth shut, flattened my ears, and tucked my tail.

"That's better. Don't even think about biting

me, either. We have a long ride ahead of us, and I'd rather not have to fend you off. It'd be warmer for you in my jacket than forcing your male to carry you down the entire mountain."

My wolf's contentment warmed my head. I couldn't tell if she was satisfied Dad wanted to carry us or pleased with his acknowledgement Ryan was ours, but it didn't matter to me either way.

Even the thought of trying to walk to the living room seemed like too much work to me. I relaxed in my father's grip. After several long moments of staring at me, he tucked me in the crook of his arm and strode down the hall, bumping large wolves aside with his legs.

There was only one snowmobile parked behind Ryan's cabin. Dad straddled the seat, started the engine without hesitation. He shoved me into his coat, zipping it up so it pinned me to his chest, leaving my head exposed to the cold air.

The wolf I recognized as Ryan sighed, staring at the snowmobile wistfully.

"No, you can't ride with me. You have legs, use them. Don't worry. I'll give her back to you once we reach the vehicles. Dalton said she should stay as a wolf until we reach the city."

While Ryan flicked an ear back and sighed again, he nodded and joined the other wolves gathered where the yard made way for pine forest. Dad followed the wolves, and I was astonished at how fast they could run; the snowmobile was faster, but the Fenerec had no trouble keeping up with him despite having to plow their way through the snow.

By the time we reached a group of SUVs and cars parked at the end of the road, my fur was frozen, the cold bit my nose, and I shivered despite Dad's warmth and his coat. Killing the engine, Dad slid off the snowmobile. One of the cars, dusted with wind-driven snow, was on, and its headlights illuminated the forest.

Sam stepped out of the vehicle. "Everything okay?"

"It's fine. Sorry to call you back. The two had decided to play in the cabin and trashed the place."

"Which two?" Sam asked, his tone wry.

"My daughter and her male," Dad replied, pulling me out of his coat. "I'm not really sure how she contributed to the destruction, considering she weighs maybe five pounds."

"Her male? Does he have a name, or are you going to play the role of disapproving father?" Kicking his way through the snow, Sam approached and held out his hands. Dad passed me over. "She's not going to stay this small or cute for long. Enjoy it while you can, Ralph."

Snorting, Dad headed for the car, brushing snow away from the back door with his hand. "He's the one who helped her at the airport."

"He has my approval."

Dad shot Sam a glare. "I'm pretty sure they don't need your approval. They need mine."

"So you're going the disapproving father route?"

"I'm thinking about it. He did something to annoy her, and I'm not sure what."

Sam shook his head and draped me over his shoulder. "Ignore him, Matia. He just needs something to complain about. The car's warm, so why don't you relax while we get the other vehicles ready."

Neither Dad nor Sam paid attention to my warbled complaint. They left me locked in the car, and I was too small to reach the window to watch them. Howling earned a tap at the window and a glare from Dad, and I snapped my teeth at him despite being aware I couldn't reach him even if I wanted to.

According to the car's clock, I was imprisoned for half an hour before Dad opened the back door. I launched my way towards freedom, only to have my scruff grabbed. I twisted around and paddled at his arm with my hind paws, which only made him laugh. "It's too cold and dark for you to go romping in the snow."

"She hasn't been over ritual sickness for very long, so it's not surprising she has pent up energy. She handled hunting with Ryan for several hours, too," Dalton said, coming to stand beside my father. "Ryan will be a few more minutes, and I wouldn't be surprised if he falls asleep during the drive. You want to take him in your car?"

"He's not staying with my daughter if he doesn't come in mine," Dad snarled.

"Behave yourself, Ralph," my grandmother demanded. I had always thought she looked young, but I had never believed she was anything other than my grandmother through adoption, justifying her appearance with the simple explanation of having my dad when she was really young.

Knowing differently didn't change all that much for me. Dad presented me to my grandmother, and my wolf was intrigued by the pleasure in my father's scent. "She hasn't been this cute since she was little."

"Ralph, that's rude," my grandmother scolded, taking me out of my father's hand and cradling me in her arm. "Give her a couple of weeks. She'll be big enough to sit on you."

Dad sighed. "You're ruining my fun, Mother."

"Don't you mind your father, Matia. He's just relieved you're alive and well. We all are. He'll calm down by tomorrow, or I'll be forced to have his father give him a stern reminder of his manners. For tonight, let's get somewhere we can talk, make plans, and show the fools who dared to hurt you the real meaning of fear."

## TWENTY

*It'll be one of life's great unsolved mysteries.*

---

RYAN FELL asleep moments after buckling his seatbelt, and I made myself comfortable on his lap, draping my front paws over his leg so I could stare at Dad and his mother. Grandmother won the argument over who would sit beside me and Ryan with a single snarled threat.

It wasn't until I watched her snap her teeth and growl at Dad I realized they had all been very careful about their behavior around me, wearing masks to hide the truth of who—and what—they were. Even Dad was more relaxed, as though a great weight had been lifted from his shoulders, and I doubted it was just from knowing I was alive and well. At least Dad hadn't shown up while I'd been too sick to do anything other than sleep and throw up.

It was bad enough I was hungry again. It hadn't been that long since I had gorged on deer during the hunt with Ryan. My stomach growled its complaints, and my wolf whined in my head.

"You shouldn't be surprised a male courted her, Ralph. You've raised a beautiful girl, and any wise Fenerec would want her," my grandmother declared.

"He's submissive," Dad complained. "Submissive!"

I growled, flattening my ears. Ryan slept on, oblivious to my father's scornful tone.

"Son, if you don't behave, I'm going to have Sam pull over so I can beat some manners back into you," my grandfather warned from the front seat. "First, if her mate was dominant, they'd probably both be dead right now. Dominants are not exactly subtle, and what Mr. Cole did in La Guardia required far more subtlety than most dominants possess. Second, she obviously likes him."

"Matia asked for my help finding him after she came home from the hospital," Sam added.

"He's still submissive."

"Ralph," Grandfather growled.

"She knows nothing about being a Fenerec. I've already been warned—repeatedly—I will get bitten, probably mauled, and otherwise put in my place before she learns to control her instincts. How is a submissive supposed to protect her during the transition? I've also been told if I have an intact apartment by the time they're done, it'll be a miracle."

"Lots of sex, probably. If he's keeping her busy in the bedroom, then she won't be able to put you in your place, no matter how much you deserve it for being rude," my grandmother replied. "Stop worrying. I'm sure the destruction at the cabin was them just playing. We do that. If he took her out on her first hunt, he was probably just trying to teach her, and they got carried away. Then again, maybe they destroyed everything while having sex. It'll be one of life's great unsolved mysteries."

"Mother!"

I covered my eyes with my paws and sighed. While my wolf and I were very interested in Ryan for a lot of things, sex included, the last thing I wanted to do was talk about it with my family. My grandmother slipping condoms in my purse and informing me I needed to sleep around more was bad enough, but would I spend the rest of my life listening to her discuss my sex life?

Having a sex life was a new enough development I didn't want it to be a topic of family discussion. If Ryan woke up and heard the conversation, would my grandmother be enough to drive him away?

"You're such a prude, Ralph. Where did I go wrong? Did I not leave enough condoms out for you? Did I not encourage you to date enough? You're one of New York's most eligible bachelors. Every bitch this side of the Mississippi would love a chance with you. I can make a few phone calls. You can't use Matia as an excuse, either. I promise you, submissive or not, her male will take good care of her. She'll transition just fine. I'm more worried about you. When was the last time a nice woman took you to bed? You're really tense, son. Stop bothering the newly mated—and for pity's sake, call the poor boy by his name."

Dad sighed. "How did this become about me?"

"You're the eligible bachelor. Once I'm done making plans for Matia's wedding, I in—"

"Wedding? What wedding?" Dad twisted around in his seat, and his dismay and shock were so potent I sneezed.

I flattened my ears and glared at my grandmother.

"The one I will plan for my beautiful granddaughter, of course. As if I'd let some wolf cart her off without marrying her first. She shall be properly chaperoned, too, Ralph Daniel Evans. Am I understood? No couples will be sneaking out of New York to elope. Take responsibility."

"How is this my fault?"

"You refused to let me bring in suitors for her. If you didn't want her with a submissive, then you should have let me arrange courtships. This is entirely your fault."

I turned on Ryan's lap, nosed my way

under his shirt, and hid, wishing I could disappear.

Things had been so much easier before I had become a Fenerec, but I couldn't help but think I had dodged a very nasty bullet.

---

THE HIGH RISE apartment building wasn't home, but it smelled like Ryan, although his scent had faded. Someone had dusted the place recently; to a human nose, the offensive lemon cleaner was probably pleasant.

A sleep-befuddled Ryan staggered into the suite, fumbled for the light switch, and made it to the couch before collapsing, half his body hanging off the cushion. I wanted to fall into a stupor with him, but Dad refused to put me down, cradling me in his arm.

"This is Ryan's place?" Dad asked, turning to Dalton, who was hanging his coat on the rack beside the door.

"One of them. He has at least one place in every major city along the east coast. He has three apartments in New York City. I picked this one because it's closest to your residence. The Inquisition owns most of them, though."

My grandmother swept past my father, slowing long enough to snag me by the scruff and take custody of me. "That's unusual. Why?"

Dalton strode into the kitchen and sat on one of the stools surrounding the island. "It makes his work easier. If he doesn't have to worry about where he'll be staying, he can focus on his assignment. He can give you more details about it later, if you're interested. For now, I'd like to lay out our current assignment and find out what you know."

The rest of Dalton's pack came in, beelining for the living room. Most, like Ryan, found a place to flop and were asleep within moments. Gavin remained awake, sitting beside Dalton in the kitchen, his attention focused on my grandmother, who set me on the island counter.

While my grandmother was a force to be feared all on her own, my grandfather was even worse, and he stood tall and straight, his arms crossed over his chest, glaring down his nose at Dalton. "Explain the assignment."

"The Inquisition wants Ryan and Matia to hunt down Harthel and deal with him. Once he's gone, they're to track down the rogue pack responsible for bombing La Guardia."

"The Inquisition is sending Fenerec to kill a Normal?" my grandmother shrieked.

Dalton sighed. "If necessary. The first phase of the assignment is to find out if it's possible to get sufficient evidence to incarcerate him. If it isn't possible, yes, the Inquisition is sanctioning the death of a Normal. He's too much of a risk to your son, your granddaughter, and the entirety of their business, which employs a substantial number of witches and Fenerec."

"Risk management," my grandmother spat.

The anger in my grandmother's scent worried my wolf, and I retreated across the counter. While I was tempted to jump and make a run for it, it was a long way to the floor. With a huff of dismay, I sat, curled my tail around me, and flattened my ears.

"Necessary risk management. My pack has been given authorization to help. I can put in a request for your pack's assistance if you can convince your Alpha to help."

My grandparents exchanged long looks, and my grandfather growled before saying, "He won't. She's not a part of our pack, and neither is Ralph."

The silence stretched on, broken by the hum of the refrigerator and the faint honking of a horn somewhere far below on the streets. Gavin thumped his elbows to the counter and clutched his hair. "Your Alpha is a waste of air. A coward, a worthless mutt. He acts like he's entitled to his territory and does nothing to protect it. La Guardia is part of his turf. He should have been the first in line seeking justice and putting an end to the rogue pack."

"Gavin," Dalton warned.

"Damn it, it's true, sir. We're limited to a fraction of Long Island while that so-called Alpha cries if anyone tries to edge in on his territory. If he can't protect it, he doesn't deserve to have it."

"While I'm not disagreeing, be respectful. He does let us infringe on his territory."

"Don't feel like you need to hold your tongue," my grandmother said, offering her sweetest smile.

I knew trouble when I saw it, and between my wariness and my grandmother's expression, my wolf retreated to the recesses of my head, leaving me to cope with her on my own.

If she decided to join forces with my grandfather, I doubted even Dalton would be able to withstand them. On her own, my grandmother was enough to worry me, but my grandfather was the quiet, stealthy type, biding his time for the perfect moment to strike.

Most of the time, he orchestrated pranks on his victims. Sometimes, he revealed his most potent weapon: his sharp but honest tongue.

The truth was difficult to fight against, and my grandfather only picked battles he knew he would win.

"I fully intend to pressure Ryan into joining my pack," Dalton declared, matching my grandfather's stiff posture and cold expression. "Your Alpha is incapable of safeguarding someone so submissive, nor is he capable of handling someone like Matia."

My grandfather relaxed. "Now you're talking sense, Mr. Sinclair. You're correct. Our pack is ill suited for a submissive, and of course my son's girl would be dominant. We raised her right."

Dad sighed. "Can we get back to business, please? Some of us have to go to work tomorrow."

I twisted around in search of Sam and spotted him near the door. With an arched brow, our driver said, "How are you going to handle that, by the way? Everyone knows she was kidnapped."

"I'll tell them she was found and is recovering, and I'll do a good job of complaining about how she cruelly forced me to work. I'll come up with something. I'm not going to let Chuck get away with anything, which means I need to keep going to work and close every last loophole he might use to infiltrate Pallodia. I also need to keep searching for anyone who might be one of his accomplices." Dad clacked his teeth together and shook his head. "Until I can figure out how to hide the fact Matia is well, it's best she doesn't come to the office at all."

Dalton nodded. "You have to maintain appearances, too, Mr. Little."

Sam sighed and nodded.

"One of my pack will be tailing your car to make sure nothing happens to either one of you. With your permission, I'd like to use you as bait. If those responsible for Miss Evans's kidnapping are still around, there's a chance they might follow you to find her."

"Those?" Dad demanded. "Chuck has accomplices?"

"We have no way of knowing. Until there is evidence he's working alone, I'm going to assume he has people helping him. That's safer for everyone involved."

"How is Matia going to be involved?"

"For the moment, her exposure to the assignment will be limited to intel gathering and drawing Harthel out. Infiltration is more Ryan's specialty than mine. Consider me the firepower of the operation."

During the long silence following Dalton's words, everyone stared at the Fenerec sprawled on the couch. I wanted to join Ryan, but I wasn't willing to sacrifice the opportunity to learn more.

Watching him sleep was enough to make me yawn.

"I wasn't expecting him to pass out like that," Dad admitted.

"Ritual sickness," Dalton explained. "Normally, the entire pack would have helped, but since he doesn't have a pack, he's been doing the work alone. I doubt he got more than a few minutes of sleep since he found her. I was hoping he'd stay awake longer, but I can't say I'm surprised. Tomorrow, we'll begin the groundwork, find out what we're up against, and start building a plan. I'll contact you about the insider information we'll need regarding Harthel and his activities. Someone is already going through all the correspondence we have on him. Until Ryan's back on his feet, there's not a whole lot we can do, and we could all use some sleep."

I was relieved when everyone agreed with the Alpha, although it was almost another hour before Dad and my grandparents left with Sam. Dalton and his pack stayed and stood guard over Ryan, which my wolf was grateful for.

With so many others around, others she believed wanted to keep Ryan safe, we were able to sleep.

---

HUNGER WOKE ME. Ryan's scent filled my nose, and it was tempting to fall back asleep, but the nearby presence of so many other Fenerec roused my wolf and put her on edge. The males slept on the living room carpet, their snores and fainter whistles filling the silence between horns honking on the busy streets outside.

I wiggled out of Ryan's arms, worked my way to the edge of the couch cushion, and jumped down to the floor. The landing jarred my bones, and my sore muscles protested. Ignoring the ache, I dodged around the sleepers littering the floor and padded my way into the kitchen.

Staring up at the refrigerator and distant cupboards, I understood the pleading stares of dogs far too well. If I wanted food, I needed hands. My wolf agreed, but if she knew how to begin the painful transformation process, she didn't reveal the secret.

Since wishful thinking wasn't going to satisfy my stomach and I wasn't quite hungry enough to resort to cannibalism, I explored Ryan's apartment, nosing open doors and breathing in the scents.

His presence was strongest in the bedroom. I nosed the door closed and sat, huffing my annoyance at my ignorance. Ryan and the other Fenerec had no difficulties shifting shapes, and while he had assured me it would take time and practice, feeling so helpless and small was driving me to the end of my patience.

All I wanted was breakfast—and coffee.

Coffee could fix anything, or at least make it tolerable. I had so many questions and no way to ask them, which didn't help my mood in the slightest. I wanted to return to work and retreat to the comfortable familiarity of my life.

Until Harthel was dealt with, I'd worry about everyone around me. The man had used me to hurt my father once, and I had no doubts he'd try to do something again. I had no idea what I could do about the Fenerec behind the bombing of La Guardia, but I'd ask as soon as I was a human again.

But how?

When Ryan forced me to shift, he always looked me in the eyes. A split second before the pain began, there had been a tugging in my head. Closing my eyes, I focused on my memories of transformation, tensing in anticipation of my bones breaking and muscles snapping.

My wolf whined her hunger and impatience in my head, and I voiced a growl at the distraction. The noises I made only served to reinforce the fact I was no longer human.

If I managed to shift, I would be one step closer to being able to resume my life. It could be done. My family had proven that much to me.

While Dad wasn't a Fenerec—a werewolf—his parents were, and they had hidden the truth from me all my life. What else didn't I know?

The life of a Fenerec seemed brutal and dangerous. If they had lied about being human, leaving me in the dark about the reality of their life, what else had they hidden from me?

I blamed my worries on my inability to unlock the trick of transformation. Shame at my failure to become human drove me into hiding under Ryan's bed, and the fear of doing something I would regret while a wolf kept me there.

## TWENTY-ONE

*Overcoming limitations had been an integral part of my life.*

---

OVERCOMING LIMITATIONS HAD BEEN an integral part of my life before the bombing of La Guardia airport. My inability to become human was another failure in a string of them, and I hated myself for my helplessness and ignorance. Anger and frustration boiled in my veins, and my wolf retreated, wary of the rage kindling under my skin.

If I couldn't control which shape I took, how could I regain any control over my life? How could I do anything? I would be a risk to those around me. Ryan didn't seem to mind, but Dad had been convinced I would hurt him before I learned how to control myself.

I had hurt Dad enough. I wanted to go home, where everything was normal—except there was nothing normal waiting for me at home.

My grandparents were Fenerec, too, and Dad knew far more about the supernatural than I ever had believed possible.

The hardest day at work was far easier than trying to adapt to life as a Fenerec. Despite being aware of my wolf and her impulses, I couldn't control them—or her. How long would it be before she took control of me?

Worse, how long would it be until she ate away at my humanity? Knowing Ryan would one day fade away and be killed as a dangerous, uncontrolled beast was bad enough. The fear he'd be killed stabbed me deep.

The solution seemed so simple but so difficult at the same time. A pack would solve everything, but as long as Ryan feared being constrained and restricted, there was nothing I could do.

I had given my word, and I already regretted it. If I couldn't master transforming between wolf and human, I had no hope of doing anything to help him, no matter how much I wanted to.

There were shoe boxes and storage containers under the bed, and I hid among them, curling up so I could tuck my nose under my tail. I still hungered, but I didn't want anyone to see my failure, to see me unable to do as they did, shifting at will despite the pain of transforming.

It was a lot easier to pretend I wasn't afraid of my inadequacies when I stood on two feet, could speak, and take care of myself. How could I protect Ryan from those who would cage him if I couldn't handle life as a Fenerec—as a werewolf?

What could I do?

Nothing.

---

I HAD no idea how he did it, but Ryan found me with ease, snaking his arm between the boxes to grab hold of my scruff. With a triumphant huff, he pulled me out from beneath the bed. "What are you doing?"

I pinned my ears and bared my teeth at him.

Unperturbed by my display of aggression, Ryan set me on the middle of the bed and flopped onto the mattress beside me. "I sent the others away for a while. They'll be back tonight with your father. I suggested it might be wise to give you a chance to make yourself at home before they come stomping in your territory."

I sighed.

"You're upset. Ah, you want to shift?" Shaking his head, Ryan gave my head and ears a brisk rub. "Don't be so hard on yourself. It could be several months before you get the hang of it. It took me almost six months to shift without someone helping me. Once you get the hang of it, you'll be able to influence other Fenerec to shift, too. It's easier for dominants."

I sighed again.

"We'll talk about it once you're human again."

Ryan took hold of my muzzle and forced me to look him in the eye. A sense of something being tugged in my head was all the warning I had before the pain of shifting took hold. When it finally faded, I panted to catch my breath.

Sweat covered me, and I shivered in the room's cool air. Ryan leaned over me and pressed his lips to the side of my neck. My body relaxed under his touch.

"I'll make you something to eat. There are sweats that should fit in the dresser. I'll be in the kitchen if you need me."

It was tempting to stay nestled in the blankets. While my wolf's presence remained in my head, she dozed. I trembled from the aftermath of transformation, but I worked up the willpower to crawl out of bed and dig through the dresser for a pair of sweats.

Black and grays dominated the collection, although one of the gray hues seemed brighter the rest. I picked the set and pulled it on. Stifling a yawn, I headed for the kitchen.

Ryan dumped a cutting board's worth of meat into a frying pan. He glanced at me out of the corner of his eye, flashed me a smile, and returned to his work.

"What color is this?" I asked, gesturing to the sweats.

"Neon pink."

I stared down at the shirt and plucked at

the soft fabric. While the hue—*color*—seemed bright, I had been under the impression neon colors could blind with their intensity. "You have neon pink sweats?"

"I try to keep a collection of clothing suitable for all ages and genders; makes it easier when another Fenerec comes calling. We tend to destroy clothing."

"I thought neon colors were a lot brighter than this."

"It's bright." Ryan picked up a bottle next to the sink and held it up. "What color do you see?"

"Gray."

"It's bright blue. Pinks are a part of the red spectrum. I avoid the color red usually." Ryan set the bottle down, looked around the kitchen, and held up a knife. "Do you see any color?"

I shook my head.

"It's yellow. Give it time. Maybe you're not really seeing the actual color yet. We can do some experiments later if you'd like. I hope you like stew. I'm a one-trick pony when it comes to the kitchen."

"I don't mind stew." I was hungry enough I would've considered eating the meat raw. "Want any help?"

"There are potatoes in the cabinet there." Ryan pointed. "Ten should do."

Despite knowing how much I could eat, the potatoes hammered home how becoming a Fenerec had changed me. Before, one would have filled me. Instead of complaining about it, I rinsed them in the sink. "Skins on?"

"Please."

I found a second cutting board near the knives. Content with having a task, I went to work, chopping while Ryan watched the meat. The silence comforted me, as did the knowledge I didn't have to speak.

My questions could wait until I figured out what I *needed* to know first. Unfortunately, I had no idea where to begin. My ignorance felt limitless, and every question I had led to twenty others.

Starting somewhere was better than spinning my wheels going nowhere fast. "You don't like the color red?"

"I see too much blood as it is."

I swallowed and nodded my understanding. There had been so much blood at La Guardia, although to my eyes, it had been charcoal rather than red. Did color make such a terrible thing even worse?

"This Inquisition wants us to deal with the people responsible for what happened at La Guardia, don't they?"

"Yes."

"How?"

Ryan poked and prodded at the meat in the frying pan. "I'll probably work with the FBI on this. We'll look for information on where they went, why they did it, and then we'll eliminate them so they don't kill anyone else. I'm an operative, which is a nice way of saying I'm a hired killer—an assassin. As long as you're with me, that's what you'll be, too."

My wolf stirred at the doubt in Ryan's voice. I sniffed, and my wolf pinpointed the unease in his scent. "So there won't be a formal trial?"

"No. Part of my job is to verify guilt."

"If no one is supposed to know what we are, how can you work with the FBI?"

"The Inquisition runs portions of the FBI, that's how. The upper management are all in the know or are Inquisitors. It's part of how we have managed to keep the supernatural hidden for so long. The Inquisition is involved at all levels of government."

I frowned, staring at the cutting board. "All levels? How high up?"

"The Inquisition cultivates people for politics, but their primary focus is on law enforcement, the Supreme Court, and the military. While there are Fenerec politicians, they're usually local-level. It's difficult to hide our nature when we're too close to the top. Most Inquisition politicians are witches."

"So the people behind La Guardia will die."

"Yes."

I nodded, clenched my teeth, and lifted my chin. "And we're going to be the ones who do it."

"Yes."

While I had never been a supporter of the death penalty, I remembered too well how many had been killed or suffered as a result of the explosions, myself included. If it hadn't been for Ryan, I would have died.

Death seemed too easy of a way out, too gentle of a punishment for those who would ruin so many lives. My wolf growled in my head.

She didn't speak with words, but I felt her desire to obtain justice for those who had been hurt and killed. "I'm under the impression it's hard to kill one of us. How are we going to do it?"

"We heal faster and live longer than humans, but a bullet to the head will kill us. Silver will, too. Some exposure to silver isn't lethal, but a silver bullet often is. They don't penetrate as far as standard rounds. Unless they're removed, they'll kill a Fenerec. The older the silver, the faster it kills. Age matters when it comes to silver. An older Fenerec is more resistant to silver, so the bullet has to be forged of older metal, preferably an heirloom of some sort—something that's been passed down through several generations."

Ryan's emotionless tone bothered me almost as much as the fact he refused to look up from the frying pan.

The scent of his discomfort and anxiety strengthened. "Anything else?"

"Broken necks will kill younger Fenerec; older ones will recover, but it takes a long time. Blood loss and extreme trauma can be fatal, too. The older the Fenerec, the harder they are to kill."

"You hate it, don't you?"

"I hate I have to do it. The fact it is necessary, the fact there are Fenerec who would lower themselves to such levels, that's what I hate. I look forward to killing the ones who hurt you. This is a hunt I want." Ryan exhaled, long and loud. "I didn't want to expose you to this part of my life like this."

"Do you kill people who don't deserve it? Innocent people?"

"No!"

I set my knife down and crossed my arms over my chest. "So, you're killing people who deserve it?"

"Yes."

"So they won't do it again? Hurt others?"

Ryan nodded.

"And you thought I'd have a problem with this?"

"Yes."

"Guess what? I don't. The only thing I'm going to have a problem with is if you tell me I can't help, or if you try to tell me I'm a good girl and I shouldn't worry my pretty head over it. If I can help, I expect to help. I am not the type of woman who will be happy if you sideline me for no reason. If I have to watch you run off and go to your mountain on your own so you can get the space you need, then you have to deal with me helping you however I can. Fine, I don't know how to use a gun. I'll learn. I'll do whatever you need me to do, just don't stop me." I picked up the knife and went back to work cutting up potatoes. "If you're expecting some stay-at-home woman, you've got the wrong girl."

"Trust me, I noticed. I noticed in the airport when you worked so hard to help the other victims. I noticed when you tore your feet to strips because you wouldn't take those shoes of yours off until there was nothing left for you to do. I don't want a trophy. I want a partner."

So did I. Satisfied we had found an understanding, I decided to cut to the chase. "Will I be able to return to work?"

Ryan took the frying pan off the burner and set it aside before turning to me. "Of course. Becoming a Fenerec doesn't mean you have to give up your life. It'll change it a bit—okay, a lot—but you'll be able to do everything you used to. I'll have to travel as needed, but I'll deal with that when it happens."

"How often does the Inquisition have you work?"

"I've been working on this pack problem for three months. They're good—too good. After the attack on the airport, they dropped off the map. Since we were trapped, I wasn't able to track them. With the scale of the attack, we'll have official FBI resources to draw on. Sinclair's pack should be enough firepower to get the job done. Normally, I prefer to do my hits in a dark, quiet alley and get rid of the evidence before anyone knows someone was killed. We've been in a holding pattern waiting for a break in the case."

I clacked my teeth together. "That changed because of me, didn't it?"

"It gave the Inquisition an excuse to call Sinclair. With a full pack on the hunt, it's a lot safer. Sinclair's pack can do a lot of the heavy work while I plan the hit."

"How can I help?"

"That's what I'm not sure of yet. With Harthel, it's easier; you'll be the bait. You'll lure him out so I can deal with him."

"We can deal with him," I corrected, narrowing my eyes.

Ryan scowled, sighed, and nodded. "We will deal with him. Sinclair will probably insist on helping, too. He's unhappy about what happened when you were under his guard."

"I was not under his guard."

"To him you were. You'll have to get used to that. Alpha males are all the same; they're protective, especially around children and young women. You were in his company, and you were hurt because he wasn't able to stop Harthel. Not all Alphas are as serious about it as Sinclair, but that's one of the reasons I like him even though he annoys me."

I had the feeling Ryan disliked all Alphas, and I was reminded of his reaction to my willingness to let him have the space he needed to be happy. I understood.

"All right. What if I can't figure out the trick to shifting?"

"You will."

"That doesn't help me now. Dad's acting like I'm going to hurt him, and he's okay with it." My frustration bled into my voice. "How am I supposed to deal with that?"

"Until you control your wolf's impulses, he'll probably get bitten a few times. It's pretty normal. Fenerec-born are tough. He can handle it."

"I don't want to bite anyone!"

Ryan scowled.

"Except you?" I corrected. "See? This is just what I'm talking about. It's okay for me to bite you. That's…"

"Not what you're used to?"

I nodded.

"We bite. I'll bite you. You'll bite me. You'll bite other Fenerec when you get into dominance battles with them. You'll get bitten, too. Honestly, I'm surprised Sinclair hasn't bitten you yet—he could have instead of grabbing hold of your neck with his hand when you were nipping at my cabin."

"Is there an instruction manual for being a Fenerec? I could use one."

"What do you want to know? Just ask."

"Before I knew it was my grandmother, why did I dislike her being there so much? I've never really cared what other women did until now."

"Competition for the only available male

around. Until you and your wolf feel comfortable and secure no one is going to steal me from you, your hackles will go up any time another female comes by. The more dominant the female, the more protective she is over her male, especially if he's less dominant than she is. Usually, females partner with more dominant males, so these instincts are reversed; normally, I'd be the one bristling around other males."

So it's normal for me to feel so possessive?"

"I'd be worried if you weren't."

I dumped all the cut potatoes into a bowl and handed them to Ryan, who in turn dumped them into a large stock pot along with the meat. "Grandmother seemed confident we're a couple. Why?"

Once the stew was situated to his liking, Ryan tapped the side of his nose. "You'll learn to identify when a Fenerec is mated from scent. Right now, you're probably still having trouble sorting out specific signatures. Mated Fenerec carry their partner's scent, so other Fenerec can tell with a few sniffs. So, in a subtle way, you smell like me, and I smell like you. Your grandmother has been a Fenerec long enough she knew right away. You'll probably start detecting subtle scents in a few weeks; most Fenerec pick it up within days of the ritual, but most don't undergo the ritual when they are as sick as you were. That affects things."

"Do I have to do anything to keep it that way?" I demanded.

Ryan laughed. "While I'm tempted to say otherwise to lure you into having your way with me, no. You're mine, I'm yours, and there's nothing anyone can do about it, not without drastic measures."

"What drastic measures?"

"We die or someone uses magic to break our bond." Ryan's mouth thinned to a line. "That's also part of what I do for the Inquisition. I hunt down those who would use that sort of magic and rid the Earth of them. No matter what anyone tells you, Matia, understand this: there's nothing good about a necromancer or a sorcerer, and don't ever let anyone try to convince you otherwise. One steals secrets from the dead and uses the bodies however they see fit. Sorcerers harvest pain, suffering, fear, and all other negative emotions and use them to fuel their magic. They can also steal away a victim's will and life, making it their own. I have met a sorcerer once, and I hope I never do again."

TWENTY-TWO

Secrecy reigned supreme.

THE WORLD HID a lot of secrets, and while the Fenerec topped the list, witches came a close second. While breakfast cooked, Ryan cleaned and told me about the types of people he killed, the conditions required for an execution order to be issued, and the rare circumstances when someone might avoid death.

Ryan and I fit in as the rare exceptions. Since he had violated only one taboo, prevented other Normals from witnessing his deed, and secured my cooperation, we weren't a risk to the Inquisition and the supernatural community as a whole.

Until the day the supernatural could live openly among Normals, secrecy reigned supreme.

I still had too many questions. Determined to be less of a liability, I asked, "Can you explain why it's okay to be a Fenerec or a witch, but it's dangerous to be both?"

"Balance of power. Fenerec witches have two types of power. Fenerec are strong, fast, and difficult to kill. Witches can control a Fenerec's stronger impulses, balancing the human and wolf halves. Depending on the type, witches have other powers, too. Witches align with the four elements. Put them together, and you have a very potent combination. Once upon a time, Fenerec with witch powers were kept under close guard. Caged. Fenerec with witch powers began hiding their abilities to prevent themselves from being imprisoned, let out only when the Inquisition needed them. That ended some fifty years ago or so—I was a puppy back then."

"What changed?"

Ryan paced the length of the kitchen, pausing to check on the stew. "Fenerec with witch powers are a lot more useful to the Inquisition when they cooperate willingly. They're becoming more common, but knowingly turning a witch into a Fenerec is as close to taboo as it gets without technically being one. Witches run a high risk of losing control of their powers when they become a Fenerec. If the witch doesn't already have control of their powers, becoming a Fenerec can have destructive—possibly lethal—consequences."

Something didn't add up; I remembered Dalton talking to Ryan about me, hinting I had been something before becoming a Fenerec. Every now and then, I caught a glimpse of the shadows surrounding people, shadows I had seen long before I had met Ryan.

"What if I'm something else, too?"

For the first time since we had started the discussion, Ryan grinned at me. "Don't worry. Even if you are, you'll be given a chance to prove yourself—or learn how to control your powers should you have them."

"I see things," I confessed.

"When I first met you, I smelled smoke on you—not like cigarette smoke; it's more like wood smoke in the winter. It's a sign of a fire witch. The stronger the witch, the stronger the scent. Talented, sensitive witches can learn to mask the scent, but it takes time and practice. Fenerec witches, ironically enough, are usually the best at hiding their nature. Fire witches are often sensors. They see things, usually auras. You're the first color-blind witch I've met, though."

I stared at him, my mouth gaping open. "Then I'm a witch? There are other people who can see things, too? You knew?"

"Harthel wasn't the one who torched the cabin he had you in. It was you. He probably put you in the tub, but then you shifted, and when you shifted for the first time, you manifested your witch powers. Fire witchcraft is common, but it's often dangerous. There are few truly powerful fire witches. Why? They combust. Those instances of self-combustion that sometimes crop up? Fires with unknown causes that kill one person? Often a fire witch losing control of their powers during their first manifestation. You survived. That's all that matters. After initial manifestation, it often takes a new witch two or three months to recover enough to begin training."

My wolf whined in my head, and her worry bled into me.

"I burned the cabin down?"

"Too much too soon?" Ryan grimaced. "I know a lot about witches because it's my job to deal with them if one goes rogue. I can't teach you how to control your powers; another witch will have to—or you'll figure it out on your own. Many do, once they manifest."

"But I've always seen those shadows." I heard the whining quality of my voice, swallowed, and lifted my chin. "I refuse to be a liability."

Ryan chuckled and checked on the stew again. "You'll be fine. You have me to help you, and I can help prevent you from manifesting again."

"You can?"

"Breakfast first, then I'll show you."

※

I HAD to be more careful about underestimating Ryan. If preventing accidental manifestation of witchcraft involved exhausting us both, his idea of spending the day in bed would work. He contented me and my wolf, and without her whining anxiously in my head every other minute, I was also able to relax.

"However much I enjoyed that, I don't think that's appropriate if I have a problem in, say, the grocery store," I pointed out, snuggling up against Ryan's back to enjoy his warmth.

"I have other ways, but they're not nearly as much fun," he admitted.

"What other sort of ways?"

"Since you're a Fenerec, I'd just pinch the nerve in your neck. The pain would be enough to break your concentration. If you're completely uncontrolled, I'd have to knock you out or use wolfsbane."

"Wolfsbane. You mentioned that before—you used it in the airport? Am I remembering that right?"

"Yes. When I was certain you weren't doing well, I slipped it in a water bottle and gave it to you. It's an herb, and it can control Fenerec. I don't like using it, but if I need to control another Fenerec, that's the best way to do it. It makes it almost impossible to disobey an order. It's our bane because it takes away our will. That'll be part of your training. You'll need to experience wolfsbane, learn its symptoms, and learn to protect yourself if you're dosed with it." Ryan stretched. "In a way, you're fortunate. You're going to be dominant enough you won't need to use things like wolfsbane to protect yourself. You'll go toe to toe against other Fenerec and beat them by the force of your will alone."

"Do you use wolfsbane on other Fenerec?"

"Whenever possible. I try to prevent unnecessary deaths. Wolfsbane helps me do that. Sometimes the Inquisition will consider alternative punishments. I try to make those happen as often as possible."

Ryan sighed, and I pressed my nose to his throat and breathed in his scent. While I didn't want to hurt anyone, I couldn't deny there were a few I wanted to kill, including Harthel.

"I have a confession."

Ryan tensed. "What?"

My wolf's influence explained my blood thirst, although wanting to rip a man's throat out with my teeth unnerved the human half of me. "I want to kill Harthel for what he did. Not just to me, but to Dad. He did it to hurt Dad."

With a soft laugh, Ryan pulled away and rolled over to face me. "That's what Sinclair and his pack are coming over later to discuss. We're going to figure out how to lure the bastard out and put an end to him. He picked the wrong family to attack, and the Inquisition doesn't appreciate when safe holdings for Fenerec are compromised; your company is one of four major corporations in the United States set up to handle witches and Fenerec."

"I had no idea."

"That's the beauty of it; you weren't supposed to know. Your father knew, of course. Young Fenerec-born often share instincts with their Fenerec parents, and from my understanding, he founded your company when he adopted you. Fenerec and Fenerec-born parents tend to be very protective of children. It's stronger among Fenerec than Fenerec-born. It's actually a way the Inquisition tracks down potential rogues—ones who need to be brought in, taught, and safeguarded. They look at teachers, doctors, nurses—anyone who would be in a position to help children. It's Fenerec instinct to protect the young and helpless, so rogues naturally gravitate towards those professions."

I blinked. "And the Inquisition is okay with that? Aren't—I was under the impression we're, well, dangerous."

"We are. A Fenerec responsible for the care of children tends to be more stable. While we look like wolves, we aren't, not really. We share some instincts with wolves, but we're different. We're built different, too. For example, our fur is denser, especially under our throats. We have dense bone and muscle structure. We try to hide Fenerec bodies, especially in wolf shape, because we're different. We'd give scientists a field day. As humans, we're different, but it's easier to hide the abnormalities."

I had never been too interested in biology, but as long as Ryan was willing to talk, I'd ask him questions. If he was anything like me—and I knew he was—he'd get tired of talking, and I wouldn't want to intrude on his desire for silence. "What sort of abnormalities?"

"Blood production, for one. Fenerec regenerate blood cells a great deal faster than standard humans. Our bones have more marrow to account for the need for more blood. We have better circulatory systems, too—more developed. We also regenerate cells humans can't. For example, your vision. Optic nerves in humans don't regenerate, not normally. Ours do. Our brain cells also regenerate, so it's possible for a Fenerec to recover from otherwise lethal damage. A Fenerec has to be very old to survive a bullet to the head, though."

"How old?"

"No one is really sure. It varies. Any Fenerec in their puppy coat can't survive a broken neck; it takes up to ten to twenty years for survival to be likely. A severed spine is a different matter altogether; thirty or more years seems to be the average."

"The Inquisition has studied this?" I blurted.

"Experience."

I grimaced at the weariness in Ryan's voice. "I'm sorry."

"Don't be. It's not your fault. I don't like what I do, but I'm the best one for the job."

"Why?"

Ryan sighed. "It's because I'm submissive.

For those Fenerec who are borderline, who might be saved, I'm the difference between life or death for them. That's why I do it. If I can save even one, it's worth it."

I understood, and because I did, I nodded and said nothing.

---

DAD AND SAM were the first to arrive, and they brought several bags full of my clothes with them. Leaving Ryan to fend for himself, I dragged them to the bedroom, kicked the door closed, and changed. Maybe becoming a Fenerec would someday heal my eyes, but I'd have to risk a mismatching outfit until that day came.

Several of my blouses had the oddity Ryan assured me was some form of red. Mindful of his discomfort around the color, I stuffed them back into a bag and picked a darker gray shirt to go with my jeans. In the bottom of one of the bags, I found my jewelry box. On a whim, I pulled out the biggest necklace I had, a gaudy ensemble of random beads and baubles making up multiple strands.

When I joined the others, the sitting room was packed with people, including Dalton, Gavin, and others from Dalton's pack.

Ryan caught sight of me, squeezed his way through the crowd, and leaned down to rest his forehead on my shoulder. "Why are there so many of them?"

Anxiety soured his scent, and I narrowed my eyes, glaring at the group. "Cannon fodder."

A strained laugh slipped out of my mate. "So we throw them at the rogue pack and clean up the mess?"

"We make them do the work while we take the credit. I think that's a suitable use for them since they're in your home." My stomach gurgled in demand. "They should order food for us, too."

"Your appetite will settle down in a month or two." Ryan sighed and nuzzled the side of my throat before straightening. "Do you like pizza?"

Hunger bit at my stomach, and I was horrified over how fast I had gone from fine to starving. "If it's edible, I like it. I'll even try sushi if it means we can eat."

"Did you forget to feed her this morning?" Dalton clucked his tongue. "She might eat you if you forget to feed her."

"Despite what you might think, we had breakfast."

I scowled at Dalton. "We had stew."

"Do you know how to cook anything other than stew, Ryan?" Dalton sighed and dug into his pocket for a phone. "Gavin, while I take care of this, get the files ready. We have a lot to go over tonight."

Gavin grabbed a pair of briefcases from beside the door and took them to the kitchen island, setting them on the counter. "We've managed to get some good information on the rogue pack, and we've also gotten some good leads on this Harthel fellow."

My nose warned me of my Dad's rage moments before I became aware of the dark shadow surrounding him. "I have people working to get everything we have on Chuck at our office, too. I should have the information in the morning."

Dad's scent betrayed his emotions, but his voice remained calm and cool.

"If I might give a piece of advice, Mr. Evans?" Pausing long enough for Dad to nod, Gavin continued, "Call the man Harthel—or something less personal. If you end up in a position to pull the trigger, distancing makes it easier. Hesitating even for a moment could get you killed."

The thought of Dad being anywhere near Harthel horrified me. The man had been ready to kill me—almost had—and I had no doubt he would kill Dad given a single chance. I clenched my teeth together so I wouldn't say anything without thinking about the situation first.

Harthel wanted revenge; Dad would have to defend himself, no matter how much the idea of him being in harm's way bothered me. Acknowledging the fact Harthel might try something would give us time to prepare.

No matter how much I didn't like the possibility of Harthel going after Dad, Gavin's advice made a sickening amount of sense.

"Harthel's going to get a very unpleasant surprise if he thinks he can come after me." Dad unbuttoned his suit jacket and held it open. "One day someone will come up with a shoulder holster that isn't uncomfortable to wear."

Gavin circled my father, examining the holster and gun. "That won't do you any good if you have to unbutton your jacket to get at it."

"I'm a decent shot and quick enough on the draw. I'm more worried about Matia. She's never been interested in guns and has never wanted to take self-defense courses."

The thought of Dad with a gun, a man who had trouble enough walking across a room, worried me. "Aren't you going to shoot yourself when you trip over your own feet?"

Dad glared at me. "It's very improbable."

"I didn't know you knew how to use a gun." I frowned, wondering when he had found the time to learn.

"Let's just say I've spent an ungodly amount of time at the range after what happened at La Guardia." Shaking his head, Dad buttoned his jacket before reaching for one of the briefcases. "It's been long enough I had to qualify."

"Who qualified you?" Gavin asked.

"Some witch the Inquisition sent over from the west coast. She didn't give her name and I didn't ask for it. Mean one, though. All business."

Dalton joined us with a snort. "You know the Inquisition means business when they send one of their qualifiers from the west coast. If you didn't qualify, you would have gotten the three-day special until you did."

"Three-day special?" I asked.

"What you're going to enjoy in the next few days," the Alpha informed me.

Ryan tensed, sucking in a breath. "Please tell me you're not serious."

"Of course I'm serious. You don't think I'm going to let you take anyone out with you who isn't qualified, do you? Maybe you're coordinating the hit, but I'm responsible for each and every person involved. She qualifies before she's involved." Taking a seat at the counter, Dalton grabbed the second briefcase and popped it open. "If it makes you feel any better about it, you're expected to attend and qualify. I thought that would be suitably annoying to count as punishment for your recent behavior. The Inquisition didn't like my version of a wrist slap and demanded something quantifiable. This counted."

"Aren't I supposed to be a risk to those around me until I learn how to handle being a Fenerec?"

"This will help you—"

"I'm in." I pulled up a stool and sat next to Dad, peeking at the stack of papers in the briefcase. "What sort of information do we have to work with?"

"About half of what I want," Dalton admitted. "We have basics on financials, basic criminal records, and telephone records. We're missing a lot of history, including education, job records, and so on. While we can start a basic profiling from this, we're going to need to wait a few days for the results of the investigation to come down from the FBI."

Financials I understood; money left a trail, and those trails often led interesting places. Harthel had been planning something, and I was eager to discover what. "Dad and I are probably best off looking over the financials." I paused, glaring at my father out of the corner of my eye. "Unless you have any other hidden super powers I don't know about?"

Dad rolled up the sheets he was looking at and swatted my arm with them. "Watch it, young lady. All I have to do to make your life miserable is suggest to your grandmother various ways to ensure a wedding in the near future—one she can plan."

My face burned from embarrassment. "Dad!"

"She has to ask me to marry her first for that to be a legitimate threat, Mr. Evans," Ryan added.

"Normal men would be bribing me to let them have a chance with my daughter."

"Actually, if we're being traditional, you would establish a dowry and pay me to take her off your hands, Mr. Evans," Ryan countered.

I sighed, slumped over the counter, and rested my head on my arms.

"That's true. Cows, goats, or sheep, right? If I really want to get rid of her, I have to provide an entire herd. No wonder that tradition went away. It'd cost a fortune to provide her husband with an entire herd of cows. Where would I find one nowadays?"

Ryan cleared his throat, and in a mild tone, replied, "I believe they call them farms, Mr. Evans."

"She cost me a fortune to feed even before she became a Fenerec. Maybe I should offer him an entire farm. What do you think, Dalton?"

Dalton laughed. "A farm would be a wise investment. However, if you purchase one and put it into Inquisition care, you'd be paid back for your investment over time, have access to livestock for your daughter and her mate, and provide a livelihood for Inquisitors unable to work in the traditional job force."

I sighed. "Can we get back to serious business?"

"Feeding a bitch is serious business, Miss Evans," Dalton replied. "Do I need to remind you that you ate the equivalent of half a cow on your own yesterday?"

My shock didn't last long before it transitioned to horror. "I didn't eat that much, did I?"

"I just ordered thirty extra large pizzas. I'm having my doubts it will be enough. It'll get better in a month or two. Until then, Ryan's going to have his hands full keeping you happy."

"I hope you realize I have a savings account and can, in fact, afford to feed myself, right?"

Dad sighed and swatted me with the rolled up papers again. "I taught you better than that. You're supposed to be robbing me blind. Get your head in the game, young lady. This is your dowry we're discussing here."

"Better request two farms, Ryan," I declared, snatching the papers out of Dad's hand. "There better be a good house on the property, too. And horses. I've always wanted a horse."

Dalton grimaced. "Most livestock don't like us very much, Matia. That includes horses."

"So find me a horse that can put up with me. One for Ryan, too. They better be good, expensive horses, too." I paused, glancing at Ryan. "Horses are not for eating. They're for riding."

Ryan smiled and held his hands up in surrender. "Do you even know how to take care of a horse?"

"No, but both of my farms will have people who take care of the animals. Dad can start a new business dedicated to making my farms profitable."

With a sigh, Dad shook his head. "I should have kept my mouth shut."

Satisfied I had won the discussion, I turned my attention to the papers, smoothing them out. "Let's get back to business, shall we?"

I needed to learn as much as possible about the Fenerec able and willing to kill so many innocent people so I could help Ryan get rid of them—permanently.

## TWENTY-THREE

*Maybe I'm colorblind, but I'm not blind.*

---

DALTON CLAIMED the papers from both briefcases and went to work organizing them into seven stacks. While I waited, I breathed in deep, taking the time to make sense of the smells filling my nose. I had the easiest time identifying Ryan's markers; my wolf recognized him, which made it easier learning who was who from smell alone.

Identifying Dad's scent took the most work; the Fenerec drowned him out. I gave up trying to pick out Sam from the others. Even when I could catch a whiff of something, something my wolf believed came from the human, it slipped away before I could commit it to memory.

Dalton's scent bothered me, as the strength of it dominated everyone else's, including mine. If anything, the Alpha's presence made it hard for me to pick out my own scent because the spice of our wolves was somehow similar.

Once I figured out who was who, I focused on the subtle tones associated with everyone. Ryan's anxiety put my wolf on edge, making her want to drive the other males away from our territory so he could relax. Dad's anger bothered me, although the dark shadows surrounding him had faded to wispy smoke; some laughter and distraction would blow it to tatters without much work on my part.

From the others, I detected the eagerness of the hunt and anticipation. None of them betrayed their emotions, which intrigued me. On the surface, everyone remained calm.

I wondered what I smelled like to the other Fenerec. Did my impatience alter my scent?

Could their sensitive noses detect Ryan's scent on me? We had spent so much time together my nose could no longer pinpoint where his scent ended and mine began. My wolf liked the mingling of our spice.

"All right. Before I go into this, we have other things to discuss. Gavin, take notes." Dalton hopped onto the counter, picked up a sheet of paper, and slid it to me. "I'll start with you, Miss Evans. Have you ever seen any of these men before?"

Twelve photographs stapled to the paper showed white men in their mid-twenties. I shook my head and passed the sheet over to Dad, who took it, and after a moment of thought, also shook his head.

"These are the Fenerec we've identified as part of the pack responsible for the La Guardia bombing. There are more of them, but these twelve were spotted at the airport prior to the explosions. Before we continue, I want to build a timeline of the events from your perspectives. We're aware of the timing for our companies beginning the negotiation process, so we can skip over that. Start with when you were planning the trip to London."

"I know nothing. I knew we had a business meeting, but *someone* neglected to tell me we were going to London until we were on route to the airport."

Dad cleared his throat, and the darkness surrounding him dissipated. "But it's so much fun catching you by surprise, Matia. You wouldn't deny me my fun, would you?"

Instead of answering, I stared at him.

"Mr. Evans?"

Sighing, Dad pulled out his phone and went through his calendar. "Most times, I curse myself for the day I insisted it be company policy for everyone to note in their calendars when the arrangements for a meeting were made at the same time the meeting is scheduled. It's an extra step in the process. Lots view it as unnecessary calendar clutter. Then, something like this happens, and knowing the whens along with the whys makes things so much easier. I notified Harthel and Annamarie of the London scheduling two weeks prior to our flight. Annamarie booked the flight two days later; Harthel had scheduled a meeting in California the same day as our trip to London, so instead of taking the corporate jet, we went commercial. Was cheaper for the company, too; operational costs for an overseas flight are astronomical."

Gavin jotted notes down on the paper in front of him. "When did Harthel know he was going to California?"

"The same day he booked the plane." Dad slid his phone to Gavin. "That has the entirety of Harthel's schedule, Matia's, and mine merged together. My itinerary is in blue, his is in orange, and Matia's is gray."

"Fitting." Gavin took the phone, scrolling through the entries. "Harthel had a lot of phone appointments compared to you. If the calendar is to be believed, Miss Evans was seen and never heard."

I turned my glare on Gavin and waited.

"And she doesn't need to say a single word to get the point across," the Fenerec muttered. "That's a potent weapon, Miss Evans."

Dad laughed. "I learned to view her silence as her taking her time sharpening her verbal swords. If Matia's quiet, she's making trouble for someone. Unfortunately for me, she was silent most of the time."

Dalton held his hand out for Dad's phone. Once Gavin handed it over, he went through the calendar. "You must have had quite the time raising her. Interesting; Harthel's booking of the corporate jet was canceled an hour before your commercial flight was scheduled to leave. Do you know why?"

"No. Laura didn't know anything about the California trip. Annamarie handled the booking since it involved the corporate jet; she's the one who handles all issues dealing with the jet and sends authorization for its usage to me. Annamarie said the other party canceled."

"Any chance we can find out the identity of the other party? A reason for cancellation might help, too."

Dad straightened. "Do you think Harthel had something to do with La Guardia? Isn't that a rather large stretch?"

Maybe Dad had always been blind to Harthel's darkness, but I had seen it.

The man had over a billion reasons to want to be rid of us; with us out of the way, Harthel would be in position to inherit a great deal of the company's primary operations. While my grandparents would inherit our liquid assets, someone needed to run Pallodia—Harthel.

At the helm, Harthel would be in a position to gain the company's future wealth, a substantial sum.

I sighed. "He would do it."

Turning to me, Dad frowned. "Matia?"

"Maybe I'm colorblind, but I'm not blind,"

I snapped.

"No one said you were."

I waved my hand. "That doubtful tone. The one you were using. Look, just trust me when I say the man's filth. He'd do it. If he thought he could inherit Pallodia by having us both killed, he would."

Furrows creased Dad's forehead, and he remained silent.

Dalton cleared his throat. "Do you mind explaining your confidence, Miss Evans? I don't doubt you; we've seen exactly what he's capable of—Ryan, especially."

Grimacing, Ryan nodded his agreement. "I look forward to the day I kill him."

I could turn into a wolf, however small and unthreatening; I was no longer human. Was it so far a leap to tell them the truth about what my eyes could see? Swallowing, I stared down at the counter. "I see things."

Dalton leaned towards me. "What sorts of things?"

"Shadows."

"How long have you been able to see these shadows?"

I bit my lip and glanced at Dad out of the corner of my eye.

"I'm not going to be upset with you, Matia," he said, answering my unspoken worries.

Once I spoke, I wouldn't be able to take back the truth; I'd never been like other people. "I've seen them for as long as I can remember; for a long time, you were cloaked in them. Whenever I did something that upset you, they got darker, deeper, and clung to you. When I did well, they faded, then they disappeared altogether. I was ten or twelve or so when they went away. Maybe a little older. Harthel's shadow reaches for people. He's always after you with those dark tentacles."

Dad's eyes widened. "Dark tentacles?"

"There's no doubt about it, Ralph. I'll eat my own tail if she isn't a fire witch, and probably a strong one, at that." Dalton chuckled, slapping his hand against the table. "I'm amazed the scent isn't stronger."

"Scent?" I demanded, sniffing in my effort to discover what he meant.

The Alpha chuckled for a few more moments before grinning at me. "It's really faint, but fire witches smell like wood smoke. Your scent is pretty weak, so I'm not surprised you can't smell it, especially with so many of us in the room. You'll learn to identify smells better with experience."

Ryan slid off his stool, came up behind me, and rested his chin on my shoulder, his hands sliding around my waist. "You smell delicious. Hickory smoke, a little sweet, a lot spicy, and all for me."

Contentment radiated from my wolf, and I leaned back against him. "Should I be worried you're comparing me to barbecue?"

Dalton rolled up a sheet of paper, leaned across the counter, and smacked Ryan upside the head with it. "Stop that. There's no need to defend your claim, Ryan. Sorry, Matia. He might be clingy for a while. Even submissive Fenerec feel a need to stake public claim when they're comfortable in the company they're keeping. As Ryan and his wolf are confident no one is going to challenge him, he's taking the time to establish his position as your mate."

"Pack politics?"

"Exactly. It'd be a lot easier on him if you two did belong to my pack; my word is law, and no one would challenge him for you while I have anything to do with it."

"Challenge him for me?" I felt both my brows rise. "Please."

"Please?"

"You have it backwards, Mr. Sinclair." I narrowed my eyes to slits, watching the Alpha's every move. He sat still, his attention focused fully on me. "Do you really think I'm going to let some pathetic man I don't want touch either one of us? You say I'm a fire witch."

"You are. I've no doubts of it."

While I had no memory of doing it, the possibility I had set Harthel's cabin on fire made me wonder. "I'm a wolf. I will bite them. If that's not enough to drive them away, I will light them on fire. Am I understood?"

Anger would've been an appropriate reaction to my threat, but Dalton smiled. "I don't think you'll have any problems at all. However, I strongly recommend you avoid trying to deliberately light anything—or anyone—on fire. Fire magic can be very dangerous. Most fire witches manifest as seers of auras. In your case, the shadows you were describing. Once your eyes heal, those shadows will probably take on different colors."

"Harthel's shadows are black. It's an absolute, Mr. Sinclair—an absolute I can see without fail. Black is black. White is white. It's the grays in between I struggle with. There's nothing gray about Harthel's shadow. It's the deepest black." The words spilled out of me, and I felt my wolf's encouragement to keep speaking. I hesitated, taking in a breath. "Harthel's shadow reaches for people. I always thought he would contaminate Dad if I let those shadows touch him. I always stepped in the way, whenever I could."

Dalton sucked in a breath. "Those shadows. Did they feel like anything when they touched you?"

Shivering, I lowered my hands to Ryan's, weaving my fingers with his. "Cold."

"I wish you had told me sooner, Matia," Dad confessed. "Had you, I would have had grounds to investigate him."

I shook my head. "I didn't think you'd believe me."

Dalton patted the table loud enough to draw our attention. "She made the right choice, even if it would have changed a lot of things. Normals would have thought she had lost her mind. She had no way of knowing you would have been able to identify what she is. You had no idea she was a fire witch?"

"I always knew she was different; always a little smarter, always had a good feel for people, always was confident about who to trust and who to avoid, but I didn't think she was a witch. There were no other manifestations. I thought she had learned to judge people by watching me." Dad smiled at me before turning to Ryan. "Do yourself a favor. Don't underestimate her. She'll always find a way to surprise you."

Ryan relaxed against me. "I'll keep that in mind."

Despite the suspicious timing of the calendar changes and reservations, I had trouble believing Harthel would stoop so low as to involve himself in a terrorism attack to kill me and Dad. There were lots of ways to kill people—ways that didn't leave hundreds upon hundreds of victims. "Do you really think there's a connection between Harthel and La Guardia?"

"There are a lot of factors we have to consider, Miss Evans." Dalton flipped through the pages and pulled out a single sheet. "First, financing a large-scale attack like the one at La Guardia is expensive—really expensive. It's risky for all parties, which means the mercenaries were being really well paid. Then there's the matter of getting explosives into the airport and past security."

I sucked in a breath. "The explosions after security. Does that mean it was an inside job?"

Dalton nodded. "This has been planned for a long, long time. One of the Fenerec involved in the attack was an airport employee, one with a moderate amount of influence. He could have easily gotten the devices past security, and his position made it possible for him to go to all the terminals while carrying luggage. It would have been trivial for him to meet someone after the security checkpoints to plant the explosives."

"So Harthel's activities are probably a coincidence?" I drummed my fingers on the counters, narrowing my eyes as I considered the board meeting I had infiltrated and crashed, resulting in Harthel's firing. "He was trying to take over the company; that's why I was at the dinner meeting. He had lied to the board in order to shunt Dad out of his position."

Dad shook his head. "It wouldn't have worked, Matia; even if he got the votes to pass his motion—which he wouldn't have—he would have had almost no power as CEO. The position is designed to be crippled substantially for a period of six months following any changes to either of our positions. He would have been a glorified paper shuffler. The real power would have been in the hands of the board, and Harthel wouldn't have had a majority, not like you do."

"That might be relevant information, Mr. Evans." Dalton flipped over one of the sheets, reached over, and grabbed a pen from a briefcase. "What scenario would have given Harthel full operational rights over Pallodia?"

"Our deaths," Dad replied, sitting straighter. "The six month freeze still applies, but after that period is over, he would have taken over full powers as CEO. He would still have the issue of shares; there are quite a few people in the company with more shares, but his positional ranking would put him in the role of CEO."

"Is Harthel aware of the freeze?"

Dad chuckled. "I doubt it. It's buried in the dullest part of the legal paperwork the company lawyer could find. Annamarie knows about it, Human Resources knows, and Legal knows. Harthel would have had many a night of reading legalese to locate it."

"Clever. Where did you come up with that idea?"

When Dad pointed at me, I shrugged. "Don't put the blame on me. I'm not the one who took the advice of a toddler for operating a business."

Ryan snickered, and his breath warmed my throat. "Started early bossing people around, did you?"

"When you have a daughter who might speak a handful of words in a day, you learn to listen when she decides to say something. May you two have one just like her."

Sighing, I shook my head. While my wolf liked the idea of children, especially with Ryan, I ignored her interest. "The reason for the freeze isn't important. I think it's safe to say Harthel had the motivation, but did he have the resources to make the arrangements?"

"That's a good question. I don't have Harthel's financials, but I should be able to get them." Dalton pulled out his phone, dialed a number, and held it to his ear. "I need someone to check Harthel's financials for suspicious activity. Call it within the past two years. Pull everything you can get and send me a copy." Hanging up, he set his phone down and picked up Dad's, scrolling through the calendar. "Without something tying him to the Fenerec pack, it's only speculation. There are a lot of ways to kill a family without wiping out an entire airport. Terrorism is easy to understand; the motive is fear mongering and controlling a populace. Why kill so many to kill you?"

Dad snorted. "That's easy. If he has the resources to make it happen, can get rid of both of us at the same time, and cover his trail so no one can link the attack to him, he's in position to inherit a company worth a substantial amount. After six months, he'd have the power to sell the business for a ridiculously large amount of money. If he's the type of person I think he is now that I've seen what he's willing to do, what's a few hundred lives for that much profit? A hundred million per life, Mr. Sinclair. How's that for motive?"

I grimaced at the casual way Dad put numbers to the deaths of so many people. "Even if Harthel is involved, wouldn't it take a lot longer than two weeks to plan such a thing?"

Shaking his head, Dalton replied, "Two days."

"What?"

"With access to the right materials and someone inside, it'd only take two days to put together an operation like that. The hardest part would be having someone inside to get explosives past the security gates, but if I had someone in position, I could throw together something in two days—hell, two hours if I had the people and the supplies on hand. That's what's so frightening about something like this. It's not hard for a home-grown terrorist to get into position. It's even easier for a Fenerec. We move fast. Ryan, how far do you think you were from the detonation point?"

Ryan tensed against me, and he freed his hands from mine so he could pull me closer to him. "Twenty feet. I saw him drop the bag and run before it detonated. I don't know what happened after that. He probably survived; he made no effort to hide the fact he was on the run. He easily was thirty or more feet away before it blew."

Nodding, Dalton held his hands up in a

helpless gesture. "At twenty feet, Ryan had his clock cleaned and had to dig his way out of the rubble, but emerged relatively unscathed. Humans would have died instantly at that range. Do you have any idea how far away Matia was from the epicenter, Ryan?"

"Maybe fifty to sixty feet," he replied, his grip on me tightening. I wiggled in his hold to ease the pressure on my ribs.

Dalton clacked his teeth together, blowing air out his nose while his cheek twitched. With what I was certain was deliberate care, he pressed his palms to the counter and splayed his fingers. "At that distance, survival was questionable at best, assuming the intel I have on the explosives is correct. The estimates are seventy to eighty feet minimum for high chance of survival. So far, we believe the exits were deliberately destroyed in order to maximize the number of deaths."

"The other victims as close to the detonation point died before help arrived. Matia would have, too." Ryan's distress soured his scent, and I twisted around in his arms, staring at him, at a loss of what to say to soothe him.

I doubted I could; I shivered at the thought of how close to death I had come while my wolf whined in my head. Her anger over how we were forced to become one being for the sake of survival simmered, and I was aware of how she fought to shelter me from her emotions.

"She's practicing her non-existent telepathy skills again," Dad muttered.

I scowled, and a faint smile made an appearance on Ryan's lips. "I find it charming."

"About as charming as her taking photographs of your bare chest?" Sam smirked and joined us at the kitchen island, planting his elbows on the granite countertop. "You're never going to live that one down, Matia. I could have sworn we had taught you the art of subtle objectification."

My face burned.

"I will cherish the memory of her expression when it dawned on her she had been doing just that. Best luck I've had." Ryan's amusement washed away his anxiety, and he relaxed, stepping far enough away from me to flash me a smirk. After a moment, he sucked in a breath, and his eyes widened. "Wait. You two were on route to Mirage's headquarters in London, right?"

I nodded, as did Dad.

"Sinclair, who tipped us off something was going to happen at La Guardia?"

Dalton turned his attention to his phone, tapping at the screen. "I wasn't told. Why are you asking?"

"My cover was to take a flight to Boston. My assignment was that terminal, to those gates."

"Boston? Our flight was to Boston."

"Same flight, then. To my knowledge, there was only one flight to Boston leaving around that time. Can you confirm that, Sinclair?"

After a few taps at his screen, Dalton frowned. "You're right. The next flight out to Boston was three hours later. Anyone catching a connection would have already dealt with security."

Ryan scowled. "It's always the little details that make the most difference. Why was I assigned to their flight?"

"I don't know, but I want to find out. Gavin, get someone on it. While you're at it, pull the full list of Inquisition operatives who were at the airport. Get on the horn with headquarters, and see if you can find out the informant's identity."

Gavin hopped to his feet, excused himself, and headed down the hallway, dialing a number and holding his phone to ear.

Inside jobs, much like the scheme Harthel attempted to pull off to evict Dad from power, plagued many businesses. Pallodia was no exception, although we had taken steps to avoid the consequences of greed.

I hadn't ever considered the fact someone would want to kill me and Dad to take over our company. Harthel hadn't just been willing to kill me; he wanted my death to be as long and painful as possible, documenting it and torturing Dad in the process.

The buzzer announced the arrival of pizza, sparing me from having to answer—or ask—questions. Enough had gone wrong already.

I wasn't sure how much more I could take.

TWENTY-FOUR

*You cost me a fortune to feed.*

---

THE ARRIVAL of pizza delayed the inevitable by thirty minutes. Dad and Sam watched me with open bemusement.

Of the thirty pizzas to enter the apartment, fifteen of them fell to my appetite, and a sixteenth, unmolested by the male Fenerec, tempted me to discover the limits of my stomach. I glared at the still-closed box, my sensitive nose detecting the mouth-watering aroma of warm meat.

"If you're still hungry, eat," Dad ordered, sliding off his stool to retrieve the box. Setting it on the counter, he opened it to reveal a pizza so covered in meat I couldn't spot any cheese on it. "Well, can't say they skimp on the toppings."

"Inquisition-operated pizzeria," Dalton replied, reaching over and grabbing a slice. "Otherwise, we have to send the entire pack out to get two pizzas each from different joints to keep from looking too suspicious. I may have underestimated Miss Evans's appetite, though."

While my wolf grumbled her annoyance over Dalton taking a slice, she approved of Ryan taking a share for himself. "I ate a lot before, too."

Dad snorted. "You cost me a fortune to feed as a child. Maybe I should invest in a livestock farm of my own and sell animals to Ryan at cost. Otherwise, he might not be able to afford to feed you."

"That's entirely unnecessary, Mr. Evans. I can manage."

"While I'm sure you can, Ryan, you don't have to. I can handle my own appetite. Dad, stop instigating, or I'll start submitting proposals to make your life miserable and vote yes—and bribe someone else on the board to likewise vote in my favor." I smiled my sweetest smile in my dad's direction. "I recommend pretending I'm the adult I actually am. If threat of corporate retribution isn't sufficient, I'll just call Grandmother and tell her you're lonely without me and need a woman in your life."

Dad's eyes widened. "You wouldn't."

"Try me."

Dalton chuckled. "You should be congratulated on your successful raising of an intelligent, headstrong woman, Mr. Evans. You've lost this war. Surrender peacefully, and she might take pity on you. For some reason, I have my doubts she will, but she might."

"Back to business." I grabbed a slice of pizza for myself. "We've established Harthel has motive. We have no proof of resources or connections. What's next?"

Grabbing a paper plate from the untouched stack on the counter, Dalton dropped his half-eaten slice onto it, got up, and washed his hands before finding the page of photographs and waving it in the air. "The Fenerec behind the attack. These men are the core of the operations, as far as we can tell. Of these, five are important. While the rest were active participants, they're middling Fenerec who aren't much of a threat to trained operatives."

Ryan devoured his slice of pizza like a starved man before licking his fingers. "What do you have on them?"

"The Alpha goes by the name of Martin Dundrich, likely an alibi. No information on education, origin, or actual age. He showed up about seven years ago. At the time, his pack was small, consisting of seven members, all males. Four are still with him; the rest are presumed dead. These four and Dundrich are the core of the pack, probably the masterminds behind the attack on La Guardia. We have no information on his dominancy, either."

"Do you have anything of actual use?"

"None of them are mated."

I frowned, wondering at the significance of Dalton's declaration. Everyone else straightened, and Ryan growled, anger giving a bite to his scent. "That makes them dangerous."

"Without the stabilizing factor of females in the pack, they're a risk to everyone, Fenerec and Normal alike. Unfortunately, you're the one at most risk, Ryan. Judging from their behavior patterns and the fact none of them have mates, they're looking for Fenerec bitches. Considering their willingness to kill, it wouldn't surprise me if they decided to target Fenerec bitches—and their mates. They haven't run wild yet, but it's only a matter of time before they do."

Rage drowned out all other scents, and I sneezed several times to clear my nose. "Are women really so rare among Fenerec?"

Dalton sighed. "On average, one in seven Fenerec are women. Lately, the number has been closer to one in ten. Most of our mates don't want to become Fenerec. We're volatile, and they know it. While Fenerec have stronger instincts than humans, most mothers don't want to risk their lives to become a Fenerec. If the candidate for the ritual isn't a hundred percent willing and determined, they die during the process. You were very fortunate, Matia. Ryan gambled with your life. I still don't know how he pulled it off; even among those who say they're willing, a quarter of the hopefuls die during the ritual. Becoming a Fenerec isn't a safe bet. But, it's not all bad. With so few women of our kind, you ladies rule the roost. Most males will roll over if their female bares her teeth and growls. I think that's partly why so many females want a more dominant male for their mate; dominant males, especially Alphas, are wired to fight back. Fenerec enjoy a challenge."

"I deal with too many egotistical, wealthy men in my life already," I muttered. "So, this pack has no women. What *do* they have?"

"A submissive male with pyromaniac tendencies and a specialization in explosives. Former explosives tech with the Marines prior to a medical discharge almost two decades ago. His name is Willard Hamburg. He was the first of Dundrich's recruits. Hamburg is the real problem of the pack. He's smart, would rather avoid a fight, and skilled at dropping off the radar. The Inquisition has had an active hit order on him for at least a decade—shortly after he became a Fenerec. He's responsible for the murders of at least seven women; failed rituals from what we can tell. There are likely more we don't know about."

I clenched my teeth together so hard my jaw ached. "So he's a serial killing mass murderer?"

"The real deal, I'm afraid. Inquisition operatives aren't often given kill-on-sight orders, but Hamburg is one of them, as is Dundrich. The rest are questionable. There are three we've pinpointed as being the muscle of the pack; like to fight, and enjoy getting up close and personal. There used to be four, but one was killed at La Guardia. He didn't get far enough away from the payload."

Curiosity got the better of me. "How do you know that?"

"His body was somewhat intact, and he's been on watch lists for a long time. Cross referencing the surveillance videos confirmed he was carrying one of the bags believed to contain the explosives. We're tough, but he trusted a little too much in our ability to withstand injury. I'll spare you the details." Dalton's grim smile chilled me. "One less problem to worry about."

"That still leaves a lot of problems, Sinclair." Ryan set his phone on the counter, tapping at the screen. "We don't know where they are. We likely don't know their numbers, either. It's impossible to plan a good operation without intel."

"That's where you come in, Ryan."

Ryan stared at Dalton, frowning. "What exactly do you mean by that?"

"Until Matia's confirmed to have control over her wolf *and* her witch powers, we can't risk sending her out on any operation, especially when she's been developing as a witch for far longer than I initially believed. However, I was thinking of a way we can use her —and you—to bait them out. Dundrich will want you, Ryan, because you're submissive. Once he smells the fact you are bonded with a bitch, he's going to want both of you. He'll likely assume your bitch is submissive, since dominant bitches don't tend to want submissive males. In short, I'll take Matia into custody without telling you where I'm taking her. That way, when you claim the Inquisition took your bitch from you, it'll be the truth."

Ryan tensed, and his growls rumbled in his chest.

"Add in the fact the newly mated are always zealously overprotective of each other, easily provoked, and easily alarmed, and it's the perfect situation to add authenticity to your con, allowing you to infiltrate the enemy. Unless Dundrich is stronger than I think, I won't have any difficulty winning a contest against him. If he were a strong Alpha, he wouldn't have a problem finding willing bitches. I'm not worried. Maybe I'm not the strongest Alpha around, but I *can* subjugate other Fenerec through their bonds with their mates—even Normals."

Sucking in a breath, Ryan stared at Dalton with wide eyes. "You can?"

"I can. Matia might one day grow into a more dominant Fenerec than me, but she's not there, not yet. I can subjugate her, which means I can subjugate you through her. If something goes wrong, we'll be able to pinpoint your location through the pack bonds."

Ryan shook his head. "There won't be enough time to develop the bonds."

"While I'm not a witch, I'm sensitive. Leave the issue of tracking you, if necessary, to me," Dalton replied in a tone allowing no argument. "I've already been in discussion with other Inquisitors on how to best handle the situation. One of my pack is currently in the process of wiring some clothing with microphones and transmitters so we'll be able to hear everything. I wanted an ear piece, but they're too easy to spot, so it'll be one way only, but we'll be able to track you. The batteries on the microphones are rated for a week."

"A week isn't a lot of time," Ryan replied, shaking his head. "I might be able to find them, but it takes a lot longer than a week to get close to rogues—especially rogues on the run."

"Within a week, any Fenerec within a city block is going to pick up on your distress. They'll find you." Pausing, Dalton glanced at me. "Then again, in a week, we'll probably be testing the patience of every single local water witch putting out literal fires when your bitch's temper frays and snaps."

I crossed my arms over my chest. "I don't like it."

"Of course you don't. You're not supposed to like it. You just have to do it. In fact, the less you like it, the better off Ryan is. If his cover appears authentic and his anxiety is legitimate, most Fenerec won't be able to hurt him. He'll be safe enough. Even Normals are affected by submissive Fenerec, especially when they're as submissive as Ryan. Unless they run wild or have employed a complete lunatic, he should be safe enough. You, on the other hand, would be a liability—and at risk."

Ryan sighed. "I hate it, but he's right. That's why I run ops solo, often against what most would consider hardened criminals. They hesitate."

"That's part of what makes him so precious. A submissive doesn't just bow to more dominant Fenerec, Matia—they bring protective instincts to the forefront. No matter how far removed humans are from their wild ancestry, those instincts still exist."

"Let's assume I manage to infiltrate them. What happens then?"

"My pack will track you down, and we wipe them out. We should be able to get a feel for their numbers and abilities by listening in on the microphones. Apparently, it's easier to waterproof the microphones and their batteries than it is to create button-sized cameras that can withstand a run through the washing machine."

"Right. How many outfits will I have with built-in microphones?"

"Ten."

"Matia will be at Inquisition headquarters for the entire operation?"

"With several water witches capable of putting out any fires she may or may not set in stressful situations. I'll also change my plan for her to participate in a training course until this is over. She won't need combat training to oversee the comms, and I'd rather move on getting the location of this rogue pack and dealing with them. Once you've done your part and been extracted, Ryan, you can worry about teaching her how to handle a gun."

"Why does this seem like a disaster in the making?" I grabbed the box of pizza and tore free a slice. While I wasn't exactly hungry, eating kept my hands and mouth busy.

No one needed to hear me—or my wolf—whine over something necessary but unpleasant. Maybe there wouldn't be a chance for public justice against those responsible for destroying so many lives at La Guardia, but I wasn't going to risk my chance of helping to stop the rogue pack from striking again.

"You're smart, that's why. Try not to worry. We'll make every effort to safeguard Ryan."

"I can take care of myself, Sinclair."

"I know you can, but Miss Evans doesn't, and there's little as dangerous as a bitch in a corner. Let's not take any unnecessary risks, especially when the cornered bitch can light things on fire when provoked."

I ate another slice of pizza so I wouldn't argue with Dalton. My wolf encouraged me to challenge the Alpha, and when I refused, her snarls of displeasure filled my head.

IT TOOK every bit of my willpower to cooperate and go with Dalton instead of staying in the apartment with Ryan. I bit the inside of my cheek to keep from voicing a whine—or complaining.

"This is really for the best." Dalton guided me to an SUV parked in the underground garage. Dad and Sam waved a farewell and didn't hesitate before getting into the car and driving off, leaving me alone with the Alpha. "Ryan'll be motived to finish his part and get back to you—you'll pay close attention to the comms. Comm monitoring can be dreadfully dull, especially without video surveillance. It'll also give you a chance to adapt to your wolf without Ryan's personality suppressing you."

"He doesn't suppress me."

"Oh, but he does, Miss Evans. That's what makes submissive Fenerec so precious. You'll understand in a day or two. By then, your temper will start fraying, and you'll get a full taste of keeping your wolf controlled all the time. Fortunately, the folks you'll be with work with dominants often. They'll be able to handle you until you learn to handle yourself. Now, get in. Let's get on the road before Ryan works up the nerve to argue with me on it."

I growled but obeyed, jerking open the passenger door.

"Or you can start having frayed nerves

within five minutes of leaving his presence. They're going to be so happy with me for bringing them a cranky bitch." Dalton sighed, buckled in, and started the engine. "This really is for the better. Ryan's motivated because he knows he has a bitch to come home to. You'll be motivated because you know you can't settle down with your new mate until you have your wolf and witchcraft under basic control. You're not going to like the headquarters because there is silver in the walls, which will help motivate you to get out of there as soon as you can. You'll end up staying there for at least a week to adapt, but if you get the hang of it quickly, you'll be released."

"Released makes it sound like a prison."

"It is. I won't lie, but that's the way it has to be. Until you're no longer a threat to Normals, it's a very comfortable prison designed to encourage you to improve your control and learn how to survive. It wouldn't surprise me if they want to keep you there for a few weeks. Witch Fenerec have become a bit more common, but the Inquisition doesn't like taking risks with the more dangerous supernatural. You're now one of those. Fire witches are dangerous enough before you add in a Fenerec's enhanced strength, longevity, and violent tendencies. The more dominant the Fenerec, the more violent the tendencies, too."

Violent thoughts were second nature to

me; before the La Guardia bombing, I often had them, although I had never acted on them. With a wolf sharing my skin, I had the feeling it'd only be a matter of time before I lashed out and did something I'd regret—something my wolf wouldn't find repulsive to her nature.

Wolves hunted, wolves killed, and wolves ate what they killed.

Humans hunted and killed, too, but we did it for greed and passion rather than survival.

My wolf stirred in my head, and she made no effort to hide her smug superiority. I was just a human while she was the wolf, the predator, and the one with the morals, the one who only did the necessary.

Underneath her superiority was an undertone of resentment and doubt. She had saved my life in La Guardia, changing me into a Fenerec, and she wasn't sure she had made the right choice.

Like it or not, we were stuck with each other. Everyone had told me what to expect with becoming a Fenerec, but no one had even suggested what had been done could be undone. If my wolf didn't want me, she'd find out about the nature of two-way streets.

I had a lifetime of experience suppressing violent instincts. If my wolf wouldn't work with me, I'd work to make sure she couldn't work against me.

"There's no changing back, is there? Becoming a human again, I mean."

Dalton put the vehicle in gear and backed out of the spot. After a long, uncomfortable silence, he sighed. "No, there isn't."

"That's what I thought. I just wanted to know for certain."

"You'll figure things out. We all do. It'll take time to get used to sharing with your wolf, but everything will work out, you'll see."

I didn't believe him, but I nodded anyway. Understanding came swift and painful; I couldn't transform into a wolf because my wolf didn't want *me*. She didn't want me in her body. Until she did, I'd always require someone forcing the transformation.

We'd always fight each other.

The only thing we had in common was Ryan, and even then, we wanted him for different reasons. Mine went far deeper than the need to mate.

He had saved me. My wolf had, too, but Ryan didn't regret the risks he had taken.

My wolf did.

TWENTY-FIVE

*It's the curse of the newly mated.*

---

THE INQUISITION HEADQUARTERS was located almost an hour north of New York City where the lines between civilization and nature blurred. According to the sign, it was a large apartment building servicing the nearby town.

Did the neighbors know they lived next door to werewolves and witches? What other supernatural existed I didn't know about?

Dalton parked near the front doors. Unbuckling my seatbelt, I wrinkled my nose and opened the passenger side door. "How long should it take Ryan to finish his part of the job?"

"If all goes well, not long. It depends on how sensitive their noses are."

"What do you mean by that?"

"Fenerec can smell lies. Some are better at it than others. It's a useful trick. Some can mask their scent and prevent lies from being detected, but it takes time to learn. Ryan will have to be careful; he can be vague without any risk of discovery, but the bigger the lie, the harder it is to hide. Of course, it wouldn't surprise me if Ryan could lie his way out of trouble. He's a cunning old Fenerec. A lot of what he'll say won't be a lie, either. He has a lot of reasons to hate working with the Inquisition."

While I was aware Dalton and Ryan knew each other, I wasn't sure how close they were, if they were close at all. However, if the Alpha was willing to tell me more about Ryan, I wanted to learn as much as I could. "Why?"

Dalton chuckled. "You may not like the answer."

"I still want to know."

"Of course you do, Ryan's your mate."

It would take me time to get used to thinking of him as my mate. In a way, I appreciated the Fenerec way. Who had the time to date someone? I didn't. The simplicity of how Fenerec picked their life partners and made it work appealed to me in more ways than one.

"Tell me, please."

"Ryan's been an Inquisitor for a long time, Matia. The Inquisition has very, very few operatives who have been working as long as he has, and the ones who have are treated very carefully, put in stabilizing pack situations, and given the support they need to remain stable. Ryan's long overdue to retire. He's too good at what he does, and that's the problem.

If he wasn't so good, the Inquisition would have stepped in and found a compatible pack for him years ago."

The Alpha's words frightened me, but I didn't understand why. My wolf whined in my head, and her discomfort drove me into asking, "What do you mean by that?"

"I mean the only difference between Ryan and the Fenerec he hunts is a matter of legality. He's sanctioned. That doesn't change the fact he hunts criminals down and kills them to make sure they never have their day in court. He's judge, jury, and executioner, and he's good at what he does—too good. If there's a way to kill someone, he's used it. He's probably forgotten more about assassination techniques than I've ever learned. He's overdue to retire, and I intend to use you to make sure he lives long enough to retire. If I have my way, this will be his last job. If I had had my way, one of *my* pack would be running intel, but none of mine are as old as Ryan. If something *does* go wrong, he has the highest chance of survival."

I tensed, and my wolf's alarm ripped through me. "This wasn't supposed to be that dangerous."

"I'm one of those Fenerec with a talent for lying, Miss Evans. Ryan understands the risks. He has a damned good reason to make it out alive: you. He knows you're here, so he'll be as careful as possible. You'll do your job on the comms to make sure nothing is missed so we can get him out as quickly as possible. We can't afford to let this pack run unchecked, and Ryan's the Inquisition's best option right now."

"I know that," I spat.

"I know you do. You know better than anyone else. It's the curse of the newly mated. It's even worse for you. You're not used to having your wolf, you don't know how to manage her emotions and your own at the same time, and you haven't had a chance to find your balance with her yet. Just be glad it's not winter, Miss Evans. Fenerec are like wolves in that regard; winter is our breeding season. At least you have a chance to adapt to your bond with Ryan before your wolf's attention is completely consumed with mating."

My casual upbringing regarding sex spared me from much embarrassment, although I wasn't sure how I felt about people being interested in the man I had chosen for my partner.

I had wanted him before my wolf had come along, and he was the one thing we had in common. Ryan bound us together in more ways than one.

"Nothing better happen to Ryan," I growled, crossing my arms over my chest. "Why couldn't I go with him, anyway?"

"Matia, you're a beautiful woman. Until your mating bond has time to strengthen, there are males who would risk anything to have a chance with someone like you. In a few weeks, the mating bond will be strong enough no sane Fenerec would even consider touching Ryan in order to get you. Until then, let's not push our luck."

The idea of someone even attempting to steal me away from my mate shocked me into silence, and my wolf raged.

———

DALTON MEANT business when he said he wanted to act fast to deal with the rogue Fenerec pack. Within five minutes of stepping through the front doors of the Inquisition headquarters, he led me into a basement room that reminded me of a smaller version of NASA's command center. Three tiered rows of desks ringed a massive display flanked with stacks upon stacks of electronic equipment. Two people were seated in the first row wearing headsets, tapping away at their computers.

Hopping down the steps two at a time, Dalton approached the working Inquisitors and sat on one of the desks, waiting until one of them noticed him. Both were older women with graying hair, and they removed their headsets in unison.

"Mr. Sinclair," the woman nearest him said, rising to her feet. "We've been expecting you."

Instead of shaking with her like a normal person, Dalton kissed the back of her hand.

"To be expected by two of the Inquisition's most beautiful women is an honor."

The woman freed her hand, took hold of her headset, and slapped Dalton upside his head with it. "I'm telling your mate on you so she can deal with you herself."

"Oh, please tell her. I like when she puts me in my place. Audrey, if I kiss your hand, too, will you tell on me?"

"You won't have a hand or a mouth if you try that stunt with me, Dalton," the other woman replied. "You're going to be in trouble enough when you go home with the scent of so many of us ladies on you—especially a bitch's scent."

"I know, and it's wonderful. She's so jealous."

"One of these days, she is going to rearrange your face for you, sir, and you'll deserve it."

"It'll heal."

"You got us to come out on our day off. What do you have for us?"

Dalton turned to me, waving me over. I took the steps with more care than he had. "This is Matia Evans, a new Fenerec. She underwent a rather haphazard ritual during the La Guardia incident."

"That explains why you wanted a witch." After wiping her hand off on her jeans, the first woman reached out to shake with me. "Pleased to meet you, Miss Evans. I'm Harriet. My sister is Audrey."

I nodded and shook their hands. "Pleased to meet you."

"Miss Evans is also a fire witch who manifested flame during her first transformation."

Both women glared at Dalton, and if looks could kill, he would have been a smoldering pile of ash within moments.

Harriet braced her hands on her hips. "We make house calls, you know. Why would you bring a new witch wolf to such a stressful place?"

"Cole's her mate."

Audrey's eyes widened while Harriet's mouth dropped open. Both women gaped at Dalton before spluttering and staring at me. I tensed, uncertain of the reason for their reaction and painfully aware of Dalton's warnings about Ryan's role in the Inquisition.

"He moves slow, but when he makes a move, hot damn, does the boy make a move." Audrey clucked her tongue, looking me over from head to toe. "You a model?"

I blinked, opened my mouth, and then closed it when I couldn't think of a single reply. Me? A *model*?

"A rather successful businesswoman, actually," Dalton replied, grinning at me. "She's Ralph Evans's girl."

Audrey frowned. "I would have thought their pack's Alpha would have claimed her. Why is she with you?"

"Because Ryan performed the ritual, and I fully intend to lure Ryan into my pack. I want you two to teach her the ropes, get her comfortable on the comms, and set up to be on the team monitoring Ryan's operation. She's used to working, so the normal method of easing her into things won't work. She needs a purpose. She's going to shake out dominant, she's newly mated, and if she isn't given something meaningful to do, she'll be clawing her way through the walls within hours. I'm going to be on the move with my pack waiting for the order to extract Cole. I've got Gavin doing the final equipment checks and preparations." Dalton slid off the desk. "Matia, I'll leave you in their capable hands. If you have any trouble, the twins know how to get in touch with me."

Without a single look back, Dalton left. I fisted my hands and pressed them to my hips. "The coward just ran away, didn't he?"

Harriet laughed. "He sure did. Welcome to the Inquisition, Miss Evans."

"Matia, please."

"Have a seat so we can get started. We have a lot to cover."

---

UNTIL MEETING HARRIET AND AUDREY, I had believed myself intelligent. They wasted no time establishing I knew nothing, reinforced my ignorance, and handed my pride to me on a platter. Their quick, sharp wit accompanied a rigid sense of honor. Their tough love was tempered with a sense of fairness, which made it possible for me to hold onto my fraying patience.

I wanted to be useful, but the complicated system thwarted me. In three hours, I learned two important things: frustrated fire witches could start smoking from the ears and singe their hair, and water witches could summon water at will.

The keyboard, at least, seemed impervious to harm and didn't care it had been drenched in water.

I admired the sisters' work ethic. The only piece of equipment I was comfortable with was the only one that mattered to me: the headset. With a click of a button, I could dial in to the microphones hidden in Ryan's clothing. The system automatically recorded every sound.

My lack of technical competence with the monitoring equipment didn't bother either twin. Harriet wrote a list of notes to remind me what I needed to do during my shift while Audrey grilled me about my witchcraft.

"If you mess up on surveillance, it won't hurt anything—really, it won't." Harriet looked up from her notes. "If something goes wrong, you just have to run up the steps, go into the hallway, and give a howl. Security knows you don't know the system, so someone will run over to find out what's wrong. Better than accidentally breaking anything."

"I can do that."

Audrey rapped her knuckles on the desk. "Forget the equipment for a few minutes. Look, you'll be on shift by yourself for at least two or three hours; there'll be some overlap, but you're going to be our filler in the typical slow times. We don't expect anything to happen, and nothing is quite as rattling as silence. The last thing we need is for you to set off the fire alarms or destroy hundreds of thousands of dollars of equipment losing your cool."

"Be fair," Harriet chided. "The poor girl had no idea she was a witch until she became a Fenerec. That's hard on a soul. She didn't start to smoke until the two and a half hour mark. She should be all right. Anyway, silence is the best sound for her to hear, unless he snores, then she wants to hear that. Normal noises are good. Now, if Ryan gets into a dispute with anyone or there's gunfire, that's when we should worry about her burning her pretty hair to a crisp."

I touched a hand to my head, grimacing at the lingering stench of burnt hair. "I'm sorry."

"Not your fault. Fire witches have it the roughest; your manifestations are dangerous and put everyone on edge. At least you won't have to worry about many pissing contests with other witches; no one wants to piss off a fire witch capable of manifesting. Only the really strong ones manifest even smoke, and if Dalton brought you to us, he wants to make sure no one's hurt—you included."

"You handle your side of things, and let me give the girl the basics on avoiding any unfortunate manifestations." Audrey huffed, shook her head, and rapped her knuckles against the desk again. "Rule one: do not think in warm colors. No imagery of fireplaces, nothing yellow, red, or orange."

I groaned and hung my head. "You ask the impossible."

"Why is that impossible?"

"My sister likes to think she's smarter than everyone else, but then she sticks her foot in her mouth and proves she wasn't paying attention to the briefing papers we were given. I read them. She's colorblind, Audrey. She doesn't know red from yellow, blue, or green, and good luck explaining it to her. From my understanding, it was caused by physical injury when an infant. If she's true to form, her colorblindness will gradually fade. Dalton was worried about sensory issues once she begins comprehending color."

"Well, fuck me with a stick."

"I seem to have left my sticks outside today. Sorry, Aubrey. Next time."

I decided the best way to handle the old witch's twisted sense of humor was to ignore it. "I'm so glad I don't have to explain that," I confessed. "Don't think about anything I associate with fire is what you want, correct?"

"Correct."

"I think I can do that. My only job is to

monitor Ryan's microphones. What about Dalton and his pack?"

"They're being handled by a second team in the building; we have five of these stations in the building for operations, and considering the delicacy of Mr. Cole's position, only limited people work on his surveillance. This is a new setup for us, but we've already done the basic sound checks on all the equipment. Harriet will leave you a list of extensions. Do you know how to use a conferencing phone?"

I glanced in the direction of the phone positioned beside my monitor. The make and model was almost identical to the ones we used at Pallodia. "I know how to use one."

Harriet flashed me a smile. "Good. Normally, we'd put you on a set schedule, but if Dalton says you're to be kept busy, you'll stay in here unless you have to take a piss or get a bite to eat. No hungry Fenerec allowed in the building. If you or your wolf get peckish, you head over to the dining hall and get something to eat. We're prepared to feed packs of Fenerec, so you won't do much damage to the supplies."

"I eat a lot," I mumbled.

"And I'm willing to bet Ryan adores feeding you. Male Fenerec live to provide for their females, so don't you worry yourself about it at all. I'll delay the inevitable and have someone bring you something to eat to take the edge off while you listen in on your mate. Audrey, let's leave the poor girl to settle; she knows enough to get by, and all we're doing now is unnerving her. We can show you your suite later. You'll like it. It's designed for a mated pair, so once your mate's back, you two can relax and enjoy each other's company."

I liked the sound of that, as did my wolf. When the two witches left, I sighed my relief, adjusted my headset, and went to work.

---

I DIDN'T APPRECIATE Ryan's love of quiet until I listened to him prepare for the operation. Without words, he managed to communicate everything Dalton had tried to tell me, but I hadn't understood.

Ryan hated his work, and his disgust rang out in the silence other men would have filled. My wolf whined in my head, and I kept careful control of her. Whining wouldn't change anything. Luring Ryan away from Inquisition operations would become my first priority. If I read Dalton right, he could help me pull it off.

Harriet and Audrey had spoken the truth about my role; the Inquisition knew Ryan's habits so well there was always someone in the room with me during active times. After eight hours of monitoring, the twin witches came to fetch me, herding me out of the room. A young woman took my place.

"I thought I was supposed to stay." My

wolf resented leaving our one connection to Ryan. I had no idea where he was going, but he was on the move, and his activity had the Inquisitors buzzing with nervous energy.

The microphones hadn't picked up anything about a location, although I recognized Gavin giving my mate a final rundown on what would happen when Dalton's pack came to extract him. I liked Ryan's orders; unless told otherwise, he was to stay low, stay out of trouble, and wait for the fireworks to end.

Harriet leveled a glare at me. "You've been at it for eight hours. It's time to get you fed. We'll show you to the suite and give you a chance to get settled. There'll be plenty of time for monitoring after you've eaten and had some rest. Last thing we need is a cranky bitch suffering from a lack of sleep lighting someone on fire."

I understood; I raised my hands in defeat and ignored my wolf's disgruntled complaints. I followed the twins as they led me to my suite, wondering how long it would be until they allowed me back into the monitoring room to listen and wait for Ryan's return.

---

SOMETHING WOKE me from a sound sleep. I bolted upright, my heart racing from a surging sense of wrongness and apprehension. Chilled sweat beaded my brow, and while sleepy, my wolf whined anxiously in my head. Early-morning light streamed in through the window; when I had fallen asleep, it had been night.

I paced, nervous energy coursing through me until I shifted my weight even when I managed to force myself to stay in one spot. Unable to tell what was wrong, I flexed my hands and stared at the silver bars over the windows, a reminder the plush, otherwise comfortable room was a prison designed to contain Fenerec.

I remembered Ryan hunting; Fenerec could kill, and witches couldn't heal like I could. If I—or any other Fenerec—turned on them, a witch would likely die. They had ways of protecting themselves and ways of controlling Fenerec, but neither Harriet nor Audrey had opted to enlighten me on the method.

Until someone came for me, I was forced to endure my anxiety alone. At the rate I paced, I'd wear a trench in the plush carpeting long before anyone remembered I was trapped in the room. The wait annoyed growls out of me, and by the time someone knocked at the door, I was surprised I wasn't smoking from the ears again.

"Yes?" I turned to the door, forcing myself to relax my hands. Inquisitors didn't appreciate tense Fenerec; even I and my wolf picked up on the scent of anxiety when I appeared nervous.

The door opened. Harriet and Audrey let themselves in.

I didn't need any help identifying the stench of their nervousness.

Jumping straight to the chase had worked well for me in the business world, so I put my experience to good use. If everything was normal, the witches wouldn't be anxious, and while I hadn't been a Fenerec for long, I had trusted my gut feelings as a human. I saw no need to change my approach. "What happened?"

The sisters exchanged a look. I recognized Harriet only because she wilted; Audrey, true to what I knew of her, kept her chin up, her eyes sharp, and maintained the appearance of calm confidence.

"There's a problem."

My wolf stilled, her attention consumed by the witches, waiting and listening for the news. My gut feeling and sense of wrongness offered insight. Whatever the problem was, it dealt with Ryan. I didn't know where my confidence came from, but my wolf agreed.

"It's Ryan, isn't it?"

Why else would both witches seem so nervous and smell so anxious? Dad was far from harm's way; he wasn't welcomed on Inquisition missions. He wasn't a witch. He wasn't a Fenerec.

Unless someone had gone hunting Dad, he was safe. Ryan wasn't.

Harriet refused to meet my gaze, and even

Audrey hesitated, which answered my question without them needing to say a word. It took every scrap of my willpower to keep my body relaxed.

If I wanted answers, I couldn't afford to frighten off the people who could tell me what was going on. I inhaled, held my breath, and then released it. The witches weren't responsible.

"Please tell me."

Audrey sighed and nodded. "Dalton and his pack are on route now, but none of us know if they'll make it in time—or if they even have a chance to. I'm sorry. Something went wrong, and we don't know what. We didn't have time to relay the communications to Dalton; we sent the extraction order and the last known location, and he was on the move before we could ask him if he recognized any voices on the tape."

Something had happened to Ryan, something the microphones I should have been monitoring picked up. It took a lot of effort to avoid clenching my teeth or otherwise displaying my growing anxiety. "Maybe I've heard them before. Can I help?"

Both witches stared at me in disbelief, and I recognized their reactions from business negotiations. Being reasonable in stressful situations surprised people, and while I worried for Ryan, I couldn't afford to shut either woman out.

They were the only ones who could tell me what was going on.

"We brought a part of the recording," Audrey admitted, pulling her phone from her pocket. "Why don't we sit and go over it? If you know anything at all, it might help."

The room had a small table barely large enough for three to sit around. I offered both armchairs to the witches while I grabbed a stool from the suite's kitchen. Audrey set her phone in the center of the table and tapped the screen.

"Why my pack?" I didn't recognize the male's voice, but I tensed at the suspicion in his tone.

"Tired of the bullshit." The vehemence in Ryan's tone made me wince, and my wolf whined her worry.

"They'll kill you if they find out."

"I know."

"I don't need any trouble in my pack."

Ryan didn't reply, but I imagined him shrugging without even trying to meet the other Fenerec's gaze.

"Get rid of him before someone follows him."

I sucked in a breath, recoiling from the phone. After so many years of working with him, and especially after the days I had spent as his captive, I'd never forget the sound of Harthel's voice.

"He's got a mate, sir. Can smell her on him. Not wise; getting rid—"

The crack of gunfire blasted from the phone's speakers, and I flinched away from the sound. Moments later, I heard a sickening thump.

"Must I really do everything myself?"

Audrey reached over and tapped on the phone's screen, heaving a long sigh. "We believe the man who pulled the trigger is a human."

A numbing cold took root in my bones. I recognized the feeling from work. "Charles Harthel. He used to be Vice President of Pallodia Incorporated."

Both witches straightened, and Audrey asked, "You're sure?"

"I've known him most of my life, Audrey. I'm sure. I have no doubt it's him."

The women stared at each other without saying a word. I clenched my teeth, forcing myself to remain silent when I wanted to open my mouth and scream. I wanted to howl, as did my wolf.

I wanted to cry, but the numbing cold within robbed me of my tears. Instead, I watched the witches and waited.

Harriet bit her lip, her gaze fixed on her sister's phone. "Dalton's doing everything he can. If anyone can work miracles, it's him. He didn't waste any time leaving. They've been given orders to shoot to kill. If something can be done, he'll do it."

"Is there anything I can do?"

Harriet grimaced. "For now, wait. I know

it's hard, but please be patient until we find out more. Right now, we know nothing. When Dalton reports in, we'll let you know. If there's anything you can do, we'll tell you. For now, let us do our jobs without distraction. If we can bring him back to you, we will."

Mindful of Dalton's warning Fenerec could smell lies and uncertain if witches could sense them, I nodded and stared at the tabletop. I stayed that way, motionless, until the women left, locking me in the suite meant for two.

TWENTY-SIX

*You want me to respect you? Fucking earn it.*

---

IF HARRIET and Audrey thought I was going to wait like an obedient dog told to sit and stay, they were insane. Glass and metal stood between me and the outdoors, and I had no intention of remaining a prisoner any longer than necessary. I grabbed hold of the bars. My hands throbbed from contact with the silver, blistered when I held on too long, and bled black before the pain drove me back.

A wolf's strength wouldn't get me through the window. Burning the building down wouldn't help me, either. All setting a fire would do was draw unwanted attention. Melting the bars and shattering the glass would get me out, but how long would I have before the Inquisitors hunted me down and dragged me back?

Once outside, I needed to get away, fast and far—too fast and too far for any Inquisitors to hunt me down. Harthel's voice and the deafening blasts of gunfire replayed in my head and ignited my fury.

A wolf could run fast and far; nothing would stop me from hunting Harthel down and ripping him into bite-sized pieces and scattering his broken body for the vultures. In that, my wolf and I were of one mind.

Harthel would die for hurting Ryan, for taking him from me—from us—when we were too far away to defend him. My throat tightened and my eyes burned. I couldn't even tell if Ryan lived.

The cold spot in my chest, born the instant the gunfire blasted the microphones, refused to ease. It hurt to breathe.

My life narrowed to one point, one man: Harthel.

The Inquisitors could take their precious taboos about killing Normals and shove them up their asses. I would earn whatever punishment they deemed fit, even death.

But first, I needed to get through the bars and glass. Maybe the silver was impervious to my wolf's strength, but it wasn't invincible. I hadn't manifested any flames, not since my purported destruction of Harthel's cabin in the mountains.

Fire could melt silver if I could make it hot enough—if I could summon it without burning myself and everyone around me in the process—if I could summon it at all.

If Ryan lived, I would find him. If he didn't, I would find Harthel, and I would show him I wasn't sick, weak, or defenseless, not anymore. I clenched my teeth, reached out, and clutched the silver bars. The metal seared my fingers, and I welcomed the pain.

It anchored me to what I needed to do, what I desired, and what I needed to do to accomplish my task. If it became my final mission in life, I was prepared.

Until I watched Harthel's world burn around him, I wouldn't quit. Closing my eyes, I fought to hold on until everything narrowed to my burning hands and the metal barring me from freedom.

It didn't take long for the silver to burn me so badly I couldn't grip the bars, and my fingers twitched, peeling free of the metal. An acrid stench scorched my nose, triggering a coughing fit.

I cracked open an eye, grimacing at the blackened state of my hands. Skin wasn't supposed to smoke, but mine did. Drop by drop, molten silver streamed down the wall, trailing a dark path to the floor. It should've burst into flame, but I remembered the witches' reassurances the room was safeguarded against fire.

Maybe the silver would've flamed, too, without those protections, but their magic wasn't enough to stop the two bars from puddling on the floor, leaving a gap large enough for me to wiggle through.

Hope revitalized me, and I fisted my abused hand, drew on my wolf's strength, and elbowed the glass as hard as I could. A web of cracks appeared. On the second blow, it broke enough fresh air washed over my face.

Once the window was too broken to use my elbow, I resorted to my fists. I stopped counting my strikes, but it took longer than I liked to bust a gap large enough for me to climb through. To escape, I'd have to cram myself between two bars of silver. With time against me, I couldn't afford to stop long enough to clear away the glass shards.

A few cuts and burns wouldn't stop me. I wanted Harthel's throat between my ruined hands. I'd put my wolf's strength to the true test when I strangled the life out of him.

I grabbed hold of the window sill, sucked in a breath at the pressure on my blistered skin, and put every last one of my gymnastic lessons to good use as I scrambled through the window.

The silver scorched my arms and legs, but it didn't stop me from pushing through. I dropped several feet to the ground, smacking face first into the gravel. The impact stunned me, and my wolf howled her anger in my head, her fury at my incompetence stinging more than my burns.

I snarled back, aware of gravel sticking to my cheek and chin. "Stuff it, bitch."

Maybe if she had helped me figure things out, I would've been with Ryan instead of locked in a room shielded with silver. Maybe if she hadn't retreated whenever I tried to assume her shape, I could have done something to stop Harthel.

In that, she was to blame, and instead of shielding her from my resentment, I allowed it to simmer so it could boil over the boundaries dividing us.

Without Ryan, I'd be dead.

Without me, Ryan wouldn't have been put into a position to face Harthel alone.

Killing Harthel wouldn't bring Ryan back, but it would prevent him from hurting anyone else, including Dad. I loved my father, but he wasn't the one I wanted.

I wanted Ryan back. I had so many questions I wanted to ask, so many things I wanted to see with him, so many things I wanted to experience with him at my side. My lack of control had ruined everything.

My wolf's grieved howl stuck in my throat, and I swallowed it back. Until I found Harthel, I couldn't afford to waste a single breath. I scrambled to my feet and ran.

---

LONG AFTER I should have collapsed from exhaustion and blood loss, I ran. The Inquisition's headquarters skirted the New York mountains, allowing me to avoid the roads. Mud specked with thin patches of melting snow reminded me of the late-season blizzard, making me remember everything Ryan had done to help me.

I stumbled to a halt and gasped for breath, bracing my hands on my knees. Wolves ran faster than humans, didn't they? Speed mattered.

While I doubted Ryan still lived, if I didn't hurry, Harthel would escape me. If he did, I'd have to hunt him, no matter where he went. I'd been warned what the Inquisition did to those who broke the rules and violated their taboos.

I couldn't die without taking Harthel with me, not just for myself, but for Ryan, for Dad, and for those Harthel would target in the future. A wolf could do what I needed, no matter how badly I wanted to strangle the life out of the man.

Wolves could run fast and far.

Once again, I was aware of my wolf's resentment.

I straightened, taking in the forest. The thick canopy blocked a lot of the sunlight, but the sky darkened with the promise of night. Her eyes saw better in the dark than mine, too—yet another reason I needed to rely on her.

Maybe other Fenerec had amicable relationships with their wolves, but I didn't. She didn't want me; her interests narrowed to mating, hunting, and being the top dog of the pack.

Her anger flared, and I smirked at how calling her a dog stirred her ire. "As long as you treat me like a living mule for you to re-side in, I'll call you a dog. That's how things are going to work from here on out. You want me to respect you? Fucking earn it. You saved my life. I get that. Nice of you, but you didn't have to—*you* decided to. *You* regret the decision. Don't expect me to roll over and treat you like a delicate little princess in a glass tower. If you wanted someone to push around, you should have picked someone else."

My wolf stilled and quieted, and I was aware of her listening, her curiosity stronger than her dislike of me.

"I want to kill Harthel, and I need your help to do it. However satisfying strangling him would be, you run faster. You have teeth. You heard what he did to Ryan. Fine, you're pissed at me. I'm not the ideal little pack mule for you to ride around on. I'm not going to always do what you want. Maybe you liked it when you could make me dance to your tune, but your tune? It'll get people *I* care about hurt. I won't let you do that. Get used to it. You want to hunt? Fine. We'll hunt deer. *Not people*. Not my dad, not Ryan, not anyone. Maybe we're supposed to posture for other Fenerec, but we can figure that out later."

Sucking in deep breaths, I straightened and balled my hands into fists. "I want Ryan back."

Maybe I was no longer human, but my desires were as human as it got; I wanted what I couldn't have. Harthel had taken Ryan from me, and I'd never forget the crack of gunfire and the thump of his body hitting the ground.

My wolf wouldn't forget, either.

It wasn't a lot, but it was enough.

---

PAIN DISTORTED TIME, and my fear of Harthel escaping before I could catch him drove me forward. My bones broke, my muscles tore, and my body reformed, and I needed it to go faster, no matter how much it hurt.

I needed to kill Harthel and watch the life die out of his eyes. I longed to watch the black aura surrounding him fade and wink out along with his existence. When I caught up to the man, I would do as Ryan had threatened and shred Harthel to pieces so small investigators would need tweezers to gather his remains.

When the transformation completed, my front paws throbbed. The sharp, metallic stench of blood hit my nose. With a single sniff, I identified it as mine.

My wolf worried, but I remembered what the witches had said; silver burns took a long time to heal, and wounds opened with silver bled longer than they should.

It didn't matter if I left a trail of blood for others to follow. All that mattered was reaching Harthel first and killing him before anyone stopped me. My wolf's agreement warmed my head. Her desire for the hunt strengthened.

The only evidence of Ryan's involvement in my life was a faint tug. At my wolf's encouragement, I broke into a lope and followed it, pausing to breathe in deep to hunt for Harthel's wretched odor.

Night made way for dawn, and in the early morning light, I found where my mate had been shot, his blood left to dry on the gravel of an abandoned lot. A gutted, decaying building reeked of Fenerec. My wolf fixated on Ryan's scent.

His fear lingered, staining the ground as much as his blood did. I lifted my nose and inhaled. Harthel's scent went one way while a trail of Ryan's blood went the other. The hope Ryan somehow lived froze me in place.

If I followed the blood trail, I might find Ryan.

If I followed Harthel, I might never find Ryan, dead or alive.

My wolf whined her distress in my head. Grief cloaked me, smothering me and numbing me inside. Wolves couldn't cry, not like humans, and my throat itched with the need to voice a mournful howl.

Instead, I gathered my resolution, turned away from the blood trail, and followed Harthel's rancid odor. My memories of the man and his vile miasma haunted me. The thought of the cold, black tendrils touching Ryan infuriated me.

Had Ryan been chilled by the man's presence in his final moments? Had Harthel somehow done something to my mate in the moments before firing?

If I had been with him as I had wanted, would things have been different? Guilt and regret chased me every step of the way. The pain in my paws intensified the longer I ran. The scent of my blood made it difficult to pick out Harthel's odor, but whenever I lost the trail, I stopped, concentrated, and circled until I found it again.

For such a fat man, he managed to hike a significant distance. The trail took me up into the mountains, and when his rancid odor grew so strong it choked me, I slowed to a prowl.

I allowed my wolf to voice a single growl, which promised violence against the human who had caused me—and her—so much misery.

---

HARTHEL'S TRAIL led to the outskirts of a decaying town tucked away in the valley of two mountains. A single street led through boarded up homes and shops. The acrid bite of burning gasoline guided me to a dirt road twisting through the trees and up a steep hill.

Rusted out cars overgrown with weeds dotted a cracked and broken parking lot. The garage had survived better than the buildings in town. A thin trail of smoke rose from the roof, and it smelled of cooking meat.

I licked my muzzle and approached. The spice of Fenerec teased my nose, so varied I couldn't isolate a single wolf nor count their number. The garage's three bay doors were closed, but light shone through the clouded glass. I skirted the parking lot, hiding in the dense weeds surrounding the place. When I reached the side of the building, I spotted a door with clouded panes of glass. Instead of concrete or pavement, a gravel walkway stretched from the door to the asphalt. I placed my paws with care, choking back my whines when the small stones dug into my ruined, silver-burned pads.

Harthel's stench strengthened with each step, and I bared my teeth and pinned my ears as I drew closer to my—our—enemy. My wolf quieted, and she demanded silence from me as well.

She reminded me of Ryan when he hunted, in the moment before he struck and felled his prey.

Shifting on my own had had an unexpected benefit; I'd grown large enough I could stand on my hind paws and peer through the window. The glass was so clouded I could only make out the dark shapes of figures moving within.

One of them was Harthel; I heard anger in his voice although I couldn't make out what he was saying. He spoke with a deep-voiced male.

Without hands, I couldn't open the door and let myself in. Backing away from the door, I considered the building's streaked aluminum siding, concrete foundation, and shingled roof.

My wolf regarded the door with disdain. Were Fenerec jaws strong enough to bend metal? If I could get a grip on the doorknob, a twist and a pull would get me in—if the door wasn't locked. I circled around the building, halting after I turned the corner.

Someone had stacked firewood along the back wall. A gap in the pile revealed another door. Those inside had plenty of ways out of the building, a fact I couldn't change. I huffed my annoyance.

If I had my way, I'd burn them all alive as they had tried to burn me alive. Setting the place on fire, however, would only flush them out. Once they were on the move—once Harthel revealed himself—I could deal with him.

I thirsted for his blood and longed to listen to his screams.

Before I could deal with Harthel and his accomplices, I needed to check if Ryan was within, dead or alive. Even if his lifeless body waited for me, I didn't want to burn him. My fear and grief welled up, and I lifted my abused and battered paws, placing them on the woodpile.

I had melted silver with magic. Wood had to be far easier to ignite than metal. No matter how much it hurt, no matter how badly I blistered my paws in the process, I wouldn't give up. I wouldn't rest until everyone responsible for Ryan's shooting died.

My wolf wanted to crunch their bones in her jaws, and I had no intentions of denying her.

I prepared for the pain, closed my eyes, and concentrated, digging my claws into the dried bark. In their efforts to prevent me from starting unwanted fires, the witches had given me a list of things not to do, including visualizing flame in my head. Colors meant a lot to fire witches, as far as I could guess.

I couldn't picture the yellows, oranges, and reds of flame, but I knew its bright warmth and feared its smoke. Shoving aside my discomfort and doubts, I focused my attention on the one thing left for me: vengeance.

Harthel's world would burn, and I would stoke the flames until nothing remained but ash.

## TWENTY-SEVEN

*If it hadn't represented everything I had lost, it would have been beautiful.*

---

INSTEAD OF BURNING ME, the heat beneath my paws soothed. Smoke tickled my nose, and I huffed to clear my nostrils of the scent so I wouldn't sneeze. Cracking open my eyes, I examined the woodpile. Dark tendrils curled around my paws while bright flickers promised flames. I hopped back, perking my ears forward while I watched the smoldering wood brighten and ignite.

To flush out my prey and gain entrance to the building, I needed to smoke them out, which meant the flames needed to enter the building without being too low to the ground.

Unless I incinerated the building, the Fenerec inside wouldn't be at risk. If Harthel didn't manage to escape, I wouldn't lose sleep over it.

The wood caught, and heat washed over me. I was aware of the flames and their hunger, and I urged them to burn hotter, faster, brighter.

Streamers of licking fire spiraled upwards, and I stared at the roof above.

The shingles and plywood beneath didn't stand a chance; they burned, and as though reading my mind, the tendrils of fire wormed into the building from above. Startled cries came from within, and I lolled my tongue, pressing as close to the woodpile as I dared.

My fires surrounded me, but they didn't singe my fur. They welcomed and warmed me. Prowling along the woodpile, I stopped at the door leading inside, glaring at the barricade. Shouts came from inside, and I bared my teeth from frustration.

Flame slithered along the gutters of the garage, stretched down the siding of the building, and snaked into the building through the door's frame. The heat grew so intense I backed away, my fur smoking. Metal groaned, crackled, and popped.

The knob's familiar gray brightened, became vivid, and surpassed the brilliance of the whitest white I knew. Yellow, orange, and red were the domains of flame, but I didn't know which color the knob was, nor was I given long to consider it. Smoke enveloped the door, and when it cleared, molten metal dripped to the ground. The door ignited, the glass panes shattering while the rest crumbled into smoldering chunks.

My abused paws throbbed, but I jumped

over the debris into the building. Smoke stung my eyes, and I huffed to clear my nose of the stench. On the outside, the garage resembled the buildings of the town. On the inside, it was a home filled with couches, a big screen television, and hammocks hung from the ceiling. Rugs covered the floor, overlapping to hide most of the concrete.

Someone had opened two of the bay doors, and through the haze, I saw figures moving outside. With a mind of its own, the flames stretched from roof to ground, keeping my enemies at bay. I snarled and limped through the garage.

The smoke killed my sense of smell, but as though aware I needed my vision, the flames stayed high and clear of where I searched, followed me, and devoured everything in my wake.

I found Ryan lying on the floor near one of the couches, and the scent of his blood overwhelmed even the stench of the burning garage. He lay still, pale, his eyes closed. Dark marks stained the front of his pale shirt, and I knew the color for what it was: crimson red.

Everyone had been right. The color was vivid and brilliant, and if it hadn't represented everything I had lost, it would have been beautiful.

My wolf's grief welled up through me, but instead of voicing her mourning cries, I sighed, grabbed hold of the back of his shirt in my teeth, and dragged him, step by painful step, towards the back of the garage.

The fire cleared a path for me, the concrete black from where the flames incinerated anything in my way. Not even the door's glass withstood the heat; nothing but a film of powder remained.

I pulled him through the gravel and over the weed-filled yard to the thick brush and the safety of the trees. My wolf's misery intensified, and when she wanted to lie down and stay with our mate, I denied her.

Before either one of us rested, Harthel had to be dealt with. Then I could mourn for what might have been. I snarled and left Ryan's body safely away from the fire I had started, limping around the building to where I had seen the Fenerec gathered.

As though understanding I had taken what I desired from the structure, my fires rampaged and a column of flame blasted skyward, roaring with a fury matching my own. Every step hurt, but the pain forced me to concentrate on my goal.

The burning building didn't matter. Nothing did, except Harthel and his accomplices. I snarled, snapping my teeth in my eagerness to be done with them all.

I turned the corner and stopped. Dalton had told me how many were in the pack, but I couldn't remember nor did I care. There were sixteen men in front of me, and Harthel was one of them. My wolf lusted for blood. While my prey stared at my flames, enraptured by them, I prowled closer.

Not even the smoke could mask the stench of Harthel's cologne. His rotund body, large enough to account for two of the Fenerec combined, was easy to pick out through the haze. The man stood apart from the Fenerec, although I couldn't tell if he was avoiding them or they wanted nothing to do with him. One of the Fenerec males spotted me, his entire body going rigid.

Instead of revealing me, he turned his gaze back to the flames, and as I drew closer, my nose detected the bite of wariness in the air. One by one, the other males noticed my approach, but none of them acted.

My wolf approved of their discretion. While responsible for more crimes than I cared to think about, they hadn't hurt Ryan.

Once I dealt with Harthel, I would deal with the Fenerec males. Satisfied with my decision, my wolf focused her attention on our prey, her disgust strengthening as she considered him and his rolls of fat.

The Fenerec closest to Harthel retreated, which drew the man's attention to me. The dark miasma I loathed reached out, coiling around the nearest male, who stopped and voiced a low whine.

"I thought I said none of you were to become animals," Harthel snapped.

Most of the Fenerec flinched, and I displayed my teeth but made no noise. Ryan had taught me that.

Hunting wolves made no noise.

The Fenerec males exchanged looks.

One took a step towards Harthel, and while his smile showed his teeth, there was nothing friendly about the Fenerec's expression. "I warned you the male you shot had a mate. I warned you it wasn't wise to bring him. I told you to leave him, but you insisted on bringing him. To study."

I took a step closer, judging the distance separating Harthel and I.

"Get rid of her," Harthel snapped.

"You shot her mate. Take care of her yourself." The male shoved his hands in his pockets, his body appearing relaxed, but my wolf was aware of the tension in his stance and the way he balanced his weight, poised to act.

I couldn't tell if he meant to help or hinder. My wolf didn't care. She wanted Harthel's blood and had no interest in the other males—not yet, at least. I couldn't mimic Ryan's fluid grace, not on bloodied, blistered paws, but I burst into a sprint, gathered myself, and lunged for Harthel, snapping my teeth at his face.

I scraped his cheek before sinking my fangs deep into his shoulder. With my front paws, I clawed at his neck and face. The surge of heat and stench of charred flesh heralded the man's shrill screams.

While I was no longer small, I wasn't large

either, and with a heave of his arm, Harthel threw me off him. My fangs tore through him as I was forced to release him. I hit the ground on my side, rolled, and scrambled to get my feet under me.

"Matia, *sit*," Dad ordered. Startled by the command in his voice and the fact he was somewhere behind me, I planted my hindquarters on the ground. My wolf's disgust grated, but like me, she hesitated to defy him. I recognized my dad's tone; he meant business and wouldn't tolerate anything other than obedience.

"R-Ralph," Harthel stammered.

Dad lifted a handgun, the kind I'd only seen in movies. "Fuck off and die, Chuck."

The instant Harthel's name left my dad's lips, he pulled the trigger. Harthel jerked and toppled to the ground, his eyes open and staring. The bright, vivid crimson of blood sprayed while Dad aimed and fired three more times.

"Shit. I was supposed to tell him why I was shooting him in the face before I fired." Dad sighed, clacked his teeth in his frustration, and stowed his gun in a hip holster. "I'm pretty sure I wasn't supposed to give him a name and humanize him, either."

My dad had lost his mind, he had a gun, and he was a good shot. Being obedient seemed wise, so while I flattened my ears, I stayed put.

My wolf wanted to retreat and return to

Ryan's side; fat, sick meat didn't appeal to her, and she had no interest in the other males. She wanted Ryan, and her grief melded with my own.

"Inquisitor." The male who had the courage to speak to Harthel relaxed his stance. "You've come for us."

It wasn't a question, and the relief in the man's tone startled me into turning my head in his direction. I flicked an ear at Dad, shifting my weight from front paw to front paw in an effort to relieve the discomfort.

"He's not an Inquisitor," Dalton announced, emerging from the trees. "We are, though. He's just a very angry Fenerec-born father with a puppy to defend."

"So I see. If you're after the male, he was in the garage." The Fenerec glanced in the direction of the gutted building, which still burned with unnatural intensity. "I request a full investigation and stay of execution for the majority of my pack. I acknowledge my guilt and the guilt of my Second, Third, and Fourth."

Dalton crossed his arms over his chest. Fenerec, as wolves, emerged from the forest and surrounded the Alpha, their hackles raised and fangs bared. "Reason?"

The male pointed at Harthel's still twitching body. "Sorcerer."

"Sorcerer," Dalton echoed, his eyes narrowing, focusing on Harthel's corpse before glancing in my direction. "Ralph, if any of them move so much as an inch, shoot them. The rest of the pack will stay here. Matia, where's Ryan?"

I lowered my head and whined.

Dad waved me off with one hand while unholstering his gun with the other. "Go on, Matia. Between me, Dalton's pack, and my parents, I don't think these pups are going to give us any trouble—not if they're serious about a stay of execution."

My wolf's need to see Ryan again drove me to my paws despite the pain. I limped several steps before Dalton grabbed hold of my scruff with one hand, knelt down, and grabbed my foreleg with the other.

"Those are going to be a long time healing." Releasing me, he rose and waited for me to lead the way. "Show me where Ryan is."

Sighing, I made my way around the burning building. The flames were dying down, no longer stretching in spiraling columns to the sky. Smoke darkened the air and deadened my sense of smell whenever I got too close to the ruined garage. Dragging Ryan through the weeds hadn't left much of a trail, but I found the spot where I had left him. Nothing had disturbed him in the time I had gone after Harthel.

Dad had stolen my kill and chance for vengeance, giving Harthel a far more merciful death than my wolf and I believed he deserved. I sat beside Ryan and whined, pawing at my mate's still arm.

Crimson red, so vivid, stained the gray of his skin where my paw touched his arm. My blood was far brighter than the stains on his shirt, although I wasn't quite sure what color it was; it wasn't red. I didn't want to know, either.

If the price for seeing color was Ryan's life, I wanted my safe, comfortable world of black, white, and gray—a world with him in it. Dalton knelt beside me, digging his fingers into the fur of my scruff. With his other hand, he reached out and touched Ryan's throat.

His gaze focused on his wrist. Had the Alpha always worn a watch? The detail seemed so meaningless, but I couldn't look away from it. Unlike most people, he wore an analog, and I watched the second hand tick its way around the face.

"Matia, remember what I told you about older Fenerec being difficult to kill?"

I sighed, turned my attention to Ryan's bloodied shirt, and pressed my paw over his heart, marked by the center of the dark stains. If he had a heartbeat, I couldn't tell; the throb from my burns ruined any chance of feeling it, if he had one.

Dalton sighed. "Old Fenerec shut down their biological functions when they're critically injured. He's old enough they'd have to shoot him in the head to kill him, Matia—they didn't. Your mate's going to be fine. Wouldn't surprise me if he's back on his feet within a week."

I pinned my ears back and glared at Dalton. No one recovered from being shot in the heart, let alone within a week. My wolf wanted to growl, and I heeded her wishes. I removed my paw from Ryan's chest, sat, and glared at the Alpha.

"You really don't believe me, do you?" Dalton shook his head, worked his arms under Ryan, and rose to his feet with a grunt. "Damn, he looks scrawny, but he weighs a ton."

I whined. If there was life in Ryan's limp body, I couldn't tell. The subtle discoloration to his nails bothered me. It wasn't white, black, or gray, and my inability to comprehend what I looked at stoked my anxiety.

Everything, including my mate, looked *wrong*.

"He'll be all right, Matia. The Inquisition has everything needed to speed his recovery. You can stay near him the entire time. When the witches aren't trying to make sure you aren't a menace to society—or destroyer of even more buildings—you can nurse him all you want. He'll probably heal faster than you will. I'd carry you, but I'd rather not drop Ryan trying."

I huffed, turned my head away from him, and forced myself into a lope. I made it a dozen strides before I slowed to a limping walk. By the time I reached the front of the garage, I had to swallow my whimpers.

The rogue pack of Fenerec hadn't moved.

Dad was crouched beside a row of firearms, dismantling them and leaving the pieces in nearby piles. He glanced up at my approach and focused on Dalton. "How is he?"

"Heart shot, and I think it went through. I didn't want to jostle him. No idea if there's any spinal damage. Gavin, go shift. You're in charge of Matia. She's got silver burns on her paws. You better bring one of the muzzle sets with you; once the adrenaline wears off, we're going to have our hands full with her."

I growled at the thought of wearing a muzzle like some domesticated dog. My wolf snarled her displeasure.

A dark-colored wolf, which I assumed was Gavin, trotted off in the direction of the town.

Echoing my growls, Dalton balanced on one foot and gave me a kick in the ribs, hard enough to stagger me but gentle enough it didn't hurt. "It'll be ten times worse if you fight us on this, Matia. Enough. Cooperate, or I'll have you locked on the other end of the headquarters in a room not even you can break out of. Don't test me right now. I'm not in the mood for games."

My wolf believed him, and before I could stop her, she wrested away control long enough to turn my head so I wouldn't meet the Alpha's gaze.

"How bad are the silver burns?" Dad straightened, narrowing his eyes.

"Bad enough. She'll be fine; looks like she

bled out any silver poisoning if there was any. It'll hurt, but she'll heal. I'll keep an eye on our new friends, Mr. Evans. Why don't you go make some calls? We're going to need reinforcements, I think. Taking them alive wasn't in our original plan."

Dad snorted, rose to his feet, and pulled his phone out of his pocket. Regarding the device with a disdainful scowl, he shrugged, wound up, and threw it on the ground as hard as he could.

"Or you can trigger the homing beacon on your phone and get us all in trouble." Dalton shook his head. "Calling them would have worked."

"And lose a chance to get a new phone at someone else's expense? Nonsense. It's far more fun this way, and apparently I'm out of people to shoot, unless you're volunteering."

Dalton knelt and lowered Ryan to the ground. Digging out his phone, the Alpha tossed it to Dad. "If you're going to give them collective heart attacks, I could use a new phone, too."

With no evidence of his clumsy nature, Dad caught the phone. He shifted his weight and lobbed the phone into the air, unholstered his gun, and shot it. The device toppled into the ruins of the burning garage. "So, pups. Are you gonna sit like good wolves, or will I need to practice my shooting some more?"

I had never seen a group of men move so

fast in my life. Before I could do more than blink, the rogue Fenerec pack sat and waited. Dalton snorted.

With no threats nearby, my wolf retreated, her exhaustion bleeding into me. Whining, I shuffled to Ryan's side, bumping my nose to his neck. His faint warmth promised life. With a heavy sigh, I stretched out beside Ryan and rested my head on his shoulder to wait.

## TWENTY-EIGHT

*Heaven's busy right now, so they sent me instead.*

---

DALTON WIELDED the muzzle like a weapon. He sat on me and forced it over my head while I snarled, snapped, and growled warnings of how I'd rip him to shreds if he dared put the leather and silver contraption on me. The leather basket surrounded my nose and created a barrier I couldn't get through. While I could smell the silver affixed to the leather, it didn't burn me.

Completing my humiliation was a leather and silver harness, a collar, and a leash. The muzzle clipped to the collar. The instant Dalton released me, I rolled onto my back, hooked my hind claws in the leather, and tried to yank the accursed restriction off my head.

The silver stung my pads, and I howled my displeasure for the world to hear.

"Fight it all you want, but it isn't coming off," the Alpha informed me.

I howled my fury and snapped my teeth,

which amused a chuckle out of the man. He kept a firm hold on the leash. While he came in contact with the silver bound to it, the metal didn't seem to bother him. I growled, flattening my ears.

"Want me to take charge of her?" Dad asked.

"If she gets a mind to run, she might rip your shoulder right out of its socket. Probably not a wise idea. Why don't you keep watch over Ryan? You're a good shot. If anyone gets too close to him without permission, make them dance."

"Making them dance implies I can't kill them."

"Are you sure you're not a Fenerec?"

"Mother reminds me how disappointed she is I'm not every chance she gets," Dad muttered.

"We can change that whenever you're ready. You score a passing grade for your protective instincts. I'll leave Ryan to you. I'm going to take your daughter to headquarters. The last thing we need is for Ryan to wake up while we're treating her hands. Burns this bad are nasty to begin with, and if she doesn't feedback to him during the process, I'll be shocked. I want to get it done before he's healed enough to put up a fight."

"And the rogues?"

"How many silver rounds do you have left?"

"Four magazines worth."

"They give you any trouble, shoot them before they're on their feet." Dalton reached down, hooked his arm under me, and lifted me up. Howling my fury, I clawed at him, snapping and snarling despite knowing I couldn't reach him while muzzled. "She's plenty angry we're separating her from Ryan."

"You could just toss him in the back of your SUV and take them both. It's not going to matter if you wait for the med team. I know it, you know it, and they know it. Don't underestimate Matia's determination. She's patient and isn't against waiting a few years to get her revenge." Dad stepped to me, reached out, and gave my ears a brisk rub. "I already miss when she was small enough to stuff in my coat."

"Trust me, so do I. She's a lot more dangerous now. She's upgraded from an annoying ankle biter to capable of breaking bones without much effort."

I snarled and howled, promising I'd do exactly that when I escaped the muzzle and got a hold of the Alpha.

Dad and Dalton ignored me.

"Why don't I carry her mate down to your SUV and load him up, then you can take them both in? If he wakes up during treatment, they'll be better able to handle him. Gets him there faster, too. Surely your pack can keep these mutts in line for a few minutes."

"All right. I'll leash her to the front seat and put him in the back. Last thing I want is to have him reacting to silver during the drive. This is just a great idea. Ah, hell. Why not? What could possibly go wrong with two injured Fenerec in the vehicle while I'm driving?"

"A lot," Dad replied, his tone wry. "I tried to warn them she had a temper, Dalton. I tried to warn them she's headstrong. I really did."

"I tried to warn them she'd burn the place down around their ears if anything went wrong. Maybe next time they'll listen."

Dad and Dalton looked at each other and burst into laughter.

Shaking his head, Dalton carried me down the hill towards the decaying town. "Sure. Pigs will fly first."

I growled the entire way to Inquisition headquarters.

---

DALTON FORCED me to transform from wolf to woman before I realized what he was doing. As soon as I began to shift, he unbuckled the muzzle and harness and tossed them aside. When I finally finished, a white-coated doctor plunged a syringe into my arm. I had no idea what the man injected me with, but it subdued my wolf and numbed me.

The doctors slathered my hands in some kind of cream, wrapped my hands in thick bandages, and left me with Dalton, who shook his head disapprovingly and clucked his tongue at me. "I warned them to never underestimate a determined bitch. I also warned them you could manifest. Apparently, the twins believed you could only make yourself smoke and ran the risk of igniting your hair. Of course, that's dangerous enough."

My thoughts scattered as though blown by a strong wind, leaving me unable to do anything other than stare at him.

"Wolfsbane and ketamine. On young Fenerec, it's pretty effective—too effective, really. It'll wear off eventually. Until then, to be safe rather than sorry, you're to obey either me, your father, or Ryan. Understood?"

My mouth moved without any input from me, and I mumbled, "Yes, sir."

"Good girl. While we wait for word about Ryan, why don't I take you to your new suite —that you'll be sharing with Ryan—and explain what'll happen in the next few days. Hopefully, this will keep you from lighting anything else on fire."

Wolfsbane and ketamine made it difficult for me to walk without tripping over my own feet. Without Dalton's help, I never would have made it to the posh room, which smelled of freshly squeezed lemons.

He guided me to the couch in the living room and pushed me onto it before taking over an armchair. "Rule one: you will not light anything on fire. Rule two: no howling. Rule three: no escape attempts of any sort.

Let's not give the witches anything else to worry about. A severely injured Fenerec as old as Ryan is going to stress them all out. With you also hurt, they're going to be at wit's end trying to prevent any accidents."

I stared at him, blinking as the meaning of his words slowly sank in. Nodding, I settled back on the couch, stifling a yawn.

"First, the drug you were given will suppress your wolf. It also suppresses will, which makes it easy to control a Fenerec. Until Ryan's back on his feet, I expect they'll keep you dosed with it. The ketamine is what's making you woozy, but that'll wear off in a couple of hours at most. The ketamine just makes the wolfsbane more effective. You'll feel a bit more like yourself once the ketamine wears off."

"What about Ryan?"

"Ryan will be fine. The first step is for him to recover full heart function. When a Fenerec is critically injured, they shut down to preserve their bodies. By limiting oxygen requirements, a Fenerec can preserve brain function. In the case of a Fenerec as old as Ryan, so long as his brain isn't damaged, he'll recover. While it varies from Fenerec to Fenerec, heart, lung, and brain functionality are restored first. If his spine was damaged, unfortunately, it'll recover last; spinal damage is tough to heal, as is nerve function. Unlike humans, a Fenerec's entire body can regenerate given sufficient time."

Dalton sighed and propped his feet up on the coffee table, staring at his muddy shoes.

"That's disgusting." I pointed at his feet, snapped my fingers, and gestured to the door. "Don't be a pig."

Snorting, the Alpha kicked off his shoes. They landed halfway to the door and left smears on the carpet. "Someone will be by to clean up. Gives the bored witches something to do. Anyway, in Ryan's case, if the gunshot wound didn't damage anything other than his heart, he should be back on his feet within a day or two. Once the doctors have a better idea of when he'll recover, they'll likely bring you in so you're nearby when he wakes up." Dalton hesitated. "Of course, that'll be a little dangerous since he'll wake up remembering he'd been shot, and most Fenerec fly straight into fight mode, and while submissive, he'll defend himself. Don't be surprised if you're battered a bit before he clues in he's safe."

I didn't care if Ryan smacked me around if it meant he woke up. "How long?"

"For the doctors to have a better idea of when you can see him? I'd give it a few hours. They're going to run him through every machine they have and run tests. After they have the results, they'll decide when it'll be safe to bring you in. He's too injured to move to any of the containment suites, so they're going to have to be careful. They're already expecting to lose hundreds of thousands of dollars in equipment when he goes psychotic."

"I can replace the equipment."

"I know you can, but let the Inquisition pay for their mistakes. The first mistake was trusting in Ryan's submissive tendencies to keep him safe. Ryan's done too much for the Inquisition as it is. I'm going to take advantage of your strong witchcraft and his close call to try to push his retirement—or at least a safer role in operations. At the very least, I can have him pulled from operations to help deal with integrating the rogues to new packs. The Inquisition will need a lot of help on that score; they didn't expect a sorcerer controlling the pack. There's good news, though."

"What good news?"

"While the masterminds of the La Guardia attack will face execution, it'll be swift and merciful. The rest of the rogue pack will probably be granted a pardon. Sorcerers are bad news, and one strong enough to take over a pack is capable of removing their free will. Most of them are victims, and they'll be treated accordingly."

"They'll walk?"

"I wouldn't say they'll walk away free and clear, but they'll live. The Inquisition has harsh rules, but victims are victims, and they try to take that into consideration. The Alpha'll die, as will his stronger Fenerec. The submissive will die, too, as he was the bomb tech, but only after the pack is transferred to a new Alpha. The death of a submissive is damaging to a pack, and while brutal, the Inquisition tries not to be cruel. Sometimes it is unavoidable. To human eyes, we're a pretty cruel species at times."

I sighed and flopped onto the couch. "Humans can be, too."

"Humans often are, just in a different way. If it makes you feel better about his death, Harthel wasn't human, not really. Sorcerers may be born human, but their magic twists them into something far less—and far more dangerous. We Fenerec may be brutal and cruel in our own way, but we're angels compared to them."

I stretched out on the couch. I'd regret not being with Ryan, but I didn't regret Harthel's death. Losing the kill to Dad stung, but I shrugged it off. "He deserved it."

"He did. Your father will sleep easier tonight knowing he won't have to worry about him coming after you again. Ryan, too. For now, get some rest. There's a perfectly good bed in the other room you can sleep on instead of the couch. Just don't escape out the window again. Your hands have been abused enough."

Dalton left. I stayed on the couch. Maybe it was a mix of stubborn pride and stupidity, but I had no intention of sleeping in a bed without Ryan in it.

THE DOCTORS DIDN'T LET me see the ruined remains of my hands during the torture sessions they called treatment for two days. In some ways, my palms looked like someone had taken a meat tenderizer to them, pounding away until I was left with hamburger for hands. Dalton's orders to stay calm, quiet, and still kept me in my seat; without the orders, they would've needed to peel me from the ceiling, especially when the doctors brought out the brushes required to clean away the dead flesh and scar tissue so new, healthy skin could grow.

It hurt, and not even the order to stay quiet silenced my growls.

Dalton chuckled. "You're going to scare the witches if you keep that up."

Harriet and Audrey didn't seem frightened to me. If anything, my predicament amused them. Maybe I deserved some ribbing for breaking out of the headquarters and destroying one of the suites, but did they have to grin so much?

"I don't think either one of them is scared of anything." I turned my head so I wouldn't have to watch the two doctors at work. Someone needed to repaint the walls; the white had dulled to a drab gray. "They just don't want the place to stink of smoke. A little smoke might encourage them to repaint the place. It needs it."

Audrey clapped. "You have us figured out. We're mitigating your smoke damage so we aren't forced to repaint the medical facilities. Obviously. Maybe we're just making sure you only burn the facilities a little so you have to help us pick out paints. It'd be a good way to expose you to colors as your vision is restored without triggering anxiety attacks."

"She's really sarcastic lately, Dalton." I sighed. "How many more times do you need to treat my hands?"

I still didn't know my doctors' names; the introductions had gone by in a pain-filled blur. Each time I worked up the courage to ask, my flayed pride reared its ugly head. The pair didn't seem disgusted or put off by the state of my hands, which reassured me far more than words did.

Neither man seemed anxious, and the sweet scent of their amusement made it easier for me to stay calm. If they weren't worried, I wouldn't worry, either.

At least I didn't have to worry about my wolf; while under the influence of wolfsbane, she slept. I doubted she'd tolerate the doctors scouring my skin off to help my burns heal faster.

The older doctor, a gray-haired man who had a faint scent of spice and smoke about him, chuckled. "We're going to leave the bandages off this time and see how it goes. Within two or three hours, you should be able to use your hands normally. The brushing is to remove the silver-tainted skin and muscle as much as it is to clear away the scar tissue. Once the silver is gone, you'll heal much faster. By this evening, you'll be up for even rigorous exercise."

Breath warmed the back of my neck. "I am very interested in rigorous exercise."

Before I had become a Fenerec, startling me rarely resulted in more than me jumping in my seat. Not even the wolfsbane kept me seated, and before I comprehended who had come up behind me, I landed halfway across the room, crashed on top of one of the bulky pieces of medical equipment, knocked it over, and got tangled in its hoses and cords. I smacked against the wall and slid to the floor with a dismayed howl.

Then realization hit me, and I squeaked, "Ryan?"

Dalton cleared his throat, and I recognized the sound as an attempt to mask laughter. "That was rather mean of you, Ryan."

The older doctor chuckled. "Well, at least the good news is we needed new equipment anyway. I'm going to give her reflexes a passing grade. While I fully encourage patients getting on their feet and moving around as quickly as possible, startling an injured bitch is essentially the definition of insanity, Mr. Cole."

"She was completely oblivious to my presence in the room. I even counted to twenty. How can anyone blame me?" Ryan pouted. "When an opportunity presents itself, a wise wolf takes advantage of it."

I gaped at him. There was no evidence he'd been injured at all; everything about him was as I remembered, and he didn't even flinch away from Dalton or avert his gaze as I expected. "Ryan?"

Dalton chuckled. "I think you broke her. Since you got her tangled in that mess, you get her out of it."

"I really don't feel like bending over right now," my mate replied.

My doctor clucked his tongue. "Sit, Mr. Cole. If you try bending over, you'll fall over, which will undoubtedly hurt beyond your ability to suppress. Then the bitch will end up damaging herself and everything in a five foot radius getting to you, putting us right back to square one. If we're really lucky, she'll set the room on fire in the process. I'm sure there's something in here she hasn't already damaged or destroyed with that stunt."

With a smug smile, Ryan sat in my chair. "Your sarcasm is alive and well."

My doctor sighed. "Mr. Sinclair, please free Miss Evans so she doesn't hurt her hands."

I took in the tangle of cables, hoses, and equipment scattered around me and saw no obvious escape route. A giggle slipped out of me. Another bubbled free, and helpless to stop myself, I laughed until I cried.

"Let's just blame the drugs," Dalton suggested. "They're both higher than kites."

Ryan made a thoughtful noise. "I hear rigorous exercise is good for getting drugs out of someone's system."

"Keep telling yourself that, Ryan," Dalton muttered, making his way across the room to survey the equipment I had knocked over. "I think I'm going to need a hand with this unless we're okay with tearing the whole thing apart to get her out."

Dad stepped into the room. He stared at me and sighed. "Please tell me she's crying because she's happy to see Ryan."

"I think she's crying because she's stuck. It seems she has a very low threshold for frustration. Next time, you get to babysit the bitch. I'll take the potentially psychopathic injured operative. It's safer. Anyway, Ryan sent her into orbit when he came up behind her. Apparently, he is of the opinion she should have noticed him immediately."

Crossing the room, Dad examined the equipment, reached down, and began unplugging everything. "I swear I only left him alone for three minutes."

"You can't take your eye off the puppies for even a second. I thought you would have figured this out by now, Ralph."

"Apparently not."

Sniffling, I held up my hands. "Look, Dad. I have hands."

"So I see. They're looking much better."

Ryan made a sound suspiciously like a giggle. "The doctors encourage rigorous exercise, Mr. Evans."

My dad closed his eyes and sighed. "Heaven help me."

"Heaven's busy right now, so they sent me instead." Dalton chuckled, helping to untangle me from the mess of cables and hosing. When I was freed, he grabbed me by my elbows, hauled me to my feet, and gave me a push in Ryan's direction.

I tripped over my own feet, yelped, and twisted so I wouldn't collide with my mate. With no sign he'd been injured, Ryan hooked his arm around me and pulled me onto his lap. The sound he made was a throaty cross between a purr and a growl, and he nuzzled his nose against my neck.

I closed my eyes and relaxed against him, taking deep breaths of his scent. Without my wolf awake to guide me, I couldn't distinguish half of what I was smelling, but I recognized Ryan's contentment as the strongest scent of all, which was good enough for me.

"And now that all is right in the world, I need a stiff drink," Dalton announced. I cracked open an eye in time to watch the Alpha loop his arm around Dad's neck and pull him into a headlock. "I'll come by to check on you later, you two. No attempted escapes, no fires, and no trouble."

"How about you don't come by later and check on us. We're going to be very busy," my mate murmured, his breath warming my throat. "Too busy to escape."

The Alpha heaved a sigh and adjusted his

hold on my dad, who tolerated the Fenerec's handling with a shake of his head and roll of his eyes. "That leaves no fires and no trouble."

A single sniff was all I needed to know what Ryan had in mind, and I slapped my hand over my mate's mouth before he could say another word. Touching him stung, but my hands no longer throbbed or hurt nearly as badly as they had even an hour before. "I think we'll be just fine."

I had to admit Dalton was correct; all was right in the world, and I wouldn't have it any other way.

---

THANKS FOR READING! Enjoy the Witch & Wolf world? Beneath a Blood Moon is a standalone, or you can start the adventures of the main series with Inquisitor, which can also be found in the Witch & Wolf Complete Series collection.

## Afterword

I am often asked about how the Witch & Wolf world relates to our own. In many ways, the Earth from the Witch & Wolf novels is very much like our own. However, it is not Earth, not exactly.

While some of the events in the Witch & Wolf world overlap with our version of Earth, they are not the same. While certain events still happened, rather like fixed points in time from a certain time-traveling series, the specifics are often altered. The years and exact dates may not be the same. Some technologies have developed later—or sooner—than in our Earth.

Motivations and the execution of certain events, including terrorist attacks, have been changed. The inclusion of the supernatural would alter a great many things, including how wars are waged.

As such, there are discrepancies between the Witch & Wolf world and our Earth. No matter how hard the supernatural community tries to hide their presence, they have the power to change the world—and they do.

As always, all errors are my own, but some of those errors with history aren't actually errors at all—they are deliberate alterations to Earth's history to better fit with the inclusion of witches, werewolves, and the other supernatural.

Thanks for reading!

## About R.J. Blain

Want to hear from the author when a new book releases? You can sign up at her website (thesneakykittycritic.com). Please note this newsletter is operated by the Furred & Frond Management. Expect to be sassed by a cat. (With guest features of other animals, including dogs.)

A complete list of books written by RJ and her various pen names is available at https://books2read.com/rl/The-Fantasy-Worlds-of-RJ-Blain.

RJ Blain suffers from a Moleskine journal obsession, a pen fixation, and a terrible tendency to pun without warning.

When she isn't playing pretend, she likes to think she's a cartographer and a sumi-e painter.

In her spare time, she daydreams about being a spy. Should that fail, her contingency plan involves tying her best of enemies to spinning wheels and quoting James Bond villains until she is satisfied.

RJ also writes as Susan Copperfield and Bernadette Franklin. Visit RJ and her pets (the Management) at thesneakykittycritic.com.

Follow RJ & her alter egos on Bookbub:
RJ Blain
Susan Copperfield
Bernadette Franklin

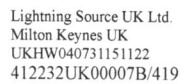

Lightning Source UK Ltd.
Milton Keynes UK
UKHW040731151122
412232UK00007B/419